I0819236

MERCY HILL

MERCY HILL

A NOVEL

Hannah Thurman

DOUBLEDAY
New York

FIRST DOUBLEDAY HARDCOVER EDITION 2026

Published by Doubleday, a division of Penguin Random House LLC,
1745 Broadway, New York, NY 10019.

Doubleday and the portrayal of an anchor with a dolphin are
registered trademarks of Penguin Random House LLC.

Book design by Anna B. Knighton

Library of Congress Cataloging-in-Publication Data
Names: Thurman, Hannah, author
Title: Mercy Hill: a novel / Hannah Thurman.
Description: First edition. | New York: Doubleday, 2026. |
Identifiers: LCCN 2025009419 (print) | LCCN 2025009420 (ebook) |
ISBN 9780385551823 hardcover | ISBN 9780385551830 ebook
Subjects: LCGFT: Novels
Classification: LCC PS3620.H876 Me 2026 (print) |
LCC PS3620.H876 (ebook) | DDC 813/.6—dc23/eng/20250331
LC record available at https://lccn.loc.gov/2025009419
LC ebook record available at https://lccn.loc.gov/2025009420

penguinrandomhouse.com | doubleday.com

Printed in the United States of America
1st Printing

The authorized representative in the EU for product safety
and compliance is Penguin Random House Ireland, Morrison Chambers,
32 Nassau Street, Dublin D02 YH68, Ireland, https://eu-contact.penguin.ie.

For Ivy & Ed

For we must all appear before the judgment seat of Christ,
so that each one may be recompensed for his deeds in the body,
according to what he has done, whether good or bad.

—2 CORINTHIANS 5:10

MERCY
HILL

PROLOGUE

If I were to pick the number one strangest thing about my childhood, which was packed to the gills with strangeness, it would be the way the sun disappeared each day at noon. If I was at home and bored—which was often—I'd track its progress against the paneled walls of our cottage, watching them gleam as the light shone brighter and higher throughout the morning in anticipation of a glorious midday zenith.

But this zenith never came. When the rays were about to reach their peak, they abruptly stopped, blocked by the largest of the stone buildings that stood at the very top of the Hill. A long shadow stretched down, covering our home and everything behind it, our daily total eclipse.

Ten minutes later, the sun popped out again and everything brightened. We'd all grown used to this routine, and although visitors might have commented on it, we almost never had visitors. I suppose if someone had ever said anything, the rest of us would have shrugged and replied that strange as it seemed, it had been happening for a very long time.

MERCY HILL ASYLUM opened its doors in 1856 on land that, at the time, was considered far beyond the city limits of North Carolina's Piedmont capital, Raleigh: the first and largest mental hospital in the South. Old pictures in the admin building showed its massive acreage: orchards, fields, livestock stables—along with the four big stone buildings that would later become the wards. As the city developed, so did the asylum, erecting a nursing college and cottages for staff across the nearly two thousand acres of land.

By the 1970s, that land began to look more precious, and the city started to reabsorb it, taking nearly all of the fields and flatlands where Mercy Hill's crops had once grown. The hospital was no less busy, filled with the insane from across the state, but everything became condensed to the steep inclines of the hill that gave the asylum its name, cut off at the base by a four-lane highway that led to Raleigh's epicenter.

The next event of historical significance, at least in the minds of my sisters and me, was the hiring of our mother. In 1984 she became the first female director of psychiatry in the facility's history and, like all full-time staff, was offered housing in one of the employee cottages that clung to the north side of the Hill.

Most of the other doctors, especially married ones, declined this offer, but our mother was never one to say no to something free. She and Daddy packed up their books and clothes and an ambitious fifty-seven-piece set of wedding china given to them by Daddy's mother, and moved into one of the staff cottages. My sister J.J. was born a year later, then Caro, then Mimi, then finally me. For many years, we four girls were the only children who lived on the Hill, which our mother called a "special privilege." Sometimes we believed her; sometimes it seemed like she was just saying that to make up for the fact that we didn't own a television.

Our mother was not like the mothers of my classmates, or the ones I read about in books. She was brilliant and not modest about it, and, although she could charm anyone she wanted to, rarely bothered. She was frequently brusque and snappish with us, even when we were very young. In return, we knew her word as bond—that she would meet us eye to eye as if we were grown-ups ourselves.

I WONDER IF, given everything that happened, she'd choose to do it again. The cottage, the isolation, the daily shadow running across our family until it darkened each one of us in turn. Was it worth it, for what we saved?

I'm sure she'd tell me if I asked. But it's taken me years to untangle myself from her version of the truth.

1999

ONE

Mimi's branch snapped like a gunshot, and all four of us began to scream.

The magnolia had been an easy climb, and so we'd gone both high and far—up into the canopy and also out, scooting along the smooth limbs that reached over the barbed wire fence. Eighteen feet below us was the recreation yard of highest-security Ward C, and up until this moment, we'd had the perfect perch to spy safely on the men below. But Mimi, like always, had gone too far, out to where her bough tapered into leaves. My own arms began to shake as I watched the bough bend and then split.

I felt a great ruffling wind as she plummeted past me, arms still locked around the limb like it would save her from what came next. Then two booms: first, as the wood made contact with the razor-wire fence, sending a wave of clanging along the chain links. Next, the thud as my sister and her tree limb landed inside the yard.

The summer air was still and wet, and the cloying scent of magnolia flower rose from the ground where Mimi's fall had knocked down a shower of moon-white blossoms. Paralyzed, I clung tight to the bark, staring down. Mimi's right leg was twisted underneath her, bent back at an angle that I'd never seen before. Her face wrenched into a grimace, and even eighteen feet up, I could hear her whisper: *Is he coming?*

For the first time since hearing the crack, I raised my head and looked around. My other two sisters, J.J. and Caro, were already beginning to make their way down the ladderlike limbs to safety. I tried to follow them, but my hands stayed locked. I had never felt fear like this before, and my heart beat wildly, like some animal was trapped inside me.

"Denise!" Mimi called up at me, louder than before: "Is he coming?"

I looked across the yard. Unlike Ward B, whose residents were allowed passes to the commissary and the post office and the tennis courts, Ward C was surrounded by a razor-wire fence, a fence ten-year-old Mimi was now trapped inside. The men inside this fence arrived on the Hill in police cars and left in prison transport vans. And yes, drawn from the shade of the building where they'd been clustered, they were now making their way toward Mimi, led by the man we all called the Scarecrow.

The Scarecrow was taller than the others, with patchy hair that stuck out in tufts around his somber face. That was why we'd given him the nickname, because you could imagine him staring off in some field for hours, flat eyes fixed on a point well beyond what you were seeing. He'd arrived at the beginning of the summer, and we'd spent the last few weeks observing him. He made even the biggest longtimers, Carl and Joe James, shy away, and we wanted to know why.

J.J. threw herself at the fence from the outside, rattling the metal. "Techs!" she yelled. "Can we get a technician?"

Usually one of the techs, big dough-faced men with army crewcuts, would be standing in the yard with the residents. But on hot days in the summer, many called in sick to go fishing.

The wards were egregiously understaffed at the best of times, and in July and August it often seemed as if no one worked there at all.

J.J. then began to call the names of the nurses: Reginald, Jamie, Noah. At thirteen, she was the oldest and tallest, but standing there against the shining fence, she didn't even reach the midpoint.

Numbly and dumbly, I thought: *I should yell too*. But my mouth was so dry I could hardly speak. I stared down at Mimi, watching as red cuts like scales appeared along her hands and arms and cheek, courtesy of the razor wire. With effort, she wrenched her arms behind her back, trying to push herself up to a sitting position. By the time she was upright, the Scarecrow was close enough to touch.

J.J. and now Caro, too, pounded the fence, their voices ringing in a twisted wail. "Mom!" Mimi sobbed, staring in vain at the ward's open, empty door. "Mom!"

This is what, more than twenty years later, chills me most to remember. Mimi was the wildest, the bravest, the one who taunted the rest of us at any sign of fear. To see her helpless sliced at my skin as if I had been the one who had toppled into the yard.

The Scarecrow crouched down. Extended a broad hand against Mimi's face, stroking his fingers through the blood on her cheek. She stopped screaming.

He held his hand up to the light, as if it weren't high noon in August. Blood dripped down his wrist and he sniffed at it like he was trying to place the scent.

"Hey, you!" J.J. shouted, addressing him for the first time. "She's Dr. Cross's daughter. You know Dr. Cross?"

The Scarecrow lowered his hand. Mimi's blood dripped from his finger onto the sun-fried grass. After a very long moment, he spoke, the first time I'd ever heard his voice. "You look like her," he said.

That wasn't surprising. We all looked like our mother: dark hair, dark eyes, narrow hips and shoulders. I felt another wave of fear shake through me. I wanted to be back on the ground, but I didn't trust myself to let go of my chokehold on the branch. My arms began to ache.

"Please," J.J. said, pressing her whole body against the fence. "Can you please go get her? Please go get Dr. Cross."

The air was so thick and still I felt as if I couldn't take in another breath. My stomach seized at the possibility of violence.

Then he turned. He walked in a broken cadence, like he could come back around at any second. But he walked nonetheless. It drove the other residents back, like a shark through a school of fish, leaving him a direct path to the dark open door of the ward. No one spoke, everything was silent.

When he stepped into the narrow shadow of the building, everything happened at once. A blue flash of men's scrubs, the snap of plastic restraints, the Scarecrow let out a high, piercing cry and thudded to the ground. His feet thrashed as one of the techs fought to bundle his kicking legs.

Lisa Cross, MD, stepped around the warring men, white coat blinding in the midday sun. She held the plastic cap of a prefilled syringe; with each step, her stethoscope flashed bright silver. She knelt down next to Mimi. "He did this?" She held her hand right where the Scarecrow had, and the gesture looked so similar that I wondered if he had simply been trying to stop the bleeding.

Mimi couldn't speak. On the other side of the fence, J.J. said, "No, it was the fence. Her leg—I think it's broken."

"Mom, he was trying to find you," Caro said, staring off

across the yard. I followed her gaze. Ernie the tech was standing again, brushing off his hands in a continued stream of *motherfuckers*. The Scarecrow lay, bound and silent, his face turned toward us. His eyes blinked slowly under heavy lashes, and his mouth, like Mimi's, was pressed tightly in pain.

"Don't worry about him," our mother said. "Mimi, you need to stand if you can."

Mimi tried once and flopped back down again, so our mother bent over and scooped her up. At ten, Mimi was only a head shorter than our mother, but she curled into her neck like she was much littler. Our mother struggled under the weight, shifting once, then turned to Caro and J.J. through the fence.

"Where's Denise?"

They answered by looking up, and she followed their gaze. Her look cut through all the waving leaves and branches until it met my own, then went further, burrowing deep into my skull. It felt like I was witnessing my own dissection.

When she spoke, her voice was tighter than usual but no less commanding. "Go home now," she said. "All of you."

I felt movement return to my arms. Clumsy and shaking, I scrambled down the tree to where J.J. and Caro were waiting. The yard was empty, my mother and Mimi and all the men gone. How had the Scarecrow been taken back inside, bound as he was by the restraints? I don't like to think about the answer.

J.J. cleared her throat and stepped between me and the fence, picking up her knit cap from where it had fallen. In the panic, all of us had stripped down to the most animal versions of ourselves and now that it was over, we were quickly reacclimatizing to our personalities. She pulled the hat on, then folded it back so you could see the sides of her cropped hair. In a few years J.J. would come out as a lesbian, and at thirteen, you could tell she was trying both to telegraph and hide the fact that she felt different, which mostly resulted in her wearing Daddy's winter clothes year-round.

Caro wiped her face with the back of her hand, elegant as a black-and-white-movie star. At twelve, just a year younger than J.J., she was the most sensitive, able to pick up on our mother's shifting moods before the rest of us. So when she took my hand and said, "We'd better go tell Daddy before she calls him," J.J. and I listened, picking up our leaden feet and starting along down the path toward home.

The graying sidewalk was pitted and cracked, and empty holes trailed alongside where railings had once stood. The whole campus was like that, filled with ghostly reminders of its former grandeur. Those days weren't the ones to idolize, our mother often told us: in the time of secrecy around mental illness, before pharmaceutical intervention, patients languished in these wards for their entire lives. But what wards they had been! We crossed into the shadow of the great limestone admin building, then wound around past the giant stone dormitories of Wards A and B.

The smoking yard for Ward B, which had only a short chain-link fence, was empty.

"Did they lock down?" I asked, hearing the squeak of fear in my voice.

"I didn't hear the sirens," J.J. said, and we continued along in silence.

On the other side of Ward B's empty yard was the identical Ward A, doors and first-floor windows blocked with peeling plywood. I was too young to remember what it was like before Ward A closed, but J.J. and our mother told us stories: the patients housed there had been ancient and sedate, born in a time when children with disabilities were sent away to institutions and left there to be forgotten. On sunny days, the staff would push their wheelchairs out in a line into the rec yard, and then after a long and silent hour, they'd be pushed back inside. The last of those patients died in 1992, three years after I was born, and the entire building was shuttered. The four of us sometimes broke in when we were bored, climbing on the old metal bed frames and writing our names on the dust-covered windows. There wasn't much to do beyond that, and the shadowy hallways felt heavy with an old sadness and a present fear: that this very thing could happen to Wards B and C, as well.

This fear lurked everywhere across the grounds, a mist so fine it crept into every brick and balance sheet. Across the country, mental health advocates and belt-tightening legislators alike were calling for deinstitutionalization, for "less restrictive accommodations." Each year the staff list grew smaller, and we watched as patients were ferried out to halfway houses and group homes. The Hill was crumbling, fast.

You could see it everywhere we walked. Past the rusting swing set and the weedy gardens and down along the dry creek bed, through the patchy woods filled with the remnants of our forts, abandoned in the heat of the summer like tiny wards themselves. Then the path sloped, taking us down through the staff cottages: twenty-five of them total, maybe ten of them occupied, all but ours by single adults, nurses and techs who didn't earn enough money to rent a place off campus.

As the director of psychiatry for the entire hospital, our mother made $170,000 a year, which to my nine-year-old self seemed almost unfathomable. She was saving nearly all of it for our tuition—undergraduate, then medical school, which we were all expected to attend. But thriftiness was not the only reason we lived where we did. In our war, as in any other, proximity was power. It's harder to steal land to which someone has chained herself.

Our feet had just touched the porch of Cottage 10 when we heard the gravel crunch behind us. We turned to see one of the ward vans pull up and our mother and Mimi get out. Mimi's arm and cheek were covered with Band-Aids, and she was leaning on a crutch that looked way too big for her. It was clear that each step she took was painful, and her foot still hung at a strange angle. Nevertheless, our mother ushered her inside with the rest of us, and we scrambled in one rush through the screen door.

Daddy was sitting at the desk in the corner of the cottage's main room, the makeshift office that housed our desktop computer. When he first saw us, he nodded only briefly, then, when Mimi and her crutches came into view, he sprang up so fast his chair toppled.

"Jesus—Mimi—girls, what happened?" He was halfway across the room when he saw our mother. "Lisa?"

Our mother stood in the doorway, silent for a long moment. With her face sweaty and her bun beginning to unravel, she looked more rattled than I'd ever seen her.

"They climbed a tree into the rec yard. Into *Ward C*." She pressed her lips tightly together. "You're all too smart to act that stupid."

"We weren't climbing in," J.J. said, which was true. "We just wanted to look, Mimi didn't know the branch would break."

Our mother held up a hand. "That man who touched you? He's one of the HB95s," she said, a term we all knew that meant he'd been tried and found not guilty by virtue of insanity. "Alexander White. He drowned three boys in a lake. He held them under with his own hands."

We stood in stunned silence. I could smell the cold, brackish water closing around me.

J.J. said, "The mentally ill are much more likely to be the victim of violence than the perpetrator." This was something our mother said often, but hearing her own words repeated back charged her into a frenzy. Caro felt it first, ducking backward and pulling me with her.

Our mother turned to face J.J. straight on. "You're the oldest," she said. "You should have known better." She stepped into the kitchen and from under the sink yanked out a black plastic garbage bag. She shook it out with hard, fast snaps.

"You know this incident will have to be reported? It'll be on Kelly's desk tomorrow. You think she needs an excuse? She doesn't."

J.J. shoved her hands deep into the pockets of her cargo shorts.

Our mother started down the hall toward the room we all shared. We rushed in after her, even Mimi, even Daddy, whose quiet protest of *Li*-sa disappeared beneath the sound of her footfalls.

The room was small, filled with two sets of bunk beds: one for J.J. and Mimi, one for me and Caro. Our mother stomped over to the top bunk where J.J. slept. I guess I knew all along she would go for the dolls.

"Maybe," our mother said, holding one of the dolls by the foot, "this will help you be less childish." She dropped it into the empty bag.

Now it was J.J.'s turn to let out a cry. "No! Please—put them back!"

I couldn't stand to look. J.J.'s dolls were her one concession to femininity, a collection of porcelain girls she asked for on each birthday and on Christmas, with ruffled crinolines and sausage-curled hair. Each night after lights-out we could hear her moving them around, setting them posed in new positions so they didn't get bored.

Each one of them—Abigail and Ruthie and Elliana and the one whose name J.J. kept a secret, even from us—our mother dropped into the bag. I could hear the snap of porcelain limbs breaking and Mimi's ragged breathing beside me. Was that how it had sounded when her own leg snapped?

"Daddy," J.J. pleaded, grabbing his T-shirt. "Tell her to put them back."

"Lisa." Daddy stepped forward, hand outstretched. Our mother hefted the sack like Santa Claus.

"She's obviously sorry," Daddy went on. "Lisa, please."

Our parents rarely disagreed. They each had their role—our mother the leader, the advocate, the zealous genius; our father the follower, the details man, the one who made sure we had mayo in the fridge and the right vaccinations for school. He'd probably been the one to purchase the garbage bag our mother now held. "Come on," he said slowly, and I knew she'd eventually say, *Okay*.

Except she didn't. She swept past us and went back out the front door. Standing beside the van, she called, "Mimi, come with me. I'm taking you to the ER."

J.J. raced onto the porch like she was going to throw herself after them, wrestle the bag from our mother's grip. Then she stopped at the top of the stairs like she'd hit glass. I knew. We all knew. It was over.

Daddy picked Mimi up in his arms, carrying her carefully to the waiting van. When he bent inside to help her with the buckle, he said something to our mother, and there was a long silence in return. Slam of two doors, spark of the engine, the van backed up and pulled away, heading down the long gravel road that led to the exit gate. Then it was just the four of us left: Daddy, J.J., Caro, and me.

Daddy turned to J.J. "I'll get you some new ones," he said. It was the first time I'd ever heard him offer something that contradicted our mother's direct instruction. It would not be the last.

J.J. dug her nails into the flaking black paint that covered the metal railing of the porch, hands turning white. Then she released a long-held breath.

"No," she said. "Don't." Then she looked at Caro and me in turn, and I felt us lock back into one unit. Listening to my sisters' breathing, feeling the warmth of their bodies as we stood side by side, felt good and familiar. I closed my eyes and bowed my head as my hands finally stopped shaking.

A WEEK LATER, a thick white envelope in our mother's hand as she made her way down the Hill well after dark. We watched her set down her keys and open the huge orange binder she kept atop the refrigerator, easily grabbable in case of fire. This was our war plan, filled with checklists and photocopies of letters we'd sent the city council, the governor, Congress. She opened the envelope and slid the contents into a folder behind a new tab.

"Kelly's sniffing around," she said. "She heard about the incident with the fence."

Of course we knew when our mother said Kelly, she meant Kelly MacLain, the secretary of DHHS, the state's Department of Health and Human Services. We knew the names of all the legislators and lawyers, the advocates and allies who with a stroke of a pen could turn Wards B and C, too, into hulking silos of empty stone. We dreamed about yanking those pens from their hands and breaking them.

We gathered around her as she flipped forward in the binder, with Mimi leaning against me so as not to put weight on her new cast.

"What do we do?" asked J.J. I had thought that the destruction of her dolls would make J.J. angry at our mother, but if she was, she had hidden it deeply. Instead, she seemed even more eager to prove herself.

Our mother exhaled. "We're going to need to move faster," she said. And then she looked back up through the tiny dark kitchen window, and we knew she was staring past the walkways and the trees to the four stone buildings: shuttered Ward A, bustling Wards B and C, and the admin building planted firmly in the middle. Four buildings to match four daughters, the shape of the grounds the same shape as our family.

People often asked our mother why she fought so hard for a crumbling institution in a state she hadn't even visited until she'd turned twenty-four. "Because it's the right thing to do," she always told us. But there are so many causes one can devote oneself to wholly, and this cause was so difficult. Was it the power she was able to wield? The respect she was unlikely to find anywhere else? Yes, and yes. But there was something else too.

Our mother's own mother had seen shadows, ones that seemed real enough that she cut her skin where they touched her. Our mother's father, Grandpa Cross, was convinced that prayer alone would save her, and when those shadows drove her car off the road and into a tree, he said simply that they must not have prayed hard enough. Our mother was nine.

It could have destroyed her but it didn't—it inspired her. She went to school, then to battle, to keep the occupants of the wards locked inside. A type of love so entirely intermixed with a desire for control that you couldn't separate the individual parts. It drove her like gasoline.

As for us, it would be wrong to say we were simply soldiers, acting out her orders. You have to understand, it was Mercy Hill. It was more than a place we lived, it was the place we were made, as if our mother had gone out and formed us from the red clay mounded beneath it. The last of its kind, an asylum for those who could go nowhere else. From our births, we had been fighting for this mission, our goal reinforced by constant attacks from the outside world.

We four pressed in tighter around our mother until the heat of our breathing felt like the beginnings of some fire. Then, after a long moment, Lisa Cross smiled.

"Good girls," she said, "I love my good girls." And we moved in close together, holding each other and holding her, unable to tell where we ended and the others began.

TWO

I'd never been in this part of town before, never even driven through. As we turned in off the highway, rows of shotgun-style houses greeted us, their yards grassy and overgrown, many of them with high chain-link fences. Then came the Chavis Heights projects, two-story brick buildings edged in with concrete, with a rusting laundry rack sunk into the cement in front of each stoop. After leaving the Mercy Hill's verdant campus, it felt particularly strange to see no trees. When the school building appeared around the corner, a vast swath of shining windows and orange brick, I got a funny feeling in my stomach, like I wasn't supposed to be here at all.

It had been six weeks since the incident with the fence, and Mimi, who sat beside me in the back seat, had graduated from cast to a walking boot. The cuts on her arms had also faded, although along her cheek you could still see a raised line, two shades whiter than the surrounding skin.

Our mother tapped the steering wheel with her nails. "J.J. and Caro, I want you to make sure the littles find out where they're supposed to go before you run off. It's not every man for himself, you're a team."

"Denise is in 1605," J.J. said without turning around. In the front seat, she held tight to the leather messenger bag she'd chosen in lieu of a backpack, and I could tell that despite her confident answer, she felt just as nervous as the rest of us about what was going to happen next.

This was the plan: rather than continue on at the local public elementary, our mother had petitioned to transfer us all to Lincoln, an academically rigorous secondary school in Raleigh's downtown. On top of the transfer, each of us would skip two grades, with J.J. starting tenth, Caro ninth, Mimi seventh—and I, who had already toured the fourth-grade classroom with my friends on Move Up Day and seen the well-stocked art corner with its bright bottles of tempera paint—well, that memory faded quicker than a dream. I'd be a middle schooler now, a sixth grader, with a locker and a morning class called Health Education.

Why our mother was executing this plan was no secret: we all needed to move faster. As she'd feared and predicted, the incident with the Scarecrow had incited Kelly's rage, and talk of a budget cut was looming. On top of that, a bitter patient advocate had sent the *News and Observer* a letter detailing a situation with two residents, a cigarette, and a length of copper wire and the resulting articles had emphasized *unsafe conditions for residents and staff*. Our mother now stayed late most nights on conference calls, and left the cottage again before dawn.

We were going to this new school, Lincoln, to learn the skills we needed to help her defend our territory—composition and history and statistics, the chemistry we'd eventually require for premed.

Lincoln was what was called a magnet school. In order to comply with legally mandated desegregation in the '60s, Raleigh began pouring resources into a few select schools in poor Black neighborhoods. These institutions, with their glut of advanced classes and professional-looking theaters, drew affluent students "like a magnet" and promised to uplift the entire student body. We'd soon learn the limitations of this promise, but today the building just seemed tall and imposing.

Our mother stopped in the carpool line and turned around, taking in our scrubbed faces and stiff new jeans, four heads of carefully combed dark brown hair—J.J.'s cropped, Caro's curled, Mimi's cinched back, and mine still damp in two braids. After an almost too-long moment, she cleared her throat. "Girls . . . if I could have done this at your age, I would have been the happiest child in the world."

We all knew what she was referring to. After our grandmother's death, our mother's father had allowed no books but the Bible to remain on his shelves. To get an education, our mother had to borrow dictionaries from the library, hitchhike to take the SAT, handwrite her application to Princeton. These stories seemed to shine through the pores of her face, and I felt my sisters do as I did, pushing our fear deep down into our stomachs, trying to find some fragment of gratitude instead.

When we said nothing, she cleared her throat. "Don't let anyone tell you you're not ready for this." Then she turned back toward the road and we scrambled out of the car as fast as we could.

We entered the building four abreast, squeezing together tight to fit through the front doors. At our old school we'd mostly ignored each other upon arrival, each settling into our own circle of friends, classmates our same age. But in this bright, crowded hallway, I pressed close to J.J.'s side like we were deep underwater. Around us, hundreds of older kids streamed in from the T-shaped entrance, hugging and shrieking as they met after a summer apart. In vain, teachers tried to corral the tide; in some cases they were not much taller than the students themselves.

A few boys I saw boasted stubbled beards, and the air

smelled different from the hallways I was used to—deodorant and cologne fighting in vain against a sweat more odorous than I'd ever encountered. I imagined my old friends, miles away at my old elementary school, smelling only construction paper and playground sand.

The grades 6–8 classrooms were in a wing off to the right, and Mimi and I allowed ourselves to be swept into that tide while Caro and J.J. continued onward to the portion of the building that housed the high school. Abruptly, a teacher grabbed my arm. "AG or GT?" she asked and I blinked up at her.

"I'm room 1605," I said, clutching the schedule that had arrived in the mail.

"Is that AG or GT?"

"I'm Denise Cross," I said, looking for Mimi, but she too had disappeared.

"Let me see that," the woman said, taking hold of my schedule. "Okay, that's AG. Those classrooms are right down there, you'll be the second door on the left."

I was so confused I didn't thank her. As I began to learn the ins and outs of the school, I'd eventually understand what she was asking. The school was divided into two tracks: Academically Gifted, which meant the magnet kids, and Gifted and Talented, the ones who lived in the blighted area around the school. These were euphemisms that allowed the administrators to strictly bifurcate the population while putting on a good face. I'd soon learn that *all children* here were Gifted and Talented, but *only some* were Academically Gifted, like I was. But on this first day, it was like everyone was speaking a different language. However, as I shuffled toward the door the woman had pointed to, I did notice one divide: all the Black students were going to the right, the white and Asian kids to the left.

My heart was high in my chest as I entered the classroom,

which did not have an art corner, only rows of beige chairs fitted with hard plastic arm desks. Kids sitting in these chairs had dragged them into little clots, and I scanned the room for one to join. It was easier to make friends one-on-one, but joining a group seemed like the bigger payout—get in with a clique, get in with all. These new kids were older than me but I had older sisters; I knew how to punch above my weight.

I walked up to a handful of girls who were seated in the back. They were all wearing the same baby doll tee from Limited Too, in coordinated pastel colors. And even though they were just as flat-chested as I was, I could see the spaghetti-strap outlines of their training bras pushing against the tight fabric.

"I'm Denise," I said.

They shrugged and I sat, dropping my new backpack on the floor with a thump. "Whew, that thing's heavy."

"You're tiny," said the girl in the purple shirt, without giving her name. "How old are you?"

"Nine and a half," I said, realizing a second later I shouldn't have said the "half."

Purple Shirt snorted. "You're younger than my brother."

"I don't know your brother," I said, not sure what else to say.

"Awkward . . ." Pink Shirt said.

I flushed a deep red. I'd soon learn that at Lincoln, *awkward* was one of the strongest insults in your arsenal. It cut deeply because it indicted every part of you at once, dismissing your looks and speech and thoughts as ill-fitting, when what you wanted most was to fit in.

I took a deep breath, and tried to explain: "I didn't want to skip two grades, but my mom made me. I've got three older sisters, she made them each skip two grades too." When no one responded to this, I felt myself begin to jabber. "Our mom's cool but it's kind of her way or the highway, you know?

When she got the job at Mercy, I think Daddy wanted to live in a normal house and commute, but she was the one who said they should try living on campus and fourteen years later, here we are."

Purple Shirt cocked her head. She was clearly the leader. "Y'all live at Mercy downtown?"

"Yeah," I said. "Not like, in the wards, but in staff housing."

"What's Mercy?" Green Shirt asked.

"Mercy Hill Mental Hospital," Purple Shirt said, her eyebrows almost disappearing beneath her bangs. "It's a jail for crazy people."

I was dumbfounded. It took me a minute to find my words.

"No," I said. "No, it's different from a jail. The HB95s may have committed crimes, but they've been found not guilty by reason of insanity. And most of the residents haven't committed crimes at all."

"And you sleep there?" Pink Tee said. "You sleep there with them?"

This play on words was too much—did I *sleep* with them? Like *sex*!

My voice rose in pitch. "No, I said that already. We live down the Hill in our own cottage."

"Oh my god," Pink Tee said. "They live in a *cottage*."

My frustration rose. "We only live on campus because my mother has such an important job—"

They kept cutting me off. "Im*por*tant," they mouthed. "Im*por*tant!"

"Why did you skip all those grades?" Purple Tee said. "Are you some kind of genius?"

My mouth felt dry. I didn't feel very smart right now.

"Oh, jeez," Purple Shirt said. "We didn't mean to make you cry."

"I'm not crying," I said, which was true at first, but then my throat tightened.

"Don't cry," said Pink Tee.

"Don't cry," said Green Tee.

"Girls!" Mrs. Owens appeared behind them, rapping on Purple Tee's desk with her knuckles. She was an imposing woman, strict and unsmiling, and I immediately thought of my teacher last year, kind old Mrs. Jenkins who sat in a circle with us to sing songs on her guitar. I felt my throat close even tighter, hot tears of shame and sadness gathering behind my eyelids.

"Girls," Mrs. Owens said. "I hope you're making all of your classmates feel welcome."

"We're trying," Purple Tee said. "We listened to her life story."

For some reason, hearing her say the word *story* tipped me over the edge. I felt a sob bubble in my throat and could not swallow it down fast enough. I tucked my chin so the others couldn't see the tears falling down my cheeks.

Mrs. Owens sighed as she addressed the rest of the clique. "Girls? I think you need to come sit in the front with me."

They raised their voices in a chorus of complaint. They hadn't been doing anything! It wasn't their fault I was crying! They didn't know what had made me cry! Mrs. Owens just stood silent until they all kicked their backpacks toward the front of the room. She followed them without looking back at me.

THAT AFTERNOON, with no credentials to drive past the guardhouse nor space to turn around at the top, our new school bus let us out at the very bottom of the Hill. As we climbed single file up the concrete steps, I felt the gaze of the other riders prickle my neck, and sank deeper into my shame.

After my encounter in homeroom, I'd tried in vain to strike

up conversations with other kids in Language Arts, Math, and French—with similar, disastrous results. Rumors had spread fast, and each time I approached, the others smirked. *We know who you are, the girl who lives with the crazies.* Judging by my sisters' absolute silence as we climbed, they hadn't fared any better. When the sounds of the bus faded and everything was quiet, I heard Caro in front of me sniffle softly. J.J. must've heard it too.

"Don't be such a fucking baby," she said without turning around. Her own voice sounded tight enough to snap.

I watched Caro's shoulders begin to shake. J.J. whirled around and I wondered if she was going to hit her. She hated when any of us cried, like it reflected some weakness in her by association.

Just then I saw another figure walking down the path toward us.

It was a man, very tall and very thin, dressed in the gray sweatsuit worn by the Ward B residents. He was holding a big blue sheet of paper that we knew had our mother's signature at the bottom, an off pass. We were used to crossing paths with residents but rarely got close enough to touch—our last face-to-face encounter had been with the Scarecrow.

"In my mind, I'm going to Carolina," he sang. He had a sweet and clear voice but the tune was entirely wrong, James Taylor's lyrics fitted against the melody of "Over the Rainbow." "Can't—you just feel the sunshine—sunshine—" He scowled as if he knew something was off but he wasn't sure what it was. When we reached him, he stopped and scowled more. "'Scuse me, girls. Heading through."

J.J. straightened and motioned for Caro to come up next to her. As if they hadn't almost just come to blows, Caro obeyed, and they stood shoulder to shoulder to block the path.

"Do you need some help?" J.J. asked. Even though the off

pass flapped like a flag, it seemed odd for him to be out here, with no clear destination.

"In my mind," he repeated, no tune this time. "I'm going to Carolina. Caroline Kennedy, world's preeminent optometrist. I'm sorry but I'm going to be late." He took a step toward us, but Caro and J.J. didn't move. We were ten yards downwind from the guardhouse, a small brick building with a long steel arm that stretched out over the road. It remained down but pedestrians could walk around it, which he of course had.

"Are you taking the bus?" J.J. asked. The street at the base of the Hill whirred with traffic and I could see the concern in J.J.'s eyes. Two minutes ago we'd been blubbering about classroom injustice, but now we each stood tall with responsibility.

"I'm—going—to—Carolina," he said, emphasizing each word. "In my mind, and everyone else's too." He tried to step around Caro, but I scrambled beside her. Up close, the man had long, dark eyelashes and hair, and gray stubble on his chin. Looking at him gave me a loose and untethered feeling that made me doubt my own reality. What was rational, anyway? To silently lug a backpack up the Hill or to be singing as you traipsed down it?

"We can help you," I said, trying to seem steady and mature. "If you can just tell us where you're going."

"Pardon my French," he said. "But I said I'm going to Carolina. With Carolina. *Inside* Carolina."

"Fucking A," Mimi said. "Do you mean the Carolina Cab Company?"

The man's face broke into a smile. "In your mind too, I suppose."

Mimi laughed, then J.J. "Okay," J.J. said, "I'm sorry, I get it now. You should go wait in the guardhouse, they'll pick you up at the gate." We'd frequently seen this cab service pick up residents to shuttle them to medical appointments that couldn't be accomplished within the wards. Preeminent optometrist—this must be for eyeglasses.

When he hesitated, Mimi said, "It's nice in there. They've got a couch and a TV." It was a white-hot August day and so humid it felt like you were breathing underwater.

The man, still smiling, shook his head. "Ain't it just like a friend of mine," he sang, "I'll go-going." And with a long, slender hand, he brushed me to the side.

We all turned to watch him walk down the steps and turn past the tangled hedge of Osage orange that had been planted centuries before to protect Mercy Hill from prying eyes. At the apex of the day, the tangled trees cast only short shadows, and when he got down to the bottom, we saw him perch himself on the weathered bench by the road, which had no protection from the sun.

Mimi was telling the truth: the guardhouse was air-conditioned, the sofa inside old but soft. It was crazy in all senses of the word to give that up. And yet my throat closed again, memories of the day at Lincoln returning. In that moment I understood why the singing man would take the boiling heat of discomfort over just one more minute of being locked up.

THAT NIGHT, our mother made us a special dinner to celebrate our first day at Lincoln, and although I'd looked forward to spaghetti and store-bought garlic bread for weeks, when I sat down I discovered I had no appetite at all—the others, too, served themselves only the tiniest portions. Our mother ignored all this, pouring deep glasses of sparkling grape juice for us and insisting we clink them against her and Daddy's glasses of wine.

"A toast!" she said, and like when she dropped us off, her happiness seemed to catch in her throat. "I have so many questions about your first day!"

Fortunately, these questions were academic and therefore easily batted back. Did any of our teachers have master's degrees? Would we dissect frogs in science or had PETA gotten ahold of the school first? Did J.J. think precalculus would be enough of a challenge, or should our mother try to get her into the AP course that came after?

"I'd be okay switching," J.J. said.

Our mother glowed with pride. Or maybe that was the wine. But Daddy looked concerned. "You know, school is about more than just academics," he said. "What about your electives? Did everyone get the electives they wanted?"

We all nodded into our noodles. Daddy, looking uncomfortable, pressed further. "Mimi, what about you? Did you get into Woodshop?"

Mimi sighed. "Daddy, they don't put magnet kids in Woodshop."

"So who takes Woodshop?" Daddy said.

"The GT kids are the only ones that get put in the technical electives," Mimi said with the know-it-all confidence of someone who had learned this today. "You know, the kids who live in the neighborhood around the school."

"Really?" Daddy said. "The—uh—"

"African Americans?" J.J. said. "They're not really in any of our classes except for Gym."

Daddy set his wineglass down. "Am I the only one who finds this odd? It's like the school is segregated."

Our mother let out a very short and sharp breath. "Tucker," she said. "This is just the way things are organized. There isn't a lot of back-and-forth between the base kids and the magnets."

"It's not all white," Caro said, sounding uncomfortable. You weren't supposed to talk about what race other people were, it was like commenting on their weight. "There are a lot of Asian kids in the magnet track."

"That's different," Daddy said.

"Why?" I said.

"Well, it's not like anyone's banned from the magnet program," our mother said.

"Then why aren't they in it?" Daddy said.

"Our children's school isn't the place to correct *all* past injustices." She craned her head to look out the kitchen window and I knew where she was looking: the empty field that once housed the old mansion. Like so many parts of our city, Mercy Hill had been built on the site of a plantation, and one of my earliest memories was watching the old mansion where the owners had lived get raised onto a flatbed truck to be hauled away. Even though the building itself now resided on the grounds of the local college, you could still feel the bumps in the grass where it had stood. Standing there made it seem like the plantation's dark history hadn't happened very long ago.

Daddy didn't say anything and for once, neither did my sisters. In the silence, I felt like I needed to defend our mother. "Guys," I said. "There's an African American girl in my Language Arts class who moved here from Senegal. She's in AG with me."

Our mother didn't respond to this, she just looked straight at Daddy. "You're just opposed to Lincoln because it wasn't your idea," our mother said. "You can say that without bringing race into it."

"But race has been brought into it," Daddy said.

"Here's a fact," our mother said. "More seniors from Lincoln go to Ivy League schools than any other school in the state. I'm sorry that your city hasn't done a good job providing opportunities for its disadvantaged students. But—"

"This is your city now too," Daddy said. "You've lived here longer than you ever did in Massachusetts."

"But our girls are not disadvantaged. It's not fair for them to miss out on an opportunity because of your high-minded commitment to . . . *ethics*."

Daddy stayed silent for a long moment. Then he turned to me. "Denise, what's the name of the girl from Senegal?"

It felt like I was being tricked, but I had no choice but to answer. "Corinne-Marie," I said.

"I want you to invite her over next time you get a chance," Daddy said. "Ask her if she'd like to come home with you on the bus and do your homework together."

"Tucker," our mother said. "Don't put Denise on the spot like that."

"I thought you said it didn't matter," he said.

They both looked at me and my face flushed. The argument was making my head swirl. I wanted to shout at them—*I couldn't ask* anyone *to come home with me, everyone hates me!* But my homeroom rejection seemed small compared to the weighty argument they were having, which felt at once taboo but also grounded in a very uncomfortable truth.

This would be my first introduction to the reality of our city's racism, although it would take years and a college course dedicated to the subject for me to be able to call it by that name. Now it was an unutterable feeling, dark and heavy and tangled in my own sadness. It was hard to pick out where the history ended and my own feelings began.

When I looked up, both our mother and Daddy were still looking at me. I didn't meet their eyes when I said, "I find it easier to do homework alone. If I had a friend over, I think it would distract me."

This seemed satisfactory enough to both of them that they left me alone after that. I think they both thought that they had won. As I watched them bring forkfuls of spaghetti to their lips, I felt a bright spike of anger rise within me. It almost seemed like I wasn't a person at all but a game piece that they were fighting over. It made me feel small, plastic, disposable.

THREE

"I don't think Denise should be allowed to give a speech," Mimi said. "She's way too young." We were all sitting on the floor of our room, making covers for our textbooks out of brown paper grocery bags. It was one of the few Lincoln assignments we'd all been given, although each of us was approaching it differently. Conscientious Caro folded the paper with origami-like precision; J.J. was using duct tape the way boys did; Mimi didn't tape hers at all, her typical performance of rebellion that sprang up each time she encountered authority. It had been this rebelliousness that had pushed her along the edge of that branch into the Ward C yard, and now that her walking cast was gone, she seemed eager to show off how little she cared about everyone else's rules.

"Shut up," I said, low enough that Daddy couldn't hear. "She said we all had a part to play."

"And yours is to look cute," Mimi said. She flipped through her textbook with a mean smile—*Introduction to American Literature*. I didn't understand what she was driving at until I saw her hold up the illustration: four girls in old-fashioned dresses beaming around a piano. An excerpt from *Little Women*.

"I'm not," I said, trying to keep my voice steady, "fucking Amy."

Due to the makeup of our family, we were often gifted or assigned to read copies of what we called Sister Stories: most familiar, of course, *Little Women*, but also the girls in the Little House series (more interesting by far, the bitchy one blinded by scarlet fever), the Pride and Prejudettes (too old, too boring), and *The Poisonwood Bible* (long, but loved the presence of venomous snakes). Ascribing someone to their dull birth-order character in one of these stories was a popular way of needling each other, but before I could turn around and tell Mimi that at least I wasn't the one who *died*, Caro broke in: "We have no idea what the council wants," she said. "Maybe Denise won't have to talk at all."

When our mother had first asked us to accompany her to a hearing for the city council and to prepare speeches, we immediately recognized that this was a request we should take seriously. A developer had recently made a proposal to rezone the empty Ward A for commercial use and planned on turning the lot into rentable office space. Although the proposal concerned only the single building, it would set a precedent that our land was for the taking. In the war we were fighting to protect Mercy Hill, this was to be a major battle.

J.J. yanked out the duct tape with a screech, wrapping a long strip around the back cover. She'd used so much tape that you could smell the flecks of rubber in the air. It was clear she was nervous—we all were.

"Denise will do a good job if she has to," she said, sounding a lot like our mother: a compliment wrapped in a warning.

Then our actual mother stepped in, opening the door without knocking. "Are you girls ready? Put those books down and get in the car, Daddy's driving." She paused, surveying our outfits and shoes and hair, gaze landing on Mimi's fingernails, which were colored black with Sharpie. "Can you get that off?"

Before Mimi could have a chance at a rebuttal, she said, "Never mind, just keep your hands in your pockets."

The entire drive down the Hill and through the guard gate and onto the wide road that led downtown, she gave a series of snappy orders: Enunciate. Don't act rehearsed. Call the adults *ma'am* and *sir*; they're Old South, these people. And don't talk too fast.

Daddy stayed silent, parking behind the Capitol Building and leading us around it. Bronze statues cast long shadows in the setting sun. Confederate generals, mostly, along with busts of Andrew Jackson, Andrew Johnson, and James K. Polk, North Carolina's underwhelming contributions to the presidency.

When we got to the municipal building where the council met, he said only, "You girls are going to do great." Then, after holding the door for us all, he let it close in front of him. I still don't understand what calculus led him to stay behind that day—a request of our mother's, surely, assuming that a squadron of females would look more sympathetic. I know now that it was a miscalculation: with both parents, we felt inspired and safe; with only our mother, that safety was gone.

Inside, the meeting had already started, with grown-ups in work clothes sitting around a table scattered with papers and an empty box of Krispy Kreme doughnuts. I think we had all imagined something grander, because as we filed into seats at the front of the room, Mimi shot me an incredulous look. This was not how we expected real power to present itself.

Besides us, the audience was sparse. A few rows back, five women wearing purple NAMI shirts waved at us as we walked in, but following our mother's lead, we did not wave back. We knew that these advocates from the National Alliance on Mental Illness were on our side, but we had often heard our mother complain that they aimed too low. *A bunch of do-gooders with schizophrenic sons and depressed daughters,* she said. They were good at organizing a bake sale, not at holding legislators' noses to the grindstone.

And were these really the legislators in question? They seemed so ordinary. A man seated at the end of the table, with bushy eyebrows and a gut that looked like it could have accommodated several of the Krispy Kremes, nodded as we entered. "Lisa's here," he said. "Now the fun can start."

Although he smiled when he said this, his voice sounded weary. I thought about the number of times our mother had left after dinner to "see the council." But if she too was fatigued by this rematch, she didn't show it.

"I'll wait my turn, Tom," she called out.

Tom looked out at us and chuckled. "Come on," he said. "Let's get this over with." He picked up a yellow folder. "I move that we discuss the zoning proposal for 1102 and 1103 South Ward Boulevard."

Our mother sprang up. "1103 only," she said. "1102 was not included in their package."

"A revised package was submitted earlier this week."

"Where's the transparency?" Our mother's voice had sharpened, and I felt relieved that it was pointed away from me. "Information like this is required to be accessible to the public—"

"Lisa, we just got it Tuesday. You're hearing about it now, along with the rest of the public." He waved his hand at the seats around us, mostly empty.

Our mother's mouth tightened into a sharp circle. "This is a big addition. Ward A is empty. But Ward B is a full and functioning wing of a state hospital."

I felt a block of ice descend into my stomach. Beside me,

Caro's head was bent low over her chest. She'd probably recognized what was happening as soon as Tom read the second address.

"Do you have a plan, *Tom,* for where these people will go when you bulldoze their living quarters? Are you going to host them all in your guest room?"

Tom sat up straighter. "It's not the job of the council to discuss accommodation for patients, that's a state matter. And, *Lisa,* it might not happen. Ask Kelly. All we are discussing is whether, at some point in the near or distant future, 1102 and 1103 can be used for commercial real estate. We've examined the proposal and it makes some fair points."

A woman with very bright blond hair in the shape of a helmet spoke up. It would be the first and last time we'd hear from anyone other than Tom.

"The hospital was built in a different century," she said. "Why not use the land for something that brings in tax revenue, not spends it?"

Our mother turned and met her eyes. Embarrassed, the woman looked down.

"I'm not going to waste my breath," our mother said. "But maybe you'd benefit from a child explaining it to you." Then her arm was under my elbow, pushing me out of my seat. "Denise has something prepared. Will you cede the floor?"

Tom's weariness returned. "Yes, Lisa. Give her the microphone."

The mic felt heavy in my hands, like a baton for an unwinnable race. Throughout my adolescence and later in my law career, I'd give many speeches. And every time, I'd feel an instant of transport, flashing back to this moment, where my words first meant something. The absolute stillness of responsibility.

"In nineteen sixty-three," I began, "President John F. Kennedy signed into law the Community Mental Health Act. He didn't like state hospitals either. His younger sister Rosemary Kennedy, who had a severe psychiatric disorder, was given a lobotomy in one. He wanted to create a network of community mental health centers so everyone could be treated closer to home. But he died before that dream could be realized.

"In the early nineteen eighties, the Reagan administration used the Community Mental Health Act to justify cutting spending on psychiatric care. Many state hospitals closed, and when they did, the residents had few places to go. Some became homeless and a lot went to prison. It's likely that ten percent of all prison inmates suffer from SMI—severe mental illness."

I paused and looked up at the blond woman, nervous about going off script. "The residents, they work in the gardens and go on trips to the art museum and to UNC basketball games. But when they come back to campus, they have a home. Even the ones who can't leave, like the Ward C population."

I looked over at Mimi's scar, which stood out white under the room's harsh fluorescents.

"They're people, too. They need somewhere to call home. So please don't tear down their homes."

I handed the microphone back but kept standing. I had gotten in all my points without trembling. J.J. could suck it.

Tom frowned. "I didn't catch your name, sweetheart, but I urge you to spend a little more time researching the facts. Many people believe that Ronald Reagan did more good for this country than any other president."

"Those *are* the facts," I said, my voice suddenly feeling very thin without the microphone. "You can look them up in any encyclopedia."

"Lisa," Tom said.

"Denise," our mother said, "you can sit down now."

Frustration bit through me. Of course this was all true, it was what she'd taught us! The years that she'd been engaged in this fight, she'd said that we should play fair, overcoming resistance by being smarter and better prepared than the other side. Now, for the first time, I saw that she could be wrong. It made my stomach twist to witness Lisa Cross fail.

"I'd like my other girls to have a chance to speak," she said. "But it sounds like you've already made your decision."

Tom leaned back, clearly more relaxed now that he was once again in control. "It may be years before it happens," he said. "The second ward, if it's so full and providing services . . . the basketball games . . . I see no reason why development would proceed. Just because they can doesn't mean they must." He turned away from the audience, showing us the thinning hair on the back of his head.

"Girls," our mother said, "it's time to leave."

Even I could tell that getting up now was against protocol. The council was forced to pause their deliberation while we gathered our things, scraping back our folding chairs and walking directly in front of them as we headed for the door. After we'd all walked through, our mother yanked it shut behind her, the slam reverberating up the frame and echoing through the room behind us.

J.J. crossed her arms in her baggy sweatshirt. "I wish Denise hadn't said that stupid thing about Ronald Reagan," she said.

Our mother cut in. "Denise was perfect," she said, pressing her hand to my cheek. Even though we had lost, and even though J.J. would surely torment me later, I didn't care. Rising to the level of Lisa Cross's praise was rare. There was nothing like it on earth, at once comforting and exhilarating.

"And," she went on, "Tom left us a pretty big loophole. If the bid is for both buildings, I doubt they'll start unless they can take both at once."

"Full and providing services," Caro echoed, and our mother smiled.

"Precisely," she said, and stepped out into the darkness without a backward glance to see if we would follow.

FOUR

Even now, as an adult with decades of painful experiences to compare it with, thinking about the next two months of sixth grade still feels like a minor form of torture. By October, Lincoln had not gotten any friendlier. Although I hadn't spoken about Mercy Hill since the day I'd introduced myself, the kids in my class all knew where I came from. They saw which bus I rode, the brief moments I crossed paths with my sisters, even the pens I brought in my backpack, the ones with spell-like names printed down their sides that our mother passed along from drug reps: Celexa, Zyprexa, Geodon.

They began calling me Psycho Denise, or PD for short. At first I played along, even signing a few of my papers with the new initials, but somehow that gesture made the game more enticing, not less. I couldn't walk past the sixth-grade lockers, or through the gym or auditorium, without hearing a phantom voice call out, "Hey! Hey, Psycho! Hey, Pee Dee!" It made me curl into myself, furious at my face for betraying me by blushing.

My sisters were clearly experiencing their own flavors of torment. When I saw them in the halls, Mimi was frequently being escorted to some sort of detention, and Caro passed by me with such silence I often didn't notice her until she was already gone. Then there was J.J. It wasn't enough to say that she was *a* teacher's pet, more like she was *the* teachers' pet. Everywhere you turned, she was in some classroom helping organize the file cabinet or clean out the library book drop, following staff members—some of whom weren't even her actual instructors—until she could be praised for assisting them. I wondered sometimes if she missed her dolls; it seemed as if she were lining up teachers the way she used to line up those figures, dutiful head down as she went about the unending tasks of keeping the adults around her happy.

ONCE EVERY COUPLE OF MONTHS, and largely without warning, we were all of us subjected to dinner with Grannie Palmer, Daddy's mother. Although she was wealthy enough to afford any restaurant in the city, the only place she ever invited us to was "the club"—a stuffy, oak-paneled dining room attached to the North Raleigh golf course at which she was a nonplaying member. Depending on traffic, it could take over an hour to get there, especially when you included the time spent hiking up the Hill to the employee lot and then waiting in line at the security gate for them to let us out onto the main road. It was hard to leave Mercy Hill and except for the bus to school, we usually didn't.

In October, we received the next one of these invitations—our first since starting at Lincoln. As we filed in, I tried to see if anything had shifted since our last visit, but nothing in the club ever changed to mark the passage of time. The dark-paneled walls, starched tablecloths, and chunky crystal water glasses looked the same as they always had, which made me feel cramped, like I was stuffing myself into clothes I'd outgrown the year before.

"I can't believe we still have to do this," Mimi said, voicing aloud what I'd been feeling. School was so painful, and the loss at the city council meeting so recent, that it seemed like surely we were owed a break.

If our mother felt the same way, she didn't show it. "Miriam," she said sharply, somehow fitting an entire paragraph's worth of warning into one word, *"behave."* Then, spotting Grannie P. at a table near the window, she smiled wide and rushed over ahead of the waiter.

Grannie P. was dressed in one of her many pastel pantsuits—periwinkle, this time—with a blouse underneath so starched and white it matched the tablecloth. She did not get up to greet our mother but smiled beatifically as the rest of us ambled over.

"My son and his family," she said to the waiter, an older Black man (at the club, only the waitstaff were Black). "The Palmers."

"Actually," Caro said. "Only Daddy is a Palmer, the rest of us are just plain Cross." Then she made an exaggerated frowning face, looking up at our mother for approval. This was the joke we told when people didn't know that we had our mother's, not our father's, last name.

Grannie P. pursed her lips and Caro looked stricken. Walking into the cavernous dining room was like entering another country, Grannie P.'s personal kingdom: a place where the rules were spoken in a different language and the power of our ruler (our mother) greatly diminished.

"It's lovely to see y'all," Grannie P. said and rose to offer her cheek for Daddy's kiss.

"It's good to see you too, Momma." Daddy's southern accent rose up whenever we were around Grannie P., but our mother would have choice words for us if we followed suit. She had been born in the North, and often told us that a drawl made you sound stupid—no matter how smart you actually were.

"Can I get you started on some drinks?" said the waiter, who had lingered. Daddy and Grannie P. ordered wine, our mother a martini. When the waiter turned to me, I felt a surge of new boldness wash over me and asked in a loud, clear voice for something both parents refused to buy us at the store: Hawaiian Punch.

"Denise," Caro said, "you can't order that at a nice restaurant."

"This is *not* a nice restaurant," Mimi said, loud enough for our mother to hear and shush her again.

I nodded at Mimi and scooted closer to her, thus forming an alliance of we youngest two, the so-called littles, against the older ones. You might think this was our most frequent way of dividing allegiances, but it was only one of many. Caro and I ("the quiet ones") often teamed up against J.J. and Mimi ("the louds"), and there were times J.J. and I threw in our lots together, because we understood our mother better than dyed-in-the-wool daddy's girls Mimi and Caro. And this only accounted for the even fights! More common than these were variations on two against one, with the fourth girl claiming impartiality in order to be wooed by both battalions, only to come in at the last second with a devastating swing vote.

"Perhaps," the waiter said, "our bartender could mix you up something—nonalcoholic, of course. Some fruit juices and something fizzy?"

I grinned at the waiter. "Yes, please. That sounds great." Caro kicked me hard under the table but I didn't care.

Grannie P. shook out her napkin. "Four beautiful girls," she said.

"Four smart girls," our mother added, and even though it sounded like she was agreeing with Grannie P., Grannie P. pursed her lips again.

"I see you're out of the brace," Daddy said. He was seated next to his mother, too close to turn to her directly, so when he spoke, he locked eyes with me instead.

"Oh, Tucker, I've had it off three months." She moved her wrist back and forth like she was holding an imaginary quill. "Has it really been that long since we last saw each other?" There was a sudden edge in her voice and I felt J.J. beside me stiffen.

"Imogene," our mother said, "we'd like to see you more, but it's busy this time of year. If you would ever come to us—"

"Here," Grannie P. said, picking over the words, "just feels safer. Call me crazy, but I don't feel right going through—"

"Three layers of security, I know." Our mother pushed her water aside without drinking it. "But Imogene, it is my *job* to keep things safe. When you say it's not, what you're saying is—"

"Good *lord*," Daddy burst in, drawing everyone's attention to the waiter, who had returned with our drinks. Set apart from my sisters' Sprites was a veritable goblet, liquid inside pink as a sunset and garnished with a wedge of orange and a matching pink umbrella. As the punch was placed in front of me, Daddy put his fist to his mouth like it was a trumpet, *do-do*-ing a reveille fanfare. Both Grannie P. and our mother laughed, the tension broken.

While our mother was billed as the brilliant one, Daddy had his own set of skills. From him, we learned how to put people at ease, the unwritten rules of who belonged and who did not, how to get someone to do what you wanted by convincing them it was their own idea. This distraction was no exception and when our mother received her martini, she clinked her glass against his, smiling a real and private smile. I relaxed and leaned forward to swirl the straw in my drink, listening to the rush of fizz. I could feel my sisters' silent jealousy pressing in on me. Then I put my mouth to the straw and sucked as hard as I could.

Oh! The drink tasted like raspberries and sugar, buoyed on a platform of sharp carbonation. I really thought I'd be lifted by it, like the forbidden concoction in *Charlie and the Chocolate Factory*. In a life marked by fourth-hand clothes and Barbie dolls that arrived with their hair already cut off, how wonderful it felt to have something the others did not!

I felt Mimi's forearm press against mine. Ugh, fine. I needed at least one of them on my side; it was suicide to alienate all three others at once. I tapped the straw in her direction so she could try it.

"Good lord," Mimi said, in a voice mimicking Daddy's. "This is *excellent*."

Caro and J.J. exchanged a dark and jealous look. Before they had a chance to respond, Grannie P. said, "Tucker, I do need an answer soon on cotillion. The fall session is almost full."

"Cotillion?" Caro said.

Grannie P. smiled. "Classes, just like your Daddy took. Etiquette, social dancing, when you're eighteen, you're thrown a wonderful ball . . ."

"We've already told you," our mother said, "we appreciate the offer but the girls are very busy. When the school moved them up two grades . . ."

I looked over at J.J. who raised her eyebrows, a quick moment of truce. When *the school* moved us up? We were watching Lisa Cross rewrite history in real time.

"You can poo-poo cotillions all you want," Grannie P. said. "But the skills they teach . . . the connections they could make . . . One of the recommendation letters for Tucker's law school came from George Fischette."

"Who?" our mother asked.

"Grace Fischette's father," Daddy said, voice soft. "I was her escort to her deb ball." Then he turned back to Grannie P. "Momma, I know cotillion is important to you, but there are other things we're doing to raise our girls with, you know, social graces."

"And history?" Grannie P. had still not touched her wine. "Tucker, your father was a cotillion graduate."

"I don't know if bringing up Dad is a good idea."

Everyone but me seemed to tense up. "Caro," I whispered in her ear, "why can't we talk about Papa Palmer?"

"Ssh," she hissed, too loudly. This wasn't typically Caro's MO, but I guess I deserved it for not letting her have any punch. Or maybe she too didn't know and was just pretending. It took a few more years before I'd get all the pieces together myself: Daddy's daddy, like Grannie P., had come from a wealthy old southern family. Their courtship, wedding, Daddy's birth—all of it had been picture-perfect and widely celebrated. Then, when Daddy was still a toddler, his father had run away to Los Angeles with another man. They got into an argument, and Papa's lover pushed him down the stairs, accidentally killing him.

Those last seven months of Papa's life were something Grannie P. refused to recognize, like our not being named Palmer. She never remarried, and to hear Daddy describe it, Grannie P. spent his childhood preparing Daddy to fulfill the destiny that his father could not. That meant cotillion, deb balls, Kappa Alpha in undergrad, Duke for law school. He took the bar but never made it into that white-shoe firm. Instead, he met our mother and threw away money and prestige and what Grannie P. called history to move to the Hill and care for the four of us. You could paint it all as an act of revenge, and maybe that was part of it. But as I got older and saw Daddy more clearly,

I began to imagine how lonely a childhood it must have been and how desperately he wanted to build something different.

The waiter came by again. Grannie P. and our mother ordered steaks, Daddy a hamburger—an argument that would play out many times over the years: how comfortable they each felt spending Grannie P.'s money. J.J. and Caro ordered the fried chicken and Mimi, trying to get a rise out of our parents, asked the waiter if the salmon was sustainably caught. He said he'd have to check but by then Daddy and our mother were both looking down darkly and Mimi huffed, clearly deflated by the lack of attention.

"I'll have the pigs in blankets," I said, which is what I always ordered.

"You're such a baby," Mimi said.

The adults didn't register the depth of the insult, but the rest of us sucked in breath. Calling a Cross sister a baby was the ultimate rudeness, attacking the very things we were most proud of—our intellect, our self-efficacy—and it ramped up the tension like an assault on home turf. It was as shocking as if she'd said, *You're such a cunt.*

I scooted my chair away from Mimi's and then reached back to remove my drink firmly from her reach. Forget the alliance.

She shot out her hand and yanked the stem toward her, straining forward to snag the straw in her lips.

"Mimi, Denise," our mother warned, which normally would have been enough to freeze the whole scene. But the prize was just too great. I felt the balance change as Mimi's strength won out, felt myself beginning to lose grip.

With no other path available to me, I let go.

The force of her pull sent the goblet smacking into Mimi's forehead, punch flying like it had been pumped from a sprinkler, covering the table, the plates, and spattering pink across the fronts of everyone's shirts.

"Jesus fucking Christ," our mother said.

"Lisa!" Grannie P.'s eyes widened.

The restaurant suddenly quieted: I hadn't realized how loud it had been before, but now there was nothing, not the rustle of silverware or the murmur of conversation.

Grannie P. raised her eyebrows at Daddy. "They do make a compelling case for cotillion lessons, don't they?"

No one said she wasn't just as funny as the rest of us!

FIVE

That month our volunteering began, the work that our mother had alluded to the night of the committee meeting. As Tom had said, Ward B's best defense was that it remain *full and providing services*. Well, here we were, to provide those services.

Our first day started cool but the flat afternoon sun roasted our backs as we trekked up the winding path to Ward B. We'd been inside before, for the Christmas party and on various errands to bring office supplies from the admin building when the staff requested it, but stepping onto the hall today felt different. I couldn't stop staring at the worn linoleum in the hallway, the sliding glass window that opened into the nursing station, the iron-barred windows painted white and the red emergency telephones dotting the walls. It felt like a foreign country that somehow existed entirely within our borders, like Lesotho or Vatican City.

Once inside, J.J. bossed us into action. At the front desk, she got directions to Francis's office, the head administrator who'd been our mother's partner on the wards for the last ten years. We'd seen him around, but mostly from afar, jogging from building to building with bulging stacks of papers, tearing out of the employee parking lot in his Acura, chasing the FedEx man for the last pickup of the day. Besides his busyness, we knew little about him, and until we showed up on his doorstep, it seemed he knew little about us.

Knocking on Francis's open door, J.J. led us in and held a hand across his desk, waiting awhile until he shook it.

"Wow," he said, pausing as he took in the sight before him: four dark-haired, stick-thin children staring at him with the same bright and focused gaze. "Y'all really do take after her, don't you?" Francis was a kind-eyed man with a thick southern accent. He wore a wedding band on his right hand, which made me wonder if he was gay. But his khakis were wrinkled, his polo shirt altogether too large. Weren't gay men supposed to be a lot more fashionable than this?

"We're looking forward to helping you out," J.J. said. "As volunteers."

"Your mother sent you," Francis said, as if he was trying to make sense of this. "Your mother sent you?"

"Didn't she tell you we were coming?" Mimi already looked unimpressed by Francis, and I was wracking my brain to try to remember what our mother had said about him. She had strong opinions about the other doctors and nursing staff but rarely spoke about this man, which I guess must have meant he was not someone she considered an obstacle to our mission.

"She says y'all are great girls," he said. Then he smiled in a way that seemed like he was trying to decide if he should treat us as children. "Who do you go for? State or Carolina?"

We stared at him blankly. Without a television, allegiance to college basketball was a concept we understood only theoretically.

"Well," J.J. said. "Our mother did her medical residency at Duke. . . ."

"Blue Devils!" His voice got higher-pitched. "I should've suspected. Go to hell, Duke!" Then he looked down at his hands. "That's just—it's something people say."

"We know," J.J. said. After a long pause that Francis did not seem eager to fill, she said, "Our mother said to come here and ask you what help you needed."

The jolliness faded quickly from Francis's face. "We don't have a volunteer program anymore. Sometimes folks come by from the old times, and we have to turn them away. We don't have the right oversight, you know? The right structure?"

"We don't need structure or oversight," J.J. said. "You can talk to our mom if you need proof."

Francis paused for an even longer time. Looking down at his hands, he said, "This ward, you know—it's not your mother's domain."

"She's the director of psychiatry," Caro said, then blushed, as if something we'd known all our lives could potentially be wrong. "The director for the whole hospital—right?"

"Yes, yes." Francis waved a hand. "Lisa is very important. But each ward has a clinical lead too, and Aaron's in charge here—Aaron Holt."

Ah, yes. We'd heard about Dr. Holt; our mother thought he spent too much time with the beautiful drug reps who rolled their suitcases of samples into the guardhouse weekday mornings. At dinner she called him a confused Freudian who couldn't hack it in private practice.

"But technically, isn't our mother Dr. Holt's boss?" J.J. had taken control again, as though our mother was speaking through her. "So, like—the whole place is her domain, isn't it?"

Francis took a long breath in through his nose. "I don't want to cause bad blood," he said.

J.J. puffed herself up. "If you don't think we can help, fine.

But once she finds out that you said no . . ." She swallowed, seeming to realize that that sounded like a threat. And it was! We could all imagine what would happen if our mother came home to find we'd been turned away: she'd be up the Hill to Ward B before the screen door shut.

"What time is it?" Francis said.

This was a funny question. "Three forty-five," I said.

"Okay." Francis put his thumbs to his temples, breathing like a squeeze-box. "Okay. Dr. Holt isn't here. If Dr. Holt isn't here, it's—it's fine." He stood up quickly. "Sorry, let's go get you started. I'll find someone to show you around." He waved his arm out the office door and after a moment, a nurse appeared. Her name was Jenny and she was one of the staffers who lived on campus with us, a plump woman with long hair hanging in a childish braid down her back.

"Hi, girls," she said. "It was good seeing you at the council meeting. Denise, your speech was very powerful."

I blinked. I hadn't realized she'd been in the audience, but then I realized she must have been wearing a purple shirt, one of the NAMIs. I eyed her with suspicion.

"Say hi to your mom for me," Francis said, and then quickly shut the door behind him.

And that was it. No instruction, no release forms, no warnings. At the time, of course, I felt perfectly capable; I'd be ten in two months, which meant I was almost a preteen, which was almost a teenager, which rubbed shoulders with adulthood. We wanted to help so badly, and hadn't everyone been telling us for years how smart we were?

When I think about it now, I want to go back and shake all these adults by the shoulders. We were *kids*—what did they think was going to happen?

WE FOLLOWED NURSE JENNY out of the office the opposite way we'd come, into the ward itself, a long hallway with doors every few feet. Inside each door was a different resident's room, which we could see into because of the peculiar way the doors were configured: each had two parts that operated independently, a lower half and an upper half. Most people had left the bottom part closed but the top part open, and some were leaning out through this makeshift window, staring at us as we walked down the hallway.

I tried not to stare into the rooms as I walked by, but it was hard not to. The residents all wore the same gray shirt and sweatpants, but many of them had accessorized further with cardigans and baseball caps and windbreakers, although it wasn't yet cold. The residents themselves were as wide an array as I'd ever seen: young and old, men and women, mostly white except for one Black man with hair shorn so short it looked tattooed on his scalp.

Nurse Jenny said hi to the residents who were standing in their doorways. Most of them didn't react at all, except one woman with a normal-looking face but only a few teeth, who called out, "Babies!" I couldn't tell if this was a conversation starter or not. No one here is dangerous, I repeated to myself. If they were dangerous, they'd be in Ward C.

We turned a corner where the smell of bleach and overcooked peas betrayed the presence of a cafeteria. Across from that was a common area where a few residents sat in folding chairs, reading or doing puzzles. An enormous tube TV played an old black-and-white movie, but no one was paying attention.

Nurse Jenny stopped here and looked us over for a moment. She seemed to be the most hesitant about this whole operation, but it was clear she wouldn't disobey Francis's orders.

"So, what do you want us to do?" J.J. asked her.

Nurse Jenny waited another long moment, then sighed. "Can you get Bethy dressed? She's in the bathroom at the end of the hall. Her clothes are in room eleven." Then she left with a quick nod, like she was walking away before she had the chance to change her mind.

"This sucks," Mimi said. "I don't want to get anyone dressed."

"Shut up," J.J. said, her bossiness amplified by the strange situation.

"I'll do it," Caro said. "I don't mind." If J.J. or I had said this, it would have enraged Mimi, but Caro's sweetness was so genuine, it was impossible to fight. Mimi scuffed her sneaker on the already-scuffed floor and began walking.

I trudged along with my head down, trying not to meet anyone's eyes as we passed the gauntlet of half doors. When we reached room 11, J.J. pushed in. It was a little smaller than our own bedroom at home and had no windows, just a low wooden bed, a nondescript dresser, and an old radiator standing in the corner. A stack of paperback thrillers sat on the floor but otherwise, nothing gave us any clue as to who this Bethy was. The name alone made me think of a child, hair braided like Nurse Jenny's.

From the dresser, J.J. pulled out a pair of sweatpants, a shirt, a bra, and some underwear, and handed it all to me. The clothing smelled sharply chemical, like not all the soap had washed out.

"At the end of the hall," J.J. repeated. She got this way when things seemed overwhelming, pulling herself together behind a shield of process and efficiency.

The bathroom was large and white-tiled, with stalls and a long trough sink, and beyond that a large open shower with eight showerheads but no dividers. The water had been turned off but the hole at the center was draining slowly, so an inch and a half of soapy water remained. Sitting in that water was Bethy.

She was a woman about our mother's age, with one white streak in her dark hair, like a witch. She was fat but only a little, the kind of weight you could hide with flattering clothes if you were not sitting on the floor of an institutional shower wearing only a hospital gown. The wet bottom of the gown spread out around her, moving with little ripples as Bethy patted the flat surface of the water.

J.J. strode up. "We're the Cross sisters," she said. "Nurse Jenny said to help you get dressed." Her tone was so commanding that I half expected Bethy to rise immediately. The woman hardly turned.

"Thank you, but no." Her voice sounded so normal I wondered if we were the crazy ones.

"Why not?" Caro stepped toward the lip of the shower.

"I really need to relax right now." Bethy looked up. "It's important for my mental health. I'm sure you ladies understand."

"You're sitting in dirty water," Caro said. "You could get sick from the germs."

If Bethy heard this, she didn't let on. "I've been working so hard," she said. "And it's just going to pick up again once we get into the busy season. They need me at peak performance."

"Who does?" Mimi asked.

"God, it feels good to relax." She closed her eyes and moved her legs in and out like she was making a snow angel. The water, gray with dirt and writhing with strands of hair, sloshed against the lip of the shower. I couldn't look at it, it was too disgusting.

"You know what would be relaxing?" J.J. said. "Taking a nap. We're here to help you get dressed so you can do that."

Bethy opened her eyes. "Who sent you?"

J.J. took the towel from me. She tiptoed into the water until she was right next to Bethy. "I think you know who," she said.

The rest of us held our breaths. Our mother often spoke

about her work, but had never instructed us on what to do specifically when someone was delusional. It seemed like J.J. was just winging it, and it was entirely unclear if this tactic would pan out.

J.J. must've done something right, because Bethy pushed herself up to stand and took the proffered towel.

"I haven't been sleeping well," she admitted. "I'm one of those people who really needs her sleep."

"I'm sure," J.J. said, offering her a hand. Bethy didn't take it but began stepping away from the drain. When she reached the dry floor, I held out my bundle of clothes. Up close, Bethy smelled bitter, like almond skin.

"You're young," she said. "You're too young to work here."

"We're geniuses," I said, only kind of believing it. "We all skipped two grades." I held out the bundle and shook it a little.

After an eternity, she reached out and took it. She stepped into the pants one leg after the other and shrugged on the sweatshirt.

"You—uh, missed some things," Mimi said. I was still clutching the bra and underpants.

"She's going to go take a nap," I said. "You don't wear a bra when you nap." I didn't wear a bra at all but that seemed logical enough.

The four of us corralled Bethy out into the hall and back to her room, where I left the undergarments laid out on top of her dresser in case she wanted them later. She stood beside the bed without climbing into it.

"Do you need anything else?" Caro asked.

"I need to relax," Bethy said. "Sorry, but it's just so important."

We let ourselves out of the room. "What are we supposed to do next?" Mimi hissed.

"Go find one of the nurses, I guess." J.J.'s bossiness was diminishing.

We wandered, dreamlike, back through the hall and into the rec room, where we saw Nurse Jenny. When we told her we'd gotten Bethy out of the shower and back into her room, clothed and mostly dry, she stopped short and looked at us like she was doing math in her head.

"You're serious about volunteering?" she said.

"If you'll have us," J.J. said.

Nurse Jenny closed her eyes. "I wish we didn't need your help," she said. Then before we could say anything else, she sent us off to collect the trays from the residents who'd eaten in their rooms.

As we moved through the ward, we began to get the lay of the land. At present, there were thirty-five residents living on Ward B, with Nurse Jenny and Dr. Holt in charge of the care for all of them. There were two other techs, Robert and Frank, two part-time social workers, and one man in the kitchen that everyone just called Chef. Francis didn't seem to do much at all; he stayed in his office typing on his computer and didn't look up when we scurried by, carrying trays or blankets or SlimFast smoothies for the residents who'd refused dinner.

We moved fast enough that the time too moved quickly and soon it was six o'clock, when another nurse arrived to relieve Nurse Jenny. Nurse Jenny walked with us into the ancient elevator, and when the doors closed, she let out a long sigh.

"Thanks for your help," she said. "Truly."

Mimi looked at Nurse Jenny with raised eyebrows. "How come Francis doesn't do anything?"

"Francis has a hard job," Nurse Jenny said. "He writes letters asking the government for all the things we need. It's a struggle."

I got the sinking feeling in my stomach that came when I thought about the failure of the city council meeting and the threat of bulldozers. Changing the subject, I said, "What was Bethy before?" In my mind, I imagined her as a successful lawyer who'd had a psychotic break after staying up for a hundred hours to win a case.

"Bethy's never been anything," she said. "I don't think she even finished high school."

Before I could fully consider this, the elevator doors opened and I heard a familiar voice.

"Is this the new class of interns?" Our mother was walking toward us, white coat swinging. "Hi, Nurse Reynolds."

Nurse Jenny's face took on a stiff mask of respect. "Hi, Dr. Cross. It's good to see you." Then she turned abruptly and went back down the hall.

Even though I was getting too big for it, I jumped into our mother's arms. She stroked my hair and smiled down at my sisters. "You all had a good time?"

"Yeah," J.J. said, speaking as usual for the four of us.

I heard the elevator doors open again, then the sound of footsteps. I felt my mother's grip slacken, releasing me to slide down to my feet.

"Lisa."

"Aaron."

I whirled around. A man was standing there with his hands in the pockets of his slacks. He was taller than my mother, with a trimmed reddish beard that made it hard to tell if he was young or old. Although he was not wearing a white coat, I knew he must be Dr. Holt.

"What are you doing here?" he asked, then seemed to realize how harsh that sounded. "I didn't expect you on the ward, is all." The way he said *the* made it sound like he was saying *my*.

Our mother didn't match his retreat to softness. "I could say the same about you." She looked down at her watch. "It's almost six fifteen."

"It's in my contract to end at three."

"And you're so precise. Never staying a moment later."

I looked over at J.J. She shrugged. I hadn't realized that there was some piece of paper, signed undoubtedly by Kelly MacLain, that listed how long our mother was supposed to be at work. Her job seemed like a deed, not a contract, a property onto which her life had been built.

"I left my distance glasses at my desk," he said. "Ellen and I going to a movie—date night." I could tell he felt embarrassed, telling us more than we needed to know. "Why are your daughters here?"

"We're volunteering," J.J. said. I sucked in breath, waiting to see how mad our mother would be that J.J. spoke for her. But J.J.'s similarity to our mother meant that she sometimes got a pass for speaking out of turn.

Our mother put a hand on her shoulder. "Yes, they just started today."

Dr. Holt put his hands together so quickly I could feel the rush of air. "No—Lisa, you don't have the authority."

"You need the help."

"Lisa, I refuse to be spied on."

Our mother smoothed the front of her white coat. "They're not spies. Jesus Christ, I don't need to send my daughters to find out what's happening on my own ward." Now she had said *my*. This felt like something Daddy would pay attention to, were he listening in, and so I began a score under my breath. Lisa Cross: 1; Dr. Holt: 0.

"I'll speak with Francis."

"Go ahead."

"I'll write to Kelly."

"Do you want an inspection? A chart audit?"

Beneath the beard, Dr. Holt's cheeks burned red with rage. "You put me in a very difficult position," he said.

I waited for our mother's comeback. Whenever we whined that something wasn't fair—which Dr. Holt was, in effect, doing—our mother was quick to remind us that circumstances didn't matter, only what we made of them. I could tell she thought Dr. Holt was soft, but something prevented her from diving all the way into a fight.

In the coming months before the terrible thing happened that ended our volunteering altogether, I'd come to realize that our mother did, in fact, need Dr. Holt. Part-time, inflexible, Freudian Dr. Holt did serve a purpose here and it was one of Lisa Cross's least favorite traps to be in—needing someone.

"They'll come only after school," our mother said, voice gentler. "Three thirty to six. You'll be long gone." It was another snipe at his contract, but he seemed too tired to take the bait.

"Okay," he said. "Fine." Then he walked quickly past us and down the hallway to the offices.

"Enjoy the movie," our mother said, quiet enough so only we could hear. Then she corralled us into the elevator.

When the doors closed, Caro said, "I can't believe he called us spies."

Our mother arched an eyebrow. Then she put her arm around me again and squeezed. "I'm so proud of you girls—you saw it, right? How much help they need?"

We all began to talk at once. Bethy and the shower and the dinner trays and the medication closet—the social workers smoking with the residents in the dayroom—the roaches, bigger than we'd ever seen, skittering from under the door to the boiler—each experience seared into our brains with unexpected newness. Even though the day had been confusing and strange, I felt taller, stronger, more adult.

The elevator doors opened and we walked out past the security desk, our mother nodding once at the guard, who straightened when he saw her and said only, *Ma'am*. It was all new and fascinating, we spilled out into the warm evening with rising voices echoing back to us from the great stone walls. Our mother's eyes gleamed in the semidarkness.

"I'm glad you had a good day," she said, starting off down the cracked path. "And you'll tell me, won't you, if you see anything wrong? Be my eyes and ears, when you can." Then she paused. "But not spies. Jesus Christ, Aaron needs a fucking Ativan." Then she laughed and we laughed with her, our voices mingling as they rose, weaving into a blanket of sound that couldn't be untangled.

This is how we had always been, the Cross sisters, identifiable only at close range as individuals, more ourselves when we were together, like those trees in the Tetons that share a single root. Growing up in such close proximity, we borrowed traits like clothing, trying on a week of moodiness or bossiness or cunning, then abandoning it when one of the others chose it for her own.

All of this began to change as we left the safety of the cottage for the new world of Ward B. The work there was difficult and scary and carried with it an impossible weight if we should fail. This adversity sharpened us in different directions, branching out to the paths that would eventually take us far away from Mercy Hill and from each other. Like distinct chemicals, we reacted differently when heated. Like chemicals, too, one of us would explode.

2000

SIX

"She's your age but she's not like you," Nurse Jenny said, in a way that made me think she wasn't telling the entire truth.

"Whose age?" Caro said. "We're all different ages."

Nurse Jenny didn't answer. "Sorry," she said. "I really have to go."

It was February and we'd been volunteering on Ward B for four months now—through Christmas, when an anemic artificial tree was brought into the dayroom; through the January blizzard, when we'd gotten an unheard-of twenty inches of snow and, because she was the only nurse on campus, Nurse Jenny had slept on a cot in Francis's office for two nights straight; through a late flu outbreak that tore through the closed-window building, the echoes of the residents' wracking coughs replaying in our heads even in our sleep.

Even though sometimes the work could be gross or tedious, I looked forward to it as a welcome break from Lincoln, which had not gotten much better. The Psycho Dee stuff had cooled down as long as I stayed as quiet and still as I could, like prey frozen in a meadow. In each of my classes, I got there early and buried myself in my notes, chanting mnemonics in my head until the teacher began to call roll.

This intense focus on academic material meant that I rarely

received less than a 100 percent on my schoolwork, but I didn't like looking at the congratulatory notes the teachers wrote on the top of my papers. To me, they were a side effect of a loneliness I didn't want to dwell on. I often carried the tests and quizzes straight home with me and dropped them into the big, messy trash can that greeted you when you entered Ward B, destroying the evidence of the intolerable part of my life as I entered a place where things became okay.

That afternoon on the ward, we were engrossed in preparations for the dinner rush, gathering all the utensils for the upcoming meal. We set Styrofoam cups, paper napkins, and a single plastic spoon at each seat. Everything served was soft enough to be eaten with the spoons—shredded chicken and dumplings, beef stroganoff, chili. The kitchen smelled vaguely foul with the scent of hot dishwater clouding the air, but if you tried the food, it was salty and good.

You could start to eat dinner at four and many of the residents did, Bethy and a woman with a shaved head moving through the line first. Immediately after them, I caught sight of her, the one Nurse Jenny had been talking about. She was the youngest person we'd ever seen in Ward B, probably closest in age to fourteen-year-old J.J., although in her overlarge sweatshirt and pants, she looked younger than that. She had long white-blond hair and nearly white eyelashes, which made her face look unfinished, like a doll waiting to be painted. She got her tray and came straight over to us, like we were saving her a seat in a school cafeteria.

"Volunteers or someone's kids?" she said, not looking up from her plate.

"Both," Mimi said. "Our mom is the director of psychiatry."

"Nice. All the male doctors are douchebags."

"What are you doing here?" Caro said.

"You're not supposed to ask that!" J.J. said.

"You're thinking of prison," the girl said, which was unexpectedly funny. "I'm here because I keep trying to kill myself. You know this place is free if your parents are poor?"

"Are your parents poor?" Caro asked.

"They are now. Don't have a depressed kid, that's my advice."

This was a lot to take in. The girl seemed so confident and magnetic—and young! I could no more picture myself trying to commit suicide than picture myself piloting a jumbo jet.

Mimi kicked me in the shins, which meant the rest of them wanted me to act too young to know better and ask the question we were all thinking.

"Why do you keep trying to kill yourself?" I said.

"Denise!" J.J. said, really pulling off the performance. "Don't ask her that!" Then they all got quiet to hear what she was going to say.

She shrugged. "I don't want to now. But sometimes I do. You know?"

"No," Caro said. "I don't think we do."

"If you don't get it, you don't get it. Do they have Mello Yello here?"

"Only Pepsi products," I said.

"God," she said. "This place sucks."

"What's your name?" Caro said.

"I don't have to tell you that," she said.

WE DIDN'T EVER call her by her name. It wasn't like it was a secret; it was on her door (although we never went in), and we often heard the nurses saying Ashley this, Ashley that. Nevertheless, we never addressed her by it and never used the name when we spoke about her among ourselves, calling her the Girl instead. It was never confusing, because everything she did was so wildly out of the ordinary that only she could have done it.

The Girl stole food. The Girl refused to shower. The Girl was mean to everyone, especially Nurse Jenny, whose kindness she cackled at. The Girl called us the shitheads and threw a pack of cards in Mimi's face.

But the Girl was funny. She had experience. She had spent the last years in and out of facilities like this one, and the stories she told were fantastic to the point of disbelief. And when one of us said, *No, I don't think that man ate two cartons of cigarettes, paper and all*—well, we weren't there, were we?

The Girl called us sheltered, which we countered by pointing out that we went to public school each day. She said that didn't count, that even from in here she could tell the way the world worked. That's why she couldn't stand it, she said. If everyone just opened their eyes to what kind of stuff was really going on all around them, they'd want to kill themselves too.

When she said that kind of thing, I made her promise not to do anything drastic without warning us first. Then she'd laugh and say she was kidding, I shouldn't take her seriously, but it took a long while to calm my fear. I looked at the others and knew without asking that they worried too, and for the same reason: she was the closest thing any of us had to a friend.

SUMMERS ON THE HILL felt like continuations of the year previous, like picking up a book with the page folded down. By mid-May, the whole city begins to steam like towels in a dryer, the itchy scent of honeysuckle and kudzu permeating the air. Because of the heat, schools finished by Memorial Day, releasing us full-time into the care of our parents, which for us meant Daddy.

Our love for Daddy was boundless. Our mother we feared,

emulated, and admired, and in turn were met with capricious reward. Daddy was the consistent one, the patient one. When posed with an argument, he strove for fairness; our mother was forever saying we lived in an unjust world, which we knew of course was true, but was deeply unsatisfying when Caro used up all the bath beads in one go.

That summer, things felt different. Daddy didn't bring the kites up from the basement, he didn't buy new baseballs to replace the ones we'd lost playing catch the summer before. There was no talk of trips to the public pool or getting up early to drive to Carolina Beach for the day. Instead, he packed us lunches to bring to Ward B, sending us off each morning the same time we would have left for school.

No one asked us to do this, we just knew we had to. The staff shortages had gotten even worse; some aides showed up for only a week before disappearing for good. When we walked by Francis's closed door, we could hear the urgent sound of his voice behind it, and it made us all walk faster.

Each morning, the laundry was overflowing, cups were strewn about the dining room, residents yelled from their rooms for blankets or magazines. The worst part was the medication schedule, which was frequently between one and six hours late. Antipsychotics, antiepileptics, all of these neurological medications required precision in administration. Give them too early, and side effects doubled, wracking the residents with back-arching muscle contractions; give them too late, and you risk delusion breaking through.

I had heard our mother's diatribes when her own staff in Ward C fell behind on this task. It put us at risk of violating the Wyatt standards, the rights to care that the Supreme Court had established in the '70s for anyone treated in an institution, which put us at risk of losing our Medicare and Medicaid funding, which spelled absolute utter disaster. And so, when a nurse gave us cups of pills to distribute, we took off at a flat run.

Now that we came earlier in the day, we often saw Dr. Holt. I was scared, initially, of incurring the wrath that we'd seen on the first day, but when we weren't with our mother, he greeted us with cautious friendliness. I could tell he still thought we were spies, but while his body strode the halls, it was clear his mind was elsewhere. It was a strange thing to witness, because at home we often saw the opposite: our mother eating a belated dinner or stepping into the shower or slumping down on the couch, her mind clearly still stuck eight hundred feet away in the ward she'd just left.

Most of the residents ignored us the way you ignore the busboy coming to take your plate, but a few of them latched on. Besides the Girl, of course, and Bethy, who called us the geniuses each time we pulled her out of the shower, there was an old woman named Mona who liked to stroke our hands and offered us pudding from her dinner tray, and Jared the singer, who caught our eyes as he belted out lyrics that did not match their melodies.

Then there was David Johnson, who always introduced himself with both names and spent his days in the rec room reading. David frequently seemed too lucid to be cooped up here, he liked talking to us about our classes, especially history, and told us he'd once written a master's thesis on Raleigh's role in the Reconstruction era. David's normalcy was tempered by the gloves he wore that were strapped around his wrists: if left to his own devices, he would pick holes in his own skin, and his face was pockmarked with these self-inflicted scars.

The characteristic each resident shared was what our mother called *resistance to treatment*. Not that they didn't take their medicine or want to get better—but as we came day after day and month after month, the men and women we saw did not seem to change, and very few of them ever left the ward. I quickly realized that this had been a sort of natural selection: over the last decades, anyone who was capable of showing even the least bit of improvement was quickly discharged. The ones we saw each day were the ones left behind.

The importance of this work cast a long shadow over every other aspect of our lives, like the midday shadow cast by the wards themselves. When we were in Ward B, we were doing something huge, and right, and good. It was like breathing a different type of air. When we left, it drained us, made us duller and irritable.

One night as we walked home in the dark, Caro began to cry.

"Caro, dude," said J.J. (That summer, J.J. was experimenting with incorporating the word *dude* into her vocabulary and it was not going well.) "What's wrong?"

We had reached the periphery of the Ward B rec yard, a grassy circle dotted with a few stone benches. Caro went over to one and touched it, but did not sit down.

"I feel so bad for her," she said. We all knew she was talking about the Girl. "We get to come in and out each day, and she *can't*, you know? It's like that door for us is made out of paper, and for her it's made out of stone."

I waited for Mimi to make fun of this clumsy metaphor, but she stayed quiet. Instead, J.J. turned back, gaze reaching up the dark hill to the Ward B building, where every light was on.

"If she gets better, she can leave," J.J. said, her voice measured and practical. "And being treated here is her best chance of getting better."

"Is it really, though?" Mimi climbed up onto the bench and hoisted herself to stand on its narrow back. She stepped along this ledge like a balance beam, arms outstretched. "We're so fucking understaffed."

This was true and getting truer by the day: a few weeks ago, the night shift workers had stood at the staff entrance bearing protest signs that read WE NEED MORE NURSES. Our mother had been called over from Ward C to talk with them, and after a few minutes, they'd dispersed, sheepish. I still don't know what she said.

"Get down," J.J. said to Mimi, who was still balanced on the bench. "If you get hurt, Mom will blame me."

"What did you mean?" I asked, ignoring J.J. "Mimi, what did you mean, just now?"

Mimi walked the length of the bench and then turned around slowly. "You think she's really gonna get better here? Or Bethy or David Johnson or any of the others?"

"None of us can know for sure," J.J. said. "But just because something is difficult doesn't mean you should give up."

Mimi stopped walking and stood poised on the bench, looking down at something on the ground the rest of us could not see. "I just wonder," she said, all the bravura gone from her voice. "Would she do better somewhere she's not locked up? *Less restrictive accommodation.*"

"But Mimi," I said, incredulous. "That's deinstitutionalization."

"I'm aware of the definition of *deinstitutionalization.*" Mimi's voice was sharp.

"So you're on their side?" J.J. said. "You want us to shut down?"

"Jesus, J.J.," Mimi said, voice flat again. "Not everything is so black-and-white."

"She deserves *help,*" Caro said, sniffing back the last of her tears. "I'm sorry, that's all I meant." She took my hand and moved us back up against J.J. so the three of us facing Mimi were a united front.

Mimi looked from J.J. to Caro and finally to me. Her gaze was so strong I had to look away. "Whatever," she said, and jumped back down to the ground. "Forget I said anything."

THEN DR. HOLT did the craziest thing we'd ever heard of: he went on vacation. Nurse Jenny reported that he and his wife had gone on a Caribbean cruise and couldn't be reached for ten days. I'm sure it had all been planned and organized and approved—*the contract!*—but the first time we heard about it was the first day we showed up and saw our mother standing with Nurse Jenny outside the office where Dr. Holt saw patients. She'd be providing coverage, she told us, splitting her time between Wards B and C. When she told us, she seemed to be looking not at our faces but only the vague outlines of our bodies, as if evaluating quickly what part we could play in helping her. *It's me,* I wanted to say, *your daughter!*

She turned back to Nurse Jenny, shaking a bottle of pills. "Who let it get so empty?" she said, and I scuttled away.

For the next week and a half, we did everything we'd been doing, but quieter and more quickly. I wasn't sure if I was worried about running into my mother, or excited—but it turned out I didn't need to prepare either way. She spent almost all her time in Dr. Holt's office, where patients were brought to her one after the other. I stayed away from the office as much as I could until day eight, a Sunday.

I was carrying one of the plastic containers of needles to Francis's office where it would stay until it could get picked up—Nurse Sonya had tripped over it during a very busy morning and screamed so foully I thought one of the residents had managed to break a window and jump. Staggering under the weight of the tub full of sharps, I was shuffling past Dr. Holt's office when I heard my mother's voice.

"It's okay to be scared," she was saying through the door. "Different is difficult."

I stopped. Her voice was familiar, but her words were careful and slower than I'd ever heard before. At home, unless it was very late or she'd had wine with dinner, her speech streamed forth without pause. And God help you if you missed one of her rapid-fire instructions or asked her to repeat herself.

On the other side of the door, she paused until a man's voice said, "I don't know. I look at it and it just looks wrong. It's always been blue. Nice things are blue."

"The sky," she said, agreeing with him. "The sea. There's some sort of instinct deep within us that feels drawn to the water."

"Evolutionary," the man said. "Exactly."

I lowered the sharps case to the floor and crept closer. Although the door to Dr. Holt's office was fully shut, like every door in the building it was warped so badly that if I tiptoed up to it and pressed my eye to the back of the hinges, I could see everything happening inside. There was an exam table covered in paper but it was unused. David Johnson, the historian, sat in a chair next to my mother. For once, he wasn't wearing his protective gloves, and his hands were clasped together so tightly they'd turned pale.

"Let me look at it again," he said.

Our mother handed him a little thing I couldn't make out, then I realized it was a vial.

"Haloperiodol," he said. "That's the same. But it's yellow."

"The needle caps are yellow, yes. The drug, however, is the same."

David Johnson held up the vial so the fluorescent light shone through the clear liquid at the base. "It's the one that works."

"It's the one that works when you take it," my mother said, firm.

David Johnson closed his eyes. "Dr. Cross," he said. "I trust you. I trust this place. But I look at that yellow and—"

This would be the only time I'd hear her interrupt him. "Take one," she said, and handed him a capped syringe. He held it out in his palm like it might explode.

"Look at it, feel it. Tell me if anything seems different."

He looked down at the needle. "I read," he said slowly, "about needles infected with AIDS. People leave them in the seats at movies. Biological weapons. Hemophiliac children—don't tell me it's not been done before. Tuskegee. I'm not Black but the government still hates me." His whole face was getting agitated, eyes squeezing shut in painful-looking blinks. "You probably think I'm not making sense."

"No," my mother said. "I think you're entirely making sense." She then moved her chair even closer toward him. I held my breath as she put a hand on his arm. She seemed tiny beside him, the whiteness of her coat making her shrink into the pale blank walls. "You're right about the government. When I came here in the eighties, we still had a eugenics board. But please believe me when I say: I ordered the yellow needles because they were cheaper, that's all. The plungers are smaller and harder to push down. I don't like them, either, but they're safe."

David turned the syringe over in his hand. The plastic around it crumpled.

"Here." My mother took the syringe from him and unwrapped it. I watched her fiddle with the back end of it, pulling out the plunger so it was hollow. Then she popped off the yellow protector and placed it back in his hand. She rolled up the sleeve of her lab coat and turned her bicep toward him.

"Give me a poke," she said. "I promise you these needles are clean." Then she looked straight at the door crack and I nearly slipped out of my skin. Although she couldn't possibly see me in the shadow, our eyes seemed to meet. I could see her lids flutter as she took a deep breath, preparing for the injection to go in. It was how I too felt when I had to get a shot—you forced yourself into a state of bravura until the pain broke through.

I thought maybe he wouldn't do it. I could see the hesitation in his face and the clawlike way he held the needle. David Johnson had what my mother called *insight,* which meant he understood what was wrong with him. But just knowing what a problem was didn't mean you could fix it.

"Dr. Cross," he said.

"Take your time," she said, not moving.

He lifted the syringe like a pen. It looked awkward and slippery without the plunger handles and as he brought it closer to my mother's pale shoulder, I felt a breaking urge to shout *stop!* I'd heard the same rumors David had about the AIDS needles, which seemed to be lurking anywhere you put your fingers in public, and two minutes in a city council meeting would show you just how much the government wished the people on the Hill would disappear. It was crazy to connect the two, but as I watched the needle disappear into my mother's arm, a prayer erupted in my throat. Please, let her be okay.

David yanked the thing out quickly like a burr and put a hand over his brow. I could tell he was about to cry, and this switch from fear to sadness made me feel whipped back and forth. As I clutched the door hinge, trying to steady my breathing, my mother unwrapped a new syringe, uncapped it, swiped a dab of antiseptic just below David's T-shirt sleeve, and administered the medication. She had the Band-Aid on before I could take another breath.

"You know what I just thought of," she said. "I think we've got half a case of those blue caps left over in Ward C."

David's hand was still covering his face, but I saw him give an almost imperceptible nod. Now that the whole ordeal was over, you could tell the weight of embarrassment was crushing him.

"I'll have them sent over for the next time Dr. Holt sees you."

David said nothing.

"I insist," she said. "Okay, let's get you back to your studies."

I knew I needed to get out of there fast; one look at my face and it would be clear I'd been spying, but I was glued to the scene. I watched my mother roll down her sleeve and when she turned her back to David, gathering a sheaf of papers, only then did I see her wince in pain. She steeled herself again and I backed away, forgetting the heavy sharps container and running down the hall as fast as I could.

ALTHOUGH MANY OF THE nurses and aides lasted only a short time on the ward, the one staff member who seemed like she'd never quit was Nurse Jenny. She greeted us each day and helped us with the worst tasks, telling us often how grateful she was for our "giving hearts." I wondered what had led her down the path to this job; the NAMIs often had a family member with a terrible form of mental illness. But Nurse Jenny rarely talked about herself until the day she invited us home with her after work.

That afternoon, we four were in the laundry room, separating a mountain of dirty linens into carts that would be picked up by the industrial cleaning service. Dr. Holt was back and things were more relaxed: we'd let the Girl follow us in while we worked. As we sorted, she rolled back and forth in an office chair, pestering Caro to give her a piece of the gum she'd made the mistake of bringing with her.

When Nurse Jenny appeared in the doorway, the Girl squirted at her shoes with a bottle of distilled bleach. Nurse Jenny jumped, then frowned.

"This room is off-limits for residents," she said. "Why don't you head down to recreation instead?"

"*They're* allowed to be in here," the Girl said.

"They're volunteers," Nurse Jenny said.

"Volunteers the same age as me," the Girl said, and squirted the bottle again, this time a little higher. Nurse Jenny sidestepped it.

"I'm going to count to three," she said.

"Fuck off," the Girl told her, kicking over the chair and slouching out the door.

Nurse Jenny was silent for a long moment, then looked at me. "The next time she's like that, just tell me and I can take care of it."

I didn't meet her gaze. It would have been impossible to explain to an adult, but I wanted the Girl to stick around. Sure, she could be rude and manipulative, but she treated us like normal people. No one else treated us like normal people.

"So." Nurse Jenny smiled. "I was actually coming by to ask you girls if you would swing by my place when I finish my shift today. I've got some Oreos and sweet tea." These incentives were either luck or a calculating side of her I'd failed to notice; Daddy never bought sweets at the grocery store.

None of us knew what to say until J.J. shrugged and said, "Okay, fine."

Nurse Jenny left quickly after that. When her footsteps had faded down the hall, the Girl ambled back in, clearly having heard the whole conversation behind the door.

"She's so pathetic," the Girl said. "What do you think she wants?"

"She probably just wants to hang out," J.J. said.

"Maybe she wants us to join the NAMIs," said Caro.

The Girl shrugged. "Maybe she's gonna steal your kidneys."

"That's just an urban legend," Mimi said, sounding annoyed. With her loudness and disregard for rules, the Girl was more similar to Mimi than the rest of us, and their sameness seemed to rankle Mimi, who didn't like being upstaged. I think Mimi was also still smarting from the conversation we'd had on the bench, the one where we'd accused her of defending deinstitutionalization. All that is to say, in these interactions with the Girl, she was often snappy and then silent.

The Girl didn't seem to notice, or care. Instead of answering Mimi, she picked up the spray bottle again. This time, she shot a line of bleach directly at my knee, and I was too slow to step aside. The wetness tickled, then burned, and I watched the coin-size spot on my jeans turn lighter and lighter. The Girl seemed surprised for a moment, like she hadn't meant to actually get me. Then she shrugged and caught my eye as if to say, *What are you gonna do about it?* She was always pushing the limits that way, seeing how far we'd let her take things.

I threw a clump of dirty pillowcases at her to let her know I was cool enough to take a joke. "Fuck off," I said, trying to make it sound exactly like it did when she said it.

NURSE JENNY had decorated her cottage like a mother out of a magazine. Each surface seemed to be covered with a runner or a tablecloth, red, white, and blue for the upcoming Fourth of July holiday, and flag-printed pinwheels stuck out of every vase. I looked at this stuff and just knew that by July 5th, the tchotchkes would be boxed up and replaced with their cousins, cornucopias and fall leaves made of the same expressed petroleum.

Her kitchen table was identical to ours, and we sat around it in our usual places, letting her have Daddy's position nearest the range. She set out paper plates and poured us all sweet tea from a plastic jug. Southern sweet tea was something our Massachusetts-born mother found abhorrent, although Daddy had been known to drink it on occasion. The kind Nurse Jenny had was very sweet and very strong, dark brown like cider, with a metallic taste of caffeine. We exchanged glances as we drank; it was like we were sipping cups of gin, this was so unallowed.

"So," Nurse Jenny said, setting her hands down flat on the table. "It's the famous Cross girls."

"I don't know if we're famous," Mimi said.

"Famous here," Nurse Jenny said. "It's a hard job—I mean, I find it hard, anyway. Your mother doesn't ever seem to get tired."

I thought again about David Johnson plunging the needle into our mother's arm. I was desperate to know more about what my mother did at work, it was like some vitamin I was deficient in. "It wasn't always this busy," I said, trying to draw her out. "Right?"

"Things were easier when I was starting out, before Ward A shut down. We had a lot of old-timers leave then—mandatory retirement, the state said. So a lot of the people who'd been on the Hill since the sixties, even the fifties, we lost them all. They had *stories,* whew."

I waited to see if she would start telling us one of those stories but she did not. Instead, she got a funny expression on her face and said: "I guess you could say I'm an old-timer now myself."

"You do a good job," Caro said.

"I'm not fishing for compliments," Nurse Jenny said, although as she said that, I realized that's exactly what she was doing. The clean, quiet, seasonal cottage suddenly seemed very lonely. I looked at Nurse Jenny again. It was still hard for me to tell adults' ages, but she looked younger than I'd originally thought—not as young as our student teachers, but nowhere near our parents' age.

"Anyway, I do think it's good work, you know? Not like going to a job where you're just making money—not that there's anything wrong with that, but there are rewards and there are *rewards*, you know?"

"What's your reward?" said Mimi, reaching for another cookie.

Nurse Jenny beamed. "My reward is in heaven."

The silence after this statement was so vast, I knocked over my cup. A shallow line of tea rolled out onto the laminated wood.

"I'm sorry," Nurse Jenny said, as if this had been her fault. She unrolled a wad of paper towels and placed them over the spill before sitting down again, flush-faced. "Girls, I know it's not quote, unquote, cool to talk about things like this, but it's important that you ask yourself where you want to spend eternity."

J.J. cleared her throat, assuming her position as spokesperson. "Like, God and stuff?"

"It's more than that," Nurse Jenny said. "A lot of folks talk about God—Catholics, Jews—but the real joy of being a Christian is the love of Jesus. He brings me so much happiness."

This seemed crazier than anything we'd heard on Ward B.

"Technically," Mimi said, "aren't Catholics Christians too? Do you mean Protestant Christianity, like Martin Luther?"

Nurse Jenny spluttered for a second. "Well—I don't want to get into a history lesson. I just know that I used to be sad all the time, it was like something was missing from my life, like I was seeing things in black and white. And once I met Him, everything was in beautiful, beautiful color."

I blinked, stunned by this bizarre statement. J.J. folded her hands and looked down, as if she were praying for this to go away as quickly as possible.

Mimi leaned forward, brow furrowed, and I knew a debate was coming. "Technically, you'd call yourself a what—a Methodist? A Presbyterian? A Quaker?"

"My church, we're nondenominational Christians—you might call us a mix of a lot of things."

"So do you think the other guys, the ones that don't go to your church, are they going to hell?" Mimi said. "Muslims believe that Christ was a prophet. Just not, like, *the* one. What about them?"

Nurse Jenny had surely not expected to be grilled on the validity of various Abrahamic religions, but nevertheless kept her cool.

"It sounds like you girls have a lot of questions," she said. "That is so, so wonderful. I knew you would, because you're all so smart. Like your mother."

Mimi shrugged and took the last cookie. "Our mom says religion comforts stupid people who don't understand science."

Nurse Jenny paused a long time. "Sometimes I think people who've never been to a church have a hard time understanding what goes on there."

"Our mom's dad made her go to church all the time," J.J. said.

"Ah," Nurse Jenny said. "I suppose I can't speak to her experience. I can only speak to what I know is true."

"You mean in the Bible?" Mimi said. "Because Muslims have their own holy book. It's the fastest growing religion in the world, and you're trying to tell me that they're all wrong, you're right, and when they die, their consciousness—whatever that means—is going to sink down into the magma core of the earth, where they're going to get poked by actual demons with pointy forks?"

"Shut up, Mimi," Caro said, voicing what we all felt. Of course Mimi was right, but I didn't want her loud mouth getting the rest of us in trouble. We had been invited over by this sweet, dumb, deluded lady, and now an eleven-year-old was insulting her. What if she cried?

So I was surprised when a smile spread across Nurse Jenny's face.

"This is exactly what I mean," she said. "When you don't have faith, you just feel so—angry, don't you?"

"I'm not angry," said Mimi, sounding angry.

"Thank you for the cookies," J.J. said, motioning for the rest of us to gather our things.

"Oh, it was no trouble," Nurse Jenny said. "And you'll forgive me, won't you, for bringing up such a big, serious topic? I just wanted to share it with a real bright, real sweet group of young women." The way she said the word *sweet* made my stomach ache, as if she were activating the crumbs of sugar she'd served us.

J.J. stood up and the rest of us followed. "We'll tell our mother you said hi," she said.

Nurse Jenny smiled, close-lipped. "You can tell her Francis is going to call her tonight about the budget. We need to find money for a new sump pump."

This seemed like a strange thing to say after her whole speech about heaven, but that was the way things worked here. Nothing—not even God—could compete with the monumental needs of the aging wards. Could God create a sewage backup so foul even He couldn't mop it?

"We'll see you around," J.J. said, and shuffled us all outside. In the time we'd been sitting there, the sun had sunk, the path home shadowed gray. Although the air was still thick and warm, it felt as if something alive were slithering just beyond my ankles.

"That woman is a goddamn lunatic," Mimi said. "I bet she gives all her money to her cult church."

"Then they don't have to pay taxes on it," J.J. said, echoing something we'd heard our mother say.

"She'd be better off on a good antidepressant," Mimi said. "Pop some Prozac in her sweet tea."

"Mimi, you can be so annoying sometimes." Caro shoved her.

"So you don't think she's out of her mind?"

"No," Caro said. "I think she was trying to be nice. She wants us to go to heaven with her."

"I'd rather be in hell," Mimi and J.J. both said. Then: "Jinx!"

They shrieked and giggled and tried to push each other into the bushes as we came up to our porch.

Once she touched the handrail, Caro turned. "Guys," she said. "Let's not tell Mom about this, okay?"

The rest of us stopped.

"But she'd think it's hilarious," Mimi said.

Caro looked to J.J. for support. "Please," she said, a note of desperation in her voice.

J.J. sighed and then shrugged. "Fine," she said. "It's not that interesting, anyway."

SEVEN

Another school year began, which for Caro, Mimi, and me meant more of the same yawning awfulness we'd left behind in May. But for J.J., who had completed enough credits to move into the twelfth grade, something had changed. Now that she was a senior, the countdown to college had begun, and it seemed our mother could talk of nothing else.

J.J.'s grades, like all of ours, were perfect, her SATs sky-high. As our mother enumerated these achievements over dinner—"Not to mention the volunteer hours!"—she grew pink-cheeked with delight. Her plan to steer our education upward had been proven a success.

J.J., too, seemed lit from within. She arrived late to Ward B one day wearing a skirt suit and actual heels, having come directly from an interview with a Princeton alumnus who worked at a bank downtown. It was so surprising to see her out of cargo shorts, and with a true, relaxed smile on her face, that it stopped the rest of us in our tracks.

What can I say about J.J.? She was neurotic, hyper-controlled. Had the added stress of maturity, having to trailblaze, mothering us when our real mother was working. Prided herself on working hard and selflessly and never letting a single plate slip. (Remember the dolls? Remember how she loved them and so quickly allowed them to be sacrificed?) In this way, she most clearly took after our mother.

In the old cottage, the one they'd lived in briefly until Caro was born, our mother and Daddy and J.J. all slept in one bed. J.J. claims to remember that time, even though she couldn't have yet been two. This was the secret wish that drove everything she did. That if she was good enough and smart enough, our mother would say: *Come back to nestle in between us. You've done a great job and now you can rest.*

It would be the thing that split us, her and me. Her bossiness, her constant domineering. It would come at a moment when I needed her—begged her in fact—to be my sister, not another mother. And she could not.

That moment was still years away, in a body I was still growing into, my skin shedding piece by microscopic piece until I would become an entirely different organism. My body that day was still that of a skinny ten-year-old, stubby fingers gripped tight around a push broom taller than I was. We were trying to sweep the floor of the Ward B dayroom, a task that was proving difficult since the Girl kept kicking over the dustpan. When J.J. came in, we all stopped and looked up, J.J.'s loose and unfamiliar expression halting all work.

"How did it go?" Caro asked.

J.J. actually grinned. "So when they said he worked at Wells Fargo, I was like, oh great, this'll be some old dude. But he was twenty-five—and he was *gay*. He even said his eating club was mostly queer people, like a queer community." J.J. ran her hand through her short hair, cracking the mousse. By then, everyone knew J.J. was a lesbian. There hadn't been one big coming out, just a lot of little things she'd said that made it feel like we'd always known. This was the J.J. way of things, matter-of-fact and undramatic. I'd never heard anyone use the word *queer* that way; at Lincoln it was too old-fashioned to be used as a slur but not yet used as an identifier.

J.J. was standing close enough to college that she could feel its climate on her skin, a place where you could live in a *queer community* for four years and emerge back into the real world to tell others, a type of evangelism just as intense as the one practiced by Nurse Jenny.

"So did the gay banker tell you if you got in?" the Girl said.

"He doesn't make the decision," J.J. said. "A good alumni interview is just a plus factor. But I've also got good scores and I'm a legacy. That means my mom went there too."

"I know that," the Girl said, but it was clear she was lying. She kicked once more at the dustpan, sending it skittering across the floor. I could see her trying to recalibrate with the knowledge that J.J. knew something she didn't.

"What if he gives you a bad grade, though?" the Girl said. "Like, what if he tells Princeton that you didn't seem smart enough?"

"Nothing happens," J.J. said, setting her mouth back in its familiar line. "As I said, it's just a plus factor." Even though it was nice to see her ebullient, it felt more familiar to see her like this. We all began sweeping again.

Flopping down onto the sagging couch, the Girl changed the subject back to herself. "I want to go to a party school. Like ECU or App State."

"Those are both *public schools*," J.J. said, spitting out the words like they had rotted on her tongue.

The Girl looked thoughtful. "You're always complaining about not having any friends. You're not going to have them in college either if you don't loosen up."

J.J. bent over the broom, sweeping furiously at an area we'd already covered. "I don't complain about not having friends."

"Yeah, but you don't, do you? None of you do."

I looked down at the linoleum, hating the Girl for her truthfulness. I was unbearably envious of J.J.'s impending escape, picturing how it would feel to ditch the stifling halls of Lincoln for a bright, grassy quad. But in my fantasies, I had not thought about the people who'd be walking alongside me. Would it be possible to step into a university and be just as alone as I was now?

The thought chilled me and, to be honest, provided a not-small amount of motivation to socialize. Years later, a girl in my freshman seminar would invite me to a party in her dorm, and I swear I heard the voice of the Girl telling me to *fucking show up, you imbecile!*

"I think J.J. will have a great time at Princeton," said Caro. "Mom did, and she's the most antisocial person I know."

From the most decorous of us, an unexpected burn! Mimi and I cracked up.

J.J. started sweeping again, scrubbing at the floor until the bristles squeaked. It made me feel nervous, this pent-up energy. Like we were on the precipice, waiting for something terrible to happen.

The Girl seemed to feel it too. "C'mon, J.J., it was only a joke." She got up and put her arms around her, but J.J. stiffened, then threw her off.

"You're a joke," she said. "A degree from ECU won't be worth the paper it's printed on." Then she took the broom with her and stomped off, too quick for us to follow.

IT FELT LIKE YOU couldn't do anything in Cottage 10 without people knowing all the gory details, but then it turned out Caro had been going to church for two months without anyone finding out.

Nurse Jenny drove her Tuesday and Thursday afternoons, the days we weren't volunteering, when the rest of us were spread out over the Hill doing whatever we could to distract ourselves from how awful school had been that day. For me, this meant reading ahead in my history text until I finished it, then going back and doing all the odd-numbered problems in Algebra I hadn't yet been assigned. It felt good to fill my head with theorems and dates, things that had an absolute right answer. If this made me an even greater know-it-all in the classroom, so be it. Better than the alternative, a mind left to its own devices.

All that is to say, I'm sure it was no greatly kept secret where Caro was going, but the rest of us had dulled our curiosities too much to find out.

Then one night at dinner she sat down before any of the rest of us and as soon as our mother pulled out a chair she said, "I have an announcement to make. I am a Christian."

You could always count on Mimi to talk first, but even she let a long moment go by before saying, "No, we're not."

"I'm not talking about you all, I'm talking about me," Caro said. Then she told us that a few weeks after the sweet tea and Oreos, she'd run into Nurse Jenny in the mail room of the admin building and Nurse Jenny had invited her over to her cottage again. ("You've been there before?" our parents asked on top of each other.)

"And she asked if I'd come to church with her to meet some of her other friends. So I did."

"Why?" J.J. asked.

"She drove you off the property?" Daddy said.

Our mother had frozen behind her chair. "That was so inappropriate."

Caro's voice rose. "I wanted to go with her. The church is called New Life Christian Fellowship, it's not too far."

"Why didn't you tell us before?" Daddy said. Our mother remained half seated, half standing, staring off toward Nurse Jenny's cottage with a wild look in her eyes.

"I'm telling you now," Caro said. "And I want to start going on Sundays. Nurse Jenny will drive me, you don't have to do anything."

"Well," Daddy said, "does her car have seat belts?"

"Every car has seat belts," I said.

"Not really old ones," Mimi said.

"Her car is fine," Caro said. "I always buckle up."

"But what's the point?" our mother said, sitting down with a huff. "If you're going to heaven?" Her mouth had twisted, pinning itself at one corner like a butterfly trapped by its wing. It wasn't a look I had ever seen directed at one of us, although I recognized it by description from our parents' stories: the time a man had tried to mug them at a Laundromat and she'd said *no thanks*, or the dinner party where the host had begun talking about women who have too many babies.

Our mother crossed her arms. "That's what they told you, right? If you stand up and say you're a Christian, when you die, you get to go to the five-star hotel in the sky?"

I expected Caro to crumple right there. None of us had ever experienced this type of rage firsthand.

"You want a real bible, I'll pull out my old neurology textbooks. That's your so-called soul. It's a biological process that stops when you die. And if you believe that, there's no need to get dressed up each Sunday to hear fairy tales from pedophiles."

Caro opened her mouth, but thank God (ha!) J.J. cut in.

"You're thinking of Catholics. They're the ones with the pedophiles."

"Lisa," Daddy said. "Let's all take a deep breath." He took one to demonstrate and then let it out in a loud and exaggerated sigh. I felt myself relax a little, sure that this would make my mother laugh.

She ignored Daddy, picking up her fork and addressing Caro directly. "Caroline, you are welcome to go to church; that's a choice every one of us can make for ourselves."

"Great." Caro stood up, plate untouched.

"You know who also thinks they hear the voice of God? Half the residents I work with. It's a trait *uncommonly associated with psychosis*. You of all people should know that."

Caro did not meet our mother's eyes, stepping quickly down the hall and into the bedroom, then closing the door hard behind her.

WE ATE QUICKLY AND QUIETLY, and after J.J. helped Daddy with the dishes, we all got ready for bed as if nothing strange had happened. When we entered the bedroom, Caro was lying face up on her top bunk, staring at the constellation of glow stars on the ceiling.

The rest of us looked at each other in silence until Mimi said, "Do you really think we're going to hell?"

Caro didn't sit up. "Why is everyone so obsessed with the afterlife? It's literally only one part of the whole freaking thing."

"It's the most unusual part," J.J. said diplomatically.

"Mom's being unfair," Caro said. "She hates everything to do with religion because Grandpa Cross said God didn't want Grandma Cross to go on antipsychotics and then she died, but that doesn't mean the whole thing is bad." This sentence came out long and breathless.

"She said you could keep going," J.J. said.

"She's always the most strict with me."

"Really?" J.J. said at the same time Mimi said, "Are you fuck-

ing kidding me?" It was clear that each one thought our mother was hardest on her.

"So," Mimi said, her mouth twisting into a smile. "Are you going to burn our Harry Potter books?" *The Goblet of Fire* had just been released and several groups had already written in to the newspaper claiming it was the devil's work.

"You're all so freaking stupid," Caro said. "Mom always tells us, think for ourselves, think for ourselves. She's such a hypocrite, she just wants us to think exactly like her."

"Except in this case, she just wants you to think, period." Mimi grinned until Caro hurled a textbook down at her. The paper bag cover just missed her cheek. Mimi launched forward to climb up the ladder to Caro's bed, but J.J. blocked her.

"Are you stupid?" J.J. said. Although our parents could hear everything happening in our room, they only intervened if things got crushingly ugly. And then, regardless of who started it, we were all punished.

Mimi sighed her you're-ruining-my-life sigh and stalked out to the bathroom. After a moment, J.J. followed and I was left alone, sitting on my bunk under Caro's. She wasn't crying, but her breath stammered like she was trying not to.

I got up and picked up her splayed textbook.

"Mimi's being cruel," I said, "I'm sorry."

"You're just saying that because she's not here."

This accusation was both frustrating and true: my alliances were usually duplicitous. But what was I supposed to do? I was too small to fight, physically or intellectually, so I stayed quiet and tried to smooth things over afterward.

Caro must've realized that she needed an ally, even if I wasn't necessarily the most genuine one. "I'm not stupid," she told me. "A lot of smart people are Christians."

"I don't think you're stupid," I said.

"Nurse Jenny's lonely," Caro said. "Some bad things happened to her family."

"Is that why she's in NAMI?"

"NAMI isn't all that bad," Caro said. "They're trying to do the same thing we are, Mom just doesn't like letting anyone else be in charge."

I thought about that for a moment. It was true our mother talked about the purple-shirted volunteers with disdain, but aside from Nurse Jenny, I'd never met any of them myself. Maybe the truth Caro was telling was different from the one I'd heard from our mother. It made me feel funny and lightheaded to think about it that way.

"And yeah," Caro said. "She had two brothers, they both killed themselves."

I lay down on my bed, looking up at the slats that held Caro's mattress. It was hard to picture any of my siblings disappearing, let alone two. It seemed like I would be here in this room forever, hemmed in on all sides by their sheets and beds and blankets. That thought felt tight around my throat, making it hard for me to breathe.

"Mom will get over it," I said, although I wasn't sure if this was true.

Just then, Mimi came back in. "I'm keeping the light on," she said, "so I can read the rest of my chapter."

J.J. barreled in behind her. "Nope, I've got to finish my scholarship stuff in the morning. We're all going to sleep."

"Yeah," Caro said, "I'm tired," and now it was two against one, one abstention, and J.J. clicked off the light. I closed my eyes, trying to imagine a place like heaven, but all I could see was darkness.

EIGHT

Inch by inch, the Washington Monument appeared through the car window, flat, white, and sharp enough to pierce the gauzy sky. It was still mostly dark; we had driven through the night, stopping only for pantyhose, which Mimi had forgotten.

It was just Mimi and me in the back seat, a choice our mother had justified by saying that J.J. had a paper due and Caro would "probably be busy with church." The way she said this made it clear that J.J.'s exclusion was protection, Caro's punishment.

The car slowed as we turned off the highway into the grid of downtown DC, streets and trees bare. It was December, the week before Congress recessed, and also the week they'd finalize the nation's budget for the next year. We were there to fight for one line of that budget.

Our mother parked the car on a side street in front of a big government building that looked like it was the same age as the wards. I had never been to Washington before, having skipped fifth grade and the accompanying field trip to our nation's capital. Everything seemed smaller and more unassuming than I'd pictured; it would be just over three more years before I'd visit New York and finally see a city that looked wholly different from my own.

She took one last look at the big orange binder, closing her eyes like she was memorizing something. Then she shut it and left it in the car. We followed her out, walking quickly in the cold, Mimi's new pantyhose squeaking like crickets.

Our mother led us toward and into a building she seemed to know by heart. When I was younger, she made a lot of visits to DC, but those had gotten sparser over the years. As Mercy Hill's budget dipped and its staffing became more thinly stretched, she couldn't spare a day away. This, of course, led to even less budget being allocated, and even thinner staffing, a cycle we planned on disrupting today.

Being here made my every nerve hum with excitement. To be brought along on a mission of utmost importance jarred me out of the dull sameness of the rest of my life, the days of trudging through the halls of Lincoln and spraying laundry in Ward B. I felt as if my senses were working double-time, taking note of each metal ridge on the door handle and the far-off squeaks of important shoes on unseen floors.

After a brief metal-detector check, an aide led us through a long series of carpeted halls and deposited us outside the open door of North Carolina's second senator. No, not the Republican with the handlebar mustache whom we saw each year smoking cigars at the entrance to the state fair. The man we were here to meet came from a long line of youthful, adulterous Democrats with exquisite haircuts; in three years, when he'd try and fail to secure a nomination for president, the press would reveal that each haircut cost $400, a fact that ricocheted around various media outlets for two weeks.

The day we appeared in his office, that run and the accompanying trichological scandal were still buried deeply in a future that must have felt full of promise. The Senator clapped his hands and stood as we came in, reaching across the mahogany desk to give our mother a kiss on the cheek.

"Lisa, it's been too long. You didn't have to drive all this way."

"Except I did." Our mother tried to smile casually, but it was clear the act pained her. "We don't have time, Senator. We have to make the case before it's too late."

He chuckled at the honorific. "If you insist, *Doctor*. But first, could you at least introduce me to your lovely assistants?"

If only he knew how true that moniker was! But our mother had warned us to say nothing about our volunteer work in the wards. This admonition made me wonder—not for the first time—exactly how illegal it was that we were there unsupervised.

"This is Miriam, she's twelve, and here's Denise, she just turned eleven. Girls, say hello. You met the Senator years ago at his fundraiser."

We smiled back, but I didn't remember any particular fundraiser—they all ran together.

"Your mother is a very special woman," the Senator said, flashing the whitest set of teeth I'd ever seen. "I always say, 'Here's the final number, it's the highest we can go.' And every time I talk to your mama, we end up tripling it."

It seemed to me that this would be the time to laugh, but our mother didn't. Instead, she picked up a folder from her lap and set in on the desk. "Senator," she said, but he cut her off.

"And to be raising *four* children. Four! It always made me wonder . . ."

"Wonder what?" our mother said. It seemed like she was humoring the Senator, playing along with his diversions and distractions so she could lull him into letting down his guard for her budgetary attack. As I watched her face, I also saw something different there, a playfulness I rarely saw even with Daddy.

"It makes me wonder if you knew what made those babies keep coming!"

Our mother reached out and slapped his arm.

"I'm sorry, Lisa," he said. "Don't hurt me!" She withdrew her hand and he kept grinning.

"We both wanted a big family," she said. "Myself *and* Tucker."

At the mention of Daddy's name, the Senator cooled. "I'm just teasing, Dr. Cross."

"The funding," she said. "It's been years since we've had any major capital improvements. The budget has been kept flat, and with inflation—that's less than we can withstand."

"This won't be popular," the Senator said. "Our mental health budget is supposed to be going to community health centers. This is going to feel antiquated. Old-school."

Our mother continued as if he hadn't said anything at all. "This is your state. A fire, a security breach, those would make *national* headlines." She didn't have to say it but I knew she was thinking of the Scarecrow and what might have happened to Mimi had help come just a minute later.

I don't know what the Senator was thinking about, but her words made him straighten, and you could tell he was actually thinking. Then he leaned back again, opened a drawer low in his desk, and came around to where we were sitting. Crouching so he was eye level with Mimi and me, he slowly opened his hand.

In it was a brooch with a long, straight pin folded against the back. It was heavy and gave off the scent of polish, although the silver filagree had turned black in places. Set into the complex swirls of metal were a dozen clear gems. From the careful way he held it, I knew they were real diamonds.

"My mother's," he said. "When I have to make a tough decision, I think of her and what she would have done. She was like you, Lisa. Always fighting hard to help people." He set it down on the desk and picked up the file folder. "I'll bring something to the appropriations committee tomorrow."

"Today," our mother said.

Ruffled once more, he paused. Then he looked at me and winked. "She's the boss," he said, and like a band had been cut, the tension dispersed.

"Come on, girls," our mother said, standing.

He smiled wide. "Doing some sightseeing today? Air and Space Museum?"

"No," our mother said. "I've got to get these girls home."

"If you change your mind, Ryan could get you into a White House tour. It's all done up for Christmas, you know—gingerbread houses, trees, Bill's going out with a whimper not a bang, but if the girls have never seen it . . ."

My heart leapt. If we were to set foot in the actual White House without them, J.J. and Caro would drown themselves out of jealousy.

Our mother shuffled us forward. "Maybe next year."

"These visits are always so short," the Senator said. We watched him watch us step back out into the carpeted hallway. "Lisa, let me just ask one thing. What was *your* mother like?"

Mimi and I stopped in our tracks. Our mother spoke often of her father and the abuse she suffered at his hands—a warning that there were monsters in the world and we should be on our guard should we encounter one. She rarely mentioned Grandma Cross, whose shadowy mental illness and early death had steered her own career toward institutional psychiatry.

I thought for a moment she might simply keep walking. But she was trapped, caught by the Senator's power over the one thing we all wanted. I watched a strange look pass between her eyes and the Senator's, something complex and adult that I could see but not understand.

Then she said, "She was graceful," and turned away again, pushing forward to usher us out of the room.

MERCY HILL

I KNEW THERE WOULD BE no changing her mind about sightseeing, no matter how much I wanted it. As we buckled in, I said, "What if we just drove by—the White House, I mean. Maybe we could see the tree from the window."

To my surprise, she said, "Sure—why not. We got what we wanted."

"Will he really do it?" The Senator seemed like someone whose promises you shouldn't trust.

"Yes," she said. "Although it's still less than we need. But it'll keep us afloat for now."

Hearing this made me feel warm and giddy, although I wasn't sure how much I had helped. I sat up, pressing my nose against the window as we turned down Pennsylvania Avenue. In the early morning, across the wide lawn, the White House looked just like it did on the front of my social studies book. No garlands, no wreaths as far as I could see.

"The decorations must be inside," our mother said. "I'm sorry, Denise."

She continued to drive. I closed my eyes, trying to imagine the fir boughs and jingle bells, the smell of peppermint. We never had room for a Christmas tree, although Daddy did his best with presents lined up along the sofa. Another year on the Hill, that was our prize. And while the victory was thrilling, I couldn't help feeling a little sad.

And so I kept my eyes closed, letting the hum of the car lull me toward sleep.

That's when I felt it. A sting, like a bee had landed on my wrist. "What—" I sprang up. Mimi's eyes held a strange look I hadn't seen before, flat and unknowable.

Our mother, who must've been tired too, concentrating on the long road ahead, didn't turn around. I looked down at my wrist—the left one, I'd remember years later, the same one that would figure prominently in her violent attack on Mr. Scott and subsequent juvenile incarceration, although of course at that time there would be much more blood involved. But on that day I knew nothing of the future. I just looked down at the tiny dot of red and knew Mimi had done this—how?

Wordlessly, she pushed both hands forward into the pouch of her hoodie, opening it for just a second so I could see inside. The image flashed so quickly. Even now I wonder. But what else could it have been? I saw silver, the sharp pin, and, sparkling in the low light of a gray morning, southbound on I-95, the flash of diamonds.

2001

NINE

Psychosis came with the heat, that's what our mother said. Twice a year, the changing of the season pushed a thumb into the residents' brains. Someone tried to jump, or hang, or run, the day the first touch of warmth permeated the air. And by April, we could feel that warmth already. The bulbs in the fenced-off beds surrounding the wards sprouted, poked shoots, and bloomed. Daffodils mostly, a cheery color that seemed out of place against the gloom of the stone buildings. The grounds were filled with them, the paths across the lawn squishy from the March rains.

Extra vigilance was required, our mother said, and because they were especially short-staffed that spring, much of it fell on her. What she'd said in Washington had turned out to be right: the Senator had made sure we'd gotten all the money we'd asked for—and it wasn't nearly enough. Each night she stayed later and later, some nights not coming home until it was already light outside.

One day I met her on the porch as I was going out to school and she was coming back in, face gray and lined from lack of sleep.

"I can go again," I said to her as we stood blinking in the sun.

"Where?" she said. "What are you talking about, Denise?"

"To DC," I said. "It'd be easy. I have perfect attendance, I could get my assignments saved for me or if not, I could even miss some. I'd still have straight As. Why don't we go again, and ask for more?" What I didn't say was: *Without Mimi*.

Something came over her face that I couldn't read, a brightening and then a darkening in two quick waves.

"No," she said. "Thank you, sweetheart." That was an unusual word for her, and it tripped me up. I wondered if the Senator had mentioned the missing brooch. I wondered if my mother suspected Mimi had taken it. Nothing in her interactions with Mimi seemed to let on that she knew, but Lisa Cross was the smartest person I'd ever met, and it did seem strange that we couldn't just go to Washington again after the last visit had been so successful.

She and I stood there on the porch for just a moment longer. "We're going to be okay," she said, and I wondered who she meant when she said *we*. Then she quickly sidestepped me and went through the screen door, letting it slam behind her like she was forever telling us not to.

THEN, IN WARD B, Chef quit. "Did you know how much they were paying me?" he said, the most words he'd ever spoken to us. "Five dollars and seventy-five cents an hour. You make more money at Burger King. And at Burger King, people ain't crazy. Not all of them, at least."

They brought in temporary cooks after that. A woman with a glass eye; a bald white guy with scars all up and down his arms; an old Black man whose first or last name was Wills, I couldn't tell which.

Unlike Chef, they let us help—needed help, actually. We cut open boxes of pancake mix and sorted oranges, dropping the rotten ones, blue with penicillin mold, down the trash compactor.

The Girl followed us more closely now. Her mother was an excellent cook, she said, which was another excuse to critique us: *Is that how you crack an egg? Why do you keep dropping the lids in those cans of soup?* She'd press on one of us until we snapped, and as soon as we yelled at her, she'd burst into loud, dramatic tears.

Sorry, sorry, sorry, we'd say in chorus. Then we'd cast around for some kind of dessert in the cupboards and split it with her as consolation. We knew we were being manipulated, but all it cost us was a handful of chocolate chips or a dry spoonful of brownie mix. At the end of each of these interactions, the air cleared with catharsis and sugar melted on our tongues.

It was nice to have a simple problem and solution, when everything else was veined with complication. Our mother rarely fought with Caro about church anymore, but the détente was so fragile that Caro snuck back in through the basement door each time Nurse Jenny dropped her off, circumventing the dinner table and closing herself into the bedroom. I didn't know what or if she ate those nights. And after DC, I tried not to look too often in Mimi's direction; there was something strange going on with her, something that had been happening since the trip to the Senator. She'd always been a rebel, but her recalcitrance had been low grade, Socratic. There was a limit, and I felt safe knowing Mimi knew where to draw the line. When she had fallen into the rec yard, that had been terrifying—but it had also been unintentional; I'd known, then, that she'd meant for all of us to stay on the right side of the fence.

Now, though. Whenever I looked her in the eye, it felt like something inside her had detached, the part of her that held back. There was no telling how far she would go.

With J.J. already packed for Princeton—three months before move-in, and yes, anal J.J. had already packed—I worried how much worse things would get when our eldest sister wasn't around to corral us all into some semblance of civility.

MAY 2ND STARTED OUT no different from any of the other days. We peeled carrots and set beans to soak, and when the Girl came by, we cut a Pangaea-looking slice out of a tray of lemon bars, spilling powdered sugar down our fronts like snow.

"Hey," she said, pinching me hard on the back of my arm right below the elbow. "Let me do the plates with you."

J.J. was using a big serrated knife to cut the rest of the lemon bars into squares, and it was slow going. The knife was very sharp but the dessert was not quite set, and lemon goo oozed around her fingers each time she tried to put one on a plate.

"Caro, can you help me?" she said, ignoring the Girl. "We are so fucking behind."

"I can help," the Girl said, wheeling over a cart stacked high with clean trays. "It's almost three o'clock, you know. People are supposed to eat lunch at noon."

"It's not our fault," Mimi snapped. She was in a dark mood—we all were. With the end of the school year days away, most of our classes had dropped the pretense of academics and allowed us free time to sign each other's yearbooks and chat. Unbound by structure, most of our peers turned to their favorite pastime: cruelty. Just that afternoon, I'd sent my own yearbook up and down the rows of my French class, only to receive a chorus of taunting scribbles—*Have an insane summer, Psycho D!*

The Girl began setting out the trays on the counter, slapping them hard against the white tile. "Let me just get Bethy's," she said. "I can do it better than any of y'all. Denise drops shit all the time."

"No," J.J. said without looking up. "You're not a volunteer, you're not even supposed to be in the kitchen."

"C'mon, J.J. I'm so fucking bored. Dr. Holt put me on this new medicine that doesn't even let me *come*."

We all stopped for a moment, distracted by this pronouncement—which was exactly the effect she wanted.

"Oh, now you want to hear, don't you?" She turned to J.J. "I just rub, and rub, and *rub* for hours until my clit feels like sandpaper, and nothing happens. What am I supposed to do if I can't even jerk off?"

"I don't believe you," J.J. said. "You're just saying that to get a rise out of us."

The Girl slid up alongside J.J. and ran two fingers under her nose. "Can't you smell it?"

J.J. dropped the plate she was holding and it landed with a thud on the rubber anti slip mat. Hands empty, she took the Girl by the shoulders and shoved her aside. "Get the fuck out of here. You're psychotic, did you know that?"

The Girl began to pout. "Ca-*roooo*," she moaned. "Did you hear what your sister just called me? Not very Christian of her."

Caro didn't look up from the box of napkins she was opening. "Come back later," she said. "We'll hang out with you when we're done."

"No, you won't," the Girl said, and shoved the stack of trays so that it teetered and fell, clanging to the ground like a building collapsing. We knelt on the floor, picking them up. That's when she must have stolen the knife.

SHE DID IT IN THE BATHROOM, in one of the stalls, slicing the artery in her neck clean through. No—none of us saw it happen. I just heard the sirens and when they got close, Nurse Jenny came running and told us she was locking us into the medication closet; every door in the ward must be shut, a procedure I had heard of but never witnessed in practice.

In the close air of the medication closet, we stood silent, frozen in fear as our eyes adjusted to the gray shelves with their haphazard collections of pill bottles. Columbine had happened just two years before, and because we did not yet know what had happened on the ward, we strained to hear gunshots.

"I hope she's okay," J.J. said, one of the few times that any of us spoke.

Even then, I think we all knew that the Girl was the thing we were being protected *from*. I kept reaching out in the closed-in space, hoping to at least accidentally brush the forms of my sisters. But they drifted away like shadows, and my hands met only air.

The rest I remember clearly. That night, standing around an empty dinner table: us four and our mother and Daddy and also Francis, khakis rumpled, looking like the knife had gone through his own throat.

"Girls," Francis said, at least twice, "did you notice anything unusual about Ashley Stillman today?"

"She was angry," Caro said. It was strange to hear someone besides J.J. answer first, but ever since our mother had opened the medication closet to let us out, J.J.'s face had gone gray and wooden. "She felt angry. She said Dr. Holt had put her on a new medication."

"The venlafaxine," our mother said under her breath. Then to Francis, "I'm going to fucking kill Aaron." Her voice was steady when she said that, and it made her words sound even more dangerous.

"Dr. Holt is suffering enough," Francis said. "Believe me, Lisa. I've spoken to him extensively. He's in crisis. I had to send him home."

"Of course." Now our mother's voice rose. "Of course he left. Extremely consistent. Very." She began pacing back and forth. "He should have had her on extra monitoring, not wandering around the kitchen."

"We didn't see her take the knife," Caro said, which had to be said but still made my stomach hurt with shame. This disaster seemed like no one's fault but ours. We'd allowed her into the kitchen, we'd fought with her, we'd pushed her out without checking her pockets. Our whole lives, we'd been told how mature we were, how responsible and wise beyond our years. If someone announced they were taking us all to jail now, I wouldn't have protested. That's what I felt we deserved.

As a bona fide adult now, I know that in many ways, this was pure fallacy. We were minors, we should not have been given any of the tasks we'd been set, it was not our fault that we failed a crucial one. It's easy to see things that way, cut and dried and absolved of all responsibility until you turn eighteen. But a part of me still thinks about the Girl and feels a hard knot of shame. Even now, even still. Because we weren't adults yet, but we were learning, weren't we? And if we'd been a little kinder or attentive or patient, could we have saved her?

"Kelly is on her way," our mother said. (Two years later, spiteful Kelly MacLain still chaired the DHHS.) "She's trying to get ahold of Tom Pritkins." Tom. The man who'd presided over the committee meeting. Lover of Ronald Reagan and Krispy Kreme. These names jangled sharply in my head.

"There's no grounds for legal action," said Francis.

"Just because there's no grounds doesn't mean they won't try. First thing they're going to do is bring up the fucking Wyatt standards—"

"Lisa, can we pause," Francis said, voice beginning to shake.

"No," our mother said. In my own shock and sadness, I had not realized how angry she was. "This was your job. Now the whole hospital is at risk."

Caro began to cry. Daddy pulled her to his chest.

Francis held a hand in front of his eyes like a shield. "They'll call for an investigation. Kelly—"

"Kelly will demand it," our mother said. "She's been gunning for cutbacks ever since she took office."

"But she's the one at fault!" Francis swallowed twice, loudly. "If I'd had the budget, I would have staff, not some classroom of volunteers."

Our mother strode over to where Francis was standing and got very close to him. "My girls will not be a part of this," she said. "You understand me?"

"There will be an investigation," Francis repeated. "There's no world in which there isn't."

"There are different scopes of investigations," our mother said.

"Yes, and some reach across the fence to Ward C," Francis said. "Are you saying there's nothing to find there? Under *state scrutiny?*"

"Francis," Daddy said.

"You're right," Francis said. "There are different scopes of investigations. Based upon the depth of response to the initial incident."

"Speak plainly, Francis. You think we should recommend a goddamn closure of the ward? They'll tear it down, you know. They've already got it zoned."

Francis let his arms hang by his sides. In the long moment of silence that followed, I caught J.J.'s eye. She was still wearing one of the blue kitchen hairnets, her short, spiky hair poking through it like new grass. When she caught me looking, she reached up and yanked it off.

"That's our only option," Francis said. "Do it now and preempt a yearlong process that results in the same exact thing."

"No," our mother said. "I won't let that happen."

Suddenly, both of their pagers began to buzz.

"That's Kelly," our mother said. "It's your call, Francis." I'd heard her tell us that before, and I knew she meant that it was absolutely *not* his call to make.

Francis stumbled out the door. I heard his lumbering feet trip down the porch stairs while our mother stood there in silence.

For a moment, no one moved.

"What's going to happen?" J.J. said.

"Francis will do the right thing," our mother said.

"Mom," Mimi said. "We can go with you to the city council again."

Caro nodded quickly. "We'll help in whatever way we can."

Our mother closed her eyes and it looked for a moment like she might even cry. I reached out and touched her white coat, smelling the familiar scents of latex and institutional food. She sidestepped me, moving toward the door as if pulled by some magnetic force. She had her hand on the latch when Daddy stood up.

"Lisa, wait." Daddy's voice was soft but solid. Her hand paused on the latch. That was the thing about Daddy: he had this magical way of getting our mother to stop what she was doing and really listen, like the moment an instrument fell perfectly in tune. Her back was toward us, but I saw the structure of her body soften as Daddy approached her. She looked tired and small.

Daddy put both his arms around her, his lips in her hair. It seemed like such an intimate moment, the two of them against the world, but we couldn't look away. "Lisa," he said, just her name, and the way he said it made you think about all the times he'd ever said it, right back up to the first moment they met. All that history sandwiched into one word.

Daddy, who was often the butt of jokes, the only male, the non-genius, the one who bought jumbo packs of tampons and made chicken salad sandwiches and drove us to school when the bus didn't come—all of that seemed to wash away as he held our mother. He seemed to grow as she seemed to shrink.

She dropped her hand from the latch and the screen door clapped quietly shut.

"Lisa," he said again, and she collapsed into him so we couldn't see her face.

TEN

That summer, I learned the hardest task is being asked to do nothing at all.

We were not allowed back into Ward B, not even to collect the backpacks we'd left hanging in the break room. When I told my geometry teacher the next day that I'd lost my take-home test, she seemed surprised—I'd never asked for an extension on anything before.

"What happened to it, do you think?" She was a young teacher and she kept her voice low enough so the rest of my classmates couldn't hear. Looking back, I think she saw how the other kids treated me and worried some bully had stolen it on the bus or in the cafeteria. It didn't help that my face was pinched with exhaustion, my hair frizzing from its braids.

I thought for a moment about telling her the truth, which might bring some kind of relief. But the more I stood there thinking, the more impossible the task of putting it into words. I could still picture the parallel red tracks where the gurney wheels had printed the Girl's blood against the white linoleum. That had been my doing, those bloody lines. The truth seemed so unreal, I doubted she would believe me.

"Someone spilled something on it," I said.

Then she either gave me another one or said it was okay

and I could just skip it; my memory fuzzes those last weeks of school. Even J.J.'s graduation I can barely picture. When I think about it, I can't tell if I'm replacing it with Caro's, or my own—a sea of green caps and green gowns, Pachelbel's Canon played by symphonic band, then Daddy driving us all back as fast as he could so our mother could begin her next shift.

A long, empty summer. We walked orbits around the grounds, lingering in the woods outside the Ward B rec yard, where, if the weather was right, we could hear the familiar voices of the residents blown toward us in the wind. Sometimes we saw white sedans parked in the visitors lot, their license plates marked with the state seal. Our mother never spoke about what these investigators did, and Nurse Jenny told Caro that when they came by, Francis brought them into his office and shut the door.

Not knowing, not helping—it was excruciating. Our mother sometimes gave us minor assignments: address these envelopes, put these lobbyists' contacts in alphabetical order in the Rolodex, get these files into FedEx boxes to send to the Senator's office in DC. But after a year and a half spent on the front lines, we yearned to do more. We knew that behind the ward doors, things were melting down, and just outside them, enemies were gathering. I often pictured their shadowy forms coming closer and closer, riding up the grassy side of the Hill on clanking machinery to tear the buildings down stone by stone.

This is what I feared would happen next. After the wards were razed, the Hill would be silent, the air thick with dust. And yet in each of my apocalyptic fantasies, I still pictured all six of us standing in the rubble, unable to leave even then. My sisters and I didn't know how to function in the real world, each hellish day of Lincoln was proof enough of that. And our mother? Her job was everything she was; if she were to get a different one, the woman we knew as our mother would be gone.

LIKE CARO'S ANNOUNCEMENT of her conversion, J.J. chose to share her news at the dinner table. July 2nd, two months exactly since the Girl killed herself.

"You can cancel those plane tickets, Mom. I'm not going to Princeton." I think she wanted us all to know at once, so there would be no rumors or confusion. And because she knew Daddy would be there to protect her from our mother's rage, which was immediate and incandescent.

"Where are you going, then?" Our mother set down her fork, still loaded with baked beans. They dripped onto the tabletop but she did not seem to notice. "You told everyone else no."

She was right. Duke, Emory, Yale—J.J.'s math SAT, her relatively weak suit, had prevented her from securing Harvard—she'd turned them all down months ago. Ever since the interview with the man whom, thanks to the Girl, we still called "the gay banker," J.J. had been single-minded in her devotion. She was going to Princeton. And our mother was so thrilled that J.J. would attend her undergraduate alma mater, a place she had experienced as an oasis after the desert of her miserable childhood and even now pictured only in the rosiest light, that she had bought them *both* plush tigers wearing festive orange T-shirts.

Now all that polyester fur seemed to be slipping through her fingers. "J.J., what's gotten into you?"

When J.J. spoke, her voice was measured and careful as ever, albeit a little shaky. "I want to stay at home. It's not too late for me to sign up for classes at Wake Tech."

"But that's a community college," Mimi said, and I think she too was remembering J.J.'s barb when the Girl had brought up

ECU. Community college was for people too stupid to get into even the worst of the state schools.

"It'll be cheaper," J.J. said. "Tuition is just sixty-six dollars per credit hour. And I could transfer those credits to a four-year college if I reapply."

"You've already applied," our mother said. "J.J., we have the money."

"Then use it for something else."

Our mother turned to Daddy. "Did you know about this?"

"Not until this moment," he said. "J.J., did something happen?"

There was a long silence. Of course something had happened! We'd been responsible for a death. Each morning, as we collected our thoughts from sleep, we remembered this reality, and our part in it, the knowledge heavy and sticky as tar. Daddy knew that, he wasn't stupid. So I guess what he was saying was: *Why has that horrible thing made you do this, in particular?*

Our mother began to throw out guesses. "Do you think I pushed you too hard? I could have done worse, you know. Some parents won't let their kids eat if they bring home a B. Are you doing this to punish me?"

J.J. said nothing. I think I would have cracked under the barrage of our mother's fury, but she just retreated into a smaller place inside herself. You could tell she wasn't really there with us, even though she blinked and nodded along. "I'm not trying to punish you," she said. "That's the truth." As she said it, I knew this was a more complicated kind of truth than any I'd seen before.

Because J.J. was, in her own way, trying to punish our mother by giving up something *she* wanted even now so desperately (the plush tiger! The queer *community*!). By hurting herself, she intended to hurt them both.

"Jesus Christ," our mother said, then with an ironic snort:

"Sorry, Caroline." And for a moment, she did seem sorry—certainly not for taking the Lord's name in vain in the presence of her second daughter's fledging Christianity, but for something deeper, all the circumstances that had led to the six of us sitting around a too-small dinner table in a too-small cottage at the base of a hill where everything was going wrong. Without clearing her plate, she went over to the refrigerator and took down the orange binder. Then she tucked it under her arm and marched outside. In the midsummer light, we watched her climb the steps, faster and faster, until she disappeared over the crest of the Hill.

Without her the room felt fuller, not emptier. Like there was no room to move at all.

"We could fly you back on weekends," Daddy said. "Work with us, J.J. It would make her so happy."

"I don't want to make her happy," J.J. said, and then she too got up and went into the bedroom, closing the door behind her.

ELEVEN

That August, there were only three of us left at Lincoln, J.J. having made good on her promise to enroll in community college. She left each day an hour after our school started, driving Daddy with her learner's permit to the downtown campus. Except it wasn't a campus, it was two side-by-side office buildings with benches out front to smoke on. J.J.'s classmates smoked all the time, she said, most of them middle-aged mothers and ex-army guys.

About J.J.'s schooling, our mother said nothing. She no longer picked fights with J.J., but you could feel her disappointment whenever she saw the big green binder that J.J. kept her class notes in, the mirror image of her own orange one. It made our mother's eyes get very black and very cold and until something else distracted everyone's attention, you couldn't look away.

Fortunately for J.J., a major distraction occurred just about nightly when Mimi's homeroom teacher called to inform our parents that she was once again in detention, suspended, or both.

The incidents were far ranging, involved mild to moderate property damage of the school itself, and were conducted solo.

Others may have borne witness to Mimi's pranks, but they were never invited to participate in feats such as:

One: Climbing out of a second-story Algebra II classroom and clambering around on the roof until shingles rained down on the sidewalk beside the carpool line;

Two: Pushing an unattended library cart down the breezeway, its momentum carrying it and its books into the holly bushes that flanked the school's sign, causing, if the vice principal's report was to be believed, "Wanton Damage";

Three: Coating one of the benches in the senior hall with pink highlighter, invisible on the dark wood until someone sat down in white pants.

I was in eighth grade, still in the middle school wing, and therefore didn't see much of the troublemaking firsthand. Each time the phone rang, I braced myself. Our mother and father both seemed quite annoyed when this happened; they chastised Mimi and threatened to take away "privileges," but the incidents seemed to fade quickly from their memory. And J.J. and Caro were useless: they rolled their eyes and called her *the delinquent*, but J.J. wasn't at Lincoln anymore and Caro's conversion had taken over every aspect of her brain and personality; she had no time to consider or fear what Mimi would do next.

That left only me, waiting and holding my breath and letting it out in a huff of relief each time it was *only* a tipped-over Coke machine or *only* a penknife scar on the picnic tables.

To me, it was clear that Mimi was screaming, louder and louder, and wouldn't stop until someone answered her.

And maybe the reason I alone cared is because I had been the only one to see the sparkle of the Senator's stolen pin in Mimi's pocket, and I was just waiting for the day he called to claim it—or the day she decided that stealing it would not be the worst thing she would ever do.

Then even Mimi got a reprieve, because something else happened that fall that shoved her firmly out of the spotlight: our mother's father came to stay with us.

Unlike Grannie P., Grandpa Cross was almost a total stranger. He lived just outside Boston; we had visited only once, staying in a hotel and spending most of the trip touring sites from the Freedom Trail without him.

We all knew why this was: Pete Cross had always been a cruel disciplinarian, but after his wife succumbed to her insanity, he beat our mother more and more regularly. Our mother was not shy about telling us these horror stories of her past—which, looking back, were entirely too bloody and graphic for young children, but age-appropriate content had never been our mother's strong suit.

So when she announced one night that he would be coming to visit, and in fact staying in our home for a few weeks' time, I couldn't believe it. Wasn't this the man she had spent the last twenty-five years distancing herself from?

The answer, she told us, was one of practicality. An old neighbor had contacted her because our grandfather needed surgery to repair the damaged muscles of his heart. He could not have it done up north; he had been deemed incapable of adhering to postoperative care. In order to get cleared for surgery, he needed someone to vouch that they'd dole out his pills and drive him to his follow-up appointments.

"Which we can do easily," our mother said. "In fact, with Mercy's resources, he may be able to skip some of the travel back and forth to Duke."

"So you called Duke already?" Daddy seemed upset, not only by what our mother was planning, but also by the fact that he was hearing these plans at the same time the rest of us were. Back then, I thought it perfectly reasonable that we were all finding out together, but now, of course, it seems shocking that she hadn't consulted him first.

"I don't understand," Daddy said, when our mother failed to answer his question. "Why should we help him at all?"

"You're the philosopher, don't you think we have an obligation?"

I looked over at J.J. to see how I was supposed to feel about this. Usually when our mother called Daddy a philosopher—his undergraduate degree was in philosophy—it was lighthearted, appreciative. This seemed different, like she was throwing something in his face.

J.J. didn't meet my eyes and just kept playing with her hair, which she'd just gotten cut even shorter, running her hand over the back of her head like she was still surprised at how much was gone.

Daddy paused a long time. "The beatings—the cold baths—the moldy food—he locked you in the garage overnight, for God's sake!"

"Believe me," our mother said, wry. "I remember these incidents."

"What type of example is this setting for the girls?" Daddy said as if we weren't there.

"It's a chance to demonstrate being the bigger person."

After a long moment, Daddy let out a last flail. "Where would we even put him?" he said. "Space is tight enough as is."

Our mother was also ready for this question. "He'll stay here," she said, motioning to the carpeted half of the main room. "We'll get a Japanese screen."

Our mother won, like always, and so we got the Japanese screen, along with a hospital bed with broken wheels that had been collecting dust in the attic of the admin building. We also got a television.

Holy crap, that was exciting. We'd begged for a TV for years, yearning to be able to join in when the other kids at school talked about *Full House* or *Hey Arnold!* But up until now, both parents had maintained that it rotted your brain and proudly recounted the story of when four-year-old Mimi came across a stuffed Big Bird at the pediatrician's, asking loudly, "Who is this ring-legged freak?"

So it was a very special morning indeed when our mother left and returned with a massive cardboard box from RadioShack. J.J. helped her maneuver it out of the car and onto a little end table, where it perched precariously like an egg in an egg cup.

Just a few hours later, Grandpa Cross himself arrived. Our mother drove him from the airport and instead of parking in the main lot, went up the gravel service road that passed directly behind the cottage. She helped him out of the back seat as Daddy stood cross-armed on the porch, scowling in disapproval.

Grandpa Cross was wearing gray sweatpants and a sweatshirt and his face was slashed with deep wrinkles. As he peered up toward the cottage, shielding his eyes from the sun, he caught our gaze one by one. His eyes were dark like our mother's but smaller, like the pinprick aperture of a camera.

"Now, this is J.J., and Caroline, and Mimi, and Denise," our mother said.

He seemed so much smaller in person! It was hard to imagine Grandpa Cross hitting anyone, his wrists were thin and pale.

"We hope you feel better soon," Caro said, kindly.

"Maybe I will and maybe I won't." When Grandpa Cross spoke, I felt myself shiver. His voice held the kind of command that you could imagine made people do as he said. "Lisa, this place is a dump. When you said you lived in staff housing, I thought town house, not slum."

In the past, J.J. would have been the one to speak for the rest of us and defend Cottage 10. But ever since her rejection of Princeton, she said very little.

I cleared my throat instead. "It's a lot nicer on the inside," I said. "And you can't beat the commute." I nodded up the Hill to the grand stone buildings, but Grandpa Cross didn't follow my gaze.

"So she's got you brainwashed too." Then he stopped to cough.

"Take it easy," our mother said, placing a hand on his arm. "Girls, why don't you come down and unload the suitcases?"

"She's so kind!" Grandpa Cross said. I couldn't tell if he was serious or not, and it made my stomach feel funny to look at him for too long. It was hard to reconcile the two pictures of him: the abuser and the weak old man. They overlapped in parts, but when squished together made something chimeric and unsettling.

When we brought the luggage up onto the porch, Daddy was still standing there with his arms crossed.

"I don't want you to go near him," he said to us.

How were we supposed to accomplish that? The cottage was tiny, we'd be breathing the same air the moment we set foot inside.

When we protested, he just shrugged. "Stay outside, then. Or stay in your room."

"He can't do anything to us," J.J. said. "He's too old."

"I don't want you exposed," he said, which made it sound as if Grandpa Cross had a contagious disease. "Go on, play outside. I'll take care of his bags."

"I have coursework," J.J. said, reminding him that she was too mature to engage in playtime.

Daddy shot her a look and she backed down.

"C'mon," J.J. said, leading us down the steps and up the Hill. For a moment, I thought we were headed once more toward Ward B, imagining how good it would feel to set foot on the wide sidewalk that led into that familiar building.

That, of course, was strictly off-limits, and J.J. would never stray from our mother's rules. Instead, she veered away from the steps and into the woods, where we used to build forts as children. It had seemed like a long time ago that we used to play out here, but it couldn't have been more than two years. When I started at Lincoln, I felt as if a gaping chasm had appeared between my current self and a childhood I only half remembered.

J.J. pried a rake out of a patch of clay and began to sweep away a layer of leaves from the perimeter of one of the forts, a tepeelike structure half fallen into ruin. "I don't know how he thinks we're going to stay away from him," she said.

"Daddy's just trying to look out for us," Caro said, falling to her typical defense of our father.

"I can't believe we finally got a TV and now we can't fucking watch it," Mimi said.

"Don't say that word," Caro said. "It's revolting."

"Fuck fuck fuck fuck fuck," Mimi said.

"I'm asking you *nicely,*" Caro said.

"Why don't you pray about it?"

"Guys," I said. "Guys, stop fighting."

The two of them whirled toward me. "You never take sides," Mimi said, which stung because it was true. I would be twelve in a few months, and here I was, still too afraid to choose one person over the other. I bent down and began prying up the dead moss on the fort's floor, trying to distract everyone by being useful.

THAT NIGHT, we set the table for seven, which I couldn't remember ever doing before and which we would never do again, Grandpa Cross insisting on eating in his bed after that first meal. We put Daddy's cup and big fork next to our mother's and placed Grandpa Cross facing them on the other side of the table. Although our parents' side sat two people, the table's balance felt wildly uneven in the other direction, like the frail body of our grandfather tipped the thing down like a slide. Or maybe it was the empty space beside him that held so much weight: our mysterious, *graceful,* killed-in-the-throes-of-psychosis grandmother—the reason we all lived where we lived and fought for what we fought, even though we had seen no pictures of her, heard no stories—whose absence felt so heavy.

Our mother had roasted a turkey, spatchcocked flat. Alongside the bird she'd made mashed potatoes and the kind of breadcrumb dressing we ate only at Thanksgiving, although it was clear we weren't supposed to comment on its rarity. Our mother set the bowls passing just as if it were a regular night of meatloaf.

"Will you say the blessing or will I?" We had not heard Grandpa Cross speak since his arrival, but he now fixed our mother with a clear and direct stare. The rest of us snuck glances at Caro, who was looking pointedly ahead.

"We don't say a blessing," our mother said and I could tell in the measured lightness of her voice that she was warning him. I'd seen this before when people underestimated her, an initial coiling that preceded a deadly strike.

"Just this once," he said and in his broad smile, I could sense the same rearing back.

Daddy waved his hand to break the tension but before he could speak, our mother answered: "In this house we do not say a blessing. We prefer to eat before the food gets cold."

The irony, of course, was that as we all sat there waiting, the steam had ceased rising from the potatoes.

"So you dismiss gratitude for haste?" I was surprised to hear how oratorical our grandfather sounded.

"It's rich of you to denigrate us for lack of gratitude."

At this, Grandpa Cross put down his fork. "If your mother were here, she'd be ashamed of you."

"If my mother were here, I think there would be more things she'd be ashamed of." She turned to Mimi and in a loud voice said, "Why don't you have some stuffing?" She reached forward with the plate, and I felt like I could see Grandpa Cross slapping it out of her hands, a vision of the future—or perhaps of the past. It was one of those times when I could tell the others were thinking the same thing; we all took in breath at once.

Then Caro of all people spoke up. "Guys," she said. "Guys, let me say the blessing." Then before anyone could stop her, she began: "Dear Jesus, thank you for this delicious food before us. Thank you for helping our grandfather get here safely. And help keep him healthy while we all enjoy each other's fellowship." She paused, as if she were considering adding something else, then stopped short. "Amen."

"Amen," Daddy said, and then J.J. said it, then me, then even Mimi, and with five voices down, two abstaining, it felt as if we'd ratified something.

The food smelled good, so we quickly got to eating. It was delicious and salty, the way I liked, but it felt like it was missing something essential. Cranberry sauce, I realized later. But to serve that would have meant acknowledging that this day was special, or that we had something to be thankful for, and as much as I know our mother believed both of these things, she was too proud to mark it explicitly.

"That was a very nice blessing," Grandpa Cross said, but it sounded like he was saying the opposite. "Your mother said your church—it's very modern, isn't it?" The word *modern* sounded like an insult.

"I don't think we're any more modern than anyone else."

"Tell me again what you call yourselves."

"The full name is New Life Christian Fellowship," Caro said. "But most people just call it New Life."

"Nondenominational," Grandpa Cross said. It wasn't a question.

"Pete," Daddy said, the first and only time I ever heard him address his father-in-law.

"I haven't heard of it, of course," Grandpa Cross said. "But I know the type. Bunch of girls and limp wrists who think the Lord Christ is their little best friend." He said it so evenly that it took a moment for me to register the insult. I snuck a look at J.J., but if she was going to go to bat for her queer community, it wouldn't be today.

Caro's brow furrowed. "Most evangelical doctrine includes the concept of Jesus as a personal Lord and Savior."

Grandpa Cross broke into a toothy smile. "Smart," he said and it was clear he meant *smart-ass*. "Just like your mother."

"They're all very bright," Daddy said, attempting to reroute the conversation to a different road entirely. "Sometimes I wonder where they get it—"

"I'm interested in knowing," Caro broke in. The shyest among us, this persistence was unlike her. I could tell Grandpa Cross had hit a nerve. "What is your relationship with Jesus if you don't see him as a friend?"

I watched Grandpa Cross's mouth moving, although he had

not yet put any food on his plate. I was scared of what he might say. It was like an instant inherited memory that made my heart pump faster and the hairs on my arms raise up. This was the way our mother had obviously felt her whole childhood, and even though I'd not been there, it gave me a terrible sense of déjà vu.

Our mother set down her fork and addressed them both while looking at neither. "A judge," she said, so curtly I almost didn't realize she was answering Caro's question. "'For we must all appear before the judgment seat of Christ, so that each one may be recompensed for his deeds in the body, according to what he has done.' Isn't that right, Dad?" The way she said it was very pointed, on the border of rudeness, designed to put both warring Christians in their place.

When I looked over at her with her hand clenched tight on her fork, it was achingly clear that she wanted an answer from him. It was etched in her face, her downcast head, the hunched shoulders I, too, got when I shrank into myself with want.

"Yes, Lisa. That is correct," he said, and we all let out a long breath.

TWELVE

I suppose I thought Grandpa Cross would get wheeled into surgery immediately, and I was surprised when weeks went by without anyone setting a date. Our mother drove him to Durham for several preparatory visits, but there was always some next step, a medicine he had to take until his blood pressure normalized, or a diet that involved vegetable juice in the morning and Metamucil at night. I realize now that he was extremely sick, and although our mother never told us as much, her role during these consults was to bully the surgeons into operating in the first place. Our mother was stubborn in a lot of areas, but doubly so where Grandpa Cross was concerned. She had decided to finish her father's story by fixing him—and what an ending that would have been! After his years spent trying to prevent her from educating herself, her own education would be the thing that saved his life.

I wonder, now, if she was aware that the fight for Ward B was failing. Even my sisters and I, banished down the Hill, knew something bad was happening. More investigators arrived each day and either stayed very late or left within an hour, as if they had seen all they needed to see. It couldn't have been a coincidence that while things were unraveling on the Hill, Lisa Cross chose to focus her attention on a battle she thought she could win. It was also true that she trekked up those steps every day, carrying her binder, head held high. She left earlier and stayed later than she ever had before. In those weeks, I went whole days without seeing her.

WHILE WE ALL WAITED for the surgery to move forward, Daddy retreated. One day when we were all at school, he drove the station wagon across campus to the storage annex, the one where they kept the old electroshock tables and iron lungs, and brought back a set of ancient gym equipment, dumbbells and bar bells and plate weights freckled with rust. A new bench and stainless-steel clips came via FedEx the day after, then a mat, a mirror, and pullup bar. From sunup to well past sundown, we heard the sound of metal clanging against metal like some terrible old-fashioned machine, punctuated occasionally by cries and grunts that we'd never before heard our father make.

Because Daddy was no longer around to shoo us away, we quickly gravitated toward our grandfather's makeshift room, where for the first time, we could watch as much television as we wanted. Our mother had—unwittingly or not—purchased a very extensive cable package, and the sixty channels provided an embarrassment of riches. We were so thrilled with the selection that we didn't even fight over the remote, taking turns every half hour to let someone else choose the program.

J.J., who was constantly trying to prove herself a real-life lesbian, chose a lot of sports roundtables. Caro got us hooked on *ER*, and Mimi sought out *Beevis and Butt-Head*. For my turn, I frequently picked local news, which to me was more tragic and titillating than the rawest procedural. There were jealous ex-lovers committing murder-suicides, toddlers found chained to radiators, rape victims with their faces blurred. The only downside was that every so often, they'd flash a picture onscreen of the admin building, superimposed with a big question in bold text: *MERCY HILL TO BE CLOSED?* Whenever that happened, we quickly changed the channel.

THIS NEW ENTERTAINMENT was not free, and the price we paid was proximity to Grandpa Cross. Although he didn't speak often, when he did, we held our breath, for what he had to say would be deeply cruel and cutting. He said J.J.'s new haircut made her look like an ugly boy, mocked Caro's church and Mimi's laugh, and every time I walked by, he'd grab my wrist with surprising strength, digging in his fingers until I promised to get him what he wanted.

"You can just *ask*," I kept telling him. But it was clear he liked watching me wince. It seemed to satisfy him every bit as much as the food he ate, and if we'd had any doubts about our mother's awful childhood, we certainly did not anymore.

Usually, these interactions were brief, but one day—maybe it was the steroids he was taking to build up his lungs—he spoke at length.

"Jennifer," he said in a plain, clear voice. "You know, I found out about you when you were nearly two."

We all swiveled around, and then back at the TV again, which was playing an old episode of *The Beverly Hillbillies*.

J.J. said, "I'm J.J. No one calls me Jennifer."

He sucked his teeth as if she had not said anything. "A year old," he said. "And she calls. She had another on the way by then. Guess she would have felt too guilty if she'd waited to say, You have *two* grandchildren, you old bastard."

We had no idea what to say to that either.

"I didn't get a picture till this one." He pointed at Mimi. "Three girls before I got a single picture. Would've broken your grandmother's heart if she was still alive."

"A lot of things would be different if she were still alive," Mimi said.

Grandpa Cross just snorted. "You're all smart like your mother. She was always winning those ribbons, the science ribbon, mathematics. But she doesn't have a heart, does she? She can't even think of another person the way she thinks of herself."

We sat stunned for a moment. Then, Caro said in a soft voice, "In case you haven't noticed, that's what she does at work, all day every day. Care for other people."

"Her *work*!" He said it like it was a dirty word. "She's got you living here in the cuckoo's nest, acting like she's doing God's calling. She's the one who should get her head checked."

It made my throat catch to think about how much I hated him. How dare he say that about our home! "She's only doing this because of what happened to Grandma," I said.

"She doesn't care about saving lives," he said. "She just cares about being on top."

I felt righteous anger rise in me again, but his words had a painful truth. Mercy Hill needed Lisa Cross, but she also desperately needed Mercy Hill. The more I hung around my grandfather, the more I saw how much of her life my mother had built upon trying to rewrite her past.

"Only time I saw her cry was over that car. Can you imagine? Not when she was hurt, not at funerals. Just over that goddamned car."

"What car?" Mimi said.

"Punch buggy," Grandpa Cross said. "Old as sin, rusted half to death. Engine fell clean out the bottom one winter, had to have it towed away for junk. That's the only time I ever saw her cry."

"Maybe she was frustrated," J.J. said. We had all seen her

kick the bumper of our station wagon when it let itself get dinged in the grocery store parking lot or flipped on the check engine light for an expensive repair.

"No, sirree," he said. "She was wailing."

We all stared at the TV. A commercial had come on for Stouffer's microwaveable dinners and I thought about the types of people who were watching television in the middle of the day. Lonely people.

"She'll say I was the one who did everything wrong," he said. "But some people are hard as hell to love."

"Aren't Christians supposed to love everyone?" Caro said, and I was glad, for once, for her sanctimoniousness.

Grandpa Cross said nothing. He had made his point. The TV turned back to *The Beverly Hillbillies* and we all got up at once and padded outside. It was early September and the sun was high. It had beaten against the Hill all summer, browning the grass and driving all the animals into the cool shade of the woods. When I looked up, some of the windows of Ward B were open, but I didn't dare come any closer. What was inside felt like deep, dark water, with no way of knowing what horrors could grab you from beneath.

THAT EVENING, our mother came home on time, a rare occurrence that both warmed and worried me. Had the Ward B investigation gone very well or very poorly? I couldn't bear to ask, and so when we all sat down to dinner together, Grandpa Cross already in bed, I asked her about the car instead.

To my surprise, her face brightened and she laughed. "It was pea-soup green," she said, "and there wasn't any glass in the back windows. I bought it at a flea market for a hundred and fifty dollars."

I relaxed a little. It was comforting to hear our mother's past filtered through her own telling, it made me feel like we were back in control.

"Grandpa said you got upset when it died," Mimi said.

This was the wrong thing to say. Both our parents froze.

"When did he say that?" our mother said.

"I dunno," Mimi said, unable to lie quickly. "We were all watching TV."

"You've been letting them watch TV together?" Our mother's voice rose as she turned toward Daddy.

Daddy could not come up with an answer either.

Our mother's eyes flashed. "So you're just leaving them alone with him all day while you do your aerobics? Jesus Christ, Tucker." She looked over at the screen that divided the bed from the kitchen and I realized that there was a good chance my grandfather was still awake, and listening.

"Jesus Christ," our mother said again. Then she got up and took the cordless phone out onto the porch.

This is how the scene plays out in my memory: our mother found out we'd been spending afternoons with Grandpa Cross and within moments was demanding he be scheduled for surgery the next day.

Of course, it probably didn't happen just like that. Our mother's power was not absolute and after all, who at Duke Cardiology would pick up a call at seven thirty at night? But the causality, that was real. The moment she understood that he was speaking to us, she began to push her plan forward with furor. Grandpa Cross would be cut open.

ONE MORNING WE AWOKE to find our mother gone and Grandpa Cross along with her. She came back alone and spent the rest of the day whistling as she scrubbed down the windowsills with bleach. We need to all be ready for when he comes home, she said, although it was hard for me to imagine what that meant.

Then he was back, our mother helping him up the steps and into bed, his face the color of gauze and his gauzed chest the color of strawberries. He lay so still that it seemed as if he were still under anesthesia, his breath quiet enough to make you think of the olden days, holding a mirror up to see the fog.

That night, as if the wind had suddenly switched directions, Grandpa Cross began to cough. It was a dry, wracking sound almost mechanical in its preciseness: a long, whistling breath, then: *A-hew, a-hew, a-HEW,* tapering to silence only when the last wind had been expelled. I heard it start around one thirty, then footsteps from our parents' room, the creak of the Japanese screen being folded back.

"Dad." I heard our mother's voice, thin and naked with fear. That was what stirred me, I had never heard her sound like that before. I swung my legs over the side of my bed and heard the creak of Caro coming down the ladder above me. It was clear to all of us that we needed to see what was happening and clear also that we must not be seen ourselves.

J.J. pulled back on our door bit by bit and soon a crack appeared, no more than a half foot, but positioned so we could see directly into the living room. Our mother held a glass of water in a shaking hand.

"Dad," she said again. "You're going to be okay." The way she said it sounded like a question. She touched her hand to his chest, then drew it back quickly.

"Sometimes this happens, after you've been put under. You've had a tube down your throat, which can be very—irritating."

The cough stopped for a moment and I watched our mother bend down close to Grandpa Cross's face, where he was saying something too quiet for us to hear.

"I know," she said. "I'm sorry, I'm sorry, oh God, I'm sorry." It was like a foreign spirit had animated her body. I had never heard her apologize like this before. Her sorries tended to be ironic and self-congratulatory, the kind that meant *pardon me for living*. And I don't think I'd ever heard her say the word *God* without *dammit* attached.

"Dad," I heard her say again. "Tonight will be the worst of it. You'll feel better after tomorrow." A long pause in which he continued to cough.

"Lisa." Daddy's voice from across the room made us all turn. "Lisa, should we call someone?"

Our mother crouched down closer beside the bed. "He's fine. Just uncomfortable, is all."

I watched Daddy step toward her, think better of it, then back away. "I'll be in here," he said and then I heard the door to their room close.

The whole house quieted. I didn't dare breathe. The only sound was the steady *a-hew, a-hews* as Grandpa Cross struggled to take in air.

"Oh God, I'm sorry," I heard our mother whisper, and it felt no less strange the more she said it.

I don't know which of us looked away first; it was probably J.J., trying her hardest to lead the way. We slunk back toward our beds, and I shivered as I wriggled my feet in under the blankets, trying to find the pocket of warmth I'd left behind. Outside, I could still hear coughing and in counterpoint, our mother's whispered apologies. There has not been a time since then that I've heard her say those words with such sincerity or such helplessness.

THIRTEEN

In the days after that, our grandfather needed constant care.

"It's like when Denise was born," said J.J., who could remember most distinctly the way things had been when there was a baby in the house. Every two hours, he had to be turned so the blood in his legs wouldn't clot, and he had to be given a fistful of pills along with a sickly-sweet-smelling pudding. Too weak to lift a spoon, he stared at the container until one of us fed him.

Our mother told us that she would handle all of the work herself, but the first morning she stayed home from the Hill, her pager began to buzz every ten minutes and then Francis called the house.

"It's not a good time," she told Daddy as she gathered her papers. "The Ward B investigation—If you could just prep some of his meals—"

"I won't help that cretin," he said.

"But will you help *me*?" she said.

He didn't answer, just turned away and headed downstairs. On the table, our mother's pager rattled again and her eyes darted toward it.

"Girls?" she said. "I really need you."

Even Mimi couldn't say no to that.

So we lifted spoons and changed wrappings and turned up

the TV for him when he indicated he was interested in what was onscreen. Our mother did not thank us for our efforts, but she relaxed many unspoken rules to give us the flexibility to keep going. We no longer ate together each night, but grabbed whatever we wanted when we were hungry. At first it seemed a brief break in the norm due to extenuating circumstances, but that assumption turned out to be wrong. Our new regimen was not a blip but the beginning of a larger pattern that was quickly and permanently dissolving the way things had been.

I FAKED SICK A LOT THOSE DAYS, we all did, because school was wretched and now we had a television. This was another thing our mother turned a blind eye to: as long as our grades remained high, she didn't care if one of us had a headache or stomachache every week or so. Besides, if we stayed home, we could fetch things for Grandpa Cross, a task Daddy still refused.

That particular Tuesday it was my turn to skip school and I felt filled with contentment, sprawled out on the floor with the remote to myself, Grandpa Cross napping and Daddy downstairs lifting and grunting. In the years since, when people ask what I was doing on 9/11, I say to them that it was just an ordinary day, but the truth was, it was one of the few times in my childhood that I truly felt at peace.

Of course that was not the case for long, and as the news broke, I watched the smoke billow from channel to channel. I was not scared at first, I was fascinated. I often read ahead in my physics book to where the problems veered grotesque: roller coasters colliding with spheres, trains speeding too fast around a curve. This appeared to be a problem of mass times acceleration. That the news anchors were holding back tears seemed some sort of adult hysteria.

Chaos and repetition as the networks chased their own tails.

Now news from the Pentagon, and chatter that more planes had disappeared. Six planes—no, seven—and the Mall of America and the Sears Tower were evacuating.

This sent a jolt through me. I looked around the dim room, past the sleeping body of my grandfather, and out the windows to the grassy hill that led the way to Ward C. The wards looked so exposed up there, four stone buildings reaching perilously into the sky, tarnished copper gutters seeming to outline them for all to see.

I didn't even put on my shoes, I just ran. Through the screen door and down the porch steps and then up, up, up the side of the Hill. It'd been a long time since I'd played out here barefoot, and the sticks and sharp rocks jabbed into my tender feet. By the time I got to the top, my lungs ached, but I didn't stop, flailing through the empty rec yard to the front door of Ward B. Here was the door we used to walk through daily. For the first time in months, I entered.

The hallway hummed with the familiar midmorning rush. Footsteps, carts clicking over tile, the clatter of pans in the kitchen. I breathed in deep—the scent of pink disinfectant made my eyes water. I stood frozen for a moment, awash with a yearning I had not allowed myself to name. I wanted badly to be back here, here as it was before, folding towels with Mimi, scrubbing chairs with Caro and J.J., goofing off with the Girl. It felt like she could still be alive in this place, popping out from around the corner to flick me with a hard fingernail. She's not real, I told myself, the closest I could think to the truth.

"Denise." Nurse Jenny hurried toward me. "You're not supposed to be here."

"The news," I said. "Did you see the news?"

"We're listening to the radio. It's horrifying. But Denise, you can't be here. The investigation—"

"There are more planes out there," I said. "We don't know where they're headed."

Nurse Jenny pressed her lips together very tightly. "They're not coming here," she said. "We're not that important."

I looked down at my feet, feeling very childish all of a sudden. Of course the Hill was not a target—no one knew about it, no one cared. The buildings stretched long shadows in my mind, but no one else could see that.

I swallowed. "I'm sorry. Please don't tell her I was here."

She pushed me toward the door, then she turned, catching the arm of one of the residents who'd come walking around the corner. It was Jared, the man we'd once seen singing his song about the Carolina Cab Company. Recognizing me, he waved.

"Are the geniuses back?" he called, and I felt my own hope knock around painfully inside my heart.

"No," I said. I bowed my head as I ducked toward the door. "I was just bringing a message."

J.J. WAS LET OUT of her afternoon classes early, so Daddy drove her back around the same time Caro and Mimi came home on the bus. They said Lincoln had rapidly devolved into chaos in the latter part of the day, with teachers wheeling in TVs so they could watch the news themselves and not seeming to care who left and who piled in when the bells rang. A rumor had shot through the school that Fort Bragg, two hours to our east, was a target, and this had further agitated the population until a stream of seniors and juniors departed in their cars at midday, leaving the halls echoing emptily.

"Be glad you stayed home," Mimi said, full of bravura. "People were losing their fucking minds." She rolled her eyes to condemn their panic and I felt embarrassed, remembering how my own fear had threatened to overwhelm me.

"Don't be so callous," Caro said, and while Mimi was gearing up to laugh at her, J.J. took Caro's side.

"She's right," she said. "People have a right to be afraid."

"But it's all over now," Mimi said.

"I can't tell if you're deliberately being obtuse or you're just plain stupid," J.J. said, an insult that immediately made Mimi bristle. "There's never been an attack like this—ever. It's like America isn't America."

Even Mimi was quiet for a few moments. We'd never spent much time thinking about America, or what it was or wasn't. It was something we took for granted, like food or oxygen or indoor plumbing.

"There's gonna be a war," Mimi said, and what she was saying, really, was that she was sorry, she was scared as well.

"It'll be far away," J.J. said, which meant she was sorry too.

Living in Manhattan now, I know people who were there that day. My husband, who is older than me, walked from his office to the Red Cross on the Upper East Side, only to be told that there was no need for donated blood. Practically no one was injured, the nurses told him, and that's the part he remembers most, how this phrase, which on the surface seemed positive, could mean something so sinister.

"Maybe we should do something nice for Daddy," Caro said, and even Mimi agreed.

"We can get a salad ready," J.J. said.

"Yeah," we said, "yeah," and headed into the kitchen. We didn't need to explain the impulse to ourselves or to each other, we just knew. As strange and frightening as the events of the day had been to us, we understood that the adults were hit harder. The America we hardly thought of was a home they had lived in for a long time, and the more years you spend in a place, the more expectations and baggage get codified into fact.

Our brains were wetter and more flexible, better able to take in the newness and pivot to a reality in which the events that marked the next ten-plus years were expected and commonplace. I would be talking to my father on the phone from my dorm room when the papers first printed the name of the place Abu Ghraib. He was furious, I was resigned. This wasn't the way our country should be, he would say. But ask me, or ask any of my sisters? This is the way things had been all along.

FOURTEEN

Weeks wore on, and Grandpa Cross began to seem worse, not better. At first he was supposed to fly home mid-October, then before Thanksgiving, then the first week of December. As each of these deadlines approached, new complications arose: an infected surgical site, elevated liver levels, the return of the cough. Our mother seemed unperturbed by these setbacks at first, which she said she expected, but as the weather turned colder, it became clear that she was getting nervous.

"Winter is hell on the elderly," she told us often, which I think was meant to sound casual but wound tighter each time she repeated it. As if waging her own fight against the coming season, she cranked up the thermostat until the windows dripped beads of sweat and bleached the counters so often I still cannot smell Clorox without immediately being transported to that time.

As we neared Christmas, she hired an in-home nurse, a sign of just how bad things had gotten. Although Holly was professionally cheery, beaming as she cracked open cans of Ensure and calling us all *sweetheart,* I saw her hopeful expression drop each time she heard him cough.

"He's not gonna make it to New Year's," Mimi said one day

as we dug sticks through the frosty ground of our old forts. Our mother had sent us all outside while she cleaned yet again. "It's true," Mimi said louder, when no one answered her.

"He might get better," I said, because someone had to play the hopeful one.

"Fat chance," Mimi said. "He's getting worse every day."

"I'm glad he's not talking anymore," Caro said, speaking into the dirt. Most of the structures we'd built as children had fallen into ruin, but there was a big empty space that had once held a lean-to. She stood in the middle of it, gathering strands of ivy in her hands. She stripped the leaves off carefully, laying them on the packed dirt. Evergreen, they covered the dull ground around her like gems.

The rest of us said nothing, in silent agreement. I was privately grateful to no longer feel the pinch of Grandpa Cross's fingers on my wrist.

"I hate that she's so distracted by all this," J.J. said, not looking up. "They need her help with the Ward B investigation."

"Isn't Francis supposed to be running the investigation?" I said.

"Three-hole punch," Mimi said, and despite everything, the rest of us laughed. We'd once seen Francis try again and again to punch holes in a sheaf of paper with the wrong side of the tool, examining the pages each time with incredulity, then trying again the exact same way.

As soon as the laughter left my throat, something darker filled its place. What lay in wait for us should the investigation prove unsuccessful was something too dark to think about.

I set down my stick and stood up, kicking my toe instead at the frozen dirt. "You guys think we'll win, don't you?" I knew I was acting like a baby, begging for affirmation, but I didn't care. I needed to know.

Caro let out a long breath. "I don't know if anything is going to feel like we've won."

"Yeah," Mimi said. "Fuck the investigation."

"Oh, so now it's both of you?" J.J.'s eyes went wild. "I guess y'all would just go over and cheer when they knock it down. How about you, Denise? Am I the only one who still thinks we're doing the right thing?"

My eyes blurred with tears. I didn't know what to think. My whole life I'd believed in the mission, I knew the facts and stats better than anyone. And yet when I thought of Ward B, every corner of my mind filled with a dark haze.

"Denise?" J.J. asked again, but Caro came to my rescue.

"Don't be ridiculous," Caro said, gathering the leaves into a pile and stepping back. "Pastor Jonathan says that having faith in something means *welcoming doubt*. Like, otherwise you don't really believe, you just think that you do."

I felt a sigh of relief fall from me, grateful to not interrogate this more. But when I looked over at J.J. she was staring hard at Mimi, too hard. I willed Mimi to say something to break the tension, anything to reassure us that we were the same unit we had always been.

Mimi refused to deliver. "Let's go," she said. "I'm cold." In the early afternoon, the December light fell fast and her face was shadowed with deep violet. She dropped her stick onto the ground and aimed a sharp kick at Caro's pile of leaves, which flew into the air like a miniature explosion. Caro let out a short sigh, but Mimi's face was stone. She hurried out of the woods and the rest of us followed, feet crunching on whatever bits of frost we hadn't yet disturbed.

At the top of the Hill, I felt a strange urge to look back, but didn't. This would be the last time we four ever played in the forts together.

WE SAW A LOT OF three-hole-punch Francis those days, more even than when we'd worked on Ward B. Most nights, long after the dinner dishes had been put away, Francis and our mother came down the Hill together and sat on the porch to plan the next day's strategy. We were not allowed outside when they were engaged in these war games, but we could hear the click of the orange binder snap open and closed, a faithful staccato.

One evening just a few days before Christmas, Francis came over early and by himself, refusing Daddy's offers of dinner or a beer or to come inside, even though it had been a rare cold day, the morning frost still glinting on the grass. He waited there until our mother arrived and when she did, they had a short, standing conversation. We couldn't hear her words, which were measured and low, but Francis spoke loudly. "It's over," he kept saying, "I swear to *Christ*"—his southern accent sharpened by emotion—"it's over."

We were all sitting at the foot of the bed where Grandpa Cross dozed, watching *South Park* with the volume turned all the way down. When we heard the door slam open again, Caro bumped the volume back up, but it didn't seem to matter to our mother that we'd been eavesdropping.

"Girls, get up and get in the car. I've got a surprise for you—early Christmas present."

We all looked at each other. We'd assumed Christmas was another thing that would be passed over this year: after Daddy had declared the basement his personal lair, no one had dared go down to retrieve the boxes of stockings and candles.

"I'm serious," our mother said. "Go get your coats, we're going to Crabtree Valley Mall."

As we gathered our things, our mother turned to Daddy, who was standing cross-armed in the doorway. "Tucker," she said, her voice sharp. "Please, for God's sake, just keep an eye on my father. That's all *I* want for Christmas."

Daddy said nothing but he went back into the cottage, letting the screen door slam behind him.

No one spoke as we piled into the station wagon and wound our way down the Hill and past the guard station. Although it was still fairly early in the evening, it was already pitch-black through the windows, but then we made it out of campus and the road we turned onto was bright with taillights. On nights like these, you could tell just how much Raleigh's population had ballooned. Families drawn by the tech and pharma companies in nearby Research Triangle Park ushered in new developments that spiderwebbed north and east until the outer loop beltline flooded with traffic. And now here we were in the thick of it, Francis's fear still ringing in our ears.

Our mother must've sensed our discomfort because she let out a long and dramatic sigh. "Fine," she said, turning to Mimi, who'd called shotgun fastest. "We're going to get your ears pierced!"

A long pause before anyone came up with appropriate-enough feigned excitement. "Wow, thanks!" Caro said. The rest of us mumbled along in agreement.

"I know it's been a hard year," our mother continued, "so I thought, let's get you something you really wanted."

This time, the silence was even longer. It was true that in years past, we'd campaigned to wear earrings, especially Caro, whose outfits skewed the most girly. Each time we made our case, our mother told us gruesome stories from her ER rotation: piercings caught on basketball hoops, infected lobes that turned gangrenous. That bargaining and begging seemed to belong to a different world, before Grandpa Cross, before the Girl, before the first dread days at Lincoln. I think our mother prided herself on remembering this dream, but now it just made me think about how much I'd changed since then and how much all of that change had hurt.

We reached the turnoff for the mall and I watched the light turn green. The cars in front of us began to move forward, but the light was too short to let us through. It turned yellow and then red and we were stuck again almost exactly where we'd been.

"Well," our mother said. "What do you think?"

"Can I get a lip ring too?" Mimi asked.

Our mother's laugh was jolly but I thought I heard something hard underneath. "How about this: if I go another month without getting a call from your assistant principal, we'll talk about further face mutilation." Then she drummed her hands on the wheel. "How about you, Caro? Does New Life allow piercings?"

Like all things having to do with her religious conversion, this felt like a trap. Caro's answer was cautious. "Yes, even some of the guys have them. The youth pastor, John, he's got a little gold ring in his left ear."

"Isn't that the gay ear?" Mimi said.

"No," said J.J. and Caro at the same time.

Our mother shook her head. "Dare I even ask?"

To everyone's surprise, J.J. spoke. "Some gay men get their right ear pierced."

"Ohhh," our mother said. "It's like a countercultural thing."

"Yes," J.J. said, although even I could tell that our mother's answer wasn't exactly right. But it had been so long since the two of them had said anything to each other that I was ready to turn home and count the whole trip a success. It felt good to have everyone in the same place, fumbling toward some sense of normalcy. It also made me wonder: Was this the beginning of a family reunited, or one last exceptional day before things got worse?

"I remember when I got my own ears pierced," our mother said. "Your Grandpa Cross wouldn't allow it, but Mom took me anyway. While they were still healing, I'd wear my hair down at the sides of my face, like this, you know? I walked around all day like I was carrying rocks on my shoulders."

I carefully stowed away this new fact about Grandma Cross alongside the other few details I'd learned about her. She'd been an earrings rebel.

"Did he find out?" J.J. asked, and I warmed again at the sound of them talking to each other.

The light clicked to green and our mother stepped on the gas, this time making it through the intersection and into the mall parking lot. We all cheered, and it wasn't until we pulled into a spot that our mother answered J.J.'s question. "Of course he did," she said, and I realized suddenly that he was the source of the little ridged scars that jagged down her lobes.

Silence cracked through the car like ice, but our mother waved it away. "Let's not talk about him tonight," she said. "This is supposed to be fun."

I TRIED TO PUSH Grandpa Cross from my mind, but he was a hard tail to lose. He felt like a sixth person in our group, following behind as we wove our way through the mall's open atrium, strewn with fuzzy green garlands and packed with frazzled Christmas shoppers. I'd just turned twelve, yet remained the size I'd been for the last few years, and kept getting hit in the face with other people's bags. Each time this happened, I felt knocked a little further from reality, so that by the time we reached the Piercing Pagoda, my head felt far away from my body.

The kiosk was a stand-alone island outside a Yankee Candle, which leaked cinnamon scent like a dirty bomb, in between a hut that sold hair extensions and a stall where you could get your teeth whitened. None of the kiosks were done up for Christmas and none were very busy, so when we all clustered around the display case, a technician in a black smock scurried toward us, cooing.

Our mother met her enthusiasm and raised it, gesturing animatedly as we pointed to our choices, marking every selection with a *nice one* or *good job,* even though our picks were both obvious and typical. Of course J.J. chose something plain and sturdy—little silver balls—and Caro tiny crosses, and Mimi the stars that looked like explosions. When my turn came, the only options that hadn't yet been picked by one of my sisters were peace signs or hearts, which felt like the same injustice I'd been dealing with my whole life: a choice between scraps. I pointed to the hearts.

The tech insisted I go first because I was youngest and even though we all knew Caro was most afraid, it would have made her angry to reshuffle and call it out.

The smell of antiseptic. The fumbling latex digits of the technician as she fit the plastic gun around my lobe, loading the first stud.

"Hold her hands!" the woman demanded and after a brief hesitation, J.J. and Mimi each grasped one of my palms. We weren't big huggers or touchers. We lived in such close quarters that having your own space was a luxury, and when you felt someone's skin on your skin, it was most likely a prelude to a slap.

"Blow out," the technician said. "Like you're blowing out candles." As the gun jabbed through, I pictured my next birthday, a little under a year from now. It filled me with dread, because in my mind, the faces of my sisters and my mother were vague and dark. The future I imagined would not be kind to us.

As the technician loaded the second stud into the gun, I turned to lock eyes with our mother. I had to ask before the question burned me alive.

"Mom," I said, "what did Francis mean when he said it was over?"

I watched her face twist and that was all I needed to know. The gun clicked as pain shot through my other ear.

"We're going to shut down Ward B," she said, the same time as the technician said, *Hold this, you're bleeding*. A tissue in my hand, I slid off the stool onto my shaking feet.

"We're doing it to protect Ward C," our mother said. "Sometimes you have to cut the dead weight so it doesn't drag you down with it."

But Ward B wasn't dead weight, it was a real place—one of the few places we'd all been happy. Until the Girl. Until what we'd allowed to happen. I looked around at my sisters and saw the shutters closing on their faces. The fragile congeniality we'd shared just moments ago was gone. J.J. took a step back.

"I'm not going to get mine done, after all," she said.

Our mother turned to her. "Jennifer."

"This is something you wanted, not me. Pierce your own ears if you want, he's not going to pull them out this time." Then she shuffled away quickly into the crowd, head down. I knew we'd find her waiting by the car; there was no other way for her to get home. But still.

Caro, seated on the stool, began to cry.

"Honey," the technician said, "you don't have to if you don't want to."

Our mother spoke over her. "Come on girls, hold her hands."

BACK AT HOME, Daddy was standing on the porch. When we filed in, pointing to our glinting ears, he said, "I like that they're all different, really shows off your personalities." He did not say anything about J.J.'s lack of ear piercings.

"I don't know if hearts are my personality," I said.

"Think of them as leaves instead," Daddy said. "They could be morning glory leaves."

I pictured little vinelike feelers sprouting down my neck, and despite everything, it cheered me. Daddy always knew what to say.

"What are you doing out here?" our mother said. She had not spoken the whole ride home. Her grief was so large and dark, it had its own gravity, and I felt myself pulled in with it. Ward B, gone—it was unimaginable.

"What is it?" she said again, and that's when I realized how unusual it was for him to be upstairs, and outside.

"Your father," he said, his voice strange and blank. "He's gotten worse."

FIFTEEN

We heard his cough all night, a dry choking rattle that would fade just enough for you to reach the edge of sleep then burst back in like a slap. It sounded like his body was allergic to the air itself, sputtering and wheezing to get it out as quickly as possible.

When Nurse Holly came in for her morning shift, she pulled our mother aside and told her the temperature reading in a whisper. She offered to call 911 but our mother said no, she didn't want him to die in the hospital. She got out her prescription pad and scribbled a couple of lines. Morphine, which she could go up the Hill to fill at the on-campus pharmacy.

When our mother and Nurse Holly came back, they propped up Grandpa Cross so he was nearly upright, injecting him with something from a small clear vial. I noticed that the needle was one of the ones capped with blue, the expensive kind that David Johnson had preferred.

The rattle stopped, and Grandpa Cross quieted.

"Is he still breathing?" Mimi asked.

"Yes," Nurse Holly said, although her voice was very soft.

"Morphine will eventually stop his respiration," our mother said. "It will be painless."

"I'll run an IV," Nurse Holly said, standing up. "We'll monitor his dosage through a pump."

"I'm fine giving injections," our mother said.

"That's not how we usually do things."

"I'm a physician," our mother said. "I give injections every day."

Nurse Holly frowned but said nothing. "Girls," she said, turning to us. "Do you want to take a walk outside?"

"They're fine," our mother answered for us. "They're all very mature. Denise is reading at a college level." Even at her father's deathbed, she wasn't going to miss an opportunity to brag about our academic prowess.

"Okay then. I'll be in the kitchen if you need me." Nurse Holly took her purse and sat a few feet away, pulling out a big book of word searches. Our mother closed the screen behind her.

The silence became awkward, then pleasant, then awkward again. I didn't dare look at the clock; that seemed rude, like I wanted him to hurry up and die already. Although wasn't that in fact what we were waiting for?

It all felt mixed up, and our mother's expressionless face seemed most confusing of all. It had been less than twenty-four hours since she'd found out Ward B was being shut down, and now this—I would think her grief would compound, but perhaps instead the two terrible things had canceled each other out.

She sat back and closed her eyes. It made it easier for me to sneak glances at her face, which of course I did. The high nose, the dark brows, even the lips with their deep bow on the top. I felt pain abstractly in my middle but couldn't really tell where it was coming from. Stupid, I chided myself. I was too stupid to figure out why I was feeling sad.

Finally she spoke: "He really was brilliant, you know. He had a job no one understood, because he was the only one who could do it."

"He was an engineer," Caro said quietly, reminding our mother this was something we all knew.

"An electrical engineer," she said. "He was responsible for the entire power grid of northeastern Massachusetts. Any switch you flipped, that was his doing. And he never let anyone forget it."

"Can he hear us?" Mimi said, looking down at Grandpa Cross's mouth, which had fallen open.

"Perhaps," said our mother. She crossed her legs in the other direction. "Your daddy really didn't want him coming here. And maybe he was right. He was too sick to save."

It reminded me of what she'd said the night before about Ward B, the *dead weight.* I knew I was supposed to be sadder about Grandpa Cross than about a stupid building closing, but each time I thought of the cafeteria and the halls and even those gross echoey bathrooms, I felt pain radiate throughout my entire body. We had fought hard for something important, and it had been our own fault it had failed. We had left the knife on the table, and the Girl had taken it.

Our mother had such clarity of vision around our mission to keep the wards open, and it was like I could now see the future she saw. The dust fires burning through Skid Row, men and women alike freezing to death in lonely cells. As the climate lashed and boiled, these people would be first in the line of fire. Theirs would be lonely deaths after hard lives, hundreds and thousands of them.

Staring at Grandpa Cross dying, it was easy to picture the rest of these deaths, how it would feel to see thousands of people struggling for air and never getting enough.

THE TIME WE SPENT with him that morning wasn't very long—an hour, maybe, an hour and a half. But even now I have a perfect memory of exactly how I sat, the smell of Grandpa Cross's milky breath, the way our mother's hair had fallen from its bun, dark strands coiled against her cheek. I can still feel the position of my heart too, scraped raw and pressed so close against my mother's I could feel what she was feeling. The sadness, the anger, and yes, the relief.

All of these emotions wrapped me tighter to my chair while Grandpa Cross rose from the depths to cough again. Now his breath sounded like rocks in a can. Our mother drew a second syringe.

The sun was beginning to crest the Hill, a slow riser in winter. Its thin white light flashed through the trees and I wondered if we should lower the blinds.

"Well, that was it," our mother said and when I looked back down, she was holding Grandpa Cross's wrist for a pulse. "He's gone."

We all got up very quickly, for now we were in a room with a dead man, and even though he looked no different than he had a few moments earlier, it suddenly felt creepy to stare.

Nurse Holly bustled in, repeated our mother's pulse check, and took from her the vial of morphine.

"I'm sorry for your loss," she said, then looked at the vial again. "That's more than I give."

"The dose was still within range," our mother said.

"Yes," Nurse Holly said, after a moment. "I suppose so."

It was as if Grandpa Cross's last breath had dissolved all intimacy from before. Our mother stood up. "I'd better touch base with Francis. Girls, why don't you straighten up your room? And one of you go tell your father." Then she was gone.

I looked to J.J., expecting her to start heading toward the basement.

J.J. just shook her head. "Someone else do it," she said.

And so I went over and yanked open the door to the basement, stepping quickly down the dirty steps as camel crickets ricocheted away from my feet.

When I reached the bottom, the air smelled like sweat and metal. Daddy was slumped on the weight bench, shirt off, with a jumble of dumbbells scattered around his feet. I had never been very athletic, but I'd paid enough attention in gym class to know that you were supposed to use one at a time, not every weight at once.

I stood in front of him for a long moment, frozen. The camel crickets popped for a moment longer, then settled.

"Is he gone?" Daddy said.

I swallowed. "He's dead," I said, my voice creaking on the word.

Daddy put his hands on his knees and began to rise.

"Oh, but I mean, the body is still there."

Daddy sank down again. Then he shook his head. "No more grandfathers," he said, and I couldn't help myself—I looked over at the stairs, imagining Papa Palmer tumbling down, full of too much of everything: passion, anger, hope. It was such a different end than the one I'd just witnessed. They suddenly seemed so different, Daddy and our mother, parallel lives that could go on toward infinity and never touch.

I reached out toward him but he kept his hands at his sides. He looked tired to the point of exhaustion, which I suppose was the point. When you put all your energy into your body, you don't have to worry about what your mind might do.

I let my hand fall back flat against my leg.

"I'm gonna go," I said. "She's up there, you know." I wasn't sure if that was actually true, but I wanted to see what Daddy would do.

The answer was: absolutely nothing. Daddy raised his head as if even that were an effort, then sunk it back down to his chest. "Thanks, Denise." Then without anything left to try, I turned back up the stairs, plodding at first, then speeding up as if I were being chased.

BACK UPSTAIRS WITH MY SISTERS, we stayed in the kitchen until we heard the slow crunch of gravel on the service road. We watched through the tiny window as two EMTs unloaded an orange stretcher out of the back of an unlighted ambulance. They both looked very young, J.J.'s age or perhaps a little older, and the one in back had a shaggy flap of hair almost to his chin, like a girl's.

I had a sudden urge to touch that hair and when they opened the door and he moved by us with the stretcher, I hesitated before moving back.

"Watch those toes," he said. His eyes were dark, like they were all pupil.

"It's my grandfather," I said.

"I'm sorry," he said.

We all stood outside on the porch after they'd gone, leaning hard against the black metal railings until they seemed to wiggle in their concrete wells. I had a strange feeling in my wrists, like I was walking somewhere very high. I kept thinking about the EMT with the dark eyes. His face caught in my chest in a way I hadn't felt before.

"I think that boy looked like Dracula," I said. "Isn't it funny? Because his job is to work with blood."

"It would be funnier if he were a phlebotomist," J.J. said.

"He doesn't look like Dracula," Mimi said.

Caro sniffed. "I can't believe Grandpa Cross is gone."

"Don't worry, you'll see him in heaven," Mimi said.

"Shut up," Caro said, her voice getting choked up. "Don't make fun of me."

I craned my neck toward the ambulance. "Let's stay outside a little longer."

"I think Denise has a crush on that greasy-haired paramedic," Mimi said.

"Holy crap," I said. "Absolutely not." I'd never had a crush before but I imagined a strong cloud of syrupy emotion, a kind of gentle numbness that left you smiling. Whereas—I looked at this boy and I thought about him hurting me, grabbing my wrist between his fingers until it left a bruise.

Even though we all went to bed late that night, I still didn't feel tired. My sisters' breathing slowed as I kept looking toward the gray-shaded blinds. All the helplessness and sadness that I'd felt earlier had faded away, and I felt guilty for not caring about Grandpa Cross, or for Ward B, or even for myself for the twin tragedies I had just witnessed.

Instead, every time I closed my eyes, I pictured the vampire boy appearing silently by the sill. *I know where all my arteries are,* I said to him. *The femoral beats high in the hot crease of your leg.*

You're smart, the vampire said, *and I am hungry.*

2002

SIXTEEN

Grandpa Cross was incinerated with no ceremony and immediately afterward, the hospital bed went back up the Hill and the Japanese screen went out to the dumpster. Soon the smell of antiseptic went away. But even now that it was over, Grandpa Cross's stay had caused something to shift. The distance between us—it widened from a fingernail to a finger, until you could almost feel the air whistling through it.

RIGHT BEFORE THE LONG Martin Luther King Jr. Day weekend, the remaining residents were removed from Ward B in a line of black cars that seemed long at first, then shorter than I'd thought. That January morning was the coldest of the winter so far, and yet we all stood outside, J.J., Caro, Mimi, and me, our visible breath clouding into a single thick fog as we pressed against the railing to watch them all go. At the bottom of the Hill, some of the cars turned right and some turned left. It was the only time I'd seen anything in Mercy Hill move quickly.

We went up to the admin building and sat on the concrete steps, the chill from the stone numbing us through our jeans. Nurse Jenny and the aides worked with their heads down, ushering each resident into a waiting car. When the cars were gone, they stood outside for a long time, and eventually we came over to see what they were talking about. They stopped talking when we arrived. Nurse Jenny put her arms around each of us in turn and it felt good to be squeezed tight.

"You know, he asks about you," she said. "Dr. Holt. He sent me an email just the other day, wondering how you were doing in all of this."

"I didn't know you two were in touch," J.J. said, echoing what I was thinking. After the Girl's death, it had seemed like Dr. Holt had cut and run, back to a life of Caribbean cruises and private practice, which I imagined hazily as a line of sedate and civilized patients lining up one by one at his office door.

"He writes fairly often," Nurse Jenny said. It seemed like she was going to say something more, but then her head jerked like a deer spotting a lion. I turned and there was our mother, coming toward us. She hadn't returned home at all the night before, but her face did not seem tired.

"What a morning, huh?" our mother said to Nurse Jenny.

Nurse Jenny just looked down.

"I know Francis offered you a transfer," she said. "Your work speaks for itself, even if I don't particularly agree with your evangelism. We could get along in Ward C."

"That's not what I trained for," Nurse Jenny said quietly. "But I can try."

When she said this, I let out a silent sigh of relief. I didn't much care for Nurse Jenny, her NAMI do-gooderness and the way she'd stolen Caro from us, but I didn't want there to be any more change than there already had been. I kept picturing Ward B standing empty, flimsy as paper. The creeping threat of bulldozers lurked in my peripheral vision.

I looked at each of my sisters, wondering what they were thinking. I couldn't tell. This tragedy seemed to push them further into their separate skins: Mimi angry, Caro sad, J.J. distant.

They each turned away and walked down the steps a few paces apart, leaving me standing there with our mother.

"Is it going to be okay?" I asked. Our mother would not lie, and so her reassurances were ironclad. Even after all that had happened, if she said things would be fine, they would be.

Our mother said nothing. In the long moment of silence, I felt a chill come over my body as the sun disappeared behind the building. The rays that had grown brighter and brighter all morning darkened like a pinched candle, and the Hill and everything ahead of me fell into shadow.

ONE DAY, not long after Ward B emptied, Caro invited us all to her baptism. She had been attending church for more than a year now and it had become routine enough to ignore. On Sundays that Nurse Jenny was working, Daddy drove her, although he waited for our mother to be out of the house before he started the car.

Caro never once spoke about it to the rest of us, and the only real change I could see at home was the pause she took before each meal. She didn't clasp her hands or close her eyes, but I knew she was praying.

So it was surprising when she told us one day that she was committing herself to Jesus the following weekend, and we were all invited.

"That's really nice, sweetheart," said Daddy. "We'll be there."

We all turned to our mother, who was sitting at the table, head bent over the orange binder.

"I'll be working," she said.

"Will you?" Daddy asked. "You're not scheduled for Sunday."

Our mother opened her mouth, but Daddy cut in. "The investigation is over, Lisa. You can afford to come." He was right: for the first time in over a year, our mother's days were slower. There were no more late-night talks with Francis, no more last-minute pleas to the city or the state or the Senator in DC. That sudden calm, plus the demise of Grandpa Cross, had left her with more time than she knew what to do with.

She shut the binder and turned her attention toward Caro. "If this is going to be a big fight, fine."

"No one's fighting," Daddy said. He reached out his hand to touch the sleeve of her shirt and she yanked it away.

"You mean no one but me."

Daddy threw up his hands. "What am I supposed to say to that, Lisa?"

"Stop saying my name."

Daddy closed his eyes. It used to seem like he could talk our mother down from the tallest cliff, and now even these little blowups seemed beyond him to soothe. Or maybe he just didn't want to anymore.

"The rest of us are going," he said. "Come if you want."

THE DAY OF THE BAPTISM, she announced that she was going after all, but when she said it, she didn't seem to be speaking to Daddy. We drove together in the station wagon, Mimi and me sitting in the rear-facing back seats, knocking our knees against each other as we tried not to flash our underpants at the cars behind us. Daddy had insisted that we all wear our nicest dresses, which were now way too small, riding high on our thighs. Our mother had clearly not gotten such a memo, because she was wearing slacks and a button-down.

This was my first time entering a church, and I was surprised to see how ordinary it looked on the inside: no stained glass, no gargoyles, just wooden pews facing a dais with a piano and a podium on it. There were maybe fifteen or twenty other people there, families with kids Caro's age who waved to her when she came in. They smiled in a way that said *come sit with us*, but our mother chose a pew near the back and the rest of us followed her, leaving rows of empty wood between our family and the rest of the crowd. Nurse Jenny was not there; she worked longer and different hours in her new role in Ward C, and her absence served as an uncomfortable reminder that with Ward B's closure, everything had been upended.

Then a man Daddy's age came out of a door behind the stage. He was wearing a long white robe that looked like a graduation gown and slip-on shoes.

"Holy shit," Mimi said. "They're actually going to dunk her." She pointed to the right side of the stage, where a rectangular pool had been sunk, about the size of a coffin. The water was still and undisturbed.

"No, that's a fountain," I said.

"Then why does it have steps?"

I looked closer and realized Mimi was right. A metal railing stood behind the water, disappearing down into it like the steps leading into a pool.

"Caro," I hissed, "did you bring a bathing suit?"

She squinted at me and didn't answer.

"Caroline Anne Cross." The man at the front called her name, and we all sat up straighter as Caro walked slowly down the aisle. It reminded me of a wedding on TV, even more so when she got to the front and the minister pinned a white robe around her like the one he had on. They stood there together for a moment while the man beamed.

"Today is a special day," he said. "We have come here to celebrate and raise up Miss Caroline as she makes a very special commitment to herself and to our church family and to the Lord. We thank you, God, for bringing Miss Caroline to us, and for the future works she will do in your name. We pray to you, God, bless this church family, and for anyone who has questions in their heart, please let Miss Caroline stand as an example for what we can all receive when we commit to your love."

Was this aimed at us? I nudged Mimi but she was engrossed in ripping a piece of leather off her shoe.

"And on this day, God, please bless the homebound ill, and our servicemen overseas, and our president George W. Bush; please protect his health and conscience in these modern times when we so much need your care. Amen."

I snuck a look at our mother, who as expected was biting back a smirk. Although she'd voted for him because of his promises to balance the federal budgets, she frequently referred to President Bush as a moron.

Footsteps drew my attention back up to the dais. Together, Caro and the man slipped off their shoes and stepped over to the sunken pool, and it was quiet enough that even in the back row, I could hear the slosh of water meet the sides.

The minister said something to Caro that I couldn't hear, then they both descended the submerged steps, the white of their gowns pooling around them like upside-down flowers. I felt my breath catch in my throat and looked at our parents, who seemed likewise transfixed. They both leaned very far forward, straining over the empty pew in front of us to watch.

The minister turned to us. "Caroline Anne Cross, do you trust Jesus Christ as your savior?"

Caro's voice rang strong and clear. "I do."

"And will you follow him and live for him?"

"I will." It was the same voice she'd used when she argued with Grandpa Cross about the blessing, confident and sure. I wondered, suddenly, if his death had played some role in her decision to get baptized. I guess if you believed in hell, you knew that's where he was going, and you wanted to make sure you ended up somewhere different.

I watched Caro standing up there, sunk into the water like a cake topper, but it also felt very much like I was dreaming. This was too different from everyday life to be real. I wondered if I was hallucinating, and because our mother said that first hallucinations are often auditory, perhaps I was actually still at home and simply imagining the little waves on the sides of the pool, *slip slip slip*.

The minister smiled out at us, his teeth yellow against the white of his robe. "In obedience to our Lord and Savior Jesus Christ, and upon your profession of faith, I baptize you, my sister."

That part got us all blinking, because hearing the word *sister* usually meant someone was talking about us. Then he took Caro in his arms and dunked her backward into the pool, more roughly than I would have anticipated. She hit the water hard enough that little waves sloshed over the sides onto the rubber mat, and when she came up again, she gasped loud enough for us to hear it in the back pew.

"In the name of the Father, Son, and the Holy Spirit," the minister said. "Amen." He left the pool by way of the steps, striding wide to unstick his clinging robe from his legs. Caro just stood there in the water for a moment, and her eyes were closed. It felt weird, like we were seeing her naked, or weirder still, that she wanted us to. The yellow light above the stage shone in her dark, wet hair, and she smiled at the first few rows, not looking back far enough to see us.

Our mother turned to us and commented a little too loudly, "Well, at least that was short."

SEVENTEEN

In the early spring, almost a year after her death, I began dreaming each night of the Girl. This incursion was a frustrating one: once Ward B shut down, our mother rarely spoke of the building or anything that had happened there. And we followed suit. It seemed like a win of mind over matter that we could have caused such a traumatic event and decided to simply reject it, focusing our attention on the last remaining ward, Ward C. But now each night I wandered through the mundane scenes of my everyday life—school, the forts, the cottage—and she wandered with me. Although in real life she had been older than me, it felt like having an annoying younger sibling. *Stop copying me,* I told her, and of course she copied that as well.

I wanted to know if she was visiting the others, but asking Caro about ghosts felt sacrilegious and Mimi's temper was on a hair trigger these days; when I tried to sit next to her on the bus, she elbowed me hard enough to leave a bruise.

So I went looking for J.J. one day after school. She wasn't in the cottage, nor was she in the guardhouse or the forts or the little bench by the parking lot. I found her around the back of Ward A, sitting cross-legged on the flat rectangle of asphalt that had once been a basketball court. This part of the Hill was rarely mowed, and the tall seeded grasses made a kind of wall around the flat area where she sat. I could only see the top half of her face over the greenery; if she'd been lying down, I wouldn't have been able to see her at all.

I stepped carefully through the weeds and onto the blacktop, which on this spring afternoon felt warm and just a little squishy. J.J.'s backpack sat at the edge, empty: she'd fanned her books around her in a semicircle, but none of them were open. Their glossy fronts looked naked without a paper-bag cover. The thought of how J.J. would never have to go to Lincoln again pierced me with jealousy.

I walked over to her until my shadow fell across her face, and only then did she look up.

"Did something happen?" she asked in the flat voice she'd been using for the past year.

I knew what she meant, but when I tried to say no, everything was fine, my mouth dried too much to speak. I looked down at her textbooks. Two biology, one physics, and a slimmer one that looked like a required course about medieval art.

"Do you have exams?" I asked, nudging the physics text with my toe.

"Yeah," she said. "And they're real tests too. It's the same material you learn at a four-year college."

"Sure," I said, my voice sounding squeaky and fake. "Sure, that makes sense."

She put her hands on her thighs and squeezed hard. I watched her knuckles turn white. The pain seemed to buck her out of her reverie.

"I could still go to medical school," she said. "My grades are good. I'm taking all the prereqs."

The wind turned and a sharp spring breeze whistled around the corner of the dark ward behind us. I hugged myself, but J.J. didn't look cold.

"So is that what you're gonna do?" I asked. The words felt jangled and lumpy, caught up in my own hope for what J.J. would say. She and I were so alike in our ambitions, more than dreamy Caro or contrarian Mimi: the first and the last daughter tying all four of us together with a single dream of greatness. College. Med school. Coming back to work alongside our mother, finally equals.

I wanted badly for her to tell me that everything that had happened over the last year was a hiccup, and she—and I—were back on track.

J.J. looked down, pieces of her choppy hair falling into her face. "I don't know," she said. "I feel like I'm stuck. I'm supposed to choose an associate's track but I keep switching. Every quarter I pick a different set of classes. It's just sixty hours, you can do it in two years easy. But I'm not even on track for four."

She took a deep breath and let it out so hard I watched the specks of dirt dance on the asphalt beneath her. "But don't worry about me," she said. *"You"*—she emphasized the word—"you are gonna be fine."

I felt warmed. Even through J.J.'s overwhelming pain, she wanted me to feel better. It also felt like a burden: *Keep your chin up, Denise. Because I sure as hell can't do it.*

I left without asking about the Girl.

IT WAS DURING THIS TIME that our mother decided my time in Lincoln's middle school wing had come to an end. The guidance counselor, Ms. Hollis, called me into her office one afternoon to tell me that she'd just gotten off the phone with Lisa Cross, MD. Why hadn't I told her that I'd already finished the eighth-grade coursework? Why hadn't I told her how hard I'd been applying myself?

Down the hall, the other guidance counselors were laughing about something as the microwave dinged. I wondered if they stopped talking whenever Ms. Hollis came into the room, the way the girls in my gym class did when I came out of the stall after changing.

She dabbed at her eyes. "We haven't had a student like you in the twenty years I've been here. You Cross girls are all smart—J.J. at Princeton already—but I've never seen anything like you."

I decided not to correct her about J.J.'s Princeton situation and just shrugged. I'd read ahead to distract myself from all the painful things that were happening around me, not because of any type of academic enthusiasm.

"You'll be in the same grade as your sister Miriam. You'll like that, won't you?"

To be honest, the thought of running into Mimi wasn't pleasant: I pictured the long, shining needle of her thefted pin stabbing into my side. As usual though, I didn't have much choice in the matter, so I said thank you and Ms. Hollis gave me a hall pass back to social studies, telling me that she'd get everything ready as soon as possible. I could start grade nine on Monday. It was Thursday.

Without the crush of students, the halls seemed cavernous. The sound of my footfalls echoed off the lockers even when I tried to walk quietly. I felt frustration rising in my throat. No matter what I did, adults were always changing the set pieces of my life so I stumbled, then turning around and telling me I should be thankful. I passed my classroom and kept going, pushing out the side doors to the path away from school. A one-way street separated Lincoln from the housing projects on the other side, uniform brick buildings with big wire laundry racks in front. Some were full, fluttering with towels and underwear, and some were completely empty, the bare metal the same color as the fence around Ward C.

It was only mid-March, but the sky was already white and hot, insects buzzing in the bushes and zigzagging across the brick path beneath my feet. I didn't know where I was going, I just didn't want to be where I was.

As I walked on, the noise from the street dulled and in the dry space between the buildings, I began to hear echoes of what was happening inside. The clang of pots and pans, the sizzle of something frying, TV static, a boom box. From an upper window, I saw a Black woman my mother's age looking down at me, a purple scarf tied around her head.

You shouldn't be here, I told myself, it's the ghetto. *Ghetto* was the word du jour at Lincoln, used by my magnet classmates when our textbooks came to us ripped or the desks jangled loose bits of metal. Although I didn't have the friends to use it with, I often thought it. After all, the real thing was right outside our window for comparison.

Being here made me feel strange and slow. It was hard to believe that Lincoln and all the memories contained within it were so close to this other world, inhabited by the people I was now watching through the windows and who I could have sworn were watching me. And why, I asked myself, because I was *white?* It made my face flush. You weren't supposed to talk about race, you weren't supposed to even think about it. Everyone was equal now, it was illegal not to be.

On one set of concrete steps, a woman was sitting, watching two toddlers play with a toy car. I have just as much a right to be here as you do, I thought to myself, but that wasn't true and a last-minute decision to wave at them suddenly seemed too frantic. I cast my eyes down and kept going.

The next block was empty, and the next, and my heart

calmed and I slowed my pace, thinking again of what it would be like to move up to the ninth grade. I was sure my mother had done it so that we could have a little good news after Grandpa Cross and the Ward B closure; she always made these wild gestures when things went south. She'd probably make a big deal about it in front of my sisters: there would be a dinner somewhere I chose, back-to-school shopping a second time, maybe even those little silver hoop earrings I'd wanted ever since I'd gotten my ears pierced.

And buried deep within all this celebration was the understanding that I was helping—had already helped—our mission. Now I was one year closer to college, to med school, to residency and the day I stepped back onto the Hill with an MD badge clipped to my waist. Having a mission made everything easier; it meant that even though I had to do hard things, I never had to make a hard choice.

I looked up. Past another row of buildings, I could see the street, and if I exited there, I could turn and take the long way back around the projects, all the way back to Lincoln. I still had my hall pass in my back pocket and even if someone got mad at me because I'd taken my time, who cared? I was moving up soon. I trudged along, past door after identical door, until the sidewalk was in sight.

Then I heard someone say, "Hey! Can I ask you a question?" The speaker was a man, a young one, standing in the door of one of the last buildings on the block. The door swung inward, and he had wedged himself into the opening, as if he didn't want me to see what was past him.

I looked around like I was in some sort of pantomime. "Who . . . me?"

He shifted, neither toward me nor away. "Hey!" he said. "I have something to ask you."

My heart beat in my throat. I was scared, but more than that, embarrassed of being scared, of what that meant about some rotten part of me deep within. I took a small step forward.

"How's it going?" I said quietly.

The man blinked slowly. "It's been a helluva day," he said, and then something seized me: I ran. I started fast toward the street, but it suddenly seemed too far away; I made a tight circle and, feet clacking on the uneven brick, I sprinted back the way I'd come. My chest burned like I was breathing acid, and I could hear the man's laughter echo off the buildings.

When I reached the school, I stopped short. I felt ashamed and exhausted. Why had I done that—any of it? It felt like a monster inside of me was pulling the strings, and I was the unwilling puppet.

I heard the school bell ring and after a few moments' delay, kids came spilling out of the doors. No one spotted me standing by the fence, nor did they notice when I slunk down to the footpath and cut into their midst. I still had Ms. Hollis's laminated hall pass in my pocket, and when I slipped in through the doors at the other end of the school, I flung it into a trash can.

EIGHTEEN

My first day of ninth grade began with a fight—one instigated by our mother. That Thursday, she followed me into Lincoln's front office to argue with the administrators about my course load. *Why isn't Denise in the Honors English course, no, not that one, the double period taught by the woman with the master's degree, Ms. Johnson? It was full—what does that mean? You really can't fit in one more desk? What fire code, you're telling me you know the fire code for Wake County by heart? Well, I looked it up beforehand and there was nothing in it that said you couldn't add another tiny desk to Ms. Johnson's double-period English. And Algebra II, that's not right at all, Denise should be in pre-calc at the very least.* And so on.

The women sitting behind the desk seemed annoyed but resigned and told her they'd make all the changes this afternoon. For now, I could go to the classes they'd initially assigned. That seems like a waste, our mother said, and told them we'd come back tomorrow morning, when they'd gotten things right.

I followed her back out to the car, relieved to postpone reality for one more day. I got into the front seat, where I never got to sit, and waited for our mother to turn back around toward home.

Instead, she said, "I'm hungry. Are you hungry?"

"Sure," I said, even though it was only 7:50 a.m., and I'd had breakfast not an hour before.

We went the other way out of the lot, down a winding, pine-flanked street, until we hit the highway. I only had a vague idea of where things were located outside Mercy Hill, having never driven myself. Pockets of shopping centers advertised their contents in big streetside boards, but we drove past the first two and turned into a third that contained, among other things, a P.F. Chang's, a PetSmart, and a Lifeway.

"You'll have to forgive me, this is the only place I know to get breakfast around here," our mother said. Ever since her skirmish with the front desk ladies, her demeanor had become relaxed, almost gleeful.

The place was called JB's and it was set up like a diner, with waitresses carrying big platters of biscuits and gravy to patrons who were, for the most part, fat old men. The air was thick with the smells of hash browns and grape jelly.

We sat across from each other in a booth that could have fit our whole family and paged through the sticky menus. I'd decided on pancakes with strawberry topping, but when our mother ordered the country ham, I immediately felt like I should try to act more grown-up.

"You know what," I said, smiling at the waitress, "I'll have that too." Then I blushed, wondering if copying her was even more immature than ordering pancakes.

My mother just beamed at me. "Good choice."

I stuck a straw into my pebbled cup, breaking up the cylinder of crushed ice. It was rare to have this much time alone with her and happy as I was, I was also struck dumb. So I sat up as straight as I could and asked a question that I frequently heard Daddy ask: "What's on the docket for you today?"

She smiled without condescension. "I had time set up with a few residents this morning to talk about medication management, but I'm having Jenny take those appointments. So when I come back, I'll have to look through her notes and see if I agree before I write the new prescriptions."

"Do you like working with Nurse Jenny?" I asked.

"She hasn't tried to convert me, if that's what you're asking."

I stiffened, thinking of Caro's awkward baptism. My mother just laughed and rolled her eyes a little. "No, Jenny is fine. She's got her NAMI folks writing letters."

"What kind of letters?"

"There's a developer interested in Wards A and B. It's a different one than the one from before, these guys want to build condos."

"Condos?" My whole body shivered, but when I looked over at my mother, she was grinning.

"Denise," she said. "They're out of their *minds*. They'd be eighty feet away from the rec yard. I don't think they're local; they just made this bid without looking into it at all. So Jenny and I, we're educating them."

"What's in the letters?"

She smiled wider. "Do you remember when I told you girls about Alexander White? Scared the pants off you. Didn't see Mimi climbing the fence after that. It's only right that the developers know about the HB95s."

This was a lot to take in. There was so much at stake—for the buildings, for the remaining Ward C—but my mind caught on the Scarecrow. On the ground, gasping, his arms twisted back in those sharp plastic restraints. Of course I had been frightened of what he'd done, but seeing him tied up had felt like I'd done something wrong too.

My mother met my eyes, smile fading. "We don't have to talk about it. But this is a fight we're going to win."

I swallowed. "Can I come to the next city council meeting? I want to help."

"The best way you can help is to do well in school."

"I know, but—"

"I want you to know that anything you need, you tell me. Test prep, books, tutoring, rides—just ask, and I'll make it happen."

"Thanks," I said, but she didn't seem to hear.

"I've made mistakes," she said. "I'm still kicking myself for the mistakes I've made—but we can't dwell on it. We can just set you up for success the best way we can."

I put my hands under the table. She was clearly referencing J.J.'s refusal to go to Princeton. Although I felt drunk on our mother's attention, I also felt a stab of loyalty toward my sister. I wanted to tell her that J.J. was doing well at community college, but after our conversation on the basketball court, I knew that wasn't true.

Fortunately, just then, the waitress reappeared, setting a large oval platter down in front of each of us. Ham the size of a saucer pushed up against a mound of scrambled eggs. A slick of grits spilled over every untouched surface, steam rising from the pat of butter at its center.

I sliced a triangle of ham into my mouth and almost gagged at the saltiness. It was roughly the texture of jerky, the salt so intense it made my temples pound.

"So good, right?" My mother was slicing her ham into strips. "I never give southern food enough credit. Did you know I was twenty-six before I had grits?"

I didn't really like grits. To me, they tasted like dirty water, and when they cooled, they turned into rubber. I put another tiny slice of ham into my mouth and mustered a smile.

"Did Daddy serve them to you?" Some of my favorite stories were the ones she told about dating Daddy, their initial courtship.

"No," she said. "It was my roommate, Richard."

"You had a boy roommate?"

"He was gay so it didn't really count. It was when I was in my residency at Duke."

I nodded in a way that I hoped seemed casual.

"I never told you about Ritchie? He was funny, he was from a tiny town in Mississippi, Durham seemed like the big city to him. He used to come back late from parties wired and make a whole mess of food. Sometimes I'd be up already, and he'd make grits and biscuits and gravy for breakfast."

I blinked, not wanting to break the spell. This was a side of my mother I'd rarely seen: confident and casual, not moralizing over a guy who was clearly consuming alcohol and/or drugs (!).

"What happened to him?" I asked.

"He's back in Mississippi. Cardiologist." She waved her hand over her plate. "He probably doesn't eat a bunch of buttery grits anymore."

"If he did, that'd be pretty ironic."

My mother bit into another strip of ham and smiled. "See, this is why you need to be in Honors English."

WHEN I RETURNED TO SCHOOL the next day, the reactions of my new ninth-grade classmates fell somewhere in between my greatest hopes and worst fears. No one picked on me or said anything about my living at Mercy Hill the way the middle schoolers had. In class, when we had to get into groups, they remembered my real name when we had to write it down on our worksheets, none of the old Psycho Dee crap. Then the bell would ring and they'd scatter, leaving me behind, alone. But what had I expected? By the end of the year, no one wanted any new friends, especially not a twelve-year-old kid six inches shorter than the rest of them.

You can, of course, get used to anything. I learned how to slow-walk between my classes so I arrived right before the bell and wouldn't have to talk with anyone, and flipped through textbooks in the cafeteria during the interminable lunch period.

Sometimes, I caught glimpses of Mimi or Caro as I waded through the crowded halls of the high school wing. They were never alone but tied loosely to the edge of a group—Mimi trudging along with some emo kids, Caro tagging behind a set of long-haired, long-skirted girls from her church. If I caught their eye, they acknowledged it only for a second before quickly looking away. I never pursued them any further.

NINETEEN

It had been three years since I'd set foot in the drab, windowless chamber where the city council met, and it was striking how little had changed. Tom and his gut still presided at the end of the long table, and the rows of audience chairs were once again mostly empty. It gave me the impression that we were the only ones who'd left the room that night three years ago, while the rest of the council had stayed, frozen in time like a spell from a fairy tale.

I turned to Caro to see if she sensed this too, but she'd already taken a seat, her hands folded patiently in her lap. Even though our mother had told me that she didn't want us wasting our time at the meetings, she'd decided this morning that for this one it would be helpful to have an audience.

It was clear that Caro and I had been chosen because unlike Mimi and J.J. (the ear-piercing refusal! The suspensions!) we could be trusted not to cause a scene. We were just here to listen, a silent presence reminding our enemies that we weren't going away without a fight. But a polite one, no sparring about Reaganomics.

I felt a hand on my shoulder and turned around to see Nurse Jenny holding out a little metal box. "Altoid?" she said, her smile warm. She was seated with two women and a man in NAMI shirts. It felt strange to be teamed up with them, these people our mother had rolled her eyes at for years. Made the whole night feel even more unreal. But what else was there for me to do? I took the mint and popped it into my mouth, breathing in as the sharp circle of cinnamon began to burn.

The council didn't immediately jump to Mercy Hill business as it had the last time I was here. They plodded through a jaywalking bill and a proposal about historical preservation of Victorian-style homes near Mordecai Park. I wondered if they were waiting until the other party arrived, the developers who'd been on the receiving end of the NAMI letters. No one was here yet who could fit that description.

One hour stretched to two and I began to think about the homework I had yet to do. When I'd moved up to ninth grade, I'd skipped entire chunks of math and science, which meant most assignments in those subjects took twice as long as I paged back through my textbooks to get caught up.

Then Tom banged a gavel I hadn't realized he had. "Thank you all for being here, this session is adjourned." Caro jumped too, and we looked at each other, confused. Our mother stood.

"What about us?" she said, her tone sounding strange and informal after an evening of stilted legalese.

"They dropped it," Tom said, not looking up.

"The whole proposal? Demolition and construction?"

"All of it, yes. Came in a letter last week."

"Girls, we won!" Nurse Jenny clapped both of our shoulders and squeezed. The NAMIs beside her were also hugging each other. This good news felt strange and anticlimactic; I wasn't sure where to turn. Then Caro said, "Look at her."

Our mother had gotten very close to Tom Pritkins, towering over him where he sat. Her voice was controlled but furious.

"Do you have no respect for my time?" she said. "You saw

me come in, you saw all of us sit there all evening and you kept talking about—fucking—jaywalking!" Her eyes were narrowed to slits, and I clamped my mouth shut, scared to breathe.

"Lisa, sweetheart. Why don't you just enjoy your victory?"

"This isn't a game," she said, then she turned back to the NAMIs, who'd begun to gather their purses and coats. "All of you talking about winning and losing like it's goddamned college basketball. People's *lives* are at stake."

My anger rose, then settled uneasily. I thought about what Grandpa Cross had told us. *She doesn't care about saving lives. She just cares about being on top.*

I snuck a look at Caro. Her cheeks were flushed with embarrassment, and she exchanged a look with Nurse Jenny like our mother's rage was something they often talked about. I felt excluded, mad on all sides, at Tom for wasting our time, at our mother for not being able to let something go, at the unseen forces that had control over the fate of Mercy Hill.

I looked down and thought about my sisters, how they were being transformed by this same pressure, escaping from duty (J.J.), from rules (Mimi), from the logic and atheism our mother held so dear (guess who, right beside me). And the natural question then, as I stared at the cracks in the toes of my shoes where my growing feet had begun to press against the confines of the rubber: Denise Cross, now twelve and a half. What the ever-loving fuck was going to happen to me?

JUST A FEW WEEKS after the meeting, as the school year finished up, Caro dropped another bombshell: a boy at her church wanted to court her.

Laketon was eighteen and handsome in a Disney Channel way: floppy hair, dimples when he smiled, not terribly tall but stick-straight posture, like he was perpetually going on an interview. He wore a metal retainer that bisected his upper teeth and gave him just a little bit of lisp. One day in May, he showed up at Cottage 10 in his own pickup truck, which was old and beat-up but very clean.

Daddy was the only parent home, which might have been a calculation on Caro's part, but it backfired spectacularly. As soon as Laketon came in, he shook Daddy's hand and declared his intentions ("Sir, I would like to declare my intentions"). Daddy told them both to sit down until our mother came home. Then, with a very loud and very long sigh, Daddy went back to the sink and began washing dishes with such force that I could hear the water splashing onto the floor.

Caro took Laketon outside and Mimi and I followed, J.J. not yet home from her afternoon class. We had seen him before, although not in person: Caro had plastered photo prints along the wall next to her bed, almost all of them taken during activities at the church gym, the blond-yellow wood of the basketball court running from shot to shot. But here he was in person, wearing a collared shirt and dark slacks, obviously having dressed up for the occasion.

Mimi almost had a fit over what to make fun of first.

Was he born at a lake or just conceived there? Do these pants come in men's sizes as well? Would he consider himself gay for Jesus?

"This is Mimi," Caro said, "She acts out when she wants attention."

"There's no way in hell they're going to let you two go out," Mimi said, emphasizing the word *hell*.

"We shall see," said Caro, smoothing the flared sleeves of her shirt. That year, the medieval look had come into style and all the girls at school walked around looking like Queen Guinevere in low-rise jeans. Of all of us, Caro cared the most about clothes, although since her baptism she had begun wearing skirts that hung a little too far past her knees to be considered cool.

"Are you in college?" I asked Laketon.

"I've got four more months in a certificate program to get my HVAC license."

"Jesus Christ," Mimi said. "They're definitely not going to let you date a dropout."

Some of Caro's calm began to crack. "Laketon isn't a drop-out," she said. "He could've gone to a four-year college if he wanted to."

"Did you even take the SAT?" Mimi said.

"I took the PSAT," Laketon said.

"Did you take any APs?" Mimi said.

"You must really like school," Laketon said.

"I fucking hate it," Mimi said.

That got the rise out of Caro that Mimi was looking for.

"Shut up," Caro said. "Shut up and stop acting like a smarty-pants."

This insult seemed infantile compared to Mimi's f-bomb. Mimi leaned in and Caro backed away. Were they actually about to fight?

Just then, I heard the sound of our mother's shoes clopping down the concrete steps that led from Ward C down the Hill. She was still pretty far away, but her presence threw a damper on the sparking fight.

"Daddy must've paged her," I said.

"Oh, good," Laketon said, which made him seem either very optimistic or very stupid.

Once our mother arrived, we all gathered around the kitchen table, Laketon and Caro at one end and the rest of us clustered tight around the other. You could tell Laketon was nervous, but he held it together well, addressing our parents as *ma'am* and *sir* and stating once again that he'd like their permission to court their daughter.

"I know what I'm asking is big, because she's your little girl, but I promise you, I will be good to her, and communicate. Good relationships are all about communication."

Daddy's mouth twisted like he was trying to hide a smile. "That's a very nice sentiment," he said.

Our mother interrupted. "What are you asking us?" she said.

"I know y'all aren't churchgoers, but we see things eye to eye. We won't be going off alone, we won't be doing anything physical, we just—we'll get to know each other."

Laketon swallowed. "And I know you may not believe me, since I'm a teenage boy and you were once a teenage boy like me." It was clear he had practiced this as if he'd only be addressing Daddy, but he kept nodding at our mother, too.

"Anyway," he said. "I'd like to win your trust. So—uh that's it."

Our mother put a hand to her temple. "Are you two supposed to get married at the end of all this? You know she's fifteen."

"Mom," Caro said. "I'm not getting married. I'm still in high school."

"She doesn't have to do anything she doesn't want to," Laketon said.

"This is bizarre," our mother said.

"Lisa," Daddy said. "They're not going to get into any trouble."

"Mrs. Cross, I can assure you," Laketon said, "we will not do anything inappropriate."

Our mother shook her head. "There are better ways for you to be spending your time," she told Caro. "You'll have college applications due in the fall. Or do you want to end up at Wake Tech too?"

The insult stung even though J.J. wasn't there to hear it.

"So you're saying I can't have a social life?" Caro said.

"This is hardly a social life," our mother said. "And honestly, I can't tell what you're even going to do together if you can't—"

"Lisa," Daddy said again. "Can I talk to you alone for a minute?"

"No," our mother said, voice sharp. "I need to get back to work. You called me down here to give my opinion and my opinion is no."

"Maybe there's a reasonable compromise."

"So I'm the one that's being unreasonable?" She stood up. "Nice to meet you, Laketon." Then she crossed to the door and stepped out.

I looked at Caro. Her eyes were wet, and Laketon had put a hand on her shoulder. It was a small gesture, but it made my stomach drop to see it. This was something they both badly wanted.

We all turned to Daddy. He was still seated and the look in his eyes was strange. "You have my permission," he said. "That's all you need, isn't it?"

Laketon nodded one long, slow nod.

Daddy cleared his throat. "Lisa gets home at seven thirty," he said. "Drive the speed limit and wear a seat belt."

Laketon got up so fast he had to catch one of the chairs before it fell. He pumped Daddy's hand with both of his.

"Mr. Cross," he said, "I truly appreciate it."

"It's Palmer," Daddy said, loud enough to make us jump.

J.J. GOT HOME LATE that evening and we had to usher her into the bedroom to tell her all the details.

"So you're dating?" she asked Caro.

Caro sighed. "We call it courting, but yeah, that's basically it."

"Okay," J.J. said. "I fail to see why this is so interesting."

"Daddy said she could," I said. "Mom said she couldn't."

"Okay," J.J. said slowly. "So what? They're not going to get a divorce over it."

That was an outcome I hadn't even considered. My classmates who had divorced parents, their fathers wore sunglasses and blue jeans, and their mothers put on makeup to sit in the car-pool line. It was hard to imagine either of our parents letting the world see them that way.

Caro said, "I'm not going to stop seeing Laketon."

"No one cares about Lake Man," Mimi said.

"Do you really think Mom isn't going to find out?" J.J. said. It was true that our mother worked a lot less often these days; the recent win at the city council meant fewer committee meetings and letter-writing campaigns, although none of us were sure how long this tentative victory would last.

"She won't if no one tells her," Caro said, then peered over the bed to look at each of us in turn.

"Honestly," Mimi said, "I do not care in the slightest."

"Denise?" she said. "I need to hear you say it."

"Come on," I protested, but she didn't let up. "Fine," I said, spelling it out for her. "I won't say anything to Mom."

TWENTY

That summer, it seemed like no one was ever home. J.J. had chosen courses that stretched late into the evening, Caro oversaw Vacation Bible School (an excuse, undoubtedly, to see Laketon), and Mimi spent days at a stretch away. Her story was that she was sleeping over at Anna's, a friend from elementary school. It was such a flagrant lie that I half thought she was trying to get caught. Maybe she was testing our parents' limits. Or maybe she was just lazy.

In any case, no one called her on it, even when she came home smelling like bonfire smoke or weed or cologne. She'd held up her end of the bargain—straight As, 231 on her PSAT—and in return, her summer activities would not be monitored.

Cottage 10 seemed so empty I could scream. Daddy was around, of course, but he wasn't much company, downstairs knocking his weights around or up in the kitchen cooking inedible-looking post-workout meals: big pans of unseasoned ground beef, which he wrapped in lettuce and smothered in hot sauce. The smell of these concoctions lingered in the air, and the TV was full of reruns. I had to get out.

Sometimes, if I felt like pressing on a bruise, I would walk up the Hill to Ward B and stare at the boarded-up windows. Although it had only been closed for half a year, the plywood sheets had already faded and were nearly as dark as the ones nailed up on Ward A. The rainwater that pooled on the sills quickly became a breeding ground for mosquitoes, so I never stayed long, chased away by the whining swarm of insects out for blood.

Salvation came in the form of calculus. Previously, Lincoln had only offered summer school for kids who were falling behind, but an uptick in college application panic caused them to add another AP course to their roster: combined Calculus AB and BC. Kids could skip both years of calc by taking it over the summer, then qualify for the school's most advanced math class in the fall, Differential Equations. I was good at math, as we all were, and while I had no particular interest in DiffEQ, I jumped at the chance to do something—anything—to pass the time.

The course was held in one of the French classrooms, a second-floor space that looked out over the narrow line of trees behind the school. The desks were arranged with the windows behind us, probably to minimize distractions, but this backfired as my classmates spent entire mornings twisting around to stare at the greenery and freedom beyond.

They were rising seniors who had come up through the accelerated track, mostly boys and a few girls who didn't look nerdy at all, just competitive. They were all feeling the pressure of upcoming tests and admissions and talked fast to one another at breaks about their "personal statements" and who was going to be Key Club president.

They treated me like an anomaly, a doll perched in the corner. They did not tease me, they did not speak to me. And when Mr. Burroughs called my name, he rarely smiled. Like—okay, Denise Cross, let's get this over with.

The course ran two hours in the morning and two in the afternoon, with an hour and a half lunch in between. This was the worst part. The other students piled into someone's car and came back with bags from Cookout or Bojangles', and Mr. Burroughs left for the teacher's lounge, locking the door behind him. The cafeteria was open, serving a limited menu of cheese sandwiches and cartons of milk to satisfy some state requirement, but I brought my own food. I'd eat it sitting on the steps of the dark library, then kick my way around the school grounds.

With the exception of the language wing, where the summer school classes were being held, everything was supposed to be kept locked. But I soon learned that maintenance often left doors open, and so I began a circuit of the campus each day, twisting knobs until I was admitted.

I climbed each stairwell to the top, trying the doors to the roof (never successful). I slid into the empty attendance office and flipped through stacks of forms that would get you a recommendation letter, or a transfer to an alternative school, or a pass to go off campus during lunch. I marveled at the power contained within these papers, and thought about stealing them. But I had no one to share these revelations with, and that thought depressed me.

With the entire interior of the school covered, I began to spread out, jiggling the equipment shed lock at the track and examining the big electric box that provided energy to the buildings. High voltage, it said, humming with danger. I threw a stick at it, but it emitted no sparks.

Off to the side of the main building were a handful of old trailers, spillover classrooms awaiting the years-overdue construction of a new building. I'd never tried to access any of them, because I suspected the school was extra vigilant about keeping them locked.

One day as I walked by, I saw the door of one bob inward,

revealing a shadowy interior. I stopped, tiptoeing up the rotting wood steps, and pushed open the door with my fingertips.

I nearly jumped out of my skin. A boy was standing there, writing something on the whiteboard. I quickly took in the rest of the room, which I realized was the classroom for German language classes. Signs saying WILLKOMMEN had been tacked on the walls and their edges curled in the humid air.

"Sorry," I said, and he whirled around. He looked like a student, and though I'd never seen him before, that wasn't unusual: I hardly knew the names of kids in my own class, let alone the juniors and seniors, and he definitely looked like one of the latter. He was tall and pale, with a mop of dark hair like Harry Potter and a little scab on the side of his cheek that I assumed was from shaving. Slowly, he set the whiteboard marker on the metal ridge below the board.

"What are you writing?" I asked, although I could see clearly. In a spiky, narrow hand he'd written, *I am the master of my SKATE*.

He scowled. "Are you some teacher's kid?"

"No," I said, "I go here too."

"You're like, ten years old."

"I'm almost thirteen," I said. "And anyway, I'm in high school already. Is that 'Invictus'?" I pointed at the board.

The boy crossed his arms. "You shouldn't be here," he said. "If you really are a student, you could get in a ton of trouble."

"I've been everywhere in the school," I said. "And that *is* 'Invictus,' just changed a little." I began to recite:

"'Out of the night that covers me, black as the pit from pole to pole, I thank whatever gods may be for my unconquerable soul.' But the last line there, it's 'I am the master of my *fate*,' not *Skate*—"

"That's me," he said. "I'm Skate." Then he went up to the board and began erasing the letters with a long finger. I watched, mesmerized. Even when he'd disappeared them, you could still see what he'd written, because the empty line his finger made was whiter and brighter than the rest of the board.

"Are you in one of the summer school classes?" I asked. His answer would be telling, because all the courses except for mine were remedial ones.

"Yeah," he said. "Geometry."

"Regular geometry? I took that when I was nine."

"Oh shit," he said. "You're J.J. Cross's sister."

"You know her?"

"She was in tenth grade with me for a bit." I tried to remember when J.J. had passed through that grade and couldn't. In any case, this boy was at least sixteen, if not a few years older. I could have felt intimidated except I kept picturing him doing basic geometry, spinning the pencil of a compass into a circle. It made him seem earnest. "Do you guys still live in the mental hospital?" he said.

If any other student had asked me this, I would have corrected them—*we don't live* in *the hospital, we live on the grounds*—but I got the feeling he wasn't trying to be funny or mean. I voiced something aloud I'd never said before: "Yeah, but maybe not for long. The wards are closing, and the state wants to tear the whole thing down."

His stare was piercing. "I'm sorry," he said. Then after a long moment: "No offense, but I came here to be alone."

I hadn't talked to another person in so long. I stepped close to the board.

"You know Timothy McVeigh recited this right before they executed him. It's a shame, because it's a really nice poem. And now it's tainted by this awful thing."

"I like that," the boy said.

"You like Timothy McVeigh?"

"No—of course not." The boy looked up at the ceiling, which was low and water-stained. "I like that it's not perfect anymore."

The way he said *perfect* struck a ringing chord within me. It wasn't a word I would have expected him to say.

"I'm Denise," I said.

"I'm Skate."

"That's not your real name, is it?"

"We have to go," he said, holding up a shiny key. "I'm not supposed to have this."

"Okay," I said, "maybe I'll see you around." I was trying to sound casual, but it was difficult. I wanted to keep talking for a week.

"Sure," he said. "Maybe." Then he stood at the door and I had no choice but to leave. I was sure he was watching me as I stepped down the breezeway, and when I allowed myself to look back, he was gone.

THE NEXT DAY, I ate my lunch during the morning class session so I could head for the trailer as soon as our break began. I kind of regretted doing this, because I must have smelled like bologna, and although I didn't want to admit it, I wanted Skate to think I was cool. I kept thinking about him standing at that board like he was facing execution himself, straight-backed and ready. He wasn't like the other boys I knew, who whooped down the echoey halls and called each other *faggot* whenever possible.

When I got to the trailer, he was already inside, chaining paper clips together into a long and dangling string. When I came in, he scooped them back up into a pile, like it was a secret project he didn't want me to see him working on.

"You again," he said. "How's nerd math?"

I looked away so he wouldn't see me blush. "This one girl

started crying during our morning quiz. She studied the wrong thing."

"Jesus fucking Christ," Skate said. "This is what I hate about the modern educational system. It's designed to like—cram, cram, cram, get everything in your head and then regurgitate it back out. You don't learn anything."

"It's the worst," I said, eager to agree with him.

Skate tapped his fingers fast on one of the Formica desks. He seemed more animated today, like we had agreed to meet, like I wasn't encroaching on his turf. "It just totally neuters the concept of learning. Kids no longer have passion, the only thing that matters is, you know, that they're a test-taking automaton."

"But if the school doesn't administer the tests, they don't get funding from the government." I'd meant this as a statement of *Well, what are you going to do?* But Skate took it as an escalation of his own point. He slammed his hand down flat on the desk so hard the metal legs rattled.

"Exactly," he said again. "It's a system designed to—you know, bore us into complacency."

"What do you think they should do instead?" I asked.

His expression darkened. "That's a logical fallacy, you know. Just because I don't know how to fix something doesn't mean it shouldn't get fixed."

"Oh," I said. "Sorry, I didn't mean that at all."

There was a silence, then he laughed. "Did I just get too intense? My friends say I get too intense."

"Who are your friends?" I said.

"I don't think you'd know them. You're like—a freshman?"

"Rising sophomore," I said. Then before he could say anything else, I said, "I don't have any friends." I'd never said this aloud, and I'm not sure why it came tumbling out now. If anyone ever asked me who I hung out with, I made some kind of joke, humor being the easiest way to hide the way I really felt. But with Skate, somehow I felt like I could just tell the truth.

Skate's eyes softened, and after a moment he dragged the whole desk he was sitting on over next to me. It was a weirdly sincere gesture, like he was pulling me up a chair. He scooted over and motioned for me to climb up next to him, which I did. My legs swung high above the ground.

"You're short," he said.

"I just have short legs," I said. "But I've got a really long torso. See? When we're standing up, you're much taller than me, but when we sit, we're the same height."

He straightened his back; it was true. Our faces lined up. I suddenly felt very slow and stupid.

"I don't see your skateboard," I said. "Unless your real name is Skate?"

"No," he said. Then he reached into his shirt and pulled out a long chain with a silver charm dangling off the end, a tiny stingray the size of a postage stamp. "They're a type of sea creature. Have you ever seen one up close?"

"At the aquarium, maybe?"

"I like them because they're different," he said, even though I hadn't asked. "All the other fish are going forward and backward, but skates break free and glide off. I think they have more fun."

"Are they dangerous?" I said.

He took the charm between his fingers and pricked my wrist with the sharp tail. I felt my heart pick up like I'd had an injection of adrenaline. I slid off the desk, not wanting Skate to see my face flush red.

"I didn't hurt you, did I?"

"No, no," I said. "I just have to get back to class."

"Okay," he said after what felt like a very long time. "See you tomorrow."

THE NEXT DAY Skate seemed short-tempered and testy. I was sitting where I had sat the day before, hoping to recapture the moment from yesterday, but Skate kept getting up and walking over behind the teacher's desk, asking me questions that he already knew the answer to and then pacing over to the empty whiteboard, like he was trying to make sense of something.

"So why did you skip so many grades?"

"The faster I go through school, the quicker I'll be out in the real world."

"And then you're going to be some kind of doctor?"

"A psychiatrist. I want to come back to Mercy Hill and help my mother."

"That sounds like something your parents told you to say," he said, which was unfortunately true, even though I believed it.

"Well, what about you?" I said. "Where do you see yourself in five years?"

I meant it as a joke, but he stopped and looked straight at me. "I don't want what everyone else wants," he said. "They want education, I want learning. They want marriage, I want love. I don't—I just think sometimes everyone is trying to get you to, like, play this *part* without actually feeling the things that go along with it."

I bit my lip, thinking about the way he'd said *love*. I wanted very badly for Skate to see that I was on his side, the side of authenticity and truth, and I knew a calculated response would have just the opposite effect.

"So," I said. "What does your girlfriend say about all this?"

He stopped and looked over at me. "I don't have a girlfriend."

My entire face flushed. The segue was ham-fisted, I felt like an idiot. But I'd been turning the question over in my mind for days. And now that the opportunity was here before me, I couldn't stand for it to evaporate. I held out my shaking hand like I was feeding a bird. For a long moment, nothing. Then he reached out and took it.

I had seen enough television to know that when you kissed someone, you put your hands in their hair. Skate's was thick and coarse and at first I pulled too hard and he stopped kissing me. I said, *Sorrysorry,* and he said, *No it's okay,* and we clutched together like something was trying to tear us apart. His breath was dry and a little musky, and my heart beat so fast my vision kept fading in and out.

He loosened his grip and my heart sank, but he just stepped back and lowered us both down onto the thin carpet. He kept saying my name, *Denise,* and each time it made my throat nearly close. No one had ever said my name like that.

His voice was a whisper: "Can I make you feel good?"

I said yes loud enough that we both laughed, and then he was unzipping my jeans, kneeling between my ankles, and lowering his entire face down, down, down. His breath felt hot on my cool skin and I closed my eyes, picturing the dark depths of the ocean.

THAT NIGHT, everyone was home. Listening to their stupid, useless voices made me want to tear my skin off. Caro talked to Daddy about some form he needed to sign for the DMV so she could get her learner's permit and our mother and Mimi got into it about putting a paper towel over leftovers so they didn't pop all over the microwave. And meanwhile I was there, sitting around the table with them, trying to act like my entire life hadn't just changed. My body felt like it was full of sand from a rainstick, sending shivers through my joints each time I thought about what had happened. I kept hearing his voice in my ear, saying my name like the most magical spell.

As we cleared the dishes, I couldn't take it anymore, I followed J.J. over to the TV and asked if she'd ever heard of a boy named Skate. Dark wavy hair, tall?

"I know Skate," she said. "His real name's Jeremy Morgans. Really weird guy."

"What's weird about him?" I asked, trying to sound like it was the least interesting thing in the world to me. Mimi had come over and begun painting her fingernails with a bottle of Wite-Out, and I watched the tiny white spongy tip go back and forth across her nails.

"Don't put that on in here," J.J. said, snatching the bottle. "It's so toxic."

"Don't be a bitch," Mimi said, just quiet enough so our parents couldn't hear.

"J.J.," I said. "What's so weird about him?"

Mimi wrested the bottle back from J.J.'s grip and began shaking it so it rattled. J.J. stood up in a huff.

"Why do you care?" J.J. said. "Do you know him?"

"He's at summer school with me," I said. "He's going out with a girl in my calculus class."

J.J. paused and her face got serious. "Really? I heard he got held back last year, and all of his friends graduated without him. So he's a senior again but he's like, nineteen. Who's dating him?"

"This girl Sarah," I said. "I don't know her last name."

"That's not very helpful," she said, and I knew I needed to cut it out before she got angry.

That night I hardly slept. Poor sweet, rebellious Skate, isolated for circumstances he couldn't control. Just like me. What we'd done in the German trailer was without a doubt the best and craziest thing I'd done in my life, but it paled beside my memory of him saying my name. I wanted him to say it for the rest of time, I wanted to die hearing him say it. The minutes dragged on and I pinched the sides of my legs like I was punishing myself, trying to mar my own happiness so I would keep believing in it.

I WORE A DRESS the next day, both to show myself off and for ease of access. I hadn't been able to eat anything all morning, and my hands were trembling when I knocked on the door to the trailer. Fear consumed me: What if I had dreamed this entirely?

But standing there was Skate, and his own face was wrecked with fatigue.

"I thought you might not come back," he said.

"Are you fucking kidding me?" I said, and the obscenity was so funny to us that we collapsed into each other.

"I like your outfit," he said. The dress was a sleeveless yellow seersucker Grannie P. had given me last Easter, and since then it had grown sheerer and tighter across the chest so that it looked like the kind of dress (I thought) you would wear to go dancing. I wondered if Skate could dance. I wondered what he'd been like as a baby. I wanted to know everything about him but I knew that I had to play it cool; the quieter I was, the more it drew him to me. We lay on the floor again, but face-to-face this time, and he said, *What are you thinking about* and I just said his real name, *Jeremy*.

He pulled away. "Who told you that?"

"My sister J.J."

"You told her about us?"

"No, God, no—I just—is something wrong?"

"I don't like that name," he said. "It's what people who don't know me call me. My friends call me Skate."

I remembered what J.J. had said, about all of Skate's friends having graduated without him.

"I like it," I said. "I'm sorry."

"Christ, don't be sorry. I'm sorry. I shouldn't be so fucking weird." He sat up and pressed both hands to the sides of his head, like he was trying to crush it. I came over and put my arms around him.

"You're perfect," I said. "You're perfect, Skate." We sat there a long time, long enough to make my knees hurt, until he dropped his hands to his sides.

"Denise," he said. "What would I do without you?"

MEETING SKATE MADE TIME suddenly lurch forward. In an instant, summer began to speed up. What had once seemed interminable, early June stretching before me like a day with no horizon, was now in short supply. Our time in the trailer took on a bronzed hue, and I studied everything he did like I was memorizing it for a test. Each day was a similar routine: we'd sit and talk for a little while about our days and the stupid things that people did around us, the grade grubbing and boyfriend stealing that seemed superficial when compared to the soaring feeling I'd get in my chest whenever I looked at him. Then he'd turn to me and ask, "Do you want?" and I said yes before he could finish his question.

He always went down on me. *I like to do it*, he said, and *I want to make you feel good, you deserve it more than me*. It broke my heart when he said these things about himself, but his sadness made the rest of him seem to shine brighter. I decided I would help him learn to love himself the way I loved him.

We talked about school starting the way you'd talk about the end of the world. I don't want this to end, I cried on August 5th, with classes now two weeks away. We hadn't yet figured out how we'd see each other when the German trailer was occupied by people actually learning German.

Then I had an idea. "There's all these old buildings around Mercy's campus," I told him. "They're unlocked but empty—no one ever goes in them."

"You'd sneak out at night?"

I thought of the bunk beds. "No, after school."

"It could work," Skate said, but he sounded unsure.

"Do you trust me?" I asked and he said, *Yes, God yes.*

TWENTY-ONE

The school year began and with it, a new routine. After the bus dropped Mimi and Caro and me off at home, I waved to Daddy and told the others I was headed out to study in the forts. Just in case they were watching, I walked up toward the woods, then took a wide path out to the abandoned railroad spur that had once delivered coal to Mercy Hill before circling back to Cottage 21, the cottage farthest from our own. Inside, Skate was already waiting.

He'd been nervous at first; breaking into the German trailer was one thing, but this wasn't the school, it was state property and he was old enough for real consequences should we be discovered. But he had to see me, he said. He'd do whatever it took.

Hearing him say that made me feel shiny, like my whole body was made of something precious. Bit by bit, I began smuggling things from home to make Cottage 21 more comfortable: a blanket for the bed, peanut butter crackers for us to snack on, a candle and matches for when it began to get dark. The furniture may have been dusty and water-stained, but when I came in, it felt like home.

I told Skate this once and he held me tighter than he had

before. "Do you want this someday?" he said, clarifying so there could be no doubt. "A home with me?"

"Yes," I whispered. "I want that very much."

SKATE'S BODY WAS ANGLED, free of excess, surprisingly strong. The largeness of him comforted me, the way he could fit a hand around my entire fist, or my head in the nook between his neck and shoulder. I was used to being the smallest person in the room, but when we lay together twisted up tight, I felt as though our bodies were one tall, unbreakable unit. It was as if I had grown up at last.

One day as we sat on the edge of the bed, I noticed that the backs of his hands were chapped, his knuckles red and flaking.

"It got cold," he said when I touched them, concerned. "I can't find my gloves from last year." Skate didn't like to talk about his home, which seemed disorganized and chaotic: his stepfather an ex-military despot, his moody mother mostly absent.

"Do they hurt?" I said and he looked at them like he was just now considering it.

"Sometimes, I guess."

I fished around in my backpack and pulled out a tube of lotion.

"Sorry it smells like cucumber melon," I said. "But it'll make it so your skin doesn't crack." I squeezed out a line of cream onto his hand and then took it in my own, noticing for the first time his short, square nails, the callus on the side of his thumb. Each new detail sent my heart buzzing. Skate was real. Skate was mine.

I rubbed in the bright, girl-smelling lotion until his skin glistened. When I looked up, Skate had a funny look on his face.

"Are you okay?" I said.

"Denise," he said. "You're the kindest person I've ever known."

My heart seized. People often said I was smart, or bright, or quick, or witty. No one had ever told me I was kind. It made me feel as if the edges of my body had more definition. I was a person in this world.

"Did I say something wrong?" he said. "Oh, Denise. Don't cry, Denise."

The sound of my name chimed inside me, like the tongue of a bell.

WE ALWAYS SET A TIMER because my mother arrived home at six these days and I liked to be back on the couch by then, flipping through some textbook while Mimi snapped rubber bands at me. But while I would have liked more time, the brevity of our sessions made them even more delicious, each second stretching both long and short at the same time.

Skate continued to offer what he called *cunnilingus,* a word that sounded and felt like a magic spell. After it was over, as we lay together, I could sometimes feel a hard part of him pressing against my leg, but he said he was just as satisfied as I was and told me he'd take care of his own business after he got home. If this seemed strange, well, what in my life was normal?

Even though I was never explicitly included in my classmates' conversations about sex, it was all anyone ever talked about. One day on the bus, I heard the girl in front of me say she had given a blow job that made her boyfriend cry. Actual tears, she said, like he was at a freaking funeral.

I wanted to make Skate happy more than I'd ever wanted anything before. The day before Thanksgiving would be the five-month anniversary of the first time we met, and I told him I had a surprise for him.

IT'S STRANGE THINKING about the anniversary afternoon, because it still makes me a little bit excited. Even now, knowing what went wrong, and what was wrong about the whole thing from the start, it's hard to unlearn a feeling that you've carved so deep inside your skin.

That afternoon I changed quickly in the bathroom, pulling on a sweater from last year that had begun to get tight around my chest. I looked myself over in the mirror, taking in the parts of myself that Skate had said were beautiful: my dark eyelashes, the shadow of freckles you could only see if you were looking for them. I put on dangling earrings and brushed my hair back, then brought it forward so it hung down against my collarbone. I felt warm and trembly and lit from within, in command in a way I almost never felt. Then I left, kicking through the pile of dead leaves that no one had swept off our porch.

When I got inside Cottage 21, Skate was already sitting on the bed. He'd lit one of the candles on the sill and the air smelled smoky and exciting.

"How are you doing?" I asked, my own voice sounding strange in my ears.

He put his lips into my hair. "With you, I'm always good."

I swallowed. "Skate—I have something for you." It sounded much more serious than when I had practiced this line in my head. "I want—Remember when you first asked if you could make me feel good? Well"—I turned to him, watching his eyelashes flicker—"I want to make you feel good too. The way you do for me."

Skate squeezed his eyes shut. "Denise," he said. "You're too young."

I blinked. "That doesn't matter," I said.

He didn't say anything.

"Skate," I said. "You don't really care about that, do you?"

Skate knuckled the space between his eyes. "I'm a terrible person," he said.

I sat up straighter. "You aren't making me do anything. I'm literally asking you! I want to give you a blow job!" The words seemed to float in the air like phlegm on water. As soon as I said them, I wished I hadn't.

Skate slumped forward, his head in his hands. "It's not that I don't want it," he said. "I want it very badly. I think of you, Denise. Denise, I can't stop thinking of you."

"Then what's the problem? Are you scared?"

He answered immediately: "Yes."

"So you think I'm a kid? I'm not a kid."

"I know, Denise, I know. You're not."

"Stop saying my name," I said. "And news flash, everything we do is illegal. Everything." I'd searched this in the school library to prevent it from coming up on our family computer's Netscape history. In North Carolina age of consent laws, sixteen was the magic number. I was still nearly a month away from thirteen.

"It feels different if I pene—penetrate you." His voice cracked. "Jesus, Denise, I love you. Is that what you don't get? I love you more than anyone I've ever known and I wish it were all different, I wish we lived in a place where no one gave a shit about the rules. But we don't live there, Denise, we just don't." He began to cry, pressing both fists into the sides of his face.

"I love you," I said.

Skate looked up. "I'm not worthy," he said, using a term Caro had been using a lot lately.

"You're the most worthy person I know." I stepped down off the bed and knelt in front of him. He didn't stop me as I fumbled with the metal button, then the zipper. My chest was a churn of emotions, sad and determined yet still pounding with excitement. I felt like Skate and I stood back-to-back against the winds of a cruel world, and that alone made my heart beat faster. We'd prove everyone wrong. We'd do it together.

I closed my eyes and brought my whole face down toward him.

In this blindness, I only heard and did not see the door swing open.

Skate let out a strangled cry, jerking away from me so fast his knee hit my forehead. I clutched my face and fell backward, catching myself at the last moment on the splintery cottage floor. Everything looked different from down here, Skate's cycling limbs, the candle flickering, and J.J. in the doorway, hand still on the latch.

Her voice was calm and steady: "Denise, what are you doing with Jeremy Morgans?"

My whole body felt frozen, like the day Mimi fell into the rec yard. I could barely open my mouth to speak. When I did, the only thing I could say was, "Skate, his name is Skate."

"I don't care what he calls himself. Jeremy, you have to fucking leave—*now*."

Skate obeyed. He flew across the room and out the door, scrambling down the steps without a backward look. I heard the jangle of his keys as he fled into the woods, then the crunch of sticks, then nothing.

I sank back onto my heels, then sat down hard on the floor. It was like I couldn't think at all.

"Jeremy's nineteen," J.J. said. "You know that, right?"

I didn't answer.

J.J. looked around the room, taking in the crackers, the candle, the blanket. She hugged her arms around herself. "Denise, you have to say something." When I still said nothing, she clenched her fists and brought them to her sides. I wondered if she was going to punch the bed—or punch me.

"I wanted to," I said. My voice sounded like it was coming from a recording.

J.J. looked at the window, but it was too dark beyond to show anything more than our own reflections. "You're too young."

I felt rage beginning to overtake my surprise. "You don't get to tell me anything," I said. "Fuck you! You can't make me listen to you!"

"I'll tell Mom," she said.

"I'll say you made it up."

"You think you can lie to her?"

This made me pause. Our mother's gaze was like truth serum. "Please," I said, "J.J., just listen to me."

"I'm trying to protect you," J.J. said.

"I don't need protecting!" Tears fell hot and fast down my cheeks. "This is the only thing I've ever wanted!"

"That's not true," J.J. said. "Even if it feels that way, it's not."

"How would you know?" I leapt at her, scratching at her face and neck. "You don't even like boys—you're a fucking *lesbian*—"

She fought me off the best she could, grabbing hold of my wrists and pushing me away. "Denise!" she kept saying. "If you stop, I won't tell. I promise I won't tell if you stop seeing him."

I twisted forward and bit her on the arm. She dropped my wrist. "Fuck!" she said, then backed away. "Just don't see him," she said, rubbing at the tooth marks. "I promise I won't tell, just don't see him anymore."

"Get out of here," I said, and after a moment she did. I threw myself down on the bed like a child, my throat so tight I felt like I would suffocate.

I SLEPT LITTLE THAT NIGHT, waking each hour with a pounding heart. J.J. did not meet my eye at breakfast. There had to be some way around her ultimatum, and if I couldn't think of it on my own, Skate could surely come up with something. I asked for passes out of all my classes that day, checking through the cafeteria and the gym and even the old German trailer, but he must not have gone to school.

That afternoon, when I clicked on the BellSouth email icon on the family computer and typed in my name, I saw a new message in bold from an address I didn't recognize.

> Denise, I am sorry I ran. You deserve better in so many ways. The world is so stupid and F***ed up, it doesn't deserve you either.
>
> I am not going back to Lincoln, dont worry you wont have to see me around. I just think if I see you but cant be with you I'll go insane. L.O.L., just what you need another mental patient.
>
> I love you and always will. I believe we will see each other again. December 12th 2005. Will you wait for me? You dont have to. But a guy can dream cant he?

SKATE'S WRITING SEEMED halting and awkward compared to the smooth speech I was used to. But it was like I could feel his heart beating again beside mine. He loved me. He would wait for me until I turned sixteen. I stared at that date until my eyes watered. December 12th, 2005. Three years and two weeks away, when each day without him felt like an eternity.

Without even shutting it down, I jammed the Power button until the computer whined off, something we had been forbidden to do. I was furious—at the entire world, but mostly at J.J.

She was there in the bedroom just feet away, and my fingernails itched to dig into her skin.

I thought about the others. About our mother, already on her way down the Hill, a white speck descending toward us. Everyone in my family just felt like fucking *people.* Crowding me, breathing on me, telling me what to do. If I could pull a lever to make them disappear, I would. Then Skate and I would walk slowly across each inch of the Hill, holding hands as we surveyed our personal kingdom.

SKATE CONTINUED TO SEND EMAILS, first every day, then once a week, then I realized it had been nearly a month. I was too scared to write back. I composed long replies in my head and sometimes on paper, then ripped the papers up and threw them away. I sounded stupid and *young* and wasn't that what had wrecked everything in the first place?

As the weather turned cold, I felt the most crushing unhappiness, heavy from my eyelids to my toes. When someone asked me a question, I heard myself speak like an actor in the wings, catching only snippets of the action onstage.

I dreamed of falling into a coma for three years and waking at sixteen.

I thought about what our mother had said during our breakfast at the diner. If I needed anything, anything at all, she would get it for me. It made me realize how powerless she was. Time and age and society were foes less moveable than the city council.

The only thing I had strength for was trying to make J.J.'s life hell. I threw away her school notes and put staples in her shoes, elbowed her each time she passed too closely. J.J. weathered the assaults without retaliation, which just made me angrier, and even though I got more brazen every day, no one mentioned the darkness that had come between us. They were all busy with their own obsessions, our mother and Caro and Mimi.

And Daddy, who in the past could have been trusted to know first when someone was unhappy or angry, he said nothing. Over the past year, as our basement became his torturous gymnasium, Daddy had changed. Physically, he was bulkier and broader, as muscled as the Ward C aides, but there was something that went deeper than that. He no longer stepped in to redirect arguments or throw himself self-deprecatingly on a simmering conflict. You could drag him into a conversation if you tried, but it was rare that someone did. We were all moving away from each other, it seemed, inch by inch, like the aftermath of some star explosion, each body drifting farther into the increasing cold and increasing dark.

2003

TWENTY-TWO

The rest of fall and spring semesters passed, so blank and hazy that I only vaguely registered that Caro was about to graduate. At the end of April, she was chosen salutatorian to an Indian girl named Mea. She had gotten in everywhere our mother had told her to apply: Yale, Princeton, Duke, Emory, but one night our mother had surprised us all by stating that she knew that Caro would choose Duke because of its proximity to her *boyfriend*.

"You all must think I'm stupid. I see Laketon's pickup squealing out of the lot every night."

Caro turned to her, chin up and ready to fight, but our mother just took a big bite of salad. "It's fine, Caro. Relax." She looked pointedly at Daddy, whose face remained impassive. I still don't know if she'd decided she forgave him for hiding this secret from her, or if she was simply filing it away as ammunition for future battles—it was never easy to determine on which side Lisa Cross was going to come down.

"Anyway," she continued, "I'm just glad you're going to a real college. Duke's basically an Ivy."

After dinner, she pulled Mimi and me aside to clarify that that wasn't true, lest we get any ideas.

To Lisa Cross, at least, things were looking up. On top of Caro's news, she'd recently gotten a call from the Senator:

thanks to a Congress that had shifted more heavily Democrat, Ward C had been given its asked-for budget for the next twelve months. It didn't mean Mercy Hill was safe forever, but it meant that, as with Caro's college plans, we could all breathe more easily, for a while at least.

Then came the ring.

It was tiny, sleek, and perfect. White gold with four delicate prongs holding up a square stone the size of a Tic Tac, just a little too loose on her finger; Caro couldn't stop fiddling with it, twisting it around and around so different edges caught the light.

We weren't there when Laketon proposed because he did it on some church hike. She told us later that when they got to the scenic lookout, he'd asked her to grab something for him out of his backpack, which was of course the ring. Listening to her sparked a flare of pain as I remembered what Skate had said about someday having a home together. I didn't want some stupid ring, but jealousy burned like fire in my throat.

They came back to Cottage 10 together, and with all of us gathered to head out to Caro's graduation dinner with Grannie Palmer, she made the announcement.

"She said she didn't want me to ask her father's permission," Laketon said, voice high and shaky. "And I respect that."

There was a long silence, broken only after a moment with a question from Mimi. "Is this so you can have sex?"

"Mimi," Daddy said, then everyone was quiet again. We all looked to our mother. She'd rushed to shower in between work and dinner, and her hair was still wet, a daub of mousse clearly visible beneath her ear.

"Laketon," she said. "It's a lovely ring, but she's still a minor. She's sixteen."

"Mrs. Cross, that's something I absolutely understand. We

aren't saying we're getting married tomorrow, it's just a commitment that we'd like to. Later, whenever works best for everyone." He sounded like he was scheduling a potluck.

Mimi snorted again. "Later when? When Caro's graduated college? That's a long-ass engagement."

"I love Caroline," Laketon said. "Please, Mrs. Cross."

"It's Dr. Cross," our mother said. "And I still say no."

"I'm not giving back the ring." Caro held up her hand so the band wobbled. "It's my personal property."

"I'm done talking about this," our mother said. "Are we leaving or not?"

"So that's it?" Caro said. "You're just going to—what, pretend like we're not engaged? Disown me?"

Our mother took a step toward the door and then stopped, turning back. "I raised you to be a smart girl," she said, "but right now you're acting very—fucking—stupid." Her voice dipped down low with the obscenity but then she regained control. "We have reservations for dinner in fifteen minutes. Whoever's coming in my car, follow me. Grannie P. is probably already there."

After a moment, J.J. followed, then Mimi, whose loyalties toward Daddy had been overturned by her clear derision of all things Laketon.

"I'll come with you," I said to Daddy, and Laketon said he would drive Caro so we split at the parking lot into three separate cars. It felt strange to be riding shotgun with Daddy. I suddenly regretted not being in the car with our mother, whose anger tamped down tighter than his. When he peeled out of the curve onto the main road, it made my stomach lurch.

"She's going to think this is all my fault." His voice was soft then very loud.

"Caro never listens to anyone," I said.

"Yeah, well—Jesus." His hands were tight on the wheel. "Your mother should have just ignored them. They would have gotten bored and ended things. But you know Caro, she's going to dig in harder than ever. And all because Lisa can't—let—things—go."

It seemed like I wasn't in the car. He'd never called our mother Lisa in front of me.

"Same thing with that church. Same thing with J.J. Jesus!"

I stared straight ahead. I wasn't sure what I should say.

"Sorry, Denise. Ignore what I'm saying."

"It's okay." My voice was tiny. "Please drive a little slower."

"Don't tell me what to do," he snapped, then began to decelerate. "Sorry, baby, sorry. You're right, aren't you? Denise, everything is going to be A-OK. There are worse problems in the world. People are starving. People are dying." It felt like he was reading from a script. "It doesn't help to sweat the small stuff."

After a beat, I said, "Is there something I can do?"

"I told you," he said, though his voice had an edge to it, "everything is going to be fine."

THE RESTAURANT THAT Caro had picked was French, one of the first establishments toeing the waters of Raleigh's onetime warehouse district, and despite the massive space allotted, all the tables and chairs were crammed very close together. When we arrived, Grannie Palmer was seated at the head of one of these tables, pantsuit emerald green this time, collar so starched it looked as if it could slice your hand open. It was strange to see her outside of the club, although ever since Hawaiian Punch–Gate, our dinners there had become less and less frequent.

Daddy led us toward the table and when Grannie P. offered

up her cheek to kiss, he did. Then he ripped off the Band-Aid. "Momma," he said, "Caro and Laketon have some news for you: they're engaged."

Caro held up her hand and wiggled it over the table, moving it so fast you couldn't see the ring itself, just its sparkle. Laketon was holding her other hand very tight and it felt like everyone was holding their breath.

Grannie P. just smiled and pulled out the seat next to her for Caro. "Best wishes!" she said, then, with a flick of her eyes over to the rest of us, "You know, you're not supposed to tell a woman congratulations on being engaged. It's not a prize that she's won."

"That's actually pretty progressive," said J.J.

"Not all etiquette is patriarchal oppression," said Grannie P., and J.J. laughed, which surprised me. The whole night felt that way, like a joke I wasn't quite in on.

"We're not in any rush," Laketon said, ready for the same type of resistance as before.

If Grannie P. felt any of our parents' concerns, she didn't voice them. As we waited for someone to come take our order, she simply said, "Caroline will make a lovely bride. And your sisters will be bridesmaids?"

"If they want to," Caro said, matching Grannie P.'s magnanimity.

"I'll wear a dress the day hell freezes over," said Mimi but everyone ignored her.

"I've always thought you girls looked good in lavender," Grannie P. said.

"Purple is pretty," Laketon said.

"You've got a long time to talk about this," our mother spoke for the first time. "You have to turn eighteen before it's even legal."

"Without a parent's permission," Caro said, not looking up. "It's sixteen with."

A silence. I stared at the tea lights flickering before us. Their flames were too tiny to matter. It was clear what Caro meant by a parent, but I could hardly breathe, thinking about it. Daddy would never break ranks like that . . . would he? None of us looked at him.

Grannie P. said, "Now graduation, that is a fine time to say congratulations." She handed over an envelope that I knew from J.J.'s experience contained a check for $500. J.J., I was pretty sure, had saved all of hers. Caro slipped the envelope into her purse so quickly that it seemed like the money was already spent.

THAT NIGHT I WROTE SKATE AN EMAIL, the first one I'd actually send. I did it quickly, before I could lose my nerve.

My sister is getting married, I wrote, *and I keep thinking about what you said last summer.*

> In case you don't remember, you said that most people want marriage but you wanted love. I still think you're right, although I think in this case Caro and Laketon love each other, too.
>
> Please don't write a long letter back, I can't bear it.
>
> I want love, too.
>
> I will wait for you—I am waiting.
>
> 925 days until I turn 16.

THE NEXT MORNING, I woke before my alarm and tiptoed out of the bedroom. The living room was dark and when I pressed the

Power button on the desktop computer, it made a loud whine that seemed to echo off the quiet walls. Still, no one stirred. I lowered myself into the chair as the computer booted up, lines of black code like it too was waking from a dream. The background appeared, an ancient picture of the four of us at a Christmas long ago, posed in matching plaid taffeta dresses that had undoubtedly come from Grannie P. I hated that picture, how hopeful and happy we all looked. When the icons popped up, I clicked a dozen times on the BellSouth logo and typed in my name with shaking fingers. Everything seemed to dim around the edges of my vision, the only thing I could see was the one new message, bold. I clicked it.

> I waited til midnight to write this so I could cut one day off the countdown. 924.

My heart pounded so hard it was difficult to take in breath. I felt like if I closed my eyes, I would start to cry. I stared at the message until it stuck in my vision, then looked up behind the computer to the buildings on top of the Hill. The sun was beginning to come up so I could see the outlines of the shuttered Wards A and B, and the admin building, which at this hour was also dark and uninhabited.

In Ward C, every window was lit. I knew the reasons for that involved safety, not festivity, but seeing that one last building standing there, the movement and people that breathed inside, it made me feel a strange sort of hope. It was still here, I was still here, and I could write to Skate even though I couldn't touch him. We weren't any of us dead yet, and even though that seemed a low bar, it gave me a small kernel of possibility to hold tight.

TWENTY-THREE

Caro moved into her dorm in August, and the whole family drove the forty-five minutes to Durham to help her. I'd been on Duke's campus before, for the finals of a geography competition, but the narrow quad looked very different on move-in day. Cars were crammed into the cul-de-sacs and everywhere shouts rang out as parents fumbled brightly colored futons into the Gothic-style dormitories. Our arrival had preceded that of Jessica, Caro's new roommate, so while our mother and Caro and Daddy put together a bookcase, the rest of us sat on the barren bed on the other side of the room.

"I don't know why they're even bothering," Mimi said, voice far from low. "She's never gonna be here."

Our mother set down the box she was holding and turned to Mimi. "Why would you say that?"

The answer to that question was clear: Laketon had an apartment a twenty-minute drive away. We'd already borne witness to several heated conversations about Caro's plans to spend time there with him, and even now Caro was unpacking a stack of photos with Laketon on top.

Mimi opened her mouth like she was going to keep going off about Caro's plans, but I didn't want to be caught in the crossfire between her and our mother. Trying to change the subject, I stepped in front of her with a plastic crate of toiletries and said, "Can we talk about the bus situation?"

Mimi's eyes narrowed for a long moment but then she shook herself off and said, "Fine, whatever." She backed over to the roommate's empty bed and swung up on it. It was high enough that her feet didn't touch the ground, and it gave her the appearance of a much younger kid, swinging her legs back and forth.

I came over and sat next to her. Across the room, we watched J.J. and our mother and Daddy and Caro unpack the cardboard boxes of clothes and books, quietly, a coordinated machine. It felt strange to be alone with Mimi, even if temporarily. But I guess I was going to have to get used to the feeling, since we'd be the only two left at Lincoln in the fall.

"So," I said again, dropping my voice so the others couldn't hear. "The bus sucks."

Mimi grunted in assent. It was the closest she would ever get to admitting the hell our peers put us through; after a long day of teasing and snickers, we'd slouch back into the cracked vinyl seats of bus 548. Some days there would be nothing, and some days the kids would just descend. With three of us on the bus, there were more targets; now with Caro gone, it gave me a knot in my stomach each time I thought about it.

"I know you sometimes get a ride from, like, Sheila or—I don't know their names. But do you know anyone who could drive us *every* day?"

"Do you?" Mimi said.

"No, that's why I'm asking you."

Mimi kicked her feet against the metal bed frame. "I think we can get Bob and Jeremy." For a second, hearing the name

Jeremy made my throat catch, but of course she wasn't talking about Skate. Bob and Jeremy Lyons were brothers, stoners who never seemed to have weed, whom I often saw sitting in the art lab but not painting.

"Okay," I said. I'd have accepted a ride from the Grim Reaper himself if it meant avoiding those cracked pleather seats. "So, do you still need to ask them or—"

"Oh," Caro said from across the room, looking at a message on her new laptop. "Jessica isn't going to be here until five."

Mimi swiveled her head around quickly and I knew our conversation was over. I held my breath, waiting to see what would happen next.

Our mother looked at her watch. "We could see if she wants to do dinner instead."

"Lisa," Daddy said. "That's a long time to wait." I could tell that he wanted to go back home, and I agreed with him: there were too many people in this tiny space, and the springs from the bare mattress were digging into my thighs.

"I'd like to meet her family," our mother said. "They'll be spending so much time together."

"It's fine," Caro said. "Laketon was going to pick me up for dinner anyway."

I couldn't tell if she meant to inflame the situation or had simply miscalculated. Both our parents turned toward her.

"I strongly suggest you be here when your roommate moves in," our mother said.

Caro fiddled with her ring. She'd gotten it resized but it was still loose on her finger. She said nothing, sighed, then said, "O*kay*."

Daddy turned to our mother. "We can't stay here all day—I have to get back to start dinner."

Our mother let out a snort.

"Excuse me," he said, then: "What's that supposed to mean?" His voice was unnaturally loud for the small room.

Someone else might have said *It's nothing*, but Lisa Cross did not believe in passive aggression. "It's just dinner," she said.

Daddy turned to look at her. I held my breath, hoping beyond hope she would not keep going. If she stopped now, the sharp line of truth could be hidden by the words *never mind*.

This was our mother's hubris, the scorching temper I too felt in anger, and I could see it hurtling forward.

"We'll pick up McDonald's," she said. "You can throw away the buns if that's not Atkins enough for you."

Daddy looked at our mother and a pallor came over him that I had never seen before. I could not have described it until I felt it myself, years later, in a moment when all things seemed suspended until I made a terrible choice. You feel as if you are floating, not pleasantly but like when a roller coaster drops, the wretched sensation that your organs are no longer held down by gravity.

He took a long breath and then said, "You know what, Lisa? You're right. Cooking a healthy dinner isn't as important as driving to DC to suck a congressman's cock."

What! The! Living! Fuck!

I felt like my eyes were going to pop out of my skull. I whipped my head around to look at Mimi beside me. Her gaze was flat and unsurprised. Was this true? Or rather—how true *was* this? In my own fumbled and abortive beginnings with sex, I had begun to realize there was sucking cock and sucking *cock,* and what had I seen when Mimi and I had met this man in Washington? All I could remember was Mimi's theft, which now I was realizing was perhaps directly connected to all of this. Mimi, the truth sayer, wanting to take back something that she'd realized our mother was giving too freely.

I turned back to our mother. We all did. And she said nothing. Her breaths were slow and even, and as she looked at each of us in turn, it seemed like she was assessing something in us—loyalty, perhaps. When she looked at me, I held my breath, not sure what I'd say if she asked me who was right.

I would soon recognize this as a turning point, the beginning of a war waged between them. A war in which Daddy made the choice not to fight outright, but through guerrilla tactics that undermined our mother. Perhaps, even then, he was thinking about the permission he would give Caro just a few months later.

For now, there was nothing more to be said. It was all out there, the truth hanging darkly in the small and crowded room. "Let's get these boxes," our mother said, and began carefully unhooking the flaps of the one nearest her, so it could be flattened and used again when Caro moved back home in the spring. (That Caro never moved back home should not come as a surprise, although I'm sure the salvaged boxes were used by someone eventually.) She slid an empty box toward each of us, including Daddy.

Then it was like everything was being fast-forwarded. Caro gave us all hugs and promised to wait around to meet her new roommate, which I only kind of believed, and then we all headed back outside, empty-handed. In the quad, the din had intensified, competing sound systems barking out from the open windows, all the students talking and laughing as they made their way across the grass. It was the picture-perfect scene of moving into college, and we drove away quickly, like we knew the backdrop could blow over at any moment.

TWENTY-FOUR

Then, when I thought things couldn't get worse at school, I got put in Mimi's English class. We had spent the last year and a half in the same grade, but had so far managed to avoid any academic overlap. Our streak broke the day we received our fall schedules in the mail: we'd both be in eleventh-grade AP Language & Composition with Mr. Tyler Scott. My heart sank. Although Mimi and I were close in age, thirteen and fourteen, we often fought: I hated her brashness, she hated the way I caved easily. It was simple enough to stay out of each other's way at home, but now the prospect of being in a classroom together felt like being locked in a cage with some animal.

To make matters worse, Mr. Scott sucked. He was one of the younger teachers, but not one of the ones everyone had crushes on. He was fat and tried too hard to be funny, with a row of framed pictures of Emily Dickinson above his computer in the back. He often referenced this gallery, invoking her when the class got too rowdy: "Now, I know you're not going to embarrass me in front of my girl, Em. . . ."

Mr. Scott had gone to Lincoln just a few years before, and you could tell that he had not had an easy time of it. He paid special attention to the lower-caste students, diverting attention away from their awkwardness with his own self-deprecation, and when the popular kids laughed at his jokes, he got embarrassingly pleased with himself.

The first day, when he called roll, he stopped when he got to the two of us.

"Denise Cross . . . and Miriam Cross? Any relation?"

We had seated ourselves on opposite sides of the classroom, and tried especially hard not to catch each other's eye.

"We're sisters," I said.

"Twins?"

"No," Mimi said, "Denise skipped some grades."

I could feel everyone's attention zero in on me and for a moment, saw myself as they saw me: short and skinny, wearing a baby doll tee that was too big for me, baggy in all the places it should have been tight. The scrutiny felt deeply unfair, Mimi had skipped some grades too.

Mr. Scott chuckled to himself. *"Sister, Sister!"* he said. *"Sister Act!"* Neither of these elicited any response from the class, but thankfully drew everyone's eyes away from me and back to him. Mr. Scott continued down the attendance list and I sat back in my seat.

Just then, the girl in front of me turned around. "He's so retarded," she whispered.

I blinked. My classmates never addressed me unless they absolutely had to. "I know," I said.

"So you're really Mimi's sister? She was in AP World with me last year. One day when Mr. Wallace wasn't paying attention, she glued the classroom windows shut."

I vaguely remembered that suspension, but to be honest, it bled together with all the other minor crimes Mimi had been responsible for.

"She's not allowed to have superglue anymore," I said.

The girl covered her mouth to hide her laughter. "You're

funny," she said. "I'm Christine, and this is Daniel, and Jen Li." The kids sitting around her turned to wave and I waved back, cautious.

"Do y'all still live in that mental hospital?" the boy asked.

I rolled my eyes as high as I could. "Yeah," I said, echoing Christine. "It's retarded."

This made everyone draw nearer. I'd never had an audience like this before.

"Mimi's so weird," Jen Li said. "Why's she always drawing all over herself?"

I shrugged. "She gets ink everywhere. The floor of our shower is, like, always blue."

The kids cracked up.

"Okay now," Mr. Scott said. "Quiet down, Emily's watching."

AS THE FIRST FEW WEEKS of my junior year wore on, most things stayed about the same. In the rest of my classes, I was introduced, forgotten about, then subsequently ignored, sinking into my familiar routine of perfect-score quizzes and invisibility. But in English, I was suddenly the center of attention.

The other kids were obsessed with hating Mimi—her precocity, her goth-lite outfits, the way she muttered, and having me around just gave them an opportunity to stoke their rage. They asked me for stories about what she was like at home and what she'd been like growing up, and you'd think she was a long-lost princess the way they hung on to every detail I offered. Perhaps if we hadn't been shoved together into a classroom, there would have been other topics to focus on. But there weren't, and so I watched as Mimi began to swim, to flap, to drown.

Sitting at her lonely desk, pushed as far away from us as she could go, Mimi behaved like a cornered cat. She snapped when spoken to, stonewalled Mr. Scott when he asked her anything. It fueled our cruelty like blood in the water. We pulled our desks closer together and whispered in chorus.

Yes, of course I fucking know it was wrong. A courageous sister would have linked arms with her against the circling wolves, or at the very least remained a neutral party. But these kids talked to me, not through me. Jen Li played with my hair. It had been so long since Skate, and feeling someone's nails on my scalp sent me into near ecstasy. I knew that being adored was different from being loved. I had been—was still—loved by Skate, but the feeling of attention skimmed that same surface.

"Do you think she's having sex with David French?" Christine asked me one day. David was a tech theater guy I sometimes saw Mimi with, but I got the feeling that she was only using him for his set of keys that provided access to some of the more off-limits portions of the school.

"No flipping way," I said, just loud enough so Mimi could hear we were talking about her without hearing the details. "She's not having sex with anyone. She's, like, sexually frustrated."

"How can you tell?"

"I told you we share a room."

A chorus of excited whispers rose like a gathering cyclone. Eventually, another David, David Perkins, said, "She's flicking the bean," and we all lost it. (To be honest, I didn't understand what he was referring to; Skate's introduction to sexual pleasure had been thorough and widespread, but none of it involved flicking.)

"Mimi," Jen said, "do you like beans?"

And Mimi, on guard but not nearly enough said, "Sure, whatever. I like beans."

Mr. Scott, who'd been up at the board writing out a passage from *The Crucible,* turned.

"Guys," he said. "Guys, I promise you, nothing is funny about this scene."

We burn a hot fire here; it melts down all concealment.

It was a disease that kept reinfecting us. We'd mostly stop laughing and then someone would whisper *beans* and it'd start up again. Mr. Scott looked at us, then looked at Mimi. She was sitting up ramrod straight and staring ahead like she had been frozen.

"Guys," he said again, quieter this time. He knew this was directed at her. He felt for her, he'd been there before, the object of ridicule. His pity for her wrapped both of them in the same blanket of patheticness.

"Mimi," he said. "Why don't you tell the rest of the class what this means?"

We burn a hot fire here; it melts down all concealment.

There was a long pause, but then Mimi settled back into her chair. "On one level they're talking about the witch trials. But he's actually alluding to the McCarthy hearings. Miller's saying that in both places the questioners have an outsize thirst for judgment, and they're willing to damage a lot of people if it means rooting out the truth."

"*Rooting* out," said David Perkins.

"Rooting for beans," I said, which made everyone crack up louder.

"Let's read aloud from act three," said Mr. Scott. "Y'all have got to keep yourselves under control."

As I flipped open my book, I looked sideways at Mimi. She wasn't smiling, but she wasn't frowning either.

BY THE END OF SEPTEMBER, the newness of the school year had worn off. Pens ran dry, the bathrooms stank, and trash collected like old leaves in the recesses of the halls. Only in Mr. Scott's class did we raise ourselves from our stupor, and the torment of Mimi boiled faster.

We gathered behind her to whisper. *Are you going to homecoming, Mimi? Who do you like, Mimi? Want some beans?*

Mr. Scott often and clumsily leapt to her defense, but his methods of rescue were never effective. We all knew he felt sorry for her, and these twin weaknesses were too tempting to let go.

Do you like Mr. Scott, Mimi? Does Mr. Scott sweat in bed? The whispers hung from our mouths like strings of spit, connected in a single gooey stream. When one broke off and splattered to the ground, we simply began again. It seemed unthinkable to stop.

TWENTY-FIVE

Mimi and I never spoke about English class, even on the rides home in the afternoon, when we sat in the back seat of Bob and Jeremy's car inches away from each other. This contributed to my feeling that what happened inside that classroom wasn't quite real; its consequences would be forgiven, though I think I knew, even then, that was not quite true.

One day, the brothers stopped at a filling station downtown. It was the place everyone knew to get cheap gas, located across from the downtown bus terminal where the homeless panhandled. The boys went inside for Icees, leaving Mimi holding the gas pump.

It was hot, so I got out too and stood beside the car, staring off across the street at the row of city buses, pretending like Mimi wasn't there at all. Then I saw the figure rise from her spot on the sidewalk. Why would *she* be here?

When I found my voice, I turned. "It's Bethy—Mimi, look!"

Mimi, who had almost certainly been pretending I wasn't there, jumped.

"What?" she said, but I didn't have to say anything more because it was unmistakable. Bethy was dressed in jeans and a holey T-shirt that draped down past her knees. Her hair trailed long and matted down her back.

"Hey!" Mimi and I both called. "Hey, Bethy!"

Bethy looked startled. She'd come over toward us but clearly hadn't done so out of recognition.

I ran over. "Bethy, it's the Cross girls. We used to volunteer with you at—on Ward B."

Her face brightened. "The geniuses! Of course I remember."

"How are you doing?" I asked as Mimi came around from the other side of the car. I had often wondered what happened to the residents we'd worked with, Bethy perhaps most of all.

"They moved me to a house," she said. "It was nice enough, but so loud. You know how I like my rest."

"You always told us you needed to relax," I said.

"The other women, they didn't understand. They were so loud."

"Where do you live now?" I asked.

"Here and there." Bethy looked down at her nails, which were ringed in black.

"Are those all your things?" Mimi pointed to an overstuffed backpack by Bethy's feet.

"It's enough," she said. Then after a long moment, she smiled. "Where are the others?"

"J.J. is in college," I said, her name still bitter in my mouth. Even now, a year since she'd walked in on Skate and me, my anger at J.J. had not subsided.

"And Caro's engaged now," Mimi said. "Her fiancé is a boy from Nurse Jenny's church."

"She's too young to get married."

"That's what our mom thinks," Mimi said.

Bethy laughed an easy laugh. "Your mom is something else." Then she paused. "I hate to ask you girls for anything, when you're so young and you don't have jobs. . . ."

"No, no, we want to help." Mimi dug around in her pocket

and produced a couple of wrinkled bills. I unzipped the secret compartment of my backpack—all I had was the twenty-dollar bill Daddy had given me for emergencies, but I handed it over regardless.

When we gave her the money, Bethy just nodded.

"I'd better get going," she said.

"Are you sure you're okay?" Mimi asked.

Bethy looked like she was going to say something else, but the door to the gas station jingled open and the boys came out.

"What the fuck, Mimi?" one of them said, pointing at the gas cap she'd left on top of the car.

"Suck my literal dick," Mimi retorted, and without a word, Bethy stepped back off the sidewalk and began crossing the street. She didn't look back, but Mimi and I watched her go, dragging the backpack along the asphalt behind her.

WHEN BOB AND JEREMY dropped us off outside the guardhouse, Mimi didn't rush ahead of me to walk the path to the cottage alone.

Instead, she turned and grabbed me by the shoulder. "You can never tell her. Mom, I mean."

"I have to," I said. I'd thought of nothing else since we'd seen Bethy. "Mimi, she needs help."

"She doesn't want to go back to that shelter."

"She's not in her right mind! She's not safe!" I dug my fingernails into my palms. "And you know she'll listen to Mom. She'll go back if Mom tells her to."

Mimi's eyes turned flat, her face pinched, and she began to plead. "Denise, don't. Please don't. If you tell Mom, it will one hundred percent make things worse. Everything she touches, she screws up." As if to illustrate her point, she stomped hard on the next step and the sharp concrete edge crumbled into pieces.

Unbidden, I remembered what Daddy had said in Caro's dorm room. *Congressman's cock.*

"She's kept Ward C open," I said.

Mimi looked up the path and I followed her gaze. The barbed-wire fence curved around the big stone edifice, and although we couldn't see the rec yard behind it, in my mind I was seeing straight through all the stone to the magnolia tree we had once climbed. There would be men underneath it, pacing—some of them the same men from that day. It made me feel funny to think about.

Mimi looked back at me, as if she could read my mind. "Don't be such a baby."

I stiffened. "Don't call me a baby."

"I will if you're acting like one." This was the most Mimi and I had spoken in months, and it felt like a scab had been ripped off. The blood that flowed underneath was fast-moving and full of poison, all the injustices received and perpetrated in Mr. Scott's class.

"You don't even realize it," Mimi said, "because everyone tells you you're so smart. But you're just a parrot, you can't ever think for yourself."

This rang true enough to make my chest hurt. I turned on her. "And you're a fuckup," I said.

Mimi was ready for a fight. "You're right," she said. "I am a fuckup. We all are. Living here"—she gestured hard and slammed the back of her hand against the rusted railing—"living here has fucked us all up. Caro gets it, I think J.J. gets it, but you? You just act like everything is normal and as long as you do whatever she wants, Mom will save everything."

I shoved her. It'd been so long since I'd physically fought one of my sisters, I think she was surprised by how strong I'd gotten. At thirteen, I'd hit another growth spurt while she—

stunted, perhaps, by the clove cigarettes—had slowed down. When I pushed her, I realized we stood eye to eye.

"You're just mad because they like me." Even now I was tucking this fight securely into my memory, ready to whisper the details tomorrow afternoon to Christine and David and Jen Li.

She didn't have a retort, just an explosion of fists as she leapt toward me. But even when she hit hard, they barely registered. I'd been hurt so much by losing the Girl, and losing Ward B, and losing Skate that my skin had hardened. I thought about Skate's poem, "Invictus." *My head is bloodied, but unbowed*. It was a poem about fighting for something against all odds. Of course he'd been perfect for me, I'd been fighting that way my whole life.

Mimi scrambled up onto the crumbling step and came at me with both hands, grabbing on to my shoulders as she tried to push me to the ground. I wriggled free and the momentum of her backpack, the weight of everything she was supposed to be doing, carried her past me, falling and rolling down the steps.

I began to run up the Hill, the head start that would allow me to bypass the cottage and go straight to the heavy double doors of Ward C. It was clear how these next moments would unfold, like I had already lived them, my face red with effort as I stepped inside the caged-off lobby, asking a surprised Nurse Jenny that my mother be paged: how my mother would look, stepping into the mouth of the corridor, white coat on white shirt on white tile, saying *Thank you, Denise,* she was on her way to locate Bethy and take her somewhere—anywhere—that would have her.

And that was the right thing, wasn't it? A literal fight that I would win. Mimi was wrong, Mimi was crazy. No one should live on the street instead of in a home, even if that home wasn't 100 percent perfect. Take ours, for example.

THAT NIGHT DADDY was serving another one of his high-protein dinners. Earlier in the day he'd put some meat and several types of chopped vegetables into the Crock-Pot, but he'd cooked it too high and too long: everything had collapsed into a murky sludge, circles of bright orange oil pooling on top.

Nevertheless, he brought out four bowls, calling J.J. and Mimi and me into the kitchen.

J.J. looked at the four of us, and the number of bowls. "Is Mom not coming home?"

"She's out with Bethy," Mimi said. "*Rescuing* her."

J.J. looked at Mimi, then me. "You saw Bethy?"

"Yeah," Mimi said. "Denise can tell you all about it."

But I wasn't going to tell J.J. anything, and she knew it.

After a long moment, J.J., ever dutiful, took a bowl from Daddy's hand and spooned a small amount of the meat mixture into it. It actually did smell okay, like the trays of beef stew that we used to serve in Ward B.

Mimi approached the Crock-Pot and sniffed it. "I think I just became anorexic," she said.

"Mimi," Daddy said. "What's gotten into you?"

Mimi spun around so fast that one of Daddy's laid-out forks clattered to the floor. "You know this food is disgusting, right?"

"Your sisters don't seem to think so," he said, even though I hadn't served myself yet. "What's wrong with you?"

It was the emphasis on the last word, the separation from the rest of us. Mimi reared up. "Why don't you ask Denise?" she said.

I swallowed hard, feeling the same way I did in English each day, a mixture of pride and guilt. Daddy turned to me. "Are you going to explain this so I can understand?"

But why should I have to explain anything? I shoved Mimi aside. "Calm down," I said. "Eat your beans."

This probably confused the hell out of Daddy, because of all of the ingredients in the failed pot roast, none of them were beans. But he didn't have time to ruminate on this because Mimi yanked the Crock-Pot out of the wall and upended the whole thing into the sink.

A plume of white steam rose up and the smell of beef and onions filled the room. Mimi held the Crock-Pot by the handles for a second, then it must've gotten too hot, because she dropped it with a clank on the pile of sludge in the basin.

"Jesus Christ, Mimi," J.J. said, sounding exactly like our mother.

I watched Mimi stand there and try to stay angry. She was struggling so much her whole body shook. The rage kept cracking like cheap paint and under it, you could see the sadness plain as day. I'd always known that Mimi's tough-girl persona was just a front, but not until that moment did I truly see what lay beneath it.

My chest froze from my heart to my throat. I reached for Mimi but if there was one thing her anger couldn't stand, it was kindness. She stomped off, and I heard the screen door slam behind her.

I looked back at Daddy. He still seemed shocked, and I could see him trying to work out if this was his fault. After a moment, he threw up his hands.

"What's gotten into her?" he said, to me this time, but I stayed silent.

That night in the bathroom, as I smeared stinging cream onto my pimples, I felt like I couldn't see my own face, all I could think of was Bethy in an anonymous shelter. Did she have her own room, or was she in some bright open barracks? She hated loud noise, and it was like I could hear the clatter in my own ears. I hoped she could relax. I hoped I had done the right thing. But I didn't know for sure—my certainty had left me.

TWENTY-SIX

The next day was a Wednesday. It was sunny. Mimi hadn't spoken one word to me, not in Bob and Jeremy's car, not when I saw her at her locker, and certainly not when we filed into English class.

We'd been given a sample AP question and were supposed to be answering it at our desks, on notebook paper so we could save the school's precious blue books. Compare and contrast, stack two things up against each other. The silence pressed on my ears, or maybe I was just listening harder than before, attuned to each scratch of pencil on notebook, each scrape of desk scooting back across the floor. I wanted to say something, but what? An apology? Mimi had been the one to hit me first, and the bruise on my neck still smarted.

There was nothing more to say, or do. Life had solidified around us, packed in tight like concrete. And that's why I think I knew what she would do next. I felt my throat close and put down my pencil.

Mr. Scott paced the room, clunking heavily between the rows as we worked. I felt a tautness in my chest as he got closer and closer to Mimi. My heart caught in my throat. No one else could see it, but I couldn't breathe.

Mr. Scott stopped next to her.

He put a broad, damp hand down on her desk.

He peered over her shoulder. "Nice work," he said.

Jen Li screamed. She was the first to see Mimi reach under her desk and grab hold of the metal spike.

That was the thing about Mr. Scott's classroom: it was one of the older ones, the most "ghetto." The desks were '80s era or maybe earlier—each a single piece of furniture, a plastic chair with an L-shaped laminate top connected at the side, and underneath, a wire basket. Most baskets were in rough shape; kids would kick at them until the individual pieces of metal hung down or bent out, catching the ankles of your jeans if you weren't careful. And once they were sticking out, it didn't take much effort to reach down and snap off a six-inch piece of metal, and hold it poised above your teacher's unwitting wrist.

Like she was puncturing a balloon, Mimi brought the spike down and through the back of Mr. Scott's hand. Everything became red in what felt like an instant. I choked on the spit in my throat, Mr. Scott screamed a teakettle wail as he clutched his bloody fingers to his chest, the metal protruding almost comically, stuck in deep. I felt no pain as we scrambled out, although the next day I saw how bruised my legs were and realized I must have kicked my way through the chairs. The air smelled like defecation. The floor became slick. In the condensed spacetime of panic, we were suddenly all outside, even Mr. Scott, and he slammed the door behind him with all of his weight. The smell of feces grew stronger. Mr. Scott sunk to the floor, blood streaking across the linoleum like one wing of a snow angel. The spike was still in. I couldn't look at it. Kids were vomiting.

I closed my eyes tight and felt the first breaths come back to me. Holy shit. Holy fucking shit. Mr. Scott still wailed, it was loud and echoey, and you could tell the other classrooms were starting to hear it because doors had begun to swing open.

I turned back toward the door, standing on tiptoe to see through the rectangle of safety glass.

Blood had gotten everywhere; it was like the time I'd made a smoothie with the top off the blender—splatters coated the walls, the desk, the ceiling, and most of all, Mimi herself. Her T-shirt was so wet with it, the blue fabric had turned purple, and both her hands were red gloves. I remembered looking down at Mimi bleeding the day she'd fallen into the Ward C yard. Then she'd seemed terrified, but things were perhaps different when the blood wasn't her own.

Mimi didn't look over at the door, or out the window even as I heard the first wave of sirens. She just sat there, staring at her bloody piece of paper, and after a moment, she picked up her pen.

A boy named James peered next to me. "Oh my god, she's still writing." Kids crowded in, drawn both by the danger and the spectacle. *It's a suicide note, it's a warning, it's a poem,* they guessed. I knew better. As the police came thundering up the stairs toward us, flattening us against the lockers, I knew exactly what Mimi was doing. She was finishing her goddamned AP essay.

THAT NIGHT, while two surgeries failed to fix Mr. Scott's second extensor digitorum tendon, Mimi waited under special supervision at the Wake County Youth Correctional Facility. Our mother and Daddy both met her there but returned empty-handed well after midnight with the news that she would not be released, she'd committed an assault.

At the kitchen table, our mother interrogated me as if I were the one who'd stabbed Mr. Scott. What had I noticed in Mimi's behavior? Had she had contact with Mr. Scott outside of school? Had I ever seen him say anything to her? Her voice was hoarse and she kept getting up and sitting down again, making the same kind of jerky movements that Mimi had.

"Denise, I'm asking you if you think he was . . . abusing her."

"He was just a regular teacher," I said. "I never saw anything."

"Then why did she do it?"

"I don't know," I said.

My mother drummed her nails on the table, ignoring Daddy's exhortations to let things be.

"But what do you think it was, if you had to guess?"

The cold hard stone that had been growing in my chest grew heavier. The truth is, what Mimi did wasn't something you could blame on cause and effect. It wasn't logical in a way that our mother could ever understand, because our mother was at the heart of it, all her dreams and expectations wrapping so tight Mimi couldn't breathe. I knew I couldn't explain, so I just shook my head. "Sorry," I said, using a word that was forbidden in our household. "I guess she just went crazy."

AFTER MY PARENTS retreated to their room, I too left, slouching into the bedroom that now belonged to just J.J. and me. I stood in the doorway and looked up at J.J., who was sitting up cross-legged on her top bunk. We had barely spoken in months, but she cleared her throat when I came in.

"Did they hurt her?" she said. "The police, I mean."

"She was fine," I said. She'd followed them out calm as a tourist behind a guide, albeit one wearing shiny silver cuffs.

There was a long pause. "It's funny, isn't it?" J.J. went on, and her voice seemed high and childish. "Not ha-ha funny, but like—I wonder if Mimi got the idea from the Girl. You know who I'm talking about, from Ward B?"

"I know who you're talking about," I said.

"It's just . . . it's kind of similar, isn't it? It wasn't a knife but it was—you know, knifelike."

"I guess so," I said. I didn't think the spike was knifelike, but I guess that was the difference between seeing it in person and just having to imagine it. I felt a slight sympathy for J.J., it passed over my heart but not through it.

"I think about her a lot," J.J. said. "The Girl, I mean. Do you?"

The room felt a lot bigger with just the two of us in it. J.J. looked down at me, expectation and hope unhidden on her face. I wanted for a moment to climb up into her bed like I'd done when I was little, let her scratch my back and curl her toes into my bare feet. But the hole Skate had left still felt sharp and painful, and I knew, even then, I could not forgive her.

MIMI HAD AN INITIAL HEARING with a county judge, then an appeal after our parents hired a lawyer. I was allowed to attend neither, but our mother came home after the appeal sounding satisfied: Mimi would remain in youth detention until she turned seventeen, pending good behavior, then her record would be sealed. She could attend classes in the juvenile facility, although "obviously not any Advanced Placement courses." Daddy said very little. Sometimes I wondered if he had even fully registered what had happened.

Meanwhile, the staff at Lincoln decided they were finished with the Crosses altogether. My teachers were polled, a guidance counselor consulted, and everyone agreed that I was ready, "academically and socially," to move up to the twelfth grade. I would graduate in the spring at fourteen and a half, and we could all move on.

I was fine with this solution. I did not want to return to

Mr. Scott's classroom or face the stares of Jen Li and the others. Without the prop of teasing Mimi, our camaraderie would topple, and while I knew that was the last thing I should be worrying about, I admit I worried all the same.

Plus, of course, the whole thing delighted our mother, whose Ivy League dreams had been reignited once again. Less than a week after Mimi's sentencing, she sat down with me after dinner, my PSAT scores written on a sticky note. I had not shared them with her when they'd come in the mail, so she must have called the College Board herself.

"These are excellent," she said, "but then again, I'm not surprised. You could go anywhere you wanted."

The implied question—where did I want to go?—was impossible to answer. I could hardly picture myself next week, let alone a year from now, in some brick building on a quad.

"I don't know," I said, hoping to buy myself some more time.

That night I asked him.

Skate, I'm sorry I haven't written more often. Some terrible things have happened but I'm okay. I'm going to college early; I'm applying for next year. I have no idea where I should go. 762 days.

The reply came back instantly, while I was still at the computer.

I always pictured you in a city. Don't forget to look up.

TWENTY-SEVEN

Once Mimi had spent a month at juvie, she was allowed visitors and so we began a new weekly routine, driving on Sundays out of town, past the dump and the animal shelter, to a campus that looked like a cross between Mercy Hill and Lincoln, old brick buildings with new metal grates on all the windows. The first time we went, I was scared to go but also scared to tell our parents why I felt guilty about what Mimi had done to herself. So I hung back behind Daddy as we made our way inside.

I thought there would be jumpsuits, handcuffs, telephones to speak through glass. But the inside of the building just looked like a school. It reminded me, actually, of the old elementary school I'd missed in the transition to Lincoln, the white linoleum floor studded with primary-colored tiles and the walls fluttering with taped-up papers—choppy student art and essays written in pencil on clownish wide-rule.

We'd arrived early that first Sunday and waited silently as the foyer filled with other families. They were mostly Black, and many seemed to know each other, clustering tightly away from us as the clock switched from 12:59 to 1:00, whispers rising as it became 1:05 and then 1:10 without any sign of the staff coming to get us. I looked over at the woman standing beside me; she was holding a squirming toddler and, apart from the child, appeared to have arrived alone. I didn't mean to catch her eye but we must have both been sneaking glances at each other. Our gazes met and then she both looked and stepped away very quickly. I wondered if Mimi's infamy had followed her, or if she was doing a mental calculation of how monstrous the crime must've been that a rich—we suddenly seemed rich—white girl couldn't have lawyered her way out of it, or maybe and much more simply, our family was a sight unto itself, our mother standing tall in a brown pantsuit she wore to the city council, Daddy facing the opposite way with his three-day stubble and clenched jaw, and J.J. and me pushing apart like the wrong ends of magnets, looking anywhere but at each other.

The toddler started to huff and then to whine and the woman ducked around the corner, leaving me relieved and alone. Then, thank God, a security guard arrived and without a word led us down the hall and through two big double doors into a small cafeteria.

The juvie girls were spread throughout the room, sitting on the swiveling round stools that connected to the tables. They were all wearing khakis and white polo shirts like they were in some kind of private school, and once the doors opened, the room exploded into speech and laughter. Mimi was sitting in the middle of a table and as we passed the other families, we saw that the delinquents could get up and hug their visitors—just no climbing on the tables, the guard was saying to the woman with the toddler; she'd set the child down as she embraced a girl taller than she was, *Mama*, the guard was saying, get the baby off the table, please—and so Daddy led us to Mimi and embraced her, and then our mother hugged her and then J.J. did it too, and the momentum felt like something dark and inevitable. The last time I'd touched Mimi, she'd hit me. And now she was here because of what I'd done.

I felt my vision blur as the others parted to let me through. Mimi was wearing eyeliner, I saw as I got closer, but not the smudged raccoon-eye kind that she used to wear. No, it was very carefully done, her top lid and waterline painted in dark brown, the color of her carefully straightened hair. Some of that hair brushed my arm as we embraced, just once, quickly, and then I was back behind Daddy again, my nose full of the floral body spray Mimi had doused herself with. She wasn't looking at me anymore, and I clenched my fists deep in my pockets, trying to catch my breath.

"You look very fancy," Daddy said.

"My roommate," Mimi said. "She does everyone's makeup for visiting day." It suddenly felt like she'd been here for years, not weeks. My fault. Oh my fucking god, my fault.

"And you're still on the twenty mg?" our mother said. "Because I told them you can go higher, I have folks on the thirties or even forties—"

"Dr. Kate got your calls," Mimi said, her voice hardening. "She says I'm doing great on the twenties."

Our mother put one hand on the table then quickly drew it away, like she'd just realized how dirty it was. "And the alprazolam," she said. "That can be a good option, too, not for daily use of course, but—"

"Mom. I'm fine. Dr. Kate says I don't need any more pills."

"Kate's a nurse practitioner, not a doctor," our mother said.

Mimi's face looked hot under all its makeup. For once, she said nothing, which meant we were all silent. It was the kind of silence that Daddy would usually break, and in fact I swiveled my head toward him, waiting for him to open his mouth and say something light or distracting. He remained quiet.

The cafeteria clanged with the sounds of other families, laughing, talking, reaching, kissing. And still, the Crosses said nothing. I looked up and found Mimi staring at me. Her perfectly drawn eyes didn't blink. It was the same way I looked at J.J. and our mother had looked at her father, genetics and upbringing rolled into one thread shaped like a cable, a predilection against forgiveness.

DADDY BEGAN DRIVING ME to and from school. We didn't talk about why this change in routine had happened, we didn't talk much at all. By then, no one could pretend like nothing was wrong. J.J. and I weren't speaking, Caro was engaged, Mimi was in jail, for God's sake, but it was neither a Cross nor a Palmer trait to ruminate. If I had to guess, Daddy probably remembers that time with the same gauziness, the feeling that what we were driving was only a bumper car, and if we crashed, we'd just bounce around, jostled but untouched.

He broke the silence the day after my mother announced she had bought plane tickets to tour colleges, a weeklong trek that would take the two of us through the campuses of five schools up north. She was very excited about it, particularly the stops at her alma maters Princeton and Yale, but until this moment, Daddy had treated the whole trip as if it didn't exist. So I was surprised when he turned to me at a stoplight and said, "Denise, where do *you* want to go?"

"I don't know." I was sick of answering the same question. I'd gotten letters from each school by then, some with explicit offers of admission, others winking promises to expect good news come January. Part of me had hoped that rejections would make a decision for me, but what had I expected? I was to be valedictorian. I had logged over thirteen hundred volunteer hours working in Ward B. Our guidance counselor had written a letter calling me a prodigy.

"You know you have options," Daddy said. "If you took some

courses downtown, you could live at home. State and UNC and Duke are all near enough to commute. Or you could take a gap year."

"What would I do in a gap year?" I said.

"I don't know," Daddy admitted, "but I don't want you moving away just because you think it's what your mother wants you to do. I want you to be happy, Denise."

For a moment, I felt closer to him than I ever had. I wanted to tell him about being in the mob that bullied Mimi, loving then losing Skate, all the worst and best parts of myself I'd kept hidden. I thought of all this weighed against the mission, how badly I wanted us to win. I took a deep breath and pressed on: "I want to go to school and become a doctor, and, like—come back here and help."

"I know," Daddy said. "But—you know, it's not a child's job to fulfill the dreams of their parents." He tapped his hands on the wheel like he was going to say something else, but didn't. I could tell he was thinking about himself and what Grannie P. had wanted for him, how he'd jettisoned all that to be with our mother.

You're not happy either, I wanted to say, but he had taught me that you shouldn't say the truth just because it was true, there had to be some other reason. And I didn't want to hurt him, we were all hurt so much already.

I looked down at my hands, thinking about Skate's email. "I'm excited about going away," I said, "I always pictured myself in a city."

"You did?" Daddy said. "I had no idea."

I HAD NEVER BEEN close friends with Caro, she was neither near me in age like Mimi nor similar in personality like J.J., but when she came home for Christmas that year, I celebrated. Everything had gotten so quiet at the cottage that having her back seemed as if a spell had been broken, or perhaps a new one had been cast. The weather turned cold and each morning, the dew froze on the Hill like snow. It was the perfect backdrop for the motions of the holiday, which the members of the family—sans Mimi, of course—seemed keen to execute with rigor.

We put together a plastic tree and watched the stop-motion *Rudolph the Red-Nosed Reindeer* on VHS and on December 24 drove to the club to have a ham dinner with Grannie P. At this outing everyone was on their best behavior; even though you could tell she was not thrilled that Caro had invited Laketon, our mother engaged him in topics such as: *Do you need a lot of specialized tools for HVAC work?* And, *Oh my, those are a lot of specialized tools indeed!*

Caro, too, seemed determined to keep the peace: although she wore her tiny engagement ring on her left hand, she did not refer to it in any way, nor mention anything about church. I could hear her whispered prayers each night before she went to sleep, but she brought forth no other evidence of defection. Our mother asked her about her classes at Duke, and she answered with what seemed like genuine interest. I felt my guard go back down.

That's why the blowup was so shocking: we'd all been lulled into submission. It was two days before New Year's, and early enough in the morning that I was still in bed. I heard my mother's voice and sat up, peering into Caro's bed. She was gone.

"Tucker," our mother screamed, "are you goddamned fucking kidding me?"

Kitty-corner to me, on top of the other bunk bed, J.J. stirred. She and I caught each other's eye, then turned away quickly, remembering our feud.

"C'mon," she said without looking at me.

The voices continued, our father's muffled. I followed J.J. out at a distance. Caro was in the front room with our parents, dressed in a long black skirt and a button-down like she was going on an interview. Her hair was still wet.

Our mother paced back and forth.

"What's happening?" J.J. asked, rubbing her eyes.

No one said anything. Daddy moved over to stand next to Caro, hand on her shoulder like they were some kind of united front.

"I am speechless," our mother said, although she continued to speak. "I do not consent, I do not approve."

"You don't need to," Caro said, staring at the floor. "I only need one."

"One what?" J.J. said.

There was a long pause.

"Guys," Caro said. "I'm getting married. Daddy's given me permission."

"Tucker," our mother said. "If you do this, you're going to lose her."

"If I don't do this, we're going to lose her," Daddy said.

"Caroline, we buy your textbooks," our mother said. "We pay for your dorm room."

"I don't even sleep in my dorm room," Caro said.

"I want you to think about this," our mother said. "And think if you'll regret it."

Caro said nothing. We all looked at our mother, whose mouth had straightened into a line.

"All I'm asking," she said. "All I've ever asked—is that you think for yourself."

"Jesus, Lisa." Daddy reached for her, but she backed away. "Let's—"

But she didn't let him finish.

"Go, then," she said, and I thought she meant Caro, but she was looking at Daddy when she said it. "Go ruin your life."

Our eyes snapped to Caro, waiting to hear how she'd respond to this taunt. She said nothing, just gave the rest of us a sort of half wave and then pushed out through the door. Daddy followed, holding the screen so it wouldn't slam. Neither of them looked back.

J.J. and I turned to our mother. Surely she had something—a cutting remark, an exhortation never to do the same ourselves—but for a very long moment, she was silent. She didn't look sad, just surprised. That was worse, somehow, because nothing ever surprised Lisa Cross.

"I'll see you two later," she said and my heart soared—she was going along with them! She'd give her permission after all! Of course that was ridiculous, and I felt stupid as soon as I thought it. She picked up her briefcase and her pager and nodded at us once before heading in the opposite direction, up the winding path to Ward C.

Alone with J.J. again, I turned and went back into the bedroom. I felt angry and powerless. There was a small closet in one corner of the room, and because we shared a bunk, Caro and I shared one side of the closet as well, cardboard boxes containing our old school notebooks and baby teeth marked with Daddy's block print: CAROLINE, DENISE, CAROLINE, DENISE.

I began unstacking them, dragging Caro's stuff over to her bunk and hefting them up on top. I took her dresses next, swinging the long skirts and modest necklines into a pile without even removing the hangers. I suppose I was making room for my own things, but as the closet began looking emptier, it occurred to me that I couldn't think of anything that I wanted to put there.

Still I continued, getting down on my hands and knees to

move a pile of old stuffed animals. I gathered up a soft and dusty armful and then, in the empty corner, I saw a flash of something tiny and blue catch the light. It was a marble—no, an *eye,* a chipped glass pupil the size of my thumbnail.

Like the object had summoned her, J.J. was there, peering over my shoulder at the little round thing in my hand. Years ago, when our mother had thrown away her dolls, this must have been left behind. It felt strange to be holding a tangible reminder of that day, which at the time had seemed like the worst thing that could happen to any of us. It all seemed small now, the eye included.

I shoved it into J.J.'s hand. "This is yours," I said.

She held the piece between her fingers, and for one of the first times in years, I saw her begin to cry.

"Denise," she said. Her loneliness seemed to leak out of every pore. I know because I felt it too, the feeling caught in my throat each morning and stayed until I passed into sleep. "Please say something," she said, and stepped toward me. For a moment I almost met her halfway. I missed her too.

But Skate!

"Shut up," I said, even though she'd already stopped talking. "I'm going to go study."

CARO AND LAKETON were married that day at the courthouse downtown, and afterward Daddy drove home alone. When pressed, he said only that it was very crowded, with many couples trying to make things official by year's end for tax purposes. I stacked all the things from the closet on Caro's bed just in case she came back to get them. After a few days, I realized she wasn't coming home, and covered them all with a blanket.

On New Year's Eve, Caro called Cottage 10 and spoke to Daddy, then J.J., then me. When it was my turn, I took the cordless into the bathroom and sat on the edge of the tub. "Are you having fun?" I asked her. "Now that you get to have sex?"

"Ew, Denise." She paused. "You've got to make up with J.J. I still don't know what it is you're fighting about."

I felt a sudden warmth toward J.J. She had kept her word not to tell anyone what had led to our falling-out. But I still didn't want to talk to Caro about it. "When are you coming back?" I asked.

"I'm not coming home. I'm moving in with Laketon."

"How are you going to get to your classes?" I said.

"I'm taking a semester off."

Even though it shouldn't have been a surprise, the revelation caught in my throat. "Really?"

Caro laughed. "I'm tired of school. Aren't you?"

"Mom's gonna be pissed," I said.

"Yeah, well. That's her problem."

"She and I are leaving the day after New Year's," I said. "To go look at colleges up north."

"Oh, really?" This slowed her down for a moment. "That's crazy."

I swallowed. Every time I thought about the upcoming trip, I felt whipped by the winds of competing emotions: excitement, of course, to have the rare time alone with our mother, but fear as well. This trip seemed like a flash point where one wrong move could doom all of us.

"I'll be fine," I told Caro, braver than I felt. Then I said it again, which made it seem even more like I didn't believe it.

2004

TWENTY-EIGHT

We arrived at Harvard in the dark. I'd never been so cold. Wind whipped through the empty quad, rustling desiccated leaves against the skirts of the ancient buildings.

My mother put her arm around my shoulders and rubbed hard, like I was drowning. Her hands felt strong and warm.

"Is it like this here all winter?" I said.

She laughed. "I should have bought you a warmer coat."

I don't think I'd ever heard her admit failure, even for something small like this. It was strange enough to make me stop shivering.

IN NEW HAVEN, the sky was slate gray and heavy, sagging down over the buildings like an artificial roof. We walked by many dry fountains, their smooth concave basins collecting sticks and plastic wrappers.

"There are tunnels under most of the school," she said. "It's like when you girls used to play Underground Railroad."

"I didn't know you knew about that," I said. It had been Daddy who brought out lunches for us to eat as we snuck through the trees.

"You never think about who's watching, do you?"

I turned that sentence over in my mind. At first it seemed like she was talking about us, but I soon became convinced she was referring to herself. I didn't know what to say. I hugged myself in my new coat, the one she'd bought me at the Marshalls in Cambridge. It was very warm, she'd chosen perfectly.

WE STAYED AT A Holiday Inn Express, a La Quinta, and two Days Inns. They all had the same plastic pastry case set out in the morning from which I selected a raspberry Danish, biting in so hard bloodred jam dripped down my chin.

"It's like baby food all over again," my mother said, stirring her plain coffee. Then she paused a long time. "I made it all for J.J., you know. I came home each night and cooked squash and peas and beets and put them through the food processor. But the dishes, you wouldn't believe. I still cooked for Caro, and a little for Mimi. . . . Then you, you just ate Gerber."

This admission felt rare and special. My balled-up nerves began to relax.

"You shouldn't feel guilty," I said, watching a smile spread across her face. "I turned out okay."

THIS IS PROFESSOR ANADEMS, *chair of MIT's Chemistry Department.*

This is Professor Tsu; she teaches psychology here at Harvard.

These are Professor Kenn and Professor Reynolds, I sent them your essay ahead of time. They're two of Yale's premed advisers.

This is Lucy Dickerson; she taught me during medical school.

"We can't wait to hear what choice you make," everyone said, and behind them, my mother beamed. I tried not to look at her, because the naked joy on her face seemed so private, it felt like I was spying.

After all this, I still didn't know which one I wanted. I had kind of thought that I'd step into one of the buildings and immediately feel like I belonged—like falling in love, although that concept seemed silly, too, when I considered it.

SHE SANG ALONG to the radio as we drove in the rental car, the pop station, which I found surprising. I hardly knew any of these songs, yet she could belt out all the verses to *"Hey Ya!"*?

"At work, the techs control the radio," she said. She seemed relaxed and happy, tapping her hands on the wheel as we whizzed along.

Shake it like a Polaroid picture!

"Mom!" I screeched, embarrassed and delighted at my own embarrassment. I'd never seen her sing before, and here she was, wriggling her shoulders in a goofy dance.

"Join me," she said, bobbing her head in time to the beat.

"Absolutely not," I said, rolling my eyes up at the roof.

"Suit yourself," she said, and turned the radio up louder.

Alright alright alright alright!

I put my head in my hands. "This song has never been sung worse." I had never teased her like this before and when she laughed, I felt grown up, like we were equals.

"ACTUALLY, I DO ALREADY KNOW what I want to study," I told everyone. "I want to be a psychiatrist."

"I don't know where she got that idea," my mother would say, and we'd grin at each other.

"I want to get my MD, then go back and work with my mother."

She beamed. "You'd be my favorite colleague," she said, again and again.

WE DROPPED THE CAR OFF at the Hertz in New Haven and took a taxi to the train, which I was surprised to see was aboveground.

"Why is it called the subway, then?" I asked.

She told me that this wasn't the subway but a commuter rail. People who lived outside the city rode it in each morning, sometimes multiple hours each way. I watched the other passengers with interest and awe. Where were they going that was worth such a lengthy journey?

Daddy had told me ahead of time that New Yorkers were all very fashionable and wore only black, but the men and women who sat around us looked like the parents of the kids I went to school with, just skinnier. They drank from travel mugs and rustled newspapers, largely ignoring the swell of the Hudson River to our right, which in the early sun had turned crystalline at the edges, ice covering the banks in spiky chunks.

The city rose more gradually than I expected, houses giving way to duplexes to towering X-shaped brick buildings. My mother told me these were housing projects and I imagined the entirety of Chavis Heights shifted onto its side, sprawling up instead of out.

We went into a tunnel and emerged in the dark underground. *Last stop, Grand Central.*

"Now we take the subway?"

"Now we take a cab." My mother hauled our two suitcases from the wire rack and thumped them down to the platform.

Out in the clear morning, the sounds of the city seemed amplified, traffic and construction and the rattle of something mechanical sending waves through my feet. We rode in a sour-smelling taxi with broken seat belts and at each turn I held on tight to the handhold, feeling dangerous and free.

"This place is really cool," I said, which sounded babyish, but I had to say something. I'd never seen so many people walking fast. At Lincoln everyone ambled, demonstrating that they didn't care where they were going. Here, everyone had a place to be, even the kids, bouncing along the blocks in hooded jackets, carrying messenger bags. I touched the strap of my own backpack, feeling an unfamiliar envy.

"The city's a blast," my mother said. "When I was at Princeton we used to go for the day, eat dim sum and sneak into a Broadway show. If you lit up with the smokers at intermission, the ushers would let you back in for the second act."

I still couldn't get over how relaxed she sounded, her voice light and laughing. It was as if by leaving the grounds of Mercy Hill I had been inducted into some secret club of adulthood. It was wonderful, and I kept my mind wrapped tightly around itself so I wouldn't screw it all up.

THE TOUR OF COLUMBIA was the same one we'd taken at the other colleges, a smiling student walking backward through the quad as parents and children followed: here's the main dining hall, here's the performing arts center, here's the funny thing that happens in the library during finals. The only difference here was how the city bled in around the campus walls, the sounds of honking weaving through, the spikes of skyscrapers growing behind the crenelated classrooms. It felt like something out of a sci-fi show, a college settled on a crowded planet.

That night, we ate Indian food in a restaurant so tiny the whole place could have fit into my bedroom at home. I'd never had curry before, and the flavors made my eyes water and nose run. My mother offered me a sip of her wine and as we walked back to the hotel, I wondered if I had gotten drunk accidentally. I felt sparkling and happy for the first time in many months.

"Now, Princeton is just a short ride away from the city," my mother said, as we boarded the train. "You could do this every weekend if you wanted to go there instead."

"I know," I said. But in my mind, I was already slinging a

satchel over my shoulder and striding up from the mouth of the subway into the waiting lights.

"You want to go to Columbia, don't you?" she said.

"Yes," I said quickly, surprising myself. "I really do."

"Good," she said, and she brought a hand to her eyes. She suddenly looked very tired and not at all happy. "Because I'm ready to go home."

She stayed in a funk the whole next day, through our perfunctory tour of Princeton ("She's already decided she doesn't want to go here") and back onto the plane at Newark airport. As I leaned over her seat to watch the spiked buildings disappear behind us, she pushed me back with what felt like unnecessary force.

"Denise, behave yourself. You're acting like a child."

The relaxation, the happiness—our status as equals—all of that seemed like it had happened in another dimension. The shock of change blindsided me. Was she steeling herself for her return to work, mourning the end of vacation, or just feeling tired? Or had this whole week been a performance, designed to elicit a response in me, and now that she'd gotten what she wanted, she didn't feel the need to continue? It made me feel lower than I'd felt before the trip, pressed into my seat by a force stronger than gravity.

TWENTY-NINE

I had tried everything I could to get out of giving a speech. I told Principal Kay I got nervous in front of crowds; I told my new English teacher, Mrs. Lee, that I couldn't think of anything to say. I even tried leveling with the guidance counselors, telling them the entire truth as I understood it: "They aren't my peers and they aren't my friends. No one wants to hear from me."

I expected a polite rebuttal, but the counselors were direct instead—sick, undoubtedly, of years of dealing with the Crosses.

Those are the rules, they told me, the valedictorian speaks at commencement. Don't make things more difficult for everyone than they already are.

LINCOLN WAS A BIG SCHOOL, even if I never saw half of it. We held the ceremony in North Carolina State's women's basketball arena, and the mass of mortarboards spread down the entire court, looking from the stage like uneven tiles. I was high up enough that I couldn't see too many faces, just the swaying mass, and that felt about right.

Surrounding the court, families waved signs and cheered. I didn't know where my family was sitting, but they certainly weren't making noise; it was just my parents, J.J., and Grannie P.

Caro had decided at the last minute not to come. It was now more than six months since we'd last seen her. In another lifetime, this would have been cause for alarm, but now it was by no means the worst thing that had happened to us.

I felt very numb and yawningly bored, like this was a show I'd seen too many times but there was nothing good on the other channels. Principal Kay spoke, but it was hard to catch what she was saying. I had been in the crowd for Caro's and J.J.'s commencements and although I didn't remember exactly, this seemed like a similar speech. Pride, hope, accomplishment, meant to applaud the students who would go on to college while reassuring those who would not. It felt overly long, but then everyone was clapping and Principal Kay was saying, "Denise Cross, our valedictorian."

I picked up clumps of my graduation gown. Even in my new high-heeled sandals, it was far too long for me. The podium was also too tall: I know how I looked, a tiny, capped head reaching just to the microphone. The room went quiet. *Fuck you,* I thought. *Fuck you all.* These rows and rows of kids who had teased me or ignored me or laughed at me, spun by their webs of anxiety, praying to get the grades that they thought would change everything. *You're all stupid,* I thought about saying, and wondered how long it would take Principal Kay to snatch away the mic and/or body-check me off the stage. It was a very Mimi-like thought and the fact that Mimi wasn't here, messing around with the lights or pulling the fire alarm, made me deeply sad.

There were a lot of things I could have said to ruin things, or show off how smart I was, to right indignities I had been forced to endure during the years I spent at Lincoln. *Psycho Dee. Pee Dee.* And I think that's what some people were expecting. Some strange and circuitous talk that quoted philosophers they'd never heard of.

But when you spend so much time trying to make a single person happy, you become good at the fake-out.

I put both hands in the air. "What's up, class of 2004!" I screamed into the mic.

The awkward silence broke and people cheered.

"We have worked *so* hard," I said, hearing the unfamiliar echoes of my own voice bounce back to me from each edge of the room. "And now—we are going to *party*!"

I stood up there for maybe ten seconds more. The faces in the crowd materialized, and I could see their genuine joy and excitement. It made my stomach dip, because maybe all that had been missing was my own enthusiasm. Maybe some of my alienation had been my fault.

I closed with a cheer, and when I stepped back, Principal Kay gave me a hard hug. She too, I realized, had been worried I was going to sprinkle in a little Nietzsche.

"You did it," she whispered into my hair.

And now, I thought, *you're done with us forever.*

AFTERWARD, we spilled out into a sunny courtyard to find our friends and families. A couple of kids good-jobbed me and I shrugged away as fast as I could. I scanned the crowd, telling myself I was looking for my family, but in reality, looking for Skate. I'd written to him that I was speaking at commencement and even though I knew it was a long shot, I thought he might still show. It would be safe here, in the crowd. Even if we just saw each other for a minute. Even if we never touched.

Although I looked and looked, I never saw him. Instead, I saw Caro.

She was standing to the side with Laketon, wearing a long dress with a purple paisley pattern. The material looked cheap, like our graduation gowns.

"I thought you weren't coming," I said, checking her over for signs of strangeness. She looked just as she had before, long hair shiny and curled at the edges, wearing a white bolero sweater to cover her shoulders.

"I didn't want to cause a scene," she said.

"Are you ever going to come home again?"

Instead of answering, she said, "I miss you."

"But you only call J.J."

"She's the only one who answers the phone. I guess you still aren't talking to each other?"

I dropped my hands to my sides, wishing the robe had pockets so I could clench them into fists. "No," I said.

A brief flash of pain passed over Caro's face. Even from afar, she took it personally when any of us were fighting. "You should try talking to her. She seems different now. There's this girl in her stats class, and she says they're just friends, but—"

"I don't care who J.J.'s fucking."

Caro stopped in her tracks, like I knew she would. It felt telekinetic, to be able to get her to freeze with just a word. Then I felt an echo of long-ago panic, the pressure to make an ally so I wouldn't be the only sister standing alone.

I made my voice softer. "I'm getting a cell phone," I said. "In August. When Mom and I move up to New York City. You can call me on my new number when I get it."

Caro let out a long breath. "I still can't believe she's going with you, and not Daddy."

"Daddy offered, but she said she wanted to."

"She never trusts Daddy to do anything."

"It's just for one semester." This had been a requirement of

Columbia; they would not let me move into a dorm room until I turned fifteen. The plan was to rent an apartment near campus until my birthday in December, while our mother took a sabbatical from work.

"Still. Do you remember her taking a vacation, ever?"

Damn Caro, bringing up my deepest and (I thought) most well-hidden anxiety within moments of our meeting. I, too, had been surprised at our mother's offer, which, like everything our mother offered, was not up for debate. I feared what would happen to her, being away for so long—not to mention Mercy Hill itself, which I pictured crumbling the moment she stepped away from its grounds.

As if answering my question, she asked: "How's stuff with the General Assembly?"

"It's been okay," I said. "They haven't cut the budget, but they haven't increased it either." I didn't mention that our mother had twice this spring gone to Washington, on Tuesdays with only a single week in between. She was clearly seeing the Senator while she was there, but whether for business or pleasure (whose pleasure?), I wasn't sure.

"Look, Denise," she said, her soft voice almost lost in the boisterous crowd. "It sounds like things are going to be okay for the time being. Mom wouldn't go away if they weren't." She reached for my hand, and we touched for just a moment. I felt steadier than I had for a long time.

"Please come home soon," I said, throat beginning to ache.

Caro said nothing, and then Laketon stepped between us. "Hey," he said, "I see them." We all turned and saw our mother and Daddy, J.J. and Grannie P., struggling through the sea of green robes. Caro dropped my hand and before I could say anything else, she and Laketon ducked away into the crowd.

By the time the others got to me, I was standing alone. If

they had seen Caro and Laketon, they didn't say anything. Instead, Daddy said he liked my speech and Grannie P. said, "Lisa, wasn't it wonderful?"

Our mother seemed to be looking somewhere far beyond the milling students. "Oh yes," she said. "Denise certainly gave them what they wanted."

THIRTY

As the move to New York approached, I tried to quell my fears about its impact by repeating to myself what Caro had told me. Things were undoubtedly going to be fine, because if they weren't, Lisa Cross would not have agreed to go. But while this logic would have convinced a younger version of myself, I'd grown enough to know that things could always, always go wrong.

Some days I could get through if I kept my head down, reading *Dead Man Walking* for my freshman seminar and packing and repacking my meager set of winter clothes. Other days I felt like a bird had gotten trapped inside my body and was trying in vain to get out. The thing I wanted—to walk fast through that green campus surrounded by the glistening city—by taking it, and taking our mother with me, was I consigning Mercy Hill to destruction?

And so I began moving whenever this fear seized me, tramping each square foot of the Hill as if putting my weight on it would stop it from blowing away. I went everywhere: circling each staff cottage, every one of them empty but ours and Nurse Jenny's, whose window AC unit sagged and whose bright blue checked tablecloth I could see through the gap. That felt like something in the hopeful column. Then I walked wider, down to where the Hill got steeper and steeper at the guardrails of the road. I got close enough to feel the rush of wind as cars whooshed by, intent on their destination without a single glance upward.

One day I touched the exterior of Ward B to see if I could feel any residual warmth from the time we'd spent there volunteering—surely the exertion and effort remained in some part in those stone walls—but when my hand met only the rough coolness, I felt the bird return. She was stuck in my rib cage now and each wingbeat thrashed with pain. There were ten days to go. Ten unthinkable days. I pushed off like a swimmer, intending to take the long path through the woods to the old cemetery. The last gravestone had been erected in the '70s and it was the one place on the grounds there were never any changes. But it was like the bird was controlling my movement. Instead of going straight, I turned left, taking the once well-worn dirt path, now sprouting with two years of weeds, that connected Ward B to Ward C.

Stupid, stupid, I said in my head and then aloud. You stupid baby. Bothering our mother with even a page or a phone call was a cardinal sin, it was like saying, I think I'm more important than the work you're doing. When Caro was eight and I was five, she and I were left alone while Daddy took J.J. and Mimi to the eye doctor and Caro cut her hand on the lid of a tuna fish can. We spent an hour wrapping it with paper towels as they quickly turned scarlet rather than call our mother. And now here I was, not even bleeding, shuffling toward the side entrance where Ward C got its deliveries of mail and soap. Just wait to ask her, I told myself. But waiting seemed as impossible as going backward in time.

The side door of Ward C had a buzzer and bars across the

window, but other than that looked like a normal entrance to a building. I pressed the button and heard a muffled tone inside. Then everything was quiet again. Stupid, I thought as I pressed it once more. You stupid fucking baby. My anger at myself rose until it drowned out the fear that had been rocketing around my chest. I took a step back, ashamed. Then my mother opened the door.

I was so surprised, I said nothing at first. I knew the ward was short-staffed, especially in the summer, but why was the director of psychiatry answering doors? Because Lisa Cross did what had to be done, of course. No job too small. No crusade too big.

She too seemed stunned—not angry. "Denise?" she said, as if I could perhaps be someone else. "What do you need?"

I felt my face scrunch up. "I'm sorry," I said. "I just felt funny—you know, our trip." I looked around past her at the shadowy hall. "Mom, are you really going to be able to leave?"

It was such a stupid question and my voice shook as I asked it, anticipating what I knew her reply would be: *Of course, don't be ridiculous*. Instead, she stepped back, holding open the door so I could follow her.

"Why don't you come in?" she said. "It's okay, I have time."

I stepped quickly in after her and the door closed behind us.

I'd never been inside the main part of Ward C before, only the front vestibule a couple of times, and I was surprised at how dark it was. The layout was the same as Ward B, but without the half doors on the resident rooms and the big windows letting light into the main corridors. Here, everything was much more closed off, long hallways with offshoots marked LAUNDRY and ISOLATION.

"The residents are all upstairs," my mother said, to assuage my fears or perhaps simply to explain the silence. "When we got down to sixteen, we closed the bunks on the first floor so we could reduce the guard shifts. It's easier this way."

I swallowed hard. I knew Ward C's population had dwindled considerably as some stood trial or were moved to Central Prison, which had a more intensive medical center, dialysis, and the like. But sixteen men? They wouldn't fill half a school bus. The bird in my chest began to racket around again and I looked down at my feet, taking in only the faded tile, the same big beige squares that I'd trudged over in Ward B.

My mother stopped outside a door and unlocked it with a key from an interior pocket of her lab coat. "My office," she said, flipping on a row of lights. They spluttered for a long second, then plunged the room into searing whiteness.

This office looked like it used to be a treatment room, like the one in Ward B in which I'd seen her let David Johnson plunge the needle into her arm. But the exam table, the long desk, the cabinets missing their fronts, everything was piled high or packed tight with papers. It was as if the orange binder had been breeding in secret.

"Sit down, Denise." She moved a stack of files off a chair but continued to stand herself, leaning against a counter that held a dusty, unused sink.

I sat and said nothing for a long moment, but then, looking down at my feet, I said, "Eighteen weeks is a long time. I really want to go but—I could wait, you know. Defer. So you wouldn't have to come with me."

Our mother paused a long moment, and in that pause, smiled a tired smile. "They'll be okay if I step out," she said.

I steeled myself to look her in the eye. "Who's going to do the weekend intakes?" This was one of the ironclad rules, another one of the Wyatt standards: patients had to be evaluated within twenty-four hours of arrival. We were in such a precipitous spot—MDs answering the doors! Residents in almost the single digits!—I was sure that just one mistake would doom us.

"We aren't doing any intakes," she said. "We haven't for months. But Denise, I promise you, it's going to be okay. Now, I'm going to tell you something under the condition that you don't tell anyone else. Not Daddy, not J.J." It surprised me that she still hadn't realized J.J. and I weren't speaking, but I could hardly focus on that revelation because what she told me next was the most wild and hopeful thing I'd heard in years.

"The work I'll be doing these next few months . . . I don't have to be here in person. In fact, maintaining my clinical hours would have been a distraction."

And here was why: the state was cutting its mental health budget again, no surprise there, and rumor had it that two facilities, an outpatient clinic in Greensboro and an inpatient facility in Butner, were to be shuttered completely. This abrupt closure would leave at least two hundred patients in need of services.

"And so I'm making a case," she said. "The Senator said he'd consider it. I told him we could accommodate them all—if we reopened Wards A and B."

I couldn't speak. To have Ward B back was one thing but Ward A as well? It would be like a video run in reverse, water going back uphill, dead flowers uncurling into life.

I must have let the hope show on my face because my mother uncrossed her arms. "I know," she said. "It sounds crazy—but not as crazy as you'd think. The facilities exist here, even if they'd need to do some remodeling. We'd staff differently, of course. No more Aaron Holts. More oversight, more structure."

I breathed out one word: "Wow."

"As you can imagine, there will be a lot of logistics," she

said. "As such, I don't mind having some space away to work on it."

Now I couldn't stop grinning either. It felt as if the walls of the room had cracked open and bright light was shining in through every crevice.

"It's a complicated proposal," she went on. "You know how it is, anything with federal and state money, there's people to please both in Raleigh and DC."

I bristled slightly at the juxtaposition of *please* and *people in DC*, but the rest of this news overshadowed even the shame of what Daddy had accused her of doing with the Senator. Which—fuck it. What if it was true, cock-sucking in the most literal sense? If it had resulted in this outcome . . . I pictured the Hill bustling again, hundreds of people walking the grounds—residents, aides, nurses, doctors—in such stark contrast to the barren loneliness that covered it now.

"I can't believe it," I said, reaching for her hand and squeezing it. She pulled me toward her, crushing me in a hug so tight I could barely breathe. Her blouse still smelled like the tang of cafeteria grease that I remembered from my time in Ward B, and I jolted, realizing I could perhaps someday go back through those doors again, myself. This hope was so sharp and sudden I felt like I could cut myself on it.

"Not a word to the others," she said. "There will be time to tell them soon enough." Then she went back to the door and opened it again, and I stepped with her into the dark hall, which now seemed silent with anticipation.

THIRTY-ONE

The apartment we rented on West 119th Street was called a studio, which I thought at first meant it would come with an easel. Instead, it was about the size of an RV, one long, narrow room with a window that looked out onto an internal courtyard where everyone put their trash. We had a stove, a mini fridge, and sink, but no dishwasher, and a bathroom with a tiny porcelain tub chipped all around the edges. The walls were freshly painted, although the day we arrived deliverymen banged them up while moving in two twin beds with plastic-wrapped mattresses and two identical desks.

"Looks kind of like a dorm, doesn't it?" my mother said.

I told her it was funny it looked like a dorm because neither of us was the right age to be attending college.

"You deserve to be here." Suddenly serious, she set down the ball of plastic that had come off the mattresses and clasped her hands together. "Anything the other kids can do—you got here, fair and square."

"I was just joking." I had a collection of worries about college, but none of them were academic. I mostly feared walking into a classroom and hearing whispers. I had spent the summer telling myself that this would be my chance to make friends, but now that the time had come, I had no idea how to go about doing it.

"Where do you want to set up your things?" I asked. "You should have first pick of the desks, you'll have a lot more papers than me. And I can always work in the library."

Her eyes flashed and her voice became stern. "No," she said. "Pick your desk first, don't worry about me.

"Denise," she went on, "I want you to forget about what I told you back on the Hill. About the wards proposal. That's my work, and I don't want it to distract you—you have a different set of tasks here."

"Yes, but . . ." I smiled a little. How could she ask me to put aside what would undoubtedly be the most exciting thing to ever happen to our family—not to mention all the patients across the state, Bethy and her brethren, who would finally have a home? The possibilities were so monumental it overshadowed everything else.

"No buts," she said. "If you can't pick, I'll choose for you. You take the desk by the window."

AS WE SETTLED INTO our new lives in the studio, my mother continued to work furiously on her proposal and tell me nothing about it. From early morning until well after I was in bed, I heard the click of her laptop keys as she tapped out messages and memos, but when I asked her about it, or the new pages she added daily to the famous orange binder (kept now on the top shelf inside our mini refrigerator, in case of fire), she just smiled. *Focus your attention on school,* she told me. *We're going to need all the MDs we can get.*

Since classes hadn't yet started, I began to go out each day and explore the city. Although growing up I had been allowed to walk almost anywhere on campus, my limits were circumscribed by the roads that encircled it. Going anywhere beyond the Hill required a car and someone to drive it. But here—two dollars on my MetroCard and I could step onto any train, see the sharp shards of buildings in midtown or the empty platforms in the Bronx, crush into a mass of rush-hour commuters who didn't pay a lick of attention to what I did as long as I didn't step on their feet.

It felt good to be ignored this way. Not like people saw you and dismissed you, the way it had been my whole life—but to blend in, meeting no resistance. I felt homogenous. I felt like I was a part of something.

AUGUST ENDED, classes began, and September continued with what everyone was calling a heat wave. I just laughed. The air outside was no worse than early spring in Raleigh, the complained-about humidity rarely hitting 70 percent. *Call me when the air is so thick you choke,* I said to the girl sitting next to me in freshman seminar. It came out too loud and I cringed at my own foolishness. But she just grinned and fanned herself with her course pack.

"You sound like my roommate," she said. "She's from Tallahassee." Then I felt the world turn on its axis. "You should come over tonight, it's her birthday."

"Her birthday," I repeatedly, dumbly. Was I being tricked? This girl, whom I remembered from introductions had gone to a Boston prep school, was writing her dorm number on a sticky note and handing it to me.

"She's great but, like—she doesn't know anyone yet? I want her to have a good time. We'll have some wine!"

"Ah." I put my shaking hands in my lap. Any talk of birthdays made me nervous, because it drew attention to my own age, three and a half years younger than everyone else.

She didn't seem to notice, or perhaps she just didn't care. "Please come," she said. "It'll be fun."

I TOLD MY MOTHER it was a party. She wouldn't have believed me if I lied, and part of me wanted her to forbid me from going. I told her I wouldn't drink anything and she said one drink was probably fine, just don't set it down where you can't see it. I immediately felt homesick, leaving her. She was sitting on her bed, underlining something on a stack of papers, and I longed to see what she was working on. After our many years of hardship, it seemed as if Mercy Hill was finally growing instead of shrinking—it was thrilling to contemplate, and a little sad that it was happening so far away. I told myself I was just being a baby and went into the bathroom to put another coat of mascara on my already heavy lashes.

The prep school girl's name was Tati, which was short for something Russian, and her roommate was Jessica, a quiet girl with blond hair too long to be cool. I had an almost encyclopedic knowledge of the signifiers that made someone fit in or not, and Jessica's pillows were too lacy, her laptop too expensive, a framed photo of a horse (just a horse) on her desk—these were markings of an only child who spent a lot of time calling home.

Compare that to Tati, who'd lived in dorms for four years already in high school. Tati had lofted her bed just high enough to hide a mini fridge beneath it, and when I arrived, she was pouring gulps of twist-top wine into conical paper cups, laughing when it splashed on people's fingers. She was clearly the ringleader, all the attendees were from her side of the camp, and yet there was no meanness when she embraced me at the door.

"Denise came!" she said, which made everyone cheer even though they didn't know me. "We're supposed to have a cake, but Kevin's being a fucking diva, as per usual."

I didn't know what any of this meant. Tati handed me a cup and splashed in some wine. "You're twenty-one, right?"

Her face was so serious my heart jolted, but before I could say anything, she said, "I'm kidding, I'm kidding. No one open the windows, the RA lives below us and we're already on strike one."

"Strike two," said Jessica. Her cheeks were flushed.

"Shh," Tati said, eyes bright with laughter.

The dorm room, which was even smaller than my studio, suddenly seemed very large. Holding my cup without drinking from it, I wandered from one side to another, bouncing from surface to surface like a slowed-down pool ball. If I kept moving, I wouldn't have to talk to anyone.

In front of Tati's messy dresser, I stopped because there was another person standing alone. Marion Hobson was in the freshman constitutional law seminar with Tati and me. She was the only Black girl in our small class and a very good debater, absolutely schooling this boy named Kyle in a recent roundtable on the legality of assisted suicide. But in the bumping weirdness of the party, she seemed as lost as I was. The two of us stood silently for a moment, frozen in place by the magnetic pull of recognition.

"Cheers," I said, raising my paper cup.

"Do you like wine?" she said, looking dubiously into her own drink.

"Yeah," I said.

"I'd rather have a Seven and Seven," she said. "This stuff is disgusting."

"I don't think this is very representative of wine as a whole."

She laughed. "No offense," she said, "but you seem pretty young to know much about wine. How old are you?"

All summer I'd steeled myself to respond to this question with a cool lie. I figured if I seemed nonchalant enough, I might pass for seventeen, which was totally normal—some classmates just had late birthdays. But Marion had asked the question with kindness and it threw me enough to tell the truth.

"I'll be fifteen in December," I said. "I skipped a lot of grades." Then I drained the rest of my cup, stomach clenching as I waited for her reaction, the compliment-that-was-never-a-compliment: *Oooh, you must be* so *smart!*

She just raised an eyebrow. "Wow, you must've really hated high school."

A double rush of alcohol and relief flooded through my body and I let out a laugh loud enough to break through the thumping bass.

"God, yes," I said. "It fucking sucked."

She raised her cup in agreement. "I went to Catholic school and the day after AP exams I burned my blazer in the barbecue grill." She giggled. "Hell is other people, right?"

It all came out in a rush. "I lived in—not in but, like, my mom worked there—I lived in a mental hospital. And I was stupid enough to tell everyone at school."

"Holy shit, that must've sucked."

"Yeah," I said. "Hell is other teenagers."

"Except for us," she said, and it was half a joke but half a question.

My heart contracted. I had never felt so similar to someone outside my own family. My limbs became light, like I might float away if I didn't hold tight to the bedpost.

Instead of answering her, I said, "I think you're probably the smartest person in 106H."

"Thanks," she said. "I want to study constitutional law. What about you?"

"Hang on," I said, wanting to savor this conversation as long as I could. "Let me go get another cup of this terrible wine."

THIRTY-TWO

As the air crystalized into cold, I felt my spirits rise higher than ever before. Columbia was like Narnia, Hogwarts, and the Secret Garden all rolled into one: a kingdom where other students met my eyes and I met theirs, smiling with genuine happiness when we called each other's names across the quad.

That fall, I began making footholds in several overlapping social groups: Tati and her scrum of jaded ex–prep school kids who used their embarrassing monthly allowances to keep us drenched in vodka and Thai takeout; the stressed-out but friendly group of my premed cohort; and several other looser sets of people whose parties I attended and whose names I knew, whose phone numbers I painstakingly entered into my flip phone that I now had to charge nightly because I was actually using it, calling and texting them all throughout the day.

Of all the people I met that fall, the one I found myself gravitating to the most was Marion. The more we talked, the more we had in common: she was from the South like me, except even farther (Houston), and it cracked us up to hear northerners say "wait *on* line" and complain about the humidity when to us the air felt cool and dry. And like me, she was used to feeling like an outsider: she had been a scholarship kid at her parochial school, iced out by both her rich white classmates and her old neighborhood friends. And we were both obsessed with our freshman constitutional law seminar, led by a tiny, perky sixty-something professor who insisted we call her Julia, which both Marion and I found difficult to do (southern sensibilities; every adult should be *ma'am* or *sir*). When it was just Marion and me, we'd call her Professor Julia, which was the first inside joke I'd ever had with anyone outside my family.

I don't think it was a coincidence that I began making friends when I stopped being the smartest person in class. I was trying as hard as ever, memorizing late into the night, but the questions on the tests asked me to really think. *Why* was this molecular structure more complex, *why* would you disregard acceleration in the equation, *why* did the court overturn this legal precedent? Sometimes I got back papers marked with a C, even a D+. While these failures felt at times like a sledgehammer to the heart, I liked being able to find Marion in the cafeteria and moan together—oh my god, I can't believe how freaking *hard* that was!

As if to underscore how nourished I felt, my body began to grow. Winter clothes I had picked out in Raleigh barely grazed my wrists, and I stopped having to stretch my feet when I sat in the auditoriums. It wasn't more than an inch and half, but it came with a new perspective, meeting people's eyes instead of looking up.

When I came back to the studio each night, I tried to tell my mother about my day and the people who populated it, but her mind seemed far away. She still kept most of the details of the potential reopening close to her chest, but she mentioned that the Senator himself had arrived for a site visit—I didn't like to think about what Daddy might have said, seeing him there—and that after many years, Nurse Jenny's sump pump would finally be installed.

Whenever she told me these things, my life at school seemed to fade in importance, clouded by the glow of what was happening on the Hill. Then, when I left the studio each morning, memories of Mercy Hill seemed to disappear. It was like two halves of my attention had separated, and I was stepping into a different body as I crossed through the gate onto campus, and then a more familiar one as I left school to go home.

MIDWAY THROUGH THE SEMESTER, Professor Julia announced that the class would be taking a field trip to a maximum-security prison, a concept that shocked my classmates but not me so much—I was used to adults telling you to go along with their plans even if they seemed crazy.

The girls had been warned to wear baggy clothes or risk being catcalled, so Marion and I had gone shopping together at the student store, acquiring matching men's sweatpants with the university's name down the side. We had to hike up the fabric everywhere we walked and Tati took pictures of us with her digital camera as we tripped down the aisle of the charter bus, clutching each other with laughter.

The prison was in New Jersey but close enough to the city that you could still see the tops of the tallest buildings as we traipsed across the parking lot. In fact, the shiny glass entrance felt like an extension of Columbia's new construction until we were led through security and everything darkened.

That's what I remember noticing first, the transition from sunlight and linoleum to fluorescents and gray concrete. A guard counted us all through a double door and when he closed the latch behind us, it was as if the very air changed. We could all feel it, and our giddiness ceased. The rooms we walked through were large, nondescript, institutional—more like Columbia's cafeteria than we'd care to think about, we'd joke on the way home. But there was something final about that closing door. It made me think of time itself passing, and how no matter what you did, you could never get it back.

For obvious reasons, we were kept mostly away from the prisoners, shown empty cell blocks and a recreation area that was being cleaned by a man wearing headphones hooked up to an old Walkman. As we stepped around his push broom, he looked up. Although he did not physically resemble the man my sisters and I had called the Scarecrow, his gaze was identical—hard, flat, and incurious. I shoved my hands deep into my massive pockets and shuffled forward as fast as I could.

The last part of our tour allowed us a glimpse through the wired glass of the hall that housed the death row inmates. This was the part Professor Julia had asked us to really pay attention to, since our next unit would be focusing on the ethics and legality of execution. But the hallway was empty and the window too small for us to crowd around long. I backed away first, staring instead at our tour guide. He was a youngish man but not new to the job: you could tell he'd been doing this for years, maybe since he'd become an adult, and he didn't look like he'd be going anywhere else anytime soon. It made me think of my mother, and a sharp pang of fear crept into my chest for the first time since she'd told me about the reopening. This was her job, too, and we were fighting to expand a place like this. In some ways we, too, were building a prison.

I told myself I was not thinking straight, that I'd been infected by Mimi's lofty talk of civil liberties and Caro's evangelical *doubt welcoming*. When Wards A and B opened again, they would look different than the hall I was standing in. And yet the close, chill air . . . It reminded me of my trip inside Ward C, down to the molecule.

Marion nudged me, then nudged me again. "We're about to go," she said, and her eyes were heavy too.

THE BUS RIDE BACK to campus was more subdued than it had been on the way over, but when we emerged from the tunnel into the city, much of the class began to warm up again, talking and laughing as they crowded into the back rows.

Marion and I stayed in our front seat, not speaking until she said, "I'm going to do it. I'm going to be a criminal defense lawyer. Innocent people shouldn't end up in a place like that."

"Yeah," I said, still looking straight ahead. It felt easier to shed my doubts about Mercy Hill now that we had put some space between us and the prison.

"I just don't know if I'll be able to do it," Marion said.

"That's ridiculous," I said. "You're so smart, you can do whatever you want."

"Yeah, but I get so worked up about things." I heard her sniff and out of the corner of my eye watched her wipe her hand across her face. "I can't get up on the stand and, like—cry. I wish I were like you."

"What do you mean?"

Now she turned and looked at me. "You're always so composed, Denise. You're logical and, like—detached."

"I wish I were more like you," I said, meaning it. "You remind me of my sister Mimi. She's really passionate too." Although Marion knew I had three older sisters, I'd never gone into detail on any of them specifically before.

"Oh yeah? What's she doing now?"

I laughed, unable to stop myself. "She's in juvenile detention for stabbing a teacher."

The shock of this cracked up Marion immediately. She let out a laugh even louder than mine. "Oh my god, Denise. Oh my fucking god."

Her giggles were contagious and my mood cleared—we were young and free and drowning in our clown sweatpants, exuberant with the high of a new friendship, moving quickly toward a future that was so bright you couldn't look at it directly.

THIRTY-THREE

Marion was the only one of my friends that fall who ever met my mother, but unfortunately and unbeknownst to both of us, she chose the worst night possible to do so. One evening a month after our field trip, while we were eating dinner together in the cafeteria, I realized I'd left our shared casebook in the studio. I told Marion I'd run to get it and bring it back but she said, "It's not far, is it?" and surprising myself, I said it was not.

When we entered the apartment, my mother was sitting up in her bed with a legal pad balanced against her knees. Her hands lay flat on either side of her body, and she was holding neither her pen nor her laptop. Something about this seemed immediately off: Lisa Cross did not often sit idle except to sleep. Her eyes were blank and hardly tracked us as we entered the room.

"Mom," I said, "this is Marion, she's in my law class with me."

"Miriam," my mother said. "That's my daughter's name."

"Marion," I said again, with force. I couldn't fathom why my mother didn't get up to greet her.

"What are you working on, Dr. Cross?" Marion said.

"Marion," she said, a second delayed. Then she pushed herself up to sit on the edge of the bed. "I'm sorry, you've caught me at a bad juncture."

You always know, don't you? You know when it's truly bad. Your stomach sinks faster than gravity. You try to chase it and find your whole self turned inside out.

"Mom," I said, "what is it?"

She let the legal pad slide off her knees. It slipped off the bed and onto the floor, pages splayed. "They voted against the reopening, all of them."

"Who did?"

"The *Democrats,* Denise. The ones who were supposed to save us. And now they're going to close us down entirely."

"Mom," I said again. It was all I could say, like I'd become a baby again. *"Mom?"*

She cleared her throat and her eyes focused a little. "They're still going to consolidate the residents, but they're moving them to Butner instead. It's a newer facility, small shared rooms. They're really going to pack them in."

I thought of Bethy at the gas station. All she wanted was some quiet space to herself.

"What about Ward C?"

"All of them. Denise, all of them are leaving."

I still couldn't take in the enormity of what she was saying. It was like my brain was a high-speed track, thoughts going around too fast to let in anything else. "But I thought we were winning."

Marion touched my arm, looking concerned. "What's going on?"

"The institution where I work," my mother said, speaking to her but looking at me. "It's shutting down."

I gathered myself, suddenly angry. "I thought the Senator . . . what was all of that *for?*"

"I don't know," she said.

I felt a cold dread spread through me. Forgetting Marion

for the moment, I came over to sit on the edge of her bed, nearer to her than I'd been in weeks. "It's my fault that you're here," I said, then, realizing what that would mean: "You were so close, if we go back, you can fix it. Don't worry about me, I don't have to get my degree *now,* Daddy even said I should take a gap year—"

She did not put the pad down. "No," she said. "It's over."

My throat was heavy with sorrow. Even though I knew Mercy Hill's closure was perennially a possibility, there had been so many near misses, so many last-minute saves, that I could never picture it actually happening. Especially after the last few months had been filled with such hope. I felt immediately like the hope itself was to blame, like it had allowed me to let my guard down, and the enemy through. Even now, it's still hard for me to feel hopeful about something without also expecting its destruction. In some ways, my inability to hope without fear is Mercy Hill's longest legacy.

I leaned over and held out my arms to hug my mother. It was an awkward angle, but she sat up and met me halfway.

"My good girl," she whispered into my hair. "You tried your best, we all did." Then after a long moment, she pushed me away. "I'm sure you want to walk your friend out," she said.

I stood up, not meeting Marion's eye. "Sorry," I said, to both of them.

As Marion and I waited for the creaking elevator to make its way up to our floor, both of us stayed silent. Then I felt a tentative hand touch my shoulder.

"I'm sorry," she said. "It's terrible that this is happening to your home."

I didn't say anything back, but I was glad she was there. Marion didn't say it'd be okay or try to find some way out of the silence. I appreciated that about her. It was a very different kind of strength than the one I'd grown up with, the pressure to wrestle feelings into a box.

When the elevator doors clanked open, I nodded and stepped back. I watched her walk in and watched the doors close, feeling so heavy I could barely move.

Standing there, staring at the elevator door as I heard the ancient cables move downward through the core of the building, I took breath after shuddering breath. I still felt shocked and shaky, yet my feet stayed planted on solid ground.

Now that the initial shock waves were subsiding, a strange and unfamiliar feeling was cresting. It felt like I could breathe a little more deeply than I had ever been able to before. It felt almost like relief.

HOLIDAYS NEVER SEEM to come at the right time, when you feel like celebrating. There had been so many in my lifetime marred by tragedy—Grandpa Cross dying at Christmas, Caro defecting the day before New Year's Eve, the agony that would happen on my birthday just a month later—that when Thanksgiving came the following week, it felt natural that we would be in mourning.

The campus emptied quickly, with Marion flying home to Houston and Tati and the other überwealthy meeting their parents at the Columbia gate for celebrations at Manhattan pieds-à-terre. Soon even the cafeteria darkened and I had no choice but to return to the studio, a place I'd been avoiding in daylight hours ever since we heard about Mercy Hill's fate. It felt too strange to be there with my mother without anything to do, no letters, no calls, no laptop tapping. It felt like being back on the prison tour, although at times I couldn't tell which of us was the guard and which the inmate.

Thanksgiving midday, she broke the silence with a "Let's go

eat," and led us both like sleepwalkers across the street to a bar, the Macy's Parade on replay on two big TVs. I ordered potato skins and a Sprite and watched my mother order and drink in quick succession four Cuba Libres, discarding the wedges of lime into a little pile on a cocktail napkin without squeezing them. I wondered why she didn't just ask for a rum and Coke if she didn't want the lime, but she seemed to like the act of removing the piece of fruit. Like it gave her something to do. When I thought about her empty days, my throat closed.

Just then, she spoke. "You know what I believe?" she said. "It wasn't about the proposal at all, just the land. It's cheaper in Butner. Where we are is simply more valuable."

I forced myself to nod. Growing up, the Hill had felt precious to us, but no one ever seemed to agree. I often thought of my first day at Lincoln, the mean girls who heard where I lived and said: *Ew.* It seemed that there were many things about my life that I'd underestimated.

I swallowed enough to speak. "Mom," I said. "What are *you* going to do?"

"Oh, there will be a lot of work at first," she said. "Evaluating where the residents should be sent. Some might be transferred, some released. It'll be a lot of work."

"But after that. After all the residents are gone?"

"Don't worry about me," she said. "Nurse Jenny wrote me—she's going on full-time with NAMI. Associate events director or something like that. Lobbyists and fundraisers, putting on silent auctions. Maybe they'd take me too." Her smile was higher on one side and I realized that the four cocktails were beginning to take their effect. I'd never seen my mother drunk before.

"But I *am* worried about you," I said. I swallowed, emboldened. "I know you wanted to help her," I said, not daring to say her mother's name. "Or, like—people like her. I'm sorry they aren't letting you do it."

Her gaze was steady even though the alcohol had relaxed her mouth, and it seemed for a moment like I was looking at two faces, sliced down the middle like a division sign.

I wondered in this moment for the first time how real it had all been, the great hope of this eleventh hour reopening. When I thought about it, sitting here five hundred miles away, it seemed suddenly like a fantasy, like one of the games we played in the forts as children. As I looked at my mother, I knew she hadn't been lying to me—she had believed. And she'd been wrong. Over my lifetime I'd seen her be cruel, I'd seen her blow things out of proportion, I'd seen her let her anger get the better of her. She'd never made an error like this one.

She continued talking. "It was a hard road," she said. "We all made so many sacrifices. But, Denise, you have to understand. I thought by doing this"—she swept her hands out as if to encompass the entire Hill and every other hill like it across the country—"I thought I would keep more people safe. But for you girls, I think I just made everything more dangerous."

"*Mom,*" I said. "We turned out fine."

"Even Mimi?" she said. "Even Caro?" She didn't say J.J.'s name, but I knew she was thinking it.

Together, we looked at the pile of lime wedges. She took the four of them and set them points together so they made an uneven circle. Four daughters make up a whole, I thought to myself, but I didn't say it aloud.

"What was different about you?" she said with an openness that startled me.

"I don't know," I said. And then I said something that I meant to be funny: "Maybe practice makes perfect. You finally got it right with me."

She let out a long breath, and then seemed to get ahold of herself. "Don't worry about me," she said, taking my hand. It was the same thing J.J. had said to me on the blacktop, and for a brief piercing minute, I missed her terribly. "I'm fine," she said.

And that was the thing about Lisa Cross: she wouldn't lie to you, not even to make you feel good. It was infuriating a lot of the time, but sitting there on those barstools, it comforted me greatly. I couldn't count on a lot of things, but I could count on her telling the truth.

THIRTY-FOUR

Near the end of the semester, Professor Julia called a few of us to stay after class: two quiet boys and Marion and me. Smiling at us all, she said we had had the highest grades in the class and were any of us considering law school? The others nodded but I said I had already declared premed.

"I want to be a psychiatrist," I said. Even though Mercy Hill was closing, it didn't feel right to change my own path. There would be other asylums in desperate need of staff. Maybe my mother and I would both move to Butner, just an hour away from Raleigh. Maybe being there, with her and with some of the same residents, would feel almost like being home.

Instead of looking impressed the way adults usually did when I said this, Professor Julia said, "And you think that would make you fulfilled?"

She didn't wait for my answer. There was an internship next semester with Columbia's Innocence Project and she'd be happy to write the four of us recommendations, even those of us who wanted to go to med school and become psychiatrists. We all told her thank you and headed out into the biting December air.

Outside the building, Marion and I stamped our feet in our boots until the boys left, and then I hugged her. "Congratulations!" I said. "This is exactly what you wanted!"

She clasped her hands together, excited. "Fuck, this is *so huge*! They freed four people from death row last year. Four! And we're going to get to do this as *freshmen!*"

"Well, you will." I rubbed my hands together to try to warm them. "The office is all the way downtown, and I'm supposed to take organic chemistry . . ."

Marion stopped and pursed her lips. "Do you even like chemistry?" she said.

"I'm good at it," I said, ruffled.

"Sorry," she said. "But you'd be good at this too. And, like . . . if you're good at a lot of things, you have to pick the one that you *want* to do."

I considered this as we walked through the dead grass of the quad. I thought about high school and how different I'd become since then. The old Denise would have stood her ground, insisted on being right and staying the course, doing what was hardest. But I didn't feel like the old Denise anymore.

"Okay," I said. "I guess I'll come—but only to keep you company."

She laughed, crystals of frost puffing out around her mouth and nose. "I'm so fucking cold," she said. "Can we run?"

IN WHAT SEEMED LIKE a perfect stroke of luck, Marion's roommate left for a sorority dorm at the end of the semester, and so the week before finals, we moved my stuff into her room. It took us most of a Saturday to carry it all, box by box, from the studio. When we were done we both collapsed exhausted onto the lumpy futon, moaning that we were too tired to even go to the cafeteria for dinner.

"What was in that last one I carried?" Marion asked. "Because it felt like a fucking rock collection." She paused. "It had better not be a fucking rock collection."

I stretched my sore wrists. "Mostly papers from high school."

"Are you telling me I nearly killed myself hauling your essay about symbolism in *The Great Gatsby*?"

"*A Farewell to Arms*, actually."

She snorted. "High school papers. What was the name of your high school? Please tell me, so I can be specific when I curse it."

I had felt loose and happy up until that moment, but suddenly my stomach grew cold. "Lincoln," I said. "Lincoln Magnet for the Arts, the Sciences, and the Humanities."

"Fucking . . . long-ass name," she said.

I didn't say anything. It had been so easy to write off high school as ancient history, something that had no bearing on my current life or anyone else's. During the unit on education inequity in Professor Julia's seminar, I tried not to think about my own experience growing up, the kids I saw in the halls who never shared a single class with me. But Professor Julia often said that you don't need to be racist to benefit from racism. I carried that thought around with me like a stone and at times like these, it seemed to grow heavier.

Slowly, I said. "Lincoln was a magnet school that was like—you know magnet schools?"

"Yeah," she said. "Checking the box on desegregation since *Brown v. Board of Education*."

"Anyway," I said. "Sometimes I feel like—that's the only reason I was able to make it here. Like, the base kids had to get pushed down so I could get pushed up."

"The Black and Brown kids, you mean?"

"Mostly Black. The Indian kids were in the APs with me."

Marion got a funny look in her eye. "I'm not going to, like—absolve you of your guilt."

"Oh—God—no, I didn't mean—"

"Yeah, you did," she said, but her tone was neutral. "I'll be your friend, but I won't do that."

She didn't say anything else. The silence made my stomach twist, it made me think of all the bad things I'd done or even thought about doing. I wanted to say something silly, to get us laughing again like we had about the rock collection. But I held my tongue. It's one of the first times I can remember that I didn't try to clear the air by saying something funny.

"I'm glad you're my friend," I said. "I mean it."

MY EXAMS WERE SCHEDULED from December 10th to the 15th, after which my mother and I both planned to fly back to Raleigh, leaving the studio for good. The fate of the beds we had purchased remained up in the air; no charity would take them and our landlord wouldn't let us put them out with the trash because the fifteenth was a Wednesday, which had some sort of complicated meaning in the arrangement of 119th Street's pickup schedule. Each time my mother saw him in the hallways, this little wheezing Polish man with Cold War glasses, they got into it with raised voices, with my mother telling him we'd just leave the beds in the unit and take him to small-claims court for the security deposit.

They were having one of those fights when I left the building on December 12th, the day of my fifteenth birthday and also my final exam for Professor Julia's class. "Happy birthday," my mother called over his back before turning to Mr. Wojcik: "Now, don't tell me to listen to *reason*."

The exam itself turned out to be fairly easy, asking for one essay describing a Supreme Court case we'd studied whose outcome we disagreed with. Previously, I'd been able to debate for any number of sides but now, again and again, I was surprised to find that there was frequently one I felt was right. I wrote about *Gertz v. Robert Welch, Inc.*, and the way the court had decided that the standards for libel or defamation against private citizens were lower than ones for public figures. *Why shouldn't they be the same?* I asked. *If we as a nation were going to restrict freedom of speech in cases where the speech itself was defamatory, why wouldn't we hold each case to the same standard?*

I had never had convictions like these before, and caring so strongly made me feel heavier, more solid. I finished first, faster even than Marion, and wandered out of the classroom and into the computer lab next door to wait for her.

I sat down at one of the machines and logged into my webmail account. The first email I saw was from him.

> Dear Denise, happy birthday, although next year will undoubtably be a happier one. 365 days. I'll wish them all away like nothing. All my love, Skate.

I swallowed, a strange unease coming over me. I hadn't gotten an email from Skate in months. We'd sent messages back and forth in the summer, but ever since classes started, I hadn't heard from him. And I'd been too busy to reach out, tied up in Columbia and the hope for Mercy Hill's reopening, and then despair over its closure. He was always there in the back of my mind and of course in my body, his hands my hands as I lay in bed late at night after I was sure my mother was asleep. A memory, someone I could summon at will. A fantasy, light-years away from the place I lived now.

I read it again. *Next year will undoubtably be a happier one.*

I looked away from the screen and down at my fingernails, gray with graphite from the essay I'd just written about the standards for private citizen defamation. Cut short by the clippers that I'd bought at a Duane Reade across the street from the college. These fingers, my hands, my arms, my whole self—this was me, on my first day of being a fifteen-year-old.

Professor Julia would have recommended he use *undoubtedly*, not *undoubtably*.

Skate was twenty-one, three years older than the other boys in Professor Julia's freshman seminar.

Those freshman boys were my friends, my classmates; they borrowed notes from me and invited me and Marion to their stupid case-race parties but never, not once, sat close enough to touch. Things would be different in a few years, Marion said when she saw them move toward the other girls. Everyone knows you're too young, Denise C*roff-limits*.

What did Skate know that they didn't? Or, painfully, haltingly, the realization stabbing through my navel into my stomach: Why didn't Skate know too?

Why didn't Skate know. Too.

I forced myself to picture it. The time we spent together in the German trailer, and later in the empty cottage. How his hands moved toward me every time. They had been such big hands, and of course I'd known and seen and thought I'd understood, but now it made me queasy to remember. *They were such big hands.*

I thought about his voice, in a low whisper, that I had spent so much time longing for. That pleasure now felt caked with something so disgusting, it was worse than dirt. It was worse than poison. It was like taking the stained, sodden, shit-soaked trash that overflowed out of the trash cans in the Penn Station bathroom and blending it into a smoothie. Drink this. For this is what gave you pleasure.

Twelve turning thirteen. If there had been another Cross

daughter, two years behind me, that's how old she'd be today—that's how old I'd been when I was with Skate. When I thought of Skate reaching for her, I felt an even deeper jerk of revulsion.

I'll wish them all away. Like nothing.

I still had no idea where Skate was living, what he was doing when he woke up each day. It had seemed romantic, to be wishing away your days. Now it seemed feral, not free.

Like nothing. Was I nothing? Being with Skate had made me feel larger too. But it was—and I was realizing this more clearly, waves of realization crashing while I struggled to even breathe—so outside the norm of what anyone in the real world did. I couldn't yet in that moment say to myself *it was wrong*, although that is what I believe now, of course. I had loved him for such a long time, and growing is like that: you don't notice until one day, nothing fits anymore. And Skate didn't fit. Darkly, terribly, Skate was un*fit*.

I felt hot tears falling down my face, the first time I'd cried since J.J. had walked in on us in the cottage. I cried for myself then and all that had happened to me, but also for myself in the future. There would be no more countdown, there would be no reunion. I had grown beyond where we had been, and even though I could see much more clearly that this was because what we had was ill-fitting and unmatched—still unable to think *wrong*, still for many years unwilling to categorize it with the words *statutory* and *pedophilic*—I still mourned it. This was my first love. It was fucked-up and shot to the core with rot, but it was all I had.

My sobs echoed off the walls of the empty computer lab. I didn't care who heard.

I gulped in deep breaths as I typed something that I did not yet believe. I needed him to stop and I knew anything less strong, anything that showed the hesitation that I actually felt in this moment, would keep the window open. I wanted to seal it shut.

> I'm only fifteen, Skate. Stay away from me or I will call the police and tell them everything you did to me.

Writing those words, I cried at my own cruelty, my mind racing wildly to some future where—thirty and thirty-seven, perhaps, or fifty-one and fifty-eight—we might come together again, at a time when we could fit. But that was the thing, wasn't it? Because of the way we'd started, we'd ruined any possibility of the future. At that time, it felt just as much my fault as his, too naive to have known my own naivety.

In the years to come, I would look back on every part of Skate with more clarity, even his name. I would stand on the shore in Montauk one summer and watch a fisherman drag something flat and thrashing through the surf. When he held it up, mouthing *Just a skate fish,* the other fishermen laughed at its ugliness. In the deep water, it was graceful; in the sun, an abomination. Fleshy, writhing, pathetic.

ON THE LAST DAY IN THE STUDIO, Mr. Wojcik came and removed the beds himself, muttering in English for our benefit that these ladies were sucking the life out of him. The capitulation spurred my mother into a fervor I hadn't seen in months. She leapt into the street with our luggage, waving her hands as if she were hailing a plane and not a taxi. Once inside the cab, she cranked the window down all the way, sticking her face out as if to soak up the last few molecules of the frozen city. The driver insisted she close it as we descended into a tunnel and there in the darkness, orange bands blinking over us like a stop-motion film—only then did she sit back. She closed her eyes.

"Denise," she said. Nothing else for a long time.

"Yes?" I was sitting on my hands, trying to warm them.

"Do you remember when we were touring colleges, we were singing that stupid song on the radio?"

"Yes," I said. "What about it?"

"It was a good time, wasn't it?"

"Yeah," I said. "It was a good time."

"How did it start?" she said. "It gets stuck in my head sometimes but I can only remember the middle."

"I don't know," I said.

The cab slowed as a red line of brake lights lit ahead of us.

"Sorry," the driver said as we jerked to a stop. "Today, I think many people travel for the Christmas holiday."

In the stopped vehicle, I felt antsy and I knew she felt it too. It was like I could see into the future, and this moment, stalled together in the darkness, was one I would remember. I felt soaked in strangeness: the bitter taste of the Skate email, about which I could not tell her, combined with the looping happiness of my future at Columbia, held up against the weight of my grief that while all this had been happening, we'd lost the battle that we'd been fighting my entire life.

"Mom," I said, wanting to ask for some sort of reassurance, that after all these changes something that mattered would still remain. "Mom, did they know about the proposal? Daddy and J.J. and the others?"

"They know everything's closing," she said. "It's been in the paper, and on the news."

"But did they know you were working on a plan to save it?"

The heat had kicked on, stuffy stale air that provided little warmth. "It doesn't really matter," she said. "Because it failed."

My fists clenched. I felt trapped in the hot motionless car. "But you worked so hard," I said. It felt unfair that no one else knew that, but I'd never say the word *unfair* in front of Lisa Cross.

"That doesn't matter now," she said again. Then she turned away to face the smudged and foggy window. The cab began to move again, and I felt both of us breathe out, one after the other.

THIRTY-FIVE

One of the terms of Mimi's incarceration was a points-based system that rewarded good behavior. In his phone calls to me at Columbia, I'd heard from Daddy about her recent wins—permission to wear her hair down, access to the library's desktop computer, a mini locker to store her things in her shared room. The biggest coup was the off pass, which she had obtained just in time to come stay with us over Christmas.

"She says it's not a big deal," J.J. told me over breakfast the second morning I was back. "She says they want to let staff have Christmas off, so they approved a bunch of kids to go home."

Ever since Skate's birthday email, I had begun speaking to J.J. again, but I had not told her why, and our conversation was rusty after years of silence.

"Still," our mother said. "It'll be nice to have her. Tucker?"

Daddy looked up from the magazine he'd set beside his bowl of cereal. "Oh—yes. Very much agreed."

This was now the third meal the four of us had eaten together and things were still very awkward. Daddy and J.J. looked largely the same but, having spent the semester almost entirely alone together, had developed an unspoken shorthand, passing each other things without speaking, cutting each other off midsentence. I wondered if that's how my mother and I seemed, too, although I suspected not. In fact, coming back home appeared to have erased any memory of our time as roommates. Her orders to me became stricter than I remembered: Put away your things, turn off the TV, take your elbows off the table.

I felt my phone buzz in my pocket with a text message and got up, dropping my half-full cereal bowl in the sink. Daddy gave me a look that said, *Isn't that wasteful,* but I just kept going.

Outside, the air had cooled to the beginnings of a North Carolina winter, a season I had lived through two and a half months ago in Manhattan. The sky was clear and cloudless, the air still. Under my feet, frost covered the Hill's wide lawn, furred white like mold.

My phone buzzed again. Two texts from Marion, two from Tati.

My uncle's been telling everyone I moved to COLOMBIA, Marion said. Then: *He doesn't get why my Spanish sucks*

I NEED A DRINK, Tati's said. *Mom just learned what MDMA is*

Ha Ha, I said to both. Then also to both: *18 days?* I flushed suddenly as I remembered the way Skate and I had also counted down. My phone continued buzzing but I snapped it shut, turning away from the cottages and crunching through the frost as I headed up toward the forts. Although it couldn't have been colder than forty degrees, I hugged my coat around me as I passed into the shadow of the trees.

The stick fence surrounding the forts had fallen down, and the empty space where the lean-to had once stood was covered in branches. So I was surprised to see a new structure propped up against the red-clay roots of a fallen tree. It was a little nook just big enough for one person to sit under; the branches it was made out of were newly plucked, their needles still green.

It made me sad to think about J.J., nineteen now, going out

here by herself to weave greenery together. Seeing the evidence of her loneliness in front of me made me feel like our positions were reversed: I the eldest, she the child.

I continued on past the woods to the magnolia tree we had once climbed, the one Mimi had fallen from long ago. There were no buds on it yet but as I stopped, I could swear I smelled the sweet and cloying scent of the white flowers. I stared up, hypnotized by the shuffling of the waxy leaves in a high-up wind I could not feel. Then, in some shift of greenery, I saw a flash of silver white. Something was stuck into a fork in the branches, so high up I had to squint to see if I was imagining it.

I was not. It was something bright and faceted, and as the morning light got brighter, the flashes of reflection brightened too. I gauged the distance up the tree. Whatever it was had stuck—or been placed—just a little higher than a person could climb, as if someone had stood on their tiptoes to screw it into the smooth gray bark.

Or it could be trash. It was windy on the Hill, and little pieces of refuse from the dumpsters, the yard, or the surrounding freeway often found their way into the bushes and trees. It could be tinsel, the reflector from a bicycle, something wrapped in cellophane.

Or it could be the pin Mimi had stolen so many years ago. Of course she couldn't have hidden it in the cottage, or in juvie, or any of the more familiar and traveled places on the grounds. This was the one place she knew we never would return to, the one place she could keep it safe.

I pulled myself up onto the first low branch, compelled by something deeper than instinct. I felt, brightly and stupidly, that if I could confirm that it was the brooch, it would tell me something I needed to know about Mimi. Maybe touching it would absolve me of the guilt that still lingered from Mr. Scott's class, or make me feel worse. Either option felt like movement, and so I climbed higher, shaking my hair over one shoulder and then the other to keep it out of my face.

The branches felt cooler and more slippery than I had anticipated, my ballet flats finding little purchase. It had been a long time since I climbed a tree, and my center of gravity felt different too. Whenever Tati and Marion and I took the body-type quizzes in *Cosmo*, I fell into "athletic," which was to say childish: skinny straight legs with no curves to speak of. But as I tried to get my arms and legs higher, I realized I could no longer climb like a child. Then I looked down. I was only twelve feet up, maybe not even twelve feet; God, it was embarrassing to be stuck paralyzed no higher than the deep end of a pool, but I was high enough that I could see through the razor wire and into the Ward C yard.

A group of men stood a ways beyond it, shuffling in and out of an inward facing circle. With a start, I recognized the Scarecrow, still taller than the rest, his hair the same patchy blond, now streaked with gray.

I clenched the trunk of the tree and wondered: Would he end up in Butner or South Carolina or—I shivered still, thinking of my mother's threat—somehow back on the streets of regular day-to-day life? Or would he find his way to somewhere worse, the close air of a prison? I felt scared for him. It had been many years since I'd watched the plastic restraints clasp around his wrists and yet I still remember how mournful he'd sounded. Just another person on this hill, trapped and betrayed.

I didn't say anything or move but as I kept staring, I saw the group begin to notice me and swivel. They turned one by one and came quickly over to the fence. I felt my heart thump faster, even though I was behind the fence and high up a tree. Now I felt silly and very childish. I had to acknowledge them. And so

I held out my hand and waved. This was me, half grown-up and trying to seem unafraid.

The Scarecrow once again came fastest, stopping just short of the chain link and looking up at me with glassy eyes.

"Dr. Cross," he said.

I felt my whole body flush. People said I took after my mother, but no one had ever mistaken me for her before.

"No," I said, "I'm just her daughter."

He smiled wide. "But you look like her."

This was what he'd said to Mimi, when he'd been close enough to touch her bleeding face. But now his words did not carry any chill of fear.

"My mother's inside if you need her," I said, pointing back up at the doors my mother entered every workday. She was in there somewhere, through the locks and checkpoints, layer upon hardened layer separating her from the rest of the world.

"I know," he said.

"Do you . . . need anything?" I asked. I wondered if there was anything he could ask for that I could give him.

He didn't say no, but he didn't say yes either. One of the other men said, twice like he was stuck on repeat, *Gofuckyourself gofuckyourself.* If that would have bothered me once, it certainly didn't now. I was used to people shouting obscenities on the subway, or outside the corner store where Tati and I went to buy beer.

"I'm sorry," I said, because that seemed like the only thing I could say. I told myself I was trying to apologize for his circumstances, the way you say *I'm sorry for your loss* even if you weren't the one to blame. I felt the guilt deep in my bones. I hadn't done enough, or maybe I had done too much of the wrong things. Both could be true and both hurt. I thought of the Bible verse our mother had fought Grandpa Cross with: our deeds in the body. It really did feel like the things you did made their way into your body, somewhere in the spaces between the fascia and the muscles and the tendons that I had been memorizing for premed. And there wasn't any way to make them lighter; you just had to carry them around with you until you died. I looked up again at the flash of silver. It might be the brooch, but it also might not. And I could not climb high enough to tell the difference.

When I looked back, the Scarecrow was gone, the men dispersed. Being alone broke some kind of spell, and I slithered quickly down the tree and onto the frosty ground. Then, without looking back, I ran down the Hill as quickly as I could.

THE AFTERNOON OF CHRISTMAS EVE, I went alone with Daddy to pick up Mimi, with our mother and J.J. staying behind to peel potatoes and rinse the cranberries. I had been surprised that this was the way we were dividing things, that J.J. was comfortable being around our mother solo, but even in the short time I'd been home, I'd noticed that the icy distance between the two of them was thawing. It had been three years since J.J.'s refusal to go away to college, and in that time our mother had weathered many graver disappointments. Perhaps, I thought as I sat in Daddy's car, the perspective had allowed them to feel close again.

This was the kind of thing I wanted to ask Daddy about, but as we inched through traffic toward Mimi's facility, I couldn't find the right way to say it. When I was a little kid, it felt like I could ask Daddy anything. He had had this permeability to him, able to absorb and digest any question and turn it into wisdom. Now, sneaking glances at him across the gearshift, I felt like his edges had hardened. It hurt to be so distinctly on the outside. I wanted the Daddy of my childhood back the way

I sometimes still wanted to be picked up and swung high. But I was beginning to realize that Daddy's shell was a mechanism of survival, the same as Caro's faith or Mimi's destructive tendencies. I didn't blame them for doing what they had to do to make it out alive, but when I thought about all the things I'd never be able to ask him, it made my throat hurt. *No more grandfathers,* he'd said when Grandpa Cross had died, and what I should have realized was that in a way he was also saying *No more fathers.*

We chugged along. First we waited in a line of cars entering the parking lot, then behind those same people going through the metal detector, then we sat in the cafeteria while staff bustled, walking in a single girl at a time and laboriously shuffling through her paperwork. Although the scene was festive, with red-and-green paper chains taped to the cinder-block walls, Daddy continued to say very little.

When Mimi came out, I was struck by how different she looked. She had grown taller and softer, her cheeks rounder. Her hair hung in long brown curls to her shoulders. Cross hair was notoriously stick straight, so the first and obvious question was: How had someone smuggled a curling iron into what amounted to a medium-security prison?

I held my breath as she approached us. The entire drive over, I'd been replaying all the things that had happened in Mr. Scott's class last year, the cruelty I had stoked. I hadn't thought about it in months, but now, confronted with the walls and bars of Mimi's daily life, it surged in my throat. I wanted to tell her how sorry I was.

When Mimi skipped toward me, I felt knocked off-kilter. Her eyes were bright as she wrapped me in a big hug. "Denise!" she said, laughter shaking her chest. "College girl back from the big city."

"How are you doing?" I said, hardly able to meet her eyes.

She pushed back and stared at me, and I realized that the last time we had touched had been the fight on the Hill. "I'm good," she said, her voice strong and emphatic.

"Are you . . . sure?"

"C'mon," Mimi said, and though her voice sounded joking I knew it was the truth. "Would I ever lie to you?"

"Okay," I said, hoping she could hear the apology stuck in my throat. "Okay, good. I'm glad to see you."

Back in the car, Daddy relaxed, letting flow a wave of news—Grannie P. was coming; we were having both a roast turkey and tofu kebabs ("I'm vegetarian now," Mimi told me, half-sheepish); J.J. had made a big clothing donation pile but hadn't actually thrown stuff out yet, we were waiting on Mimi's and Caro's input; did she remember Barb from the front office, she was retiring after all these years.

In this way we talked about the logistics of Mercy Hill's impending closure without mentioning the thing itself. The clothing donations, the retirement parties. It made me hot with frustration, and I longed to shriek—*This is fucking awful, why aren't we talking about it?*

I couldn't bring myself to upset the strange balance. I was happy that Mimi seemed not just okay but fine, actually, her life changed but not ruined by last year's bullying. She looked and sounded so different from the Mimi in Mr. Scott's class that I wondered if it was me who was remembering things wrong.

So instead I said, "I'm doing an internship . . . thing. With the law school public defenders."

"That is so great," Mimi said. "The criminal justice system is so messed up."

Daddy said, "I'm glad you're exploring other interests, Dee. You don't want to wake up in twenty years a miserable doctor."

"I'm still premed," I said, bristling.

"Do you ever go off campus?" Mimi asked. "Do you eat at Ellen's Starlight Diner?"

"I would never go there," I said. "That's like a total tourist trap."

"Oh," Mimi said, and the cheeriness dropped from her voice for a moment.

I felt like a jerk. "I just mean—you know, it's so busy. You wouldn't like it either."

"Sure, sure," Mimi said, staring straight ahead. "You'll have to tell us where real New Yorkers eat."

"Yeah!" I said, too brightly. "I totally will!"

WHEN WE PULLED INTO Mercy Hill's parking lot, a familiar pickup truck was parked next to our spot.

"Caro must be here already," Daddy said, his tone still carefully neutral.

Inside, our mother was wiping a crust of mashed potatoes off the stove from where they'd boiled over. Mimi gave her a hug but then stepped back quickly.

"Caro's in your room," our mother said. "She and J.J. are looking through those old clothes."

Mimi took my hand. The gesture surprised me, Mimi never used to be touchy-feely. But it all seemed natural, not an act.

"C'mon, Dee. Let's go."

Inside the bedroom, Caro and J.J. were sitting on the bottom bunk of J.J.'s bed. There was a black garbage bag in front of them stuffed like a Santa sack, but they weren't doing anything with the clothes in it. When she saw them, Mimi squealed and embraced them both.

I felt strange around all this hugging.

"The convict returns!" Caro said, and Mimi laughed.

"Delinquent, please. My record is sealed."

"Prison's changed you," said J.J., grinning.

"Fuck you both. Where's Laketon?"

"At the cabin with his parents," Caro said. "They're mad I didn't come too, but . . . they get it."

"I'm the star attraction, bay-bee. One night only." Mimi was trying just a little too hard, projecting her voice to fill the empty room.

"Don't get a big head. Who knows when Denise will come back," Caro said.

I looked up. "It's really good to see you, Caro." Even in just a few minutes, I could tell that she'd changed too. Her speech was no longer clipped, biting off words she couldn't say. And the long skirt she was wearing looked more preppy than polygamist.

"Denise is a party animal," Mimi said, twirling around the pole of the nearest bunk bed. "Sneaking into clubs with her fake ID."

I must have looked shocked because Mimi hooted. "Poker face, Denise—I was just guessing."

"Do you really have a fake ID?" Caro said.

I rummaged around in my wallet and handed her the piece of plastic. "It's not very good but the bars in the city don't care. This guy at NYU makes them in his dorm."

"Oh my god," J.J. said. "Denise *Palmer,* really?"

I grinned, sheepish. "It was the first name I thought of."

"Grannie P. would be proud," Mimi said.

"You look fifteen," J.J. said when the ID passed to her.

"She *is* fifteen," Caro said.

"I really don't use it much." I snatched it back before anyone could say anything more. "My friends are more like house party people."

That sat in the air for longer than I'd intended, but then Mimi leaped over and hugged me again.

"She has friends," she said. "She actually has friends!"

"We'd been worried," Caro said. "We didn't know if you were just, like, hanging out with Mom."

I shook my head and nudged the plastic bag with my toe. I couldn't bear another moment without saying it: "I know everything's closing. Mom told me when we were in New York."

J.J. looked down at her hands. "We'll move in February, probably. Daddy's looking at places in North Raleigh."

I looked at each of them in turn, trying to see if they'd expected it or if like me they'd held on to some tough shred of hope till the end. I thought maybe I could see something flicker in Caro's eyes, but I wasn't sure what that sadness meant. And as quickly as I considered this, I realized I agreed with what our mother had said—it didn't matter, because it wouldn't change anything.

So instead I said, "Here we are, I guess." I looked to Caro, then J.J., then finally Mimi, wondering if I'd see some kind of happiness on her face. Miss Deinstitutionalization herself.

Mimi looked down at her nails. "It sucks," she said. "I think sometimes people need walls." She didn't say that she herself was one of those people, but even in her silence it was clear to me that she credited walls for her current happiness. I felt my guilt rise again, but this time it was easier to push down.

"I wish there was something better out there," Caro said.

"Yeah," J.J. said.

"Yeah," Mimi said.

I swallowed hard. "Does anyone else feel relieved?" When I looked around at each of their faces, I realized I already knew the answer. We were so alike, even separated. It felt like we shared a nervous system, blood and breath and a strange guilty happiness flowing from one synapse to another.

HALF AN HOUR LATER, Grannie P. arrived in an emerald-green peacoat, trimmed with the fur of some white animal, lobes flashing pearl earrings the size of gumballs. I suddenly understood what Daddy had meant about New Yorkers dressing differently. Compared to the dark coats and jackets I'd become accustomed to seeing, this looked like a costume. But it felt appropriate even still, because Grannie P. treated the front room like her personal stage, striding up to embrace us all in descending order.

"Denise, sweet Denise," she said into my hair. "I'm glad you came back to us."

"It's good to be home," I said.

"I'm sure! I was delighted to hear that Miriam's school let out for the holidays."

I watched the other three look at each other and then cover their mouths, unable to keep a straight face in front of this euphemism.

"Yes," Caro said, flicking her wrist as if holding an invisible spike. "I'd call it a *slashing* success."

I wondered if Mimi would be mad, but her eyes lit up and she had to cough to cover her laughter. Grannie P. frowned but just then Daddy came up from the basement with a boxful of cloth napkins and, sensing impending hurt feelings, put us to work setting the table while he got Grannie P. a drink.

"Denise will have a vodka tonic," Mimi called after him.

I snuck a glance at J.J., who was using a butter knife to try to dig the wick out of one of our red Christmas candles. She caught me looking and nodded.

"Denise, I think I forgot to tell you about my job."

"Oh yeah," Caro said. "Tell her!"

"What's your job?" I said.

"Well, it's not a definite, but there's a biotech lab in RTP that wants to hire me part-time now and full-time after I get my associate's."

I looked at her sideways. "And that'll be—"

"Next spring," she said. I warmed, thinking about our conversation on the basketball court. She sounded different now, freer and more confident.

I swallowed. "That's great," I said, and then I said again, "Really great."

Caro beamed. "The lab's all the way down 54, so when she works late, she's going to crash in our guest bedroom."

"I've seen pictures," Mimi said. "Calling that closet a bedroom is extremely generous."

"Is it nicer where you are now?" J.J. said, which seemed like a cruel and loaded question, but Mimi acted unperturbed.

"At least I've got a real window."

"With bars on it," J.J. and Caro said at the same time, and the three of them bent over the table again, snorting. The sentiment between them seemed real enough, but they were all talking just a little louder than normal, as if performing a scene for an audience. I guess that was me, I was the one they were performing for, and realizing that made me feel both powerful and distant at the same time. I didn't know how far to push Mimi—or any of them, really—so I just counted out spoons and began setting them onto the napkins. The others resumed their work and I felt for a moment like we were back in the forts, prying stones from the clay.

"That's great about your job," I said, without looking at J.J.

Just then our mother came in, carrying a platter of carved turkey and a bowl of brussels sprouts.

"Girls, girls, girls, I need plates out here, we're ready to eat.

Mimi, come serve yourself some kebabs since you're not eating the turkey. Caroline—waters for everyone?"

We hustled everything out to a waiting Grannie P. This at least felt like it usually did, our mother driven to mad perfectionism in the face of her mother-in-law, Daddy trying to smooth things over by joking that we'd made the kebabs with tofu, not seitan ("satan"), because this was a Christian holiday. I shot a look at Caro when he said this but she didn't seem offended. My memories of her divisive conversion were still fresh, but for the others, they'd been written over by recent months of normalcy, and change. As I passed him the potatoes, I realized with a start that Daddy was eating carbs again. He winked at me as he spooned them out and I blushed, wondering if our mother felt the same way, stuck behind the beat after our sabbatical up north.

It was hard to tell what she was thinking. The food assembled on the table, she ushered us to sit down and serve ourselves. After a silence descended, Caro cleared her throat.

"Do you mind if I say a blessing?"

I held my breath. The last time Caro had prayed at the table had been the disastrous night with Grandpa Cross, the fight about Christ the judge. She too looked different now, wedding ring catching the light from the candles as she held her hands upward, supplicating. The air seemed to grow thin as I waited for something to come crashing down.

Our mother let out a sigh. "Sure, sweetie," she said. "Just please be quick."

Caro bowed her head and closed her eyes, and Daddy followed suit, then Grannie P., and Mimi and J.J., then, last, our mother.

"Lord, thank you for the delicious food before us," she began. "Thank you for helping Denise and Mom get here safely, and for bringing all of us here together." She continued, something about the joy of Christmas and the true reason for the season—but I had stopped listening. Looking up from my clasped hands, I saw that our mother had turned. Head craned, she peered out through the tiny kitchen window up, up, up to the Hill and the four structures that stood on top of it. She couldn't look away from it, even for a moment. Even when everything we'd fought for was over, even when she was here again, gathered with her four real daughters, the ones who weren't made out of stone.

I turned and followed her gaze, trying once more to see what she saw. I stared until my eyes blurred but all I could see were four big dark buildings, mostly empty, mostly barren. Their history was so long, but their future so short. And yet, for now they stood. Our castle walls, for only a little while longer, still visible against the blackening night.

2024

EPILOGUE

It's satisfying to know how something ends, isn't it? There's a popular series on the internet, four sisters who took a picture together each year for decades. Then one year it's down to three. We're not there yet. No one I know, really know, has died.

Who fared the best? That's the ultimate question. A single index at the end of a psychological experiment, but also the natural question that arises in each family, geniuses or not.

J.J. first, like always. She's married now, to a woman named Kate. Kate is the head of a pharmaceutical research lab at Duke, and J.J. a stay-at-home mom to the kid Kate had through artificial insemination. Rosemary is autistic and talks only rarely, which suits J.J. just fine.

Caro got out of her church and marriage after four more years. Finished her BA online and then drove across the country to a school in California that paid for her to get a Master of Fine Arts in creative nonfiction. She published two books and many articles on the subject of modern evangelical Christianity and feminism, which over the course of a decade have netted her a total of about $35,000 and terabytes of hate mail. She works as a waitress, and each month the rest of us send her money, something we discussed only once and have never spoken of since. A reverse tithe is the joke, I think, but would never voice aloud.

Mimi did not go to college. She started working as soon as she got her GED, and now runs operations for the largest foster care agency in North Carolina. People stop her on the street, not just in Raleigh but at the beach, in the mountains, once in Barcelona, and they say—Miss Miriam, you saved my life. It's easy to pick her out of crowd: sleeves of tattoos crawl from her wrists to her neck, and her hair is short and dyed black. She has four rescue dogs and a longtime boyfriend whom she refuses to marry for reasons none of us can figure out. She, among all of us, is most happy.

Caro was right about me, I didn't go back to Raleigh after that winter break, not for a long time. Things came up: summer jobs and study abroad and friends' invitations—to Tati's massive ancestral beach house off Cape Cod, to Marion's parents' place in Houston, later on to visit the parents of boys I was dating. Whenever these boys asked to meet my own parents, I told them it could happen next Thanksgiving.

At the end of my freshman year, I dropped premed and switched to prelaw, a choice that hurt so much I cried nightly for almost a month. Ward C had closed, Cottage 10 stood empty, but the mission hadn't felt like it had 100 percent failed until now. I would never stride up the Hill—*any* hill—alongside my mother. All the sacrifice and hardship had been for nothing. I wondered if my sisters were experiencing their versions of this grief, but this was a time in which we talked little. J.J. often sent newsy group emails, but they never mentioned if she too was lining up everything she'd done and comparing it to the vast emptiness of failure.

But you can only wallow for so long, and I was in a place where it was easy to forget. At Columbia, prelaw was an easy major and meant I could have graduated early, except for the fact that I would have rather slit my throat open than skip any of my time there. So I spaced out my required classes and on a whim began coursework in something I'd never studied before: music. I took theory, history, appreciation; it seemed like entering a new country with a language I'd never spoken a word of before, and the confusion was exhilarating.

I was the only one in my classes who didn't play a single instrument, and the performance students eyed me warily but soon began inviting me to their concerts and recitals. I loved tracking the themes and motifs as they rose and resolved; it was like reading the most exciting book. For a while in my senior year, I took piano lessons, but I was uncoordinated, my rhythm clunky. The instructor told me gently that most good musicians begin when they are young children. At seventeen, I was too old to be a prodigy.

I got over it, like you do with disappointments, and continued to attend concerts even after I graduated undergrad and began law school, also at Columbia. At a concert I met Ben, a French horn grad student, who took me out to eat at the same Indian restaurant my mother had taken me to years earlier, on our first trip to the city. He was twenty-six to my just-turned-nineteen, so despite our coincidentally having the same age difference as there'd been between me and Skate, the gap was now acceptable. He was the first person I had sex with, in the apartment I shared with Marion and two other law students, and it felt both sincere and special and, as soon as it was in the rearview mirror, entirely mundane.

IN MY TWENTIES, Facebook blew the dust off all the people from your past you thought you had left behind. I found Nurse Jenny, the kids whose classes I'd passed through at Lincoln, and Mr. Scott and the other teachers—everyone I could think of except Skate, who didn't seem to exist, online or off. In the photo I uploaded for my own page I look happy, grinning behind a candle that you might think is for a birthday, but was really to celebrate my getting what I unashamedly called my dream job: associate professor of law at Columbia University. I was twenty-eight.

Summers, I traveled. I got married. He's much older than me, a dean of the humanities who'd had the sense to buy in Harlem before Neil Patrick Harris moved in. We don't have children, we have a brownstone; it's what we tell people, and it's also true. Each year, it seems a new repair project arises and we're on the phone to George the contractor, who smokes in our foyer and stamps back and forth saying, *Mrs. Cross, I don't know what to tell you, this is gonna be another big one*.

See how easy it is to change the subject? Everyone wants to hear about George, who has loud conversations about Staten Island strippers on his Bluetooth while prying out our tile. No one wants to hear about the times I've had to go see Dr. Lu for a D&C, despite my absolute devotion to my daily birth control pill—blame that clockwork Cross fertility.

Each time I have the procedure, Marion comes to stay, although this is more an excuse to visit New York than anything else. She lives in Philly now, where she's made partner at a big white-shoe firm—corporate law, specializing in antitrust for telecommunications. ("Every eighteen months we tell AT&T they can't buy Verizon, or vice versa.") She has the most beautiful clothes, a personal trainer whose hourly rate is almost as high as hers, and a much younger fiancé whose art school loans she paid off with a single quarterly bonus. She is guilty about how happy she is; we both are. Neither of us is changing the world the way we'd promised each other: me sitting in on meetings of the Association of American Law Schools, she walking the long halls of her office building in Chloé pumps.

Maybe that's the real reason I don't want kids; I don't have a mission that would require their assistance, and that kind of childhood is the only one I understand. Like all things related to Lisa Cross, it's complicated: I remain childless because I am both not enough and yet too much like her.

DADDY DID WHAT HIS father could not do, and stayed married. A few years ago, after a string of temporary rentals, he and our mother bought a condo in one of Raleigh's first downtown high-rise apartment buildings—on the site of a vacant lot that we used to drive through on our way to Lincoln.

He has a very busy schedule, going to Durham to take J.J.'s daughter, Rosemary, for outings and visiting Grannie P. at assisted living. (Yes, Grannie P. is pushing ninety-five, slower and frailer but never without lipstick, still introducing us as the Palmers.) The retirement home is a new one, also downtown, manicured green lawn butting up against the shiny new office buildings where the Lincoln projects once stood.

It's been in the news a lot lately, because Raleigh is becoming a very popular place for people to move, and the waves of gentrification that swept the more populous parts of the country are now crashing there too. The city has responded fumblingly: tore down the projects, put in a bid for Amazon. And now rows of shotgun houses downtown have been flipped and sold, their doors painted peacock blue and leafy green. Where did those people go, who lived in those houses?

What I hear about, more often than I want to, is the state's increasing importance and turmoil politically, a red state turning blue shade by shade, then doubling back upon itself to swing, again, hard right. And I've begun once more to hear the Senator's name, scandal faded, now on the long list for future presidential candidates. I wonder if they're in touch—would he invite my mother to visit at the White House? Would she accept the invitation?

AFTER WARD C CLOSED, my mother went to work in a downtown ER, then a group practice, then an inpatient facility an hour and a half north, near the Virginia border. For various reasons, none of these jobs worked out. I have not asked her specifically what went wrong, but I can imagine she did not take well to supervision or to workplace politics she did not control.

In the end, she got a job at Central Prison, which accommodated the majority of Ward C's former population. She now drives through two checkpoints and a metal detector each morning, and about once a month is delayed coming home because the entire facility is on lockdown. Mimi told me that one of her patients strangled another one and then ripped off his testes. This could of course be exaggeration, but in the photos Daddy sends, our mother's hair is very short, and I suspect that is for her own safety.

When I talk to our mother about her job, I often remember our conversation at the bar that terrible Thanksgiving, the one in which she told me not to worry about her. I still trust what she said. She is not happy with the way things turned out, but happiness was never something that she wanted, not foremost anyway. If we had won our battles and kept Mercy Hill open, perhaps she would have gotten to work on being happy. Now we'll never know for sure.

AN EMPTY MERCY HILL STILL STANDS—the main buildings, anyway. Its uncertain status is still highly contentious. Now that everyone wants to live downtown, there have been multiple attempts to permit parts of the grounds for development. Others have protested, groups like the Raleigh Historical

Development Commission and a new group called Save Our Parks, whose persistent emails I get although I do not remember signing up for them. They call for preservation of its campus and ambitiously declare that Wards A, B, and C could be turned into a performing arts complex. I sometimes click on the images of their proposals, shocked to see hash marks of green lawn in the space where Cottage 10 once stood.

Whatever plan wins out in the end, there will be no plaque with our name, nor do I particularly want one. We Crosses each remember our own version of what we did and whether it deserved commemoration. It's only fitting that we who bore the name take it with us.

Acknowledgments

A book is born when it's meant to be born. Thank you to the following people for their help in *Mercy Hill*'s gestation:

To Carolyn Williams, whose brilliant editorial eye oversaw the largest themes and the smallest details and helped them all come to fruition, and to Johanna Zwirner and the rest of the Doubleday team.

To Robert Guinsler, my agent—you were right: you never gave up!

To my Tacombi Writing Group—Amber Bryant, Michelle Hess, Laura Janka, Shefali Parikh, Jennifer McClelland-Smith, Amber Silverman, and Stephanie Whetsone—thank you for your feedback and encouragement (to drink more margaritas).

To my witches, Sofi Thanhauser and Gillian Osborne, thank you for the enthusiasm and momentum.

To the Harem—Alex Binder, Matthew Price, and Katie Williamson—thank you for never letting me forget the time I called to tell you the news and said "an imprint of Wandom House."

To Karyn Marcus, thank you for talking through each excruciating stage of the submission process—you helped me keep my sanity!

To Katherine Lyman and Mary Grayson Brook and Kristen Sanders, thank you for your wise inputs on psychiatric care, southern cotillion culture, and evangelical doctrine, respectively.

To Lucas Church for reading so many drafts. So many drafts!

To Emily Hashimoto, for introductions and friendship.

To Andrea Mosquedo for your wisdom in launching a debut—much like during our memorable evening at the Gershwin, I have been changed for good!

To Diana Spechler for your needed notes on a big revision and pivot.

To John Reed for your endless recommendations and counsel.

To Shelly Oria for sharing with me your unwavering belief in this dream, month by month and year by year.

To Jonathan Brady, and my teams at FCB Health and IPG Health: thank you for your support—you continue to show me that both a writing life and a professional one can coexist.

To Elizabeth Metzger for a poetic look at this manuscript, some early encouragement, and a thoughtful discussion on titles.

To Abby Ronner and Vinny Senguttuvan for your support, lunches, and friendship.

To my ride-or-die Ragdale house crew—Christine Hume, Rodlyn Mae-Bunting, Hallie Palladino, Em Williamson—for gym rides, fireside chats, Brita filter de-escalation, sticky notes, and to Hallie in particular for helping me *finally* title this book.

To the Corporation of Yaddo, Virginia Center for the Creative Arts, Paragraph Workspace, and Ragdale Artist's Residency for uninterrupted time to create. Thank you to the NYSCA/NYFA Artist Fellowship for the cash prize and connection to a wonderful set of writers.

To my parents and sisters, thank you for your endless support, love, encouragement, and enthusiasm—not just on this book but in all aspects of life. And thank you in particular to my mother, Rita Thurman, for the initial inspiration to set a novel on a fictionalized Dix Hill (with a *very* different family from our own!).

To Ed, who screened every agent query response for almost a year, solo parented during the multiple residencies I took while our daughter was a toddler, and enthusiastically brainstormed titles for longer than anyone would deem fair or reasonable—this book would not be possible without you. I love you!

ABOUT THE AUTHOR

HANNAH THURMAN is a New York City–based writer originally from Raleigh, North Carolina. In 2024 she was named a NYSCA/NYFA Artist Fellow in Fiction. The winner of the *Florida Review*'s 2023 Editor's Prize for Fiction, her stories have been published in *The Iowa Review*, *Michigan Quarterly Review*, *The Brooklyn Rail*, and *Southern Indiana Review*, among others. She lives in Brooklyn with her husband and daughter, where she works in an advertising agency as an engagement strategist. *Mercy Hill* is her first novel.